The Monarch in the Milky Way series
Book 2

Amerlee and the Green Void

By George Hudoba

Chapter One

Unfinished Business

"CAN YOU TURN AROUND?" Evan Smith openly admired her body.

The tall girl smiled coyly, almost giggled, and slowly turned around. Then, facing her employer, Tata Crubon, she asked joyfully, almost enjoying the show, "Would there be something else, sir?"

"Miss Fontana, you're just elevated yourself!" Tata glanced at Smith, who seemed pleased enough.

Perhaps it was the day-off jeans or the almost cute pink blouse. Frankly, he was not sure why she did have to turn around. Smith rarely picked girls from outside of his circle, certainly never an IHG (International Honor Guards) graduate.

"Miss Fontana!" Smith jumped from his seat rejuvenated, and offered his hand.

She accepted and shook on it, then brushed aside her long, golden hair to mask her embarrassment.

"You'll hear from Mr. Tata Crubon within days. I think you would be pleased by your new assignment!" The Emperor admitted.

"I'm looking to advance my carrier. I'm willing to serve long deployments!" She replied, and then as Tata dismissed her, she saluted and left.

"Stunning girl!" Smith nodded, appreciating the sight of her.

"Do you want her?"

"I like pretty girls, especially talented ones!" Smith replied diplomatically, masking whatever he really thought of her.

"You know every graduate student goes above world to serve on one of the PODs . . ." He referred to the orbiting SPD (Super Planet Destroyer) PODs the IHG has been using lately.

"She won't!" he promised.

Tata felt himself to be a step behind: "What's the plan?" he asked.

"Time to put the new graduates into harm's way, to see if they really are as good as they claim to be!"

Tata became worried. "My students, what do you mean?"

"Captain Aa's ship needs some pilots. Miss Fontana will be a liaison between you and the military, and at least thirty graduates will head to Captain Aa's SPD. They're going to get the latest gears onboard her spaceship, the Destination Unknown." he explained.

Tata wanted to discuss something else with him for a while now. He cleared his throat. "I think my granddaughter figured you out."

"Oh?"

"I think she understood our complicated relationship," Tata added.

"I hope so. After all, I did something, I don't normally do," Smith frowned.

"Why did you do it?" Tata had to ask. He meant Smith's gift to the granddaughter, and Smith knew exactly what he meant, because of the way he looked at him. "It was Aa's doing, I was just augmenting her work!" Smith tried to brush aside the concern.

"Now she thinks she's special . . ." Tata aired his dislike.

"Oh, but she is. We worked on her, made her better and smarter!"

"Why?"

"You have to ask Aa why she helped her. Perhaps something Elise said caught her attention. Maybe Aa just wanted to exercise her powers and found a good candidate. Or perhaps she wanted to help her for reasons unknown."

"So, what now?"

"What do you mean?"

"Should I watch her?"

"No more than your grandsons, but . . ."

"But?"

"Mr. Mariol is a true businessman. I guess he only cares about money and the respect it comes with."

The sudden, dark thought appeared in Tata's mind: "Have you done something to him?"

"I could have," Smith bobbed his head. "But no, I did not. For our friendship's sake."

"I see," After a while, his thoughts returned to his granddaughter. "So, Elise is going to be special?"

"Hope so. But you might have to pitch in for her tuition. Try to get her into whatever she wants!"

"University, you mean?"

"Uhm . . . and . . . talk to her."

Tata scratched his two-day-old, unshaven face. "About what?"

"Whatever she needs to. I'm not in the family, but you are. Develop a friendship with her. She's worth it!"

"She has the name of my late wife."

"I did not give her that name, her own mother did," Smith replied, but the unspoken words hung around them, the ones that begin with *don't blame me for that one*.

"So, what now, for you, boss?"

"I was given an assignment!" Smith scoffed as he thought about it.

"Oh, that's a first!" Tata chuckled.

"No. Occasionally my former mentor gives me things to do. Usually, things he can't do

or doesn't have the ability to do," he sighed lethargically.

"Former mentor?" Tata asked cynically.

"It's better to call it that way," Smith felt too tired to battle over words.

"Do you have to clean up after the Trust?" Tata asked, reading between the lines.

"Yes. It will be extremely dangerous and boring at the same time."

"How come?"

"See, for this one I can't even be in the game, because I have to provide cover for the insertion team," Smith sounded sad.

"What about Azure?"

"I haven't decided whether she should be with the team or with me. It's a dangerous mission, as I said earlier."

"I mean now. Where is she?" Tata attempted to joke around by looking behind Smith.

"Oh, she is onboard my ZON Starship, the Sky Riders. The AI, Diana, needs to upload her memory into the data crystal Johnny gave me, so in case something happens to her, the memories she formed would be preserved!"

"Ah!" Tata thought he got more than he bargained for and decided to shut his mouth.

They talked about casual things, then Smith left and Tata watched long after his friend. Somehow, he was glad it was not him who has to deal with the case.

"Your skin is so smooth, honey!" Smith caressed Azure's thigh. They were laying in the grass, Smith sneezing occasionally from the flowers, to Azure's biggest delight.

"You're smooth yourself, today!" She squinted at him, then let it all go and laid back, her black hair on the green grass, looking straight into the sparkling blue sky. Few clouds sailed across the view, while the magnificent body of the Sky Riders seemingly hung in midair to their right. Azure was beyond shocked Smith would surprise her with something so sweet, so romantic, like a picnic at a valley south of the thriving megalopolis called Ugrughughau. Actually, it was further south than Stalingrad was. Beneath them, beyond the valleys, she could see the ocean and its strip of beaches. She has never been here and could not figure out how Smith learned of this place. He seemed to be thoughtful enough to bring a lunch box, too. She probed him earlier, trying hard to figure out who he was here with before, but so far, he did not break. She giggled as he tickled her. She was not particularly ticklish, but the occasion required her to relax, to give in, to let it all go, and just to concentrate on the moment with him. He pulled up her blouse and kissed her flat belly. She almost blushed. As he began to kiss her chest, she pulled his face up to hers and looked into his eyes. It was full of uncertainty, but as he noticed her closeness, he blinked and the previous thoughts were all gone, replaced by love, joy and a form of kinkiness she had not seen before. "What?" she giggled.

"What, what?" he smiled in return.

"What's all this about?"

"What, that I care about you, that I actually love you?" Smith moved back for a second, but only to bask in her beautiful almond eyes. He so loved those. Sometimes he saw not the fighter, the suspicious girl, but the dreams she held so dear as a reflection in her eyes.

"Kiss me!" she breathed heavily.

"I so kiss you!" he joked as he bent forward. As their lips touched, the brilliant sensation of mental eruptions, the outcry of joy, encompassed them and detonated like a supernova across the valley.

*

"I can't believe it! Another mission, I'm sure!" Captain Josh Kulighan ranted in his cabin. It did not help at all that his beloved wife tried hard to give him massages around his neck and shoulder. He stared into the Admiral's orders and contemplated running away.

"It's not the Emperor's orders, it's your superiors!" she tried to calm him.

"Smith is behind this, I'm sure!" Josh raised a finger.

“Nevertheless, you must obey.” her softly spoken words came soothingly and his anger dissipated away so quick, he did not even know what happened.

“Yes, I must,” he gave in.

“Don’t forget to tell the bridge!” She reminded him, looking coyly, like she knew her bellowed husband forgot that.

“Yes, yes . . .”

Captain Gabriel stared into the screen and at first was not sure whether he should be angry or happy. He knew the day would eventually come when his past agreement with Smith would expire. He was on a Starship, a high commodity in the UNHL Space Navy (United Nations of Humanlike Lifeforms). It was bound to happen; his services would be needed. In a way, he was glad he held out for this long. His orders came from the Admiral, foretelling him the DSR (Deep Space Reconnaissance) Toxic’s arrival with Smith onboard. He was not sure whether he should get the senior crew together, but because of the warning from the Admiral did not contain an exact timetable, he opted out of it. All he done was just to wait, somewhat impatiently, for Smith’s arrival. By the afternoon Toxic arrived, docked with an unusually trigger-happy Azure and a preoccupied Smith. Apparently, Baby Haas, Jena and particularly half the Honor Guards were on board, along with four Death Squad members. That told him all he needed to know about Smith’s untold, but serious intentions.

*

“Captain?” Aa heard Commander Danek’s muffled tone from outside.

“Come on in!” She stopped reading a paper book and aimed her gaze at the door. As soon as the Commander came in, he saluted.

Aa frowned. “What is it?”

“We’ve received a coded message from the Admiral.”

"So?"

"I think you should read it, ma'am!"

"Are we at war again?" she asked as her heartbeat shot up.

"Don't think so," he shook his head, "but your expertise is required!"

"Does that mean you're in charge in my absence again?" she tilted her head.

"And Victor, of course!" Danek was quick to add.

"Good boy!" Aa nodded, and then escorted him out. Once he left, she hurried back to her desk to decode the message. She read it quickly and her heartbeat rose by every sentence she deciphered.

Commander Tri'ng's Starship was on a long endurance mission, deep inside the Zharkan quadrangle. Her refueling ship for the Space and Dream Fighters just left, and she was particularly shocked when she got wind of the Toxic's arrival. She barely had time to arrive to the airlock. The Emperor came alone. There was no Azure or Captain Aa trailing him, and that made her a bit nervous.

"We need to talk, Tri'ng!" Smith said to her quietly and darkly and that one sentence alone made her legs wobbly. She escorted him to her cabin, where he sat down in the guest's chair and stared at her.

That also made her uncomfortable.

"So how is your love life?" he asked, cordoning his lack of patience. A customary pep talk was required.

Tri'ng slightly tilted her head, but spoke nothing. Mostly because she thought she hallucinated.

"I mean, your romantic relationship with Kre'ator?" Smith elaborated.

"We're fine!" she managed to compose her thoughts.

"Come on Tri'ng, some details, any plans for marriage or kids, huh?"

She was horrified. "Those are deeply personal issues."

“Ah, the ever so compartmentalized self, I seriously don’t know what Rota’erk saw you in that market oh so many years ago when he first saw you, but hey . . .” He shrugged, referring to the Krea’tor’s child name along with the occasion of how the two first met long, long time ago. “Love is in the eye of the beholder, right?”

“Right.”

“All right, so you’re not so forthcoming with your personal life and I can understand that.” Smith recognized he failed to ease her. It actually created the opposite effect. “So enough of the pep talk and let’s get into business! I need you!”

“Um, like now?” she frowned.

“Like now. Albeit a bit later.” He winced as he realized talking with so precise a woman like an ex X-Force member could be tricky. “I need your hacking expertise. I’m on a secret mission.” he stopped in mid-sentence. She lifted an eyebrow, meaning she became interested. *Good*, Smith thought.

“Where do you need me to hack in?”

“The Central Bank of the CTP. Can you do it?”

The question shocked her. She was wondering about the target herself, but this, this was something out of a sci-fi movie.

“The Central Trade Planet’s Central Bank?” she asked for clarification.

“Yes. I need to get some information. You have to do it in a way it wouldn’t raise suspicion on the other side.”

“Banks are better protected than government agencies.” she replied, subconsciously cautioning him already.

“Hence I’m asking you!” he pressed on.

“We need direct access to their internal networks!”

“So, you need to travel into AOCP (Alliance Of Central Planets) space, right?”

“Right . . . But that’s not possible, because they monitoring the entire border!”

“The Tears of the Emperor is capable of teleportation.” Smith pushed the limits.

“That would need an authorization from the Admiralty.” Tri’ng did not like the conversation at all.

"Or a written order from your friendly Emperor!" Smith jokingly produced a smart-paper detailing his order to her. "Now that the teleportation issue is the past, when can you start?"

Tri'ng's head was spinning. "We need an elaborate deception to pull this off!" she replied thoughtfully.

"There will be a ground crew to extract whatever I need, but you have to tell them where to look for the physical vault. There are also a couple of accounts we need to syphon money off of, but that shouldn't be a problem for you, right?"

"Right," Tri'ng was cynical, and Smith heard it. "Are you turning into human now?" he smiled, while pressing his lips together, akin to wincing.

"I need a week to pull it off!" Tri'ng heard somebody saying that once. She hoped it would work on this occasion.

"Just make sure you have the location I need and that the money is transferred to us!" Smith was pleased, but knew if Tri'ng would fail, the whole mission was for nothing.

"Who should I call to report in?"

"Me, onboard the Toxic!" Smith spun around and left.

"I supposed I was let off easy," she mumbled behind him.

"So how is this going to play out?" Azure caressed Smith's back. They were on the Toxic flying to a nebula to disappear, so Toxic can teleport to the planet Qbe.

"The problem is twofold and I can't be everywhere! Tri'ng and Aa and most of my people will concentrate on the CTP (Central Trade Planet) and the location of the vault from where we must retrieve the money, but there is also the need to clean vault at planet Ciun."

"You think Agent Sasha was truthful about that?" she frowned.

"We need to find that out. Plus, I suspect we need to take her to Ciun. I'm sure she will try to delay giving up all her secrets and I need a competent mission leader who isn't afraid to bust a face or two, especially hers."

"I can be that one!" she recognized herself in it.

"Okay, so we decided you're going to run that errand. Only problem is that you can't take the Toxic and I can't go with you either."

"Why?" she sounded utterly disappointed.

"Because I need to watch over Aa and Josh. They have to land on the CTP and I have to cover them mentally. I've got some intelligence reports from Admiral Qaw regarding the use of telepaths on the CTP to root out UNHL agents. It's rather a slaughter house and I suspect only I can cover them adequately. That leaves you without me and a ride!"

"But what if the Toxic drops them off, and then I can use it too," she whined.

"No. She needs to be present in case we need to evacuate them. Sorry honey, but it has to be that way!"

"So, what kind of ride am I going to get?" she sounded disappointed.

"You can choose either an IHG asset or Captain Yoyo, or perhaps I can ask Admiral Qaw to lend us the Eclipse with Colonel Re'kl . . . We got options!"

"I want Hunter Paradise on my team!" she blurted.

"Done!" Smith was quick to agree.

As Smith was putting together the plan, he ran into another problem. Apparently, the CTP team had to have more people who were familiar with the planet and its customs. That realization led him and Toxic to meet with the Ancient Man who lent his right hand, Diesel, for the mission. As soon as the Toxic parted, Smith welcomed the headhunter.

"I understand my expertise was required. My master told me about the CTP and that there would be a physical vault I must help rob, but why are we turning into bank robbers?" Diesel asked, standing in the Toxic's corridor as the ship hurtled toward the Destination Unknown. Smith told Aa to cooperate with Diesel and Josh on this one beforehand.

"We're cleaning up after the Trust. I'll get the bank's location, but we're going to be short on time, so you and the others need to be inserted by that time!"

"On enemy territory! Bring it on!" Diesel shook his head.

"Yes. I don't like it, but the money is ours. We should have it and we will need it too!" Smith answered.

"You do realize we should run some counter warfare on this?"

"I think Josh Kulighan will be perfect for that."

"Oh, he isn't coming with us to the CTP?" It was news for Diesel, who thought Josh would go with them.

"No. I don't think so. This is a fairly large operation with you and Captain Aa running the CTP operation, Azure handling another one."

"How about you?"

"I will sit this one out," Smith was hesitant.

"Why?" Diesel's one word sounded more like an outcry.

"I'll watch over your bodies, to cover you all."

"That's a really nice gesture!" Diesel nodded.

"A prudent one, I would say." Smith responded darkly.

"So, it's the planet Qbe now, right?" Azure was hoping to spend some time with him in his house on the planet called Galaxy Qbe. Time to be alone with him. It filled her heart and head with a constant yearning.

"Not exactly. I think I should calm down a tiger."

"A what?" she watched him, startled.

"Josh . . ." Smith winced painfully and told Toxic to locate him.

He was not particularly happy to see Smith. That one was given—Azure observed the two of them. She also noticed how Smith shepherded him into his cabin while she stuck outside with another Honor Guard and a lone Death Squad member. She tried to listen in, but even for her sensitive ears, the cabin's conversation eluded her. That intrigued her beyond her wildest imagination.

"I know my role!" Josh turned around, sounding angry as soon as the door was shut.

"Do you?" Smith stopped dead in his tracks, tilting his head instead.

"You want me on whatever operation you're running."

"That's true!" Smith nodded once.

"When do I leave?" Josh tried hard to contain his anger.

"As soon as everybody is in place."

"Is Captain Aa in it too?" he tried to decipher the scale of the plan.

"Everybody is in!"

Smith's reply shocked him. He stopped for a moment, contemplating his reply, then nodded calmer: "Do I work with Captain Aa?"

"I think you misunderstood this one."

"What do you mean?"

"This is a twofold operation as far as you should think of it, but you're not in the middle of the action. There are two teams operating on two different sites, but as far as you and I concerned, we're not in it directly!"

"I . . . I don't understand," he managed to say.

"I know. This mission isn't just important for me, but also for the Ancient Man. Do you understand the complications, the ramifications of it?" Smith gazed at Josh, who swallowed hard.

"I see. Failure isn't an option."

"No, it's not. For that end, I need you to work extremely hard. But I also brought gifts to you."

"Gifts?" Josh frowned. Smith has not brought him gifts in decades, unless he meant gifts by challenges, he repeatedly had to prove himself with. Those he brought plenty of!

"I know you as a good barterer. You always get what you need, but I hear this time, your luck run out." Smith circled around Josh, who was a bit confused.

"Meaning what?"

"I have a BeamChaser medium-range freighter under government flag approaching your present location. It should be here any minute . . . Onboard I have an entire squad of Space Fighters, the 2.01 version and spare parts along with the latest, interchangeable engines you sought after for trial runs!"

Josh gasped for air. "How did you . . . ?"

"See, I know what you need and I figured if you're pleased, you're better focused running secondary operation. They're watching us. Keep tabs on us and especially on the twenty-sixth Fleet. Ghost chasing. Simply put, I need you to occupy the enemy. I cut you lose, so harass them this time. The Destination Unknown with its AI, Victor and Commander Danek is also at your service! Don't cause a war, though," he warned Josh before leaving. Josh was about to tell the great news to his wife, but Lieutenant Rick paged him to the bridge as a BeamChaser freighter just pulled out of hyperspace.

"Home sweet home!" Smith gazed at the meadows. He and Azure were standing on the deserted tarmac of the Qbe's spaceport, with the Toxic behind them. It was quiet except for the occasional cries of animals they could not see beyond the perimeter.

"Do you think it's a wolf?" she cuddled up to him.

"There are no wolves in here!" he said with scientific clarity.

"Oh, you're ruining the moment!" she scolded, and then kissed him.

"Okay honey, it's a lone wolf from Down Earth," Smith tried to joke. She giggled. It worked.

An automated hovercraft picked them up and transported back to the terminal. Hunter appeared out of nowhere and greeted them.

"I thought you would be in space," Smith said to him after the handshake.

"I heard of your coming, and I figured I would see you. We're still holding your girl in house arrest." he reminded him.

"Good, straight to the reason I'm here. Very good." Smith sounded pleased. "Oh, by the way, start packing, you gonna work with Azure!" Smith said casually.

"What? Wait . . ." Hunter tried to catch up with the stream of information.

"He said you and I are going to be a great team!" Azure winked at him, deepening his suspicion.

"Take us to the prisoner," Smith instructed him darkly.

While one of the reserved cabs hauled them into the city and around, Hunter was trying hard to extract some meaningful details out of his visitors, but Smith's answers shocked him when he said, "You're going to rob a bank!"

"Bank robbers? That's a novelty, even from you. Come on, what's the real purpose of the mission?"

"We're going to rob a bank, just as Smith said. Only that we could have some official UNHL forces to back us up this time," Azure chirped, full of excitement.

"Well . . ." Smith began, then cut it off as Azure stared at him: "You said I can have Captain Yoyo and her ship!" she sounded angry.

"Of course, you can have it, honey, but they can't help you rob the bank. They will hover near your location and occupy the media . . . Ciun is on the other side. Captain Yoyo can't cross over the border."

"But I thought . . ." she pretended to be upset.

"No blasting cities if you were thinking of that!" Smith's frown deepened.

"Okay, so how do we land, then?" she asked with defiance.

"Colonel Re'kl will assist you on the ground!"

"Re'kl is in too?" Hunter grinned. He remembered the man.

"Yes, hopefully he is. I put a request to Qaw about that!" Smith exited the vehicle as they arrived to the two-story residential building.

"How does she behave?" Smith asked, pointing toward the building and its lone occupant.

"Tried to escape the first day, so we beat some sense into her." Hunter looked away.

Smith expected some details, but Hunter did not elaborate, so he said, "Let me talk to her alone!"

"Okay."

Azure protested, but Smith needed to do this by himself, so she remained outside with Hunter, who was hungry for mission-related information.

The room was nicely decorated, turned homey with the replica paintings of an alien-human hybrid painter. A bit too much red and yellow, he concluded, but luckily it was only a couple of paintings. The walls were beige, the window sills yellow and partially open. The floor was fake wood he hated so much, but the two plants on elevated podiums in the corner were a nice touch. They seemed to flourish, so care was given to them. The table in the middle was particularly empty except for the empty vase. The sleeping quarters were to his left, and the young, slender woman emerged from the shadows. "My Lord!" She bowed deep. She wore shorts and a T-shirt. Her hair grew and was neatly combed. Smith quietly observed her makeup-less face and her re-manufactured, somewhat crude, bionic arm.

"They've done a nice job!" he pointed to the rubber cover of the skeleton fingers.

"Yes, and the neurotransmitters are finely tuned!" she tried to convince him.

"Any pain?"

"Some. Mostly ghost pain," she shrugged. "Can't get rid of those."

"I guess not! I heard you tried to escape . . ." he left open the sentence.

"It's my duty to try to escape . . ." She gazed at the floor.

"You failed!"

"I realized it was futile!" she looked away. No direct contact on that. Whatever happened, she learned her lesson, Smith noted.

"Good. I told you before that it's up to you how you will live out your life here, but an escape dented your opportunities."

"I understand," she kept her look away.

"But you can remedy this situation. Perhaps you can even get a job in the city, as we will keep this place for you to retire every night. And no, it's mandatory!" He pushed the last sentence to her hard. She seemingly understood. "You can't tell anyone who you were, although there are plenty of nonexistent people around," Smith began. He felt the need to explain, "You know, people who are dead to the outside world. Now I also said you will never leave this planet. I never lie, but we've made a decision to retrieve the misplaced goods the Trust took from the UNHL and from the Monarch by any means necessary . . ." he trailed off. As he suspected, that got her attention. Since he did not speak, she peered toward him and asked shyly, "Does that mean I get the chance to go to the CTP?"

"Out of the realm of your sinful life! All you can do is help us at Ciun. My girlfriend, Azure, will lead the team. Basically, you will be her prisoner. Cooperate and when you are done, you could have the illusion of a normal life within the city limits, without checking on you too obviously. Fail me and you will regret you were ever born!" Came the dire warnings.

"When do I leave?"

"Now!"

Captain Josh Kulighan rode with two of his SCCs (Space Craft Carriers) to the Destination Unknown's location. As he looked out the reinforced windows to the cold space and noted the sister ship's silhouette, he had to smile, albeit only lightly. The SCCs resembled a late twentieth century Upper Earth based aircraft carriers minus the four stabilizing arms on their ends. Of course there were no propellers at the ends, only engines, and the inside layout was quite ifferent, but the design paid off and used widely in the Milky Way. Cost whole lot less than a Planet Destroyer and was able to travel on water, like a regular ship, just as well as out in space. A preferred method of fighting local and regional wars since the end of the II Klon Wars. He never missed working from Planet Destroyer or their POD equipped larger cousins, the Super Planet

Destroyers like Captain Aa's space ship... He was a bit surprised to find Captain Aa onboard, but remedied his shortcoming by greeting her in person. He learned from her she was a bit worried about going to the CTP. Quietly, Josh thought he got the better end of the bargain.

"Be nice to my ship while I'm away!" she reminded him.

"Of course!"

"Any operation details you can let me on?" She always respected Josh's ways. She believed he was a true professional when it came to his job.

"Sure. I already selected the Corridor of Frantics as a place to operate. It's a tricky border region with AOCP. It contracts and expands seasonally, and it's also curved many times. I'm planning to hold exercises there. I've been getting reports on how AOCP traffic straightening their routes and I've been wondering what they will say once they spot us right there!" He clapped his big and bony hands.

"Seems you figured out some good game for yourself there!" Aa had to admit, it sounded exciting.

"I hope so! Smith said I can't start until I hear from him, but he hinted it's not your mission I'm waiting for."

"I think Tri'ng is on a special mission herself," Aa replied thoughtfully.

"Huh! That's another layer of deception entirely! I wonder what's her stake in this?"

"Only Smith knows!" Aa responded while introduced him to Commander Danek.

Tri'ng quietly watched the readouts. Her team seemed to be adept at hacking into AOCP's financial headquarters. They constantly had to change position as AOCP sentinels were good at approximating their location in space. They were persistent too. As soon as they connected to a satellite node and opened the ports, the automatic watchdogs were alert. Seconds and they were on their trails. Seventeen layers of firewalls and spoofing IP addresses were only good enough to buy five to seven minutes of time, and so they had to find another node to continue work. The first day was painfully hectic, but as she assigned another six officers to locate the satellite nodes and map a random path, things got interesting. Now they were at the retrieval phrase of the trove of information, and soon she could present something to the Emperor. *Smith*-she thought. That confused her. Perhaps when he asked her all the intrusive questions, he meant it as a friend. Perhaps she offended him. That was a horrifying thought. She had to find out whether she had done that or not. She could ask the Kre'ator about it too, but decided to delay that. She supposed to meet him sometime next week. The uncertainty of the personal meet always made her excited. She muted her feelings as Lieutenant Sheila approached her.

"Yes, Lieutenant?"

"We've got the location and all the info with it!" she seemed so proud.

"Show me!" she commanded her all of a sudden.

*

"We're on the go!" Smith announced in the Trixec's conference room. Admiral Tarbuk, Captain Aa, Diesel, Baby Haas, Jena, Captain Yoyo, Hunter Paradise, along with Azure, were all present. The collected information from Tri'ng and her crew was dancing on the screen across the room.

"Will be tricky!" Josh uttered.

"I'm leaving now to prepare the ground!" Smith said cryptically.

Azure ran after him and hugged tight, and kissed him hard.

"Be good and keep Agent Sasha alive if you can!" Smith instructed her.

"Don't get killed!" she half joked in return. She returned to the conference room to discuss her options while Smith disembarked with the DSR Toxic (Deep Space Reconnaissance).

Toxic flew him to Gabriel's Starship, the Azure, and then left. She had to pick up Aa's team.

*

"Smith!" Gabriel greeted him theatrically, then changed attitude as he spotted the four Death Squad members behind him. "What do you need them for?" he pointed to the black-robed women standing behind him, seemingly patiently.

"They will watch over me!" Smith announced, keeping his face serious.

"A visit to the galley first, perhaps?" Gabriel tried to play the host, but Smith seemed to be impatient.

"Look, let's just skip the formalities. This is a serious job here. One of my most serious ones, I need to be taken care of while my body lay vulnerable. Have you prepared the medical room I requested?"

Gabriel blinked as his superior and former direct boss cut to the chase, so to speak. He needed to switch gears too. "Yes. It's in the center of the Starship, protected by many layers of security," he uttered. Gabriel was good at his job.

"Good. Escort me there. Have the doctors prepare my body and let the Death Squad members begin their shifts."

"How will you communicate?"

"You'll know it!" Smith replied cryptically as Gabriel showed him the way. Later on, he was a bit humbled, seeing his former master on a medical bed, mostly naked, tubes running in and out of his body. The automatics job was to keep the body alive and fed during his extended mission. Smith did not say, but by the looks of it could be days. He lifted an eyebrow and returned to the bridge in a deep blue suit for measure of good luck. For old time's sake!

The crew watched him in unison.

"We have the most important package onboard and failure isn't an option, teleport!" he announced seriously, then ordered his crew into enemy space.

*

"I thought after the Global Cold War I would never step on the Central Trade Planet again!" Aa glanced thru the windows. Toxic had a yacht shape, with valid codes and real looking outer hull paintings. She just transmitted her landing request, while Captain Aa handed out the ID cards to everybody. Baby Haas and her eight Honor Guards A Team members were getting ready as they needed to disembark before they did.

Civilian Space Traffic Controller 2B acknowledged the request and designated a landing pad. As the Toxic glided down below, they had the chance to admire the incredibly beautiful sight of the densely populated planet.

"I have a bad feeling about this!" Baby shook her head.

"Relax, it will be just fine!" Diesel tried to reassure the woman. As she returned to her soldiers, Aa quietly asked him, "Why did you lie?"

"She needed a strong backing. This will be serious. If we get caught . . ."

"I know, we can't get caught!" Aa nodded.

"I just hope your master will cover us mentally."

"Smith isn't my master!" It offended Aa.

"You should hope that he is this time!" Diesel knew more than he allowed telling them. He completely understood the risks they were running and Smith was running his own. Being captured was not an option at all.

Landing went without a problem. The Shashalo backed operation, although only by name, smoothed out all pesky inquiries from the authorities. Aa only learned about Smith's high placed friend after the mission.

As Baby Haas and the Honor Guards left, Toxic started two clocks-one for mission duration, another for Baby's team. Allegedly twelve hours later, Aa and Diesel were to leave, posing as a couple. They retired to their own cabins for meditation and for rest. The next morning as Diesel dressed up into his suit, he thought he looked truly dashing until he found Aa at the airlock, looking as a gorgeous princess.

"My, my!" he walked around the tall girl.

"What?" Aa blushed.

"You always look so great out of the uniform?"

"I was told." she hard pressed her lips.

"Shall we?" he offered his arm, and she took it.

"Oh, my!" wondered Toxic, tucked away deep within the yacht's hull.

*

Smith swallowed hard as the sedatives took effect. Soon his body was nothing but a distant memory. His mind, his soul, roamed freely among the stars. It left the boundaries of the Starship Azure and homed in on Toxic and Aa. It was difficult to find Toxic, as she promised to shut down most of her mental beacons. Several regions and layers of telepaths protected CTP based on space stations, spaceships, and the planet itself. For a nation just closing borders with the UNHL, the CTP was very active protecting itself. He was sure SWEi Prime, home of the UNHL was equally protected, but still, he sensed a great and unnecessary firewall. He found Toxic's location and pinged her discretely. As she replied with a mental smile, he moved on. Finding Baby Haas, Aa, and Diesel was not so easy, especially Diesel, who had all kinds of ability to hide from prying eyes, but he was not impossible find either. He had to remind himself that it is not just his friends, it is the mission, and it is also his word that he can pull it off was hanging in the air. He had to deliver, and so he had to be vicious. One enemy agent already sensed something fishy as Smith mentally blanketed his people. He back traced the intruder and fought to get into her mind. She was extremely focused, but a tiny thought on the side got him in. He roamed around in her brain, looking for evidence, but found none. He had to throw her and her handlers off, and so he initiated a mild headache and a severe nosebleed. As he disconnected from her brain, her presence vanished.

He was back on top of Baby and the Honor Guards, as Aa and Diesel seemed competent enough. At the same time, he had to watch out for the Starship as telepaths were working hard to identify the new presence in their circles.

*

Azure has not run an operation for a couple years now, but her attitude made her a perfect candidate. Her self-esteem was running high as she boarded the DSR Eclipse 0805 as it just docked with the UNHL Planet Destroyer Trinity, Captain Yoyo's ship.

"It's a pity I can't make it to the surface!" she told her candidly.

"I know, right?" Azure tried to reassure her as she watched the Honor Guards boarding the craft. To her delight, Nyikha, who she liked, was among them too. She went after Jena, who escorted a blindfolded girl, and was greeted by Colonel Re'kl, who seemed cautiously excited to work with familiar faces again.

As the Deep Space Reconnaissance space ship undocked, Captain Yoyo called her own bridge. "Take us to the closest friendly point of the Planet Ciun immediately!"

That turned out to be three and a half light years from the planet. Far, but not too far. Luckily it was not far from the Corridor of Frantics where Captain Josh was operating with the DU. Captain Yoyo contacted them and posed as a sentry for their operation. She hoped the AOCP was listening into their partially open communications and would take the bait.

"So, Colonel, you have no problem running an incursion into enemy territory?" Azure asked Re'kl.

"It's a dangerous job, but the Admiral tasked me to assist any way I can help. As a further help, Captain Mya patrols in the neighborhood along with another DSR, in case we need their help!" he revealed.

"That's pleasant news. Tell me, are we cloaked?"

"Yes, Miss Azure, but that doesn't really help with mass detectors. Luckily Ciun isn't that developed world; its agricultural nature prohibits having expensive equipment and heavy industry. Nevertheless, the younger Emperor's decision to host a military marathon nearby surely brought unnecessary attention to us!"

"You don't like it?" she asked, somewhat surprised.

"I think we could've pulled it off without any attention, but nevertheless my ship and my supply are at your disposal!" the Colonel quickly added.

"Where have you planned to land?" Azure decided to change subject. She was torn between her boyfriend's decision and the judgment of the Colonel.

"Near the city of Obol, where your bank is located according to your prisoner. There are several large swaths of unused lands. Hopefully, we won't sink. There is a wheeled jeep in my cargo hold. Fueled and ready to go. It's also armored at certain critical points, although it isn't obvious for the untrained eye. Try not to get killed, miss!"

"I got it!" She loved when support was strong. She decided to visit Agent Sasha, who she found sitting with a straight back on the bed.

"So, you're the famous girlfriend?" she glanced up at her.

"I would be!" Azure was not sure what to make out of her.

They just stared at each other for a good minute, then Azure opened her mouth, "What can you tell me about the bank?"

"I know where it is, and I dealt with the manager. His name is Ozzie, and he has a keen interest in pens and suits."

"You trying to tell me you acted as a courier and neglected to tell that to the Emperor?" Azure was about to punch her in the face.

She must've seen her anger, because she held up her hands defensively: "He did not ask . . ."

"Perhaps you were lucky he did not probe in your head! It would look like a huge mushroom field by now!" Azure vented her anger.

"I'm trying to be useful here," she pleaded.

"We don't need you to be useful in your entire life. Tell us what we need to pull this off, to right your wrongs, and we can part. I heard the Emperor promised you a quiet life if you

cooperate . . . or else . . ." she added. She could tell it rattled her nerves. She glanced up at her.

"Do you think he will really let me live?"

"He gave you a prosthetic arm to look normal, did not he?"

"What kind of life will I have?" she sounded depressed, playing with her prosthetic fingers.

"Try to be a secretary. They have all the action!" Azure said half-jokingly.

"I'll look into that," she replied while nodding.

The room shook as the DSR landed. The comm announced just exactly that. Azure bobbed her head. "Let's go and no surprises, or I knock your teeth out!"

"Are you also working for the Emperor as a freelancer, sir?" Sasha watched Hunter Paradise's bustling muscles beneath his thin shirt with open admiration.

"I was an SES agent!" he replied proudly.

That shocked the girl. She frowned at first and then realized the past tense. "So, what are you now?"

"Honey, he is God as far as you should be concerned!" Azure yelled back. The jeep was topless, and Nyikha was an aggressive driver. It appealed to her, but in this case, her hearing was impaired by the wind, and that also irked her.

"Who is God?" Sasha asked around. Since nobody answered, Hunter said, "Humans love to believe in someone. Before emperors, there were Gods, but they never formed a human body. It was a myth."

“I see the parallel. But normally nobody resigns this young from the agency. I heard they find an accommodating job until its retirement time.”

“Well, we’re both out of the game, honey! I run things on the Qbe for the Emperor, since my appearance out in the Universe would be too inconvenient for some. And I also oversee your case.”

“I see. Sorry,” Sasha replied. She had to think about it. She hoped to escape the first day she was let alone on the Qbe, but then an injected micro implant exploded, sending her to the hospital. She understood that she was a captive and had to act nice or be dead, just as the Emperor told her. She never heard of this planet she had to call home now, Planet Qbe, but apparently the Emperor was right. People on the planet could not remain alive out in the galaxy, so they were put inside a domed city on a planet nobody ever heard of. She had to find something to be occupied with, so perhaps a job or a cute boyfriend would do it. First, she had to survive this. Ozzie was a good manager, but they left on bad terms. Her heart beat faster as they approached the city limits. One of the few places she vowed never to return. She felt a bad omen.

Suddenly Azure stared up close into her face.

“What?” Sasha tried to act innocent.

“You’re hiding something! I can sense it!”

“Great, now you’re telepathic too?” Sasha asked, annoyed. She had to swallow hard when the answer came.

*

“Please welcome to our bank!” Iros, the manager, a tall male in his late forties, welcomed Aa and Diesel with customary wide smiles at the Bank of Independence. It was nothing more than a narrow front, but in reality, it was just an architectural decision to hide between the two adjacent store fronts near the CTP's embassy zone. The golden door handles and the intricate marble tiling were a telltale sign of a bank in bed with different kind of entities. The spacious indoors, the free food court and the human security as opposed to robots further deepened this notion.

"Thank you!" Aa tried to hide her insecurity behind her smile, and it worked. It mesmerized even the security guards.

"How can I be of service today?" He sat both of them down in his own office to show up for his guests. Of course, the receptionist understood at once what the couple was representing: high class, filthy rich people who move their money when the authorities were onto them. It was so obvious to the middle-aged woman; by the time she greeted the couple, she had already sent a note to the manager.

"We would like to move our assets, to diversify our portfolio!" Diesel replied diplomatically.

"What do you have in your mind?" Iros fired up his terminal.

"We have several bank accounts we need to empty and transfer to different worlds!" Diesel played the knowledgeable husband's role.

"Everything?" Iros swallowed hard. He hoped he could keep charging storage fees, even on electronic accounts forever. Especially once he pulled up the couple's assets and realized their combined value.

"Everything." Diesel reassured him and pulled up a letter, opening it before tossing it over to him.

"I see. Several of the destination accounts are in UNHL territory. I'm afraid our bank has a rather steep transactional fee for that. It's almost two percent." Iros hoped his answer would sound remorseful.

"Listen, um . . ." Diesel tried to act laid back, while reading the manager's name tag.

"Iros. It's President Iros Form . . ."

"Listen, Iros, can I call you Iros?" Diesel flinched. He meticulously tucked away his golden sunglass, then gazed into the manager's eyes. He smiled. "Mister Iros, I really don't care about your transaction fee. All I care about is your continued discretion. We need to empty our share of the vault as well. I was hoping your company would provide the armored service for a fee, of course, but if you don't feel up to the task, I can gladly . . ." he could not finish the sentence because Iros grinned, "I can provide all the service you need!"

"Good!" Diesel was quick to reply.

"I gather the necessary forms, Ma'am. What's your occupation?"

"Excuse me?" Aa pretended to be shocked.

"Um. Well, a company I presume . . ." Iros was fishing in the dark.

"I don't work, sir!" She looked him down. "Unless you call shopping a work. Sometimes it's boring to find something truly exquisite, like this dress I bought on the Shahsalo's world last week. Its microchip vowed into the silk, and it is in direct contact with my VR implant. Cute, isn't it?" she chatted with him.

"Expensive, I would think so!" Iros was trying to navigate on a landmine. These were crazy people.

"Six grand is hardly a big price tag, right, honey?" she caressed her husband's arm, who shrugged as casually as he could muster, "Chump change, my adorable one!"

Iros almost fainted on the spot. His yearly salary was around that. "Well, all you need is to input your passwords, and we're in business."

"Certainly!" Diesel leaned forward, typed in the long and convoluted sentence, then lay back.

"Excellent!" Iros was shocked that the man was able to type it in without making a mistake. Perhaps he was a true businessman, hiding behind the richness after all. "Now, they are already placing the physical assets into crates. It will be . . ." He glanced onto his screen before continuing: "Twenty-seven crates. For formalities, I need to take your ID card, so I can safe keep it for reference!"

"Sure!" Diesel put the smart card on the table.

Iros grabbed it and left.

Diesel disciplined himself not to look at Aa, who probably was crossing her mental fingers. Tri'ng's secondary assignment was to intercept the bank's identity check request and return a fake okay from a fake server.

Iros returned shortly. “Everything was fine, just fine! Now what destination do you want me to send those cases?”

“We have a berth number where our yacht is docked!” Diesel gave Iros another pre typed paper. He wore nano gloves along with Aa, so their fingerprint identification would be impossible later, when their conspiracy would surely come to

light . . .

“Can we monitor the transportation from here, honey?” Aa played the sissy wife.

“I don’t know, honey . . .” Diesel replied with the same word, playing with it's pronunciation as if he was in love.

“Of course, you can, here is a tablet!” Iros was quick to accommodate their presumed needs.

“Look honey, all those moving red dots!” Aa giggled.

Diesel shot a look across Iros’s desk, and the administrator had to look away to cover his smile. It was obvious he did not choose her for her brain.

Diesel was already in contact with Baby and her team via his neural implants. Naturally, he did not give the correct berth number for security reasons. They were close, but not too close. He used his implants to highjack a messenger service and pushed real time info thru it.

Baby Haas was waiting hard for the transport vehicles to pass by the six-lane highway, but the light turned red, and the traffic stopped.

‘Wait for it . . .’ she read it in her contact lenses.

Baby was about to strike, but no truck came.

‘Are you sure?’ she uttered as the computer transmitted the message back to Diesel.

‘According to the screen, it should be on top of your location.’ Diesel replied calmly.

The highway remained relatively deserted.

'NOW!' came the entry, but all Baby could do is scratch her head. The lights turned green, and the cars, and trucks began to flood the street again.

"Nothing happened!" she uttered.

'Go back to the ship and act normal!' came the message.

They abandoned the getaway cars and converged by the van. They had to fly back to the spaceport to get there before it would be too late.

"Um, Iros, are you sure this screen is right?" Diesel worked hard to contain his anger. Luckily, the manager did not notice at all.

"It should be, why do you ask?"

"Is something wrong, honey?" Aa played along.

"Well, it's just that the red dots disappeared for a moment, then reappeared two blocks down but one set of streets up on the screen."

"Oh, I must've forgotten to turn off the security feature!" Iros grabbed his forehead. He quickly did something with his terminal and now the red dots turned green and appeared at a totally different route.

"What is this?" Diesel let loose his anger a bit. "Are you trying to fuck us?"

"Oh no! No, I would never do that. It's just a throw off thing. Usually, we don't let even our own people know where are the shipments coming from or going to. My deepest apologies!"

"Ah!" Diesel nodded while glanced at Aa who was working hard staying in character.

As soon as the green dots slowed down at the spaceport's gate, Diesel began to fiddle with the tablet.

Iros of course noticed this and asked if he could be of any help.

"Um, I think I might have given a wrong address to you, but I'm not sure. I was trying to zoom in to see if I recognize any of the building terminal's features to determine whether it's the right place your trucks are heading . . ."

"You gave me berth 144!" Iros became suspicious.

"Oh shit. It's 164!" Diesel tried hard to look innocent.

"You even had it on a printed card." Iros was not that easy to shake off.

"Yes, but I spoke to the terminal beforehand. And I must've been thinking of my lovely wife's house, residence on Sahsalo Prime, which is on Ultimate Ave 144. My deepest apology!"

"Let me tell them!" Iros left his chair. He grabbed his secretary. "Did the ID check come back okay?"

"Yes, sir. It's all good. Even AOCP state department signed off on it!"

"Okay, that will be all!" He turned around, then remembered the change of address. He grabbed his secretary's arm to tell him that.

*

"Ozzie, how's life treating you?" Sasha hoped to avoid seeing the manager at all, but to her worst luck, he was outside of the bank, smoking a cigar. She managed to compose her thoughts and attack him verbally. Azure was onto her, questioning her moves and motives. She could tell it shocked Ozzie to see her again. He seemed angry, but then that faded, replaced with a flashy smile she chased after so long. His black hair seemed to be as dark and abundant as the first day she met him, when they set up protocols.

"My, my, I would have never thought I would see you again, honey!" he responded, grinning.

Azure and Hunter exchanged looks, both thinking of the same; these two had some sort of history together . . .

"You know me, always on the run!" Sasha shrugged.

"But you managed to come clean after our last encounter!" Ozzie noticed Sasha's mechanical arm and frowned: "Perhaps we all lost something permanent."

"I told you I would be back!" she shot it with her edgy voice, disregarding Ozzie's fingers poking at her rubber covered artificial arm.

“Yes, you did!” he left it at that and walked her into the building. Azure followed them closely, listening to every word coming from their mouths. She could sense a tense moment outside, anger erupting from the manager, but then all dissipated quicker than one-two-three. She glanced back, nodding at Nyikha still behind the wheel. She knew she could count on her if things went south . . .

The building was big, old and could not detect any air conditioning what so ever. She knew the vault had to be air-conditioned, and as Ozzie walked them to the back, she began to sense a light draft coming from the floor. Not that it mattered, but she heightened her senses, because she smelled trouble. It was evident to her Sasha and Ozzie had a complicated relationship and that had the tendency to blow up in one’s face the moment least expected!

“So, what do I owe the pleasure?” The fox-faced Ozzie sat down in his managerial chair. Sasha hopped to the chair opposite to him, leaving Azure and Hunter standing in the background.

“You know why I’m here. I told you the last time . . .” Sasha enjoyed her moment with him. He tried to set her up with a thug the last time, but it did not work, and Sasha then hinted that Ozzie was dirty and a snitch. Frankly, she was surprised to see Ozzie in charge at all. No scars on his face that would tell a recent battle either.

“Yes, that you would take everything. Then you disappeared for three months. Are you here to withdraw the company’s assets?”

“Exactly!” she nodded as casual as she could manage.

Azure felt the same tenseness returning. She activated her special glasses, a longtime gift from Smith. It was embedded AI; a miniature Smith lookalike came to life and gently bowed. She almost smiled.

“Do you have the proper credentials?” Ozzie placed a mechanical keyboard in front of Sasha.

“Of course, I do!” she smiled confidentially and began to type.

Azure watched every keystroke, reciting from her sharp memory what should it be. It was all correct.

"Now that you are who you say you are, how would you like to rearrange your company's accounts?" Ozzie watched them like a hawk.

"The money accounts we have here, I would like to transfer them to these banks!" she tossed a paper across the desk.

Ozzie caught it with unusual firmness. He moved the paper closer and scanned it. The computer accepted the embedded microchip's validity, courtesy of Miss Thorne's competent PR department.

"UNHL bank accounts, huh? No more trust in AOCP?" Ozzie glanced up.

"My company is relocating . . ." she half shrugged, like she did not care and was just the messenger.

"You know the deal, one and a half percent transaction fee in all accounts!"

"Give me that keyboard!" Sasha demanded. It was outrageous that he charged more than a percent!

Azure observed the transactions thru her special glasses. It seemed legit. Yet the dark features of the room gave her the creeps. The miniature holo-Smith behind his holo-desk from the corner of her eyes on the back, reflective part of her special glass waved at her. 'What's up?' she asked mentally.

"Something is wrong!" came the reply.

'What is?'

"As soon as the full transaction began, a backdoor opened up, and the manager sent an automated message to the web."

'Can you see the recipient?' Azure began to worry. There was no way to warn Hunter unless she wanted to let the manager know she discovered something.

"Trace is in progress . . ."

"We need to clear your vault as well!" Sasha pretended she did not know the protocol at all. Ozzie warned her before that would never happen. The man pretended to be surprised, but only lightly. “Presumably only what your company has in here, right?” he tried to joke.

“Right . . .”

“Not much. Seven tons of platinum. How do you plan to transport it? Or you need our generous service for that?”

“I can’t wait days!” Sasha shook her head.

“I thought you missed me!” Ozzie tried to smile and fondle her lower shoulder, but Sasha looked away, further deepening Azure and Hunter’s suspicion.

“Now, Ozzie, now!” Sasha warned him.

“Okay, okay! I will get the stuff together and this afternoon we can . . .”

“Everything is together, stop lying Ozzie! My company sealed the caskets upon delivery. You try to tell me they were opened since?”

“No!” Ozzie immediately backed down.

“Good! I have got two more haulers on their way with crews. We’ll take it ourselves!” Azure suddenly entered into the conversation.

“I’m sorry, I did not get your name, miss!” Ozzie turned toward her.

“And you won’t! All we need is what’s ours, and we’re on our way!” she replied defensively from behind the safety of her special glasses.

“Miss Sasha represents the company. If her passwords are correct, there is nothing further to discuss!” Ozzie excused himself, opening his arms, signaling to give up. According to the holo-Smith, that was definitely not the case . . . His trace penetrated the planetary internet, bore thru the firewalls and landed at the planet’s military headquarters’ front doorstep. Different agencies, mostly Internal Affairs, were involved in the sham. That meant federal and definitely not good for them!

Ozzie’s secretary knocked on the door, telling him that eight women arrived on two antigravity sleds, and that they’re with Sasha.

“My people!” Sasha announced.

"Well, well . . ." Ozzie flinched. "Did you know that since your last interaction, we seceded from the UNHL?"

"What that's got to do with me?" Sasha pretended to be dumb.

Azure flinched. She mentally interacted with the holo-Smith, told him to take over the bank's electronic systems. He advised stalling for a minute or two.

"Or with us?" Azure pitched in.

Hunter frowned and turned to Azure, who forcefully pronounced, "Be" for plan B, although they never discussed what that would be.

"We are under AOCP protectorate now, and as such further percentages have to be deducted from any physical currency removal."

"How much . . . ?" Sasha growled at him.

"Five percent."

"That's outrageous!" she cried out loud.

"Feel free to contact your supervisors! I know you can't make this deal!" Ozzie laughed.

Sasha turned to Azure, since she no longer had her original bosses. "We need to call . . ." she mumbled.

"We don't!" Azure stepped forward, defiant, but deep inside she began to worry. Ozzie definitely had some sort of diabolical revenge shit going on! She was not sure what that was, but did not try to find out either. "We can take that hit!" she replied.

"I'm sorry, but my superiors insist you make that call!" The manager was adamant.

Azure knew it was a setup. As soon as they call out, the tracers were onto them. She could not permit that. It was an impasse, and it could go down only two ways now. She gazed into the manager's eyes: "You can give us what we're here after or we can take it. It's your choice!" Azure was plain and clear about her intention.

Upon hearing that, Hunter flexed his muscles and slowly moved his hands behind his back where his knife and the gun were stashed.

"I can assure you we aren't in the same ballpark! After my Sasha's last encounter, I had to make concessions to some very powerful entities who doesn't let this physical monetary instrument walk out of here without getting its owners, so I'm afraid I have to insist!" Ozzie replied, openly mocking Azure. By that time, she had already made her choices.

"Be it your way!" Azure's lips curled downward. *"Fight it is . . ."*

The manager tossed a phone across the desk, but Azure stated the word clearly: "Cut!"

The next moment, the lights went out and the bank's power access was cut. Backup generators powered down, thanks to the holo-Smith's expertise.

"Duck!" Azure yelled at Sasha as she pointed her sleek laser gun at the door and pulled the trigger once. The secretary went down hard.

Hunter grabbed Ozzie's collar before the man could hit the dead man's switch and yanked him backward with such a force, he hit his head in the desk.

"You'll never leave this planet!" Ozzie laughed but not for long, as Hunter's expert knuckle hit his jaw. A single, audible pop signaled the jaw got either dislocated or outright broken.

"Now what?" Hunter asked Azure, fire and excitement in his eyes.

"We take what's ours. We're in deep shit, you know!" Azure jumped to the door and glanced out into the dark. Luckily, she could see much better than a human, and thanks to her special glasses, infrared was her best friend!

In the meantime, while Hunter grabbed Ozzie's ailing body like it was just a paperweight, Sasha trailed them, looking for trouble. "Give me a weapon!" she insisted.

"Fuck no!" Azure yelled back and jumped out into the dark hallway. People around them seemed to be confused, bumping into each other and into them. It was relatively easy to reach the vault's entrance, but there another problem presented itself; the door was locked, and it had a battery-operated identification system, still active despite the building wide power outage.

Azure grabbed Ozzie by his hair and dragged to the console: "Open it!"

"Ou bhoke mah haw!" he whined.

"Look at the console, dipshit, and put your hand on the screen!" Azure knew voice recognition was not in the system.

Since Ozzie had loyalty problems, Hunter helped him out by placing the man's hand on the screen and aligning his face at the biometric reader. Azure popped open his eyelids, and the approving chime was not far behind.

"Finally!" Azure could not wait for the big door to open. The Honor Guards stormed the vault.

"Only what is ours . . ." Hunter mumbled, but the girls knew. They scanned the crates and hauled them out one by one.

"I'm glad they're so strong!" Sasha worked her muscles, moving the crates to the door.

"What the fuck is this?" Hunter pointed to the side room, with the full chrome cobbled together thing. It was about a meter tall and almost like a bunch of toasters wielded together.

"I don't think we have time for that . . ." Azure glanced at the complicated-looking item.

"Oh, ho, this is the thing!" Sasha stood at the archway, mesmerized by the object.

"Do you know what that is?" Hunter turned around, scrutinizing the manager.

"Nofing!" Ozzie tried hard to talk.

"Lying sack of shit, what the fuck is that?" Azure pounded his stomach. The man yelled in pain and curled up on the floor.

"It's protected all right . . ." Hunter walked closer to the separate security, powered by something inside the unit; it had its own force field!

Azure asked the holo-Smith to divide his attention. The unit analyzed the security, then responded that it was a military-grade protection system, four layers deep and whatever it was, it was important to the enemy, therefore it should be even more important for them.

"Can you disable the security?" she asked him. He nodded and began to work.

"Do you think it's a setup?" Hunter tossed another crate of platinum to the vault's door.

"You mean Ozzie or that toaster headquarter?" she nodded toward the alcove.

"Both."

"I think he did not lie; he got in bed with some serious fellows." Azure watched the first of the four layers of security vanishing. The Honor Guards were quick and efficient, but not fast enough.

"Do you think we have another half an hour?" Hunter counted at least five minutes passed since the cut of the power.

"Police will be here in another ten minutes, but if this shit is real, the military will be onto us before!" Azure pointed at the chromed object.

"What is that anyway?"

"Huper Heapon!" Ozzie whined from the corner.

"Super weapon? For what?" Sasha hovered over the man.

"Ahainht the Hempehohss"

"Who?"

"Hemphehohss!" Ozzie yelled as much as he could, eyes squinted, nose pulled up.

"Let our boss know!" Hunter turned to Azure, looking serious. She immediately made a mental call for her boyfriend.

*

The Emperor inside the Starship Azure slowly gathered the updates from the complex mission. He received the update from Aa and Diesel via the cloaked Toxic. Honor Guards moved the heavy crates via antigravity sleds into the yacht's belly. From there, holo emitters moved it deeper, into one of the Toxic's compartments. Aa and Diesel safely left the bank, and they were on their way to the yacht as well. There was not much Smith needed to do; military telepaths were thrown off. He made sure of it. It was professional, and he felt satisfied when a mental image knocked him out. It was so strong his physical body twitched for a second, attributing to the nervous looks of two of the Death Squad members inside the room, deep within the UNHL Starship. It was a garbled image, laced with anxiety and nervousness. He tried to make sense of it and noticed Azure's mental touch. Something went wrong with her mission; that was certain. His mental aura, projected onto his beloved ones beneath the planet, expanded then contracted, but did not break. He tried hard to analyze the picture. It was familiar; he did see it before once. It had something to do with the late Admiral Csex and his betrayal . . . He felt the urgency embedded in Azure's mental claim and forwarded the entire message to Victor; AI of the Destination Unknown in hopes it would do something about it. He had to concentrate to his own mission.

It surprised the AI at first to receive a mental communication. They did not set him up for that one. A nanosecond later, he analyzed the message and decided with 99.98 percent probability that it came from the Emperor. After running the calculation to the conclusion and coming to the same answer, he needed to warn competent people around him of the possible danger.

*

Captain Josh was delighted upon seeing the AOCP freighter running back to their side of space. The Moronor, the AOCP light cruiser that protected the convoy, did the same.

"Nice job, people!" he shot an approving nod at his lieutenant, overseeing the operation.

"Incoming! Encrypted call from the DU, Captain!" communications promptly reported.

Josh frowned. "What does Commander Danek want?"

"Its ID is something I never seen!" the officer yelled from his seat.

"Complications, huh?" Josh grabbed his seat handle and activated his holo screen. Soon he faced with a wavering image of the Destination Unknown.

"Who is this?"

"I am Victor, the ship!"

"What, who?" Josh stared at the picture, confused.

"Victor!" The ship morphed into a tall, skinny man in his early fifties; bold head and neatly trimmed mustache around his face. He wore a beige leather coat and military pants.

"Victor? Victor . . . What can I help you with?" Josh was not sure if this was a deception from the AOCP. He signaled for his lieutenant to trace the call.

"Azure is in trouble according to the younger Emperor!"

"Why would I believe in you?"

"He sent me this image . . ." a meter-tall cobbled web of chrome toasters replaced the man's picture.

"What is that?"

"A direct threat to the Emperors. It is presumed that Azure found it and wants to bring it back to us. Probability calculations shown that AOCP should have substantial forces wherever this object is located!"

"Why are you showing that to me? Isn't Commander Danek your immediate superior?"

"You are more competent than him! The younger Emperor was clear on that! By the way, I'm only the messenger!"

"Let me talk to the Commander!" Josh turned impatient. It stroked his ego that Smith would finally proclaim his superiority. Not to mention he felt definitely more competent than Commander Danek!

*

"Almost done!" Azure spoke in the dark quietly.

Hunter looked around. The crates were all gone, transported outside by the Honor Guards. Three tons each to the antigravity sleds, one ton to the jeep. One of the antigravity sleds was on its way to the cloaked DSR. Azure hoped they would be back soon to transport away the funny-looking thing too.

Her holo-Smith clapped his hands as the last of the security fell and the alcove housing the strange object lit up.

"Move it!" Azure pointed at the heavy object.

"What is it anyway?" Hunter pushed it slowly. It was really heavy.

"Direct threat to the Emperors . . ." Sasha responded, her lips twitching. Now she was nervous. What the object was, she had no clear idea, but Ozzie seemed to be frightened enough for her to know it was a big problem.

"Over the door!" Azure helped them out with her extra strength.

Sasha nodded approvingly. "I did not think you have such strong muscles!"

"Honey, I am a superwoman!" Azure laughed, then turned to the manager: "Why is this here in your vault?"

"Ahaiting hor thansphotation. Hafe houhe hor AhOFP Mihihahy . . ."

"Safe house? Do they know we're here?" Azure bent forward suspiciously.

"He mohent ou shepped in!"

"Fuck!" Azure grabbed her gun and shot the man in his chest. She then began to help Hunter frantically, pushing the object outside. From the corner, she turned around and burned another hole into the man's brain.

"Why did you do that?" Deep down Sasha hoped Ozzie would survive this.

"AOCP telepaths would extract any information left in his brain. I can't allow that!"

"That means everybody we met . . ."

"Yes," Hunter responded, pushing aside a man's body, facing the floor.

Sasha had to catch her breath. All around her, people were lying on the floor, dead! The Honor Guards took care of them already.

"This is horrible!" Sasha was weeping, "Innocent people!"

"Don't be in the killing business if you can't take it!" Azure frowned.

Hunter flinched, "Emperor's orders!"

"I'm sure this is exclusivity from the Ancient Man . . ." Azure did not like it either.

Nyikha impatiently waited for them outside. "The sled is almost here!" She started the engine and turned the jeep around. As soon as she had done that, the antigravity sled turned in the corner. Traffic was light, but a lone cop car's siren could be heard approaching from the distance.

"We need to prepare for more of them!" Azure ordered the Honor Guards to take up defensive positions while she helped Hunter and Sasha up-righting the device onto the sled.

"Go, go, go!" Azure yelled. The sled was heavy. Taking off was not happening as quickly as she hoped it would. She hopped into the jeep and Nyikha followed the sled closely. Azure grabbed a larger weapon and aimed at the pursuing cop car. With Hunter's help, they blew its tires out. The car slammed into a truck and burst into flames.

"We've got company!" Nyikha pointed at the sky, where a military helicopter just made a wide U-turn.

"Heavy guns!" Azure yelled, desperate to counter the newly emerged threat.

"Just a turret . . ." Nyikha pointed at the second sled with its old-fashioned turret slowly turning around. One of the Honor Guards aimed at the helicopter and began to shell it.

"Don't we have a grenade launcher?" Azure looked around nervously.

"Here we go!" Hunter pulled out the pipe-like device from under a tarp. Azure wanted to do it, but it was his turn. He activated the device, aimed and pulled the trigger. White phosphorous gases erupted from the backside as he launched the grenade. It hit the side wing pod of the helicopter. Shrapnel flew everywhere and soon the helicopter was going down, uncontrollably.

"We did it!" Hunter turned around to shake hands with Azure, but something was wrong. He saw the horror in her eyes; "What . . . ?"

"Duck!" She pushed him to the floor, taking his place in the process. Hunter fell backward, and Azure fell onto him the next moment.

"Azure?" His eyes grew wide, noticing the blood gushing onto his clothes.

"We did it . . ." Her eyes shrunk and turned misty.

Nyikha yelled something in the background, but due to the sound of the whistling wind, the scream of Sasha all faded into the background. His focus landed on Azure and her beautifully engineered lips: "I love masculine men too . . ." she admitted with her dying breath.

"No!" Hunter yelled. He tried to push his jacket into her bloody chest, but the girl was dead already. Her mortal wound, the shrapnel cut pieces off her skin and ribs.

Hunter looked around helplessly. Nyikha's eyes were dry and big, and Sasha was withdrawn to the corner of the jeep. Hunter would have to explain this to the Emperor.

He could not even think . . .

He managed to call Colonel Re'kl as soon as they got onboard his DSR to let him know of the bad news. He felt it standing inside the cramped cargo bay as the ship took off from the surface. He was holding the delicate body as he made his way into the morgue. Soldiers moved aside in the narrow hallway, pointing at the body, uttering words, but it was so strange, so unlike for Hunter, he did not even pay attention. All he could do is to stare at the dead and the sad eyes of a true warrior who defied the galaxy and rescued Smith from prison against all odds. He could not even imagine what Smith could do to revive her. Maybe there was a miraculous way. After all, he was immortal, an emperor . . .

Suddenly he was thrown to the ground.

“What . . . ? What is happening?” Hunter looked around, disoriented. His head was bleeding.

“We’re under attack!” somebody yelled, but he was deep within the slightly less than a hundred and eighty meters Deep Space Reconnaissance ship, and he had no way to help the bridge from his position.

Colonel Re’kl did not like the odds at all! Somehow the two AOCP Planet Destroyers fixed up on his position, no matter that his DSR was cloaked! They shot wildly into space, and now he was on the run. They damaged his ship’s FTL. His engineers were working to at least restore partial capability, but the more than two hundred fighter planes running after him was not helping either.

“Colonel, we’ve got short range communications from Captain Yoyo’s ship. She advises us to make a run for it. She will protect us on the other side!”

“We still have to get there first!” Re’kl hissed as he took more hits; they blasted his main radar dish into pieces. The cloak was still on, but he faced the wrong direction to use the Main Gun or the alternate guns. The DSR was an attacker, not a runner. The rear quad laser guns were hopelessly outgunned for this kind of mission.

Suddenly the lead AOCP PD bow burst into flames.

“What happened?”

“Space mine, sir!” somebody yelled.

*

The needles he took out still hurt himself. Two Honor Guards and two Death Squad members helped him off the bed. With wobbly legs, he limped to the terminal and called Captain Gabriel.

“My Lord!” His shock was noticeable even thru the low-resolution screens.

"Abandon our location and head to the Corridor of Frantics, now!"

"What about the Toxic?"

"They'll join us soon. They just left the first planetary shield."

"Do you want to wait?"

"Take me to the Corridor of Frantics, now! Azure is dead!" he barked angrily at the comm.

Gabriel swallowed hard. He remembered something that she could be cloned again and again, but of course hearsay was not a solid proof. And if the Starship's name giver was dead, that was a disaster in itself.

*

"We're in a minefield?" Re'kl turned around, thinking this was the end, but their past trajectory was supposed to cross right over it.

"Somebody is trailing us!"

"We've got short range sight-to-sight communications from the 0999-Mya. She is covering us!" his second in command reported.

"Good. Shoot charges to our sides to confuse the enemy! Target every fighter closer than two clicks!" He thought that would give ample targets for his men.

His heart sunk the next moment as he heard the dreaded yell: "Radiological alert!"

"Can we jump?"

"Negative, sir!"

"Can we target the missile?"

"No, Colonel! Its heading to that w . . ." his XO pointed at the window, but the next moment, the automatics darkened the composite glass windows as the nuclear device hit its target just after the twenty-eighth rib armor, taking out the topside heat exchanger and cutting deep into the AOCP Planet Destroyer.

"Where did it come from?" Re'kl needed information, and immediately.

"The origin doesn't mark any vessel!" his XO reported, confused.

*

"Good job, Gabriel, let's get out of here! We can't be found in enemy space! That is, as you know is a direct breach of the

Treaty . . . We certainly don't need AOCP to start an open war now, do we?" Smith patted Gabriel's shoulder on the bridge. The man was proud and ordered the crew to take the Starship Azure outside of AOCP territory while they were still cloaked. They never made contact with Colonel Re'kl's DSR, but it seemed to be in one piece as it ran across the border and into the protective sphere of the Trinity, Captain Yoyo's Planet Destroyer.

*

Re'kl's ship made two micro jumps, hopping away while the reactors were operating above red line over one hundred and fifty percent. As soon as he crossed over the border, Captain Yoyo's ship, the Trinity, opened all torpedo tubes along with the Destination Unknown's own. Josh and his immediate forces were still hunting lurking AOCP freighters further out. He decided to either maintain or hide behind his cover for another while. It was obvious he enjoyed his role.

Commander Danek crossed his chest on Destination Unknown's bridge. "Weapon's Chief!"

"Solutions are loaded!" The affirmative reply was immediate.

Danek watched the AOCP PD slowly crossing the border. It identified herself as the Marcono.

"Note its hostile intention, log its position!" he commanded firm.

"Hostile enemy ship, still firing, just crossed over to UNHL space!" Victor confirmed.

"Slug it out, toe to toe!" Danek ordered his crew, and the proud warship released its lethal shelling, tearing up the AOCP

PD’s bulkheads. His team surgically took out the external firing platforms from the enemy Planet Destroyer’s side as it closed by. Its dual side guns, mounted on its planform, did not help either as the Destination Unknown slightly turned, firing from every gun, dual and quad cannons they had. As the AOCP PD sailed by, its side was on fire. Decompressions blew gaping holes into its side and soon it was derelict.

“Target its FTL ring!” Danek received the authorization from the Admiralty to capture the enemy vessel as a prize. He intended to carry out the order!

Captain Yoyo’s PD, the Trinity, took out the enemy Planet Destroyer’s right-side fin, along with its tail. The heavy objects damaged the FTL ring, and the majestic Destination Unknown released many missiles to crack the main engine’s super-strong composite metal covers. The Marcono, the AOCP PD, had to jettison the FTL ring to save the ship from complete destruction before signaling her surrender.

Chapter Two

You'll See Her Again

"I'm so sorry . . ." Hunter was alone with Smith. They were standing around Azure's corpse inside the Eclipse's morgue. Smith touched the girl's hair, gently brushed it aside. His lips pressed to each other, hard as a rock. He kissed her forehead before turning away, battling with his feelings. "It's not your fault." he said emotionally.

"Is there anything you can do for her?" Hunter's throat went dry, sounding remorseful.

Smith slowly turned around, scrutinized his friend's face before his stare returned to Azure. He straightened the white cloth covering her body. "This body is dead!" He slowly pushed the table back into the freezer.

"But . . . I thought maybe you could revive her!" Hunter was not sure this was a logical step at all. Silly by human terms, but Smith could revive dead bodies. He had seen it.

"I don't think you understand," he said hesitantly.

"Oh, you mean the wound is too big to repair. Or is it due to cell decay?" he tried to rationalize.

"Go home Hunter and take the prisoner chick with you!"

"But . . ." Hunter pointed at the freezer.

Smith wiped his eyes dry and with a melancholic tone he said, "You'll see her again . . ."

"Ah. In my memories you mean."

"No. You'll see her again in couple months." Smith left the room silently. Hunter thought about it for a good while but could not figure him out or his vague statement.

They transferred the platinum over to another UNHL military vessel before Smith congratulated Josh and Danek for the successful capture of the AOCP vessel. Aa, after hearing what happened to Azure, wanted to talk to him personally, but he avoided that entirely. Instead, he nudged her toward claiming the prize; being involved in the towing operation of the AOCP Marcono into a military Star Yard and the transportation of the strange object to another military complex. She stared at him long and hard, but he did not budge. Eventually she realized he just wanted to be alone.

Smith now understood Diana's restrictions about the Sky Riders. He must've traveled back in time to speed up Azure's re-cloning and also ordered Diana to update her memory. He had Azure's body transferred to the Toxic and with the Honor Guards onboard he left without talking to the Admiral. He did give a ride to Diesel, back to his chosen destination. Diesel mentioned how much Aa grew professional, how much he was sorry for Azure's demise. They both agreed that the AOCP Marcono's capture was a true victory and that it will go a long way as a precedent.

Once they crossed over universes via the Parallels into Down Earth's atmosphere, Smith ordered Toxic to land inside dock E1 of the Sky Riders, where Diana promptly met him.

"So, what about the body?" Smith asked her without beating around the bush.

"It's best not to let her see it. I would suggest to dump it into the main engine's incinerator. We're low on bones anyhow. . ." she responded.

"I find it morbid to do such with her body." Smith referred to the alien Starship's keen hunger toward human remains as a fuel additive for its main engine.

“The new one is being formed rapidly. Two months and she is ready. The memory forming is also ongoing. The only thing she won’t remember is from the time when you took her to the valley to have a picnic and beyond.” Diana explained without giving an avenue to Smith’s preference of how to dispose the body.

Smith flinched, “When I take her there again, she will complain. She will think I took another girl there before!”

“Did you?”

“I once intended to take Tri’ng there, but. . .” he abruptly cut the sentence before adding it, “She was not that kind of girl.” Smith remembered to another sad time in his life.

“No, she was not.” Diana agreed. “I urge you to come by every day, or at least every other day. She will sense you thru the walls; she will feel you, no matter how thick those composite walls of mine are . . .”

“I know.” Smith swallowed hard. Azure could be very passionate. “Should I pray?” he asked quietly, kind of lost.

“You should be glad Johnny constructed her such a way. She will be born again! You can monitor her vitals, but my droids will watch her day and night. We’re on a lockdown anyhow. We won’t move unless a major disaster occurs. Go on with your life, boss. She’ll be ready for you, I promise!” Diana attempted to pat Smith’s hand, but it did not come out quite right.

“I’ll leave now.” Smith announced. Diana was hoping to watch him leave thru the corridors, but Smith was sad, he just teleported back to the Toxic. The organic DSR itself teleported away the next moment, leaving the Honor Guards without a direct ride back to their compound.

Smith needed to take care of a loose end that nagged him. A trip to the planet Qbe, a short conversation with her, all he wished for. Sasha was nervous, he could tell. The girl opened the door for him, staring at the floor.

“Let’s go inside,” he tried to encourage her.

She tried to offer some tea, and he took it. It was not bad at all.

"I know you did not tell everything about your past dealings regarding to the manager on

Ciun . . ." he lay back in the comfortable chair.

"Ozzie." she responded, sadness in her eyes.

"Azure killed him. You know she was right. He had to die. He saw your face. You don't exist now, so there goes my spotless record of not lying if he talks!" He chuckled, mostly to ease the conversation.

"My deepest condolences about Azure!" he could tell she meant it with all her heart.

"Thank you, but I'm looking forward to the new her!"

"What's that mean?" she frowned, constantly playing with her rubber hand to ease her anxiety.

"It means that she did not really die, but she won't remember to this mission." Smith looked directly into her eye. He saw her confusion, then a hint of realization.

"I'm here because I want to tell you I don't hold you directly responsible for her death. If I would feel such way, you would be dead by now. I think regardless of what you did not say about your dealing with Ozzie, she would've died. That object in the bank's vault was a real shocker. Do you know what that is?"

"No." she shook her head.

"Good. It's not for you to know. Be enough that I know what it is, and I'm glad we procured one of it. It will help us devise a counteroffensive. Now about your life. Hopefully, we will never meet again. Pray that you don't. The mayor of Paradise City will come by. Her name is Melissa. She'll introduce you to your parole officer, so to speak. You'll receive an ID card and a background story of why are you here. There will be a bank account opened under your name with the initial starting of six thousand six hundred and two credits. It's how much you had under false accounts tied to you as far as I know. This is a moneyless society. Basics are free, but any extra and you have to pay. In return, you are expected to work full time. Melissa will set you up with something easy."

"Azure once mentioned secretaries get all the actions . . ." she mumbled.

Smith laughed. "Yes, she would know! Something like that. Get a boyfriend or two and a hobby. Race at night, but don't get caught! This house is your home for the rest of your life. Be at home by ten and you can leave by six AM. You can't leave the city just yet. You have to show you want to forget about your past life. This is your third in a rather short lifetime. Most people don't have the chance to have two!"

The meeting was over, and Smith was about to leave. He offered his hand to her, and she gladly accepted it. He was about to step outside, but remembered something: "Try to forget about your past and in return one day we will forget about you . . ."

Chapter Three

Amerlee

"Is that them?" Smith tried to be as inconspicuous as he could be without falling off his chair. He was in Miss Thorne's office talking about a Letter of Recognition, a smaller and less weighted sibling of a Letter of Support. The LR was a less formal version and was given more broadly. It did not require his signature, just a virtual nod. The whole case came up as Smith had more time on his hand as Azure was out of his life for the time being. He believed he handled her absence well, although Henry mentioned to him the other day he should wind down somehow. Captain Aa was on her reward mission and as such he did not want to bother her; Diana was busy reconstructing Azure's mind from the crystal, and that left him with ample of free time. He went to work to the KFT, his company regularly, and even talked to Del on an occasion utterly confusing the young man. Since the Sky Riders was on a lockdown until at least the memory formation was complete, Smith visited the cloning chamber almost every day. But after a while it became a strange ritual, and it somehow reminded him to some weird form of never-ending funeral. Here the process was the inverse, but regardless, it felt he was talking to a dead body. For the time being, it was. While Diana did not exactly let him into her books, she allegedly revised the body's age to eighteen from the original sixteen and a half. Smith had his doubts, but kept it to himself and instead he tried to be occupied with everyday things and problems. That was the reason he was sitting in the Public Relations building's eight floor, front of Miss Thorne.

"Yes, aren't they cute?" Miss Thorne leaned toward him.

"It's time you practice my full name!" Smith tried to remind her.

"Evan isn't so sexy and powerful as Mr. Smith." she responded instantly.

"It's uplifting." he responded happily, then asked: "So does Lou or Amerlee have that paper file?"

"Amerlee. Lou is a nice guy, and he is truly in love with her!" Miss Thorne uttered.

"What's the problem?"

"He is twenty-nine, and she is thirty-five."

"True love has no boundaries!" Smith reminded her, and that earned an appreciating nod from Emma.

"I did not realize you were such an expert, My Lord!"

"What a cynical response from a supervisor!" Smith shook his head, trying to appear hurt.

"We are here to work, not to socialize!" she responded.

"Best way to pick up a girl is in a workplace!" Smith disagreed.

"It's counterproductive."

"I agree. So Amerlee feels he is too young for her?" Smith gouged the last row of the open office space with intent on the man and woman sitting beside each other.

"Not just that. She has a birth defect and hates if people are feeling pity toward her."

"Birth defect?" Smith instantly frowned.

"Maybe I shouldn't say that. She is a good and adept person, a great worker. Never had a productivity issue with her." Miss Thorne was suddenly worried the Emperor might fire her.

"I don't care what's her defect. Can she do the work under the allotted time?"

"Yes."

"Then I really don't see any issue."

"Boys do. She doesn't have a left arm . . ." she turned to him. Smith frowned again. About she was calling men, boys and about Amerlee. Since he decided not asking, Emma elaborated: "Almost the entire left arm is prosthetic. Her parents are loaded, so they afforded a decent fake arm with motor functions and embedded microchip line with neuro transmitters. Pretty neat stuff if you ask me!"

". . . And hell of an expensive." Smith became interested in her, then reminded himself to take a back seat of all that. Rocking back and forth in the chair, he asked, "So what's Lou's strong points?"

Miss Thorne attempted to wince, "He is persistent with her. But I think it's the classic case of she expecting him to be her friend and not boyfriend."

"I see. Tough case. Call her in with the file, please!" Smith decided to make a run for it. If Tri'ng and the Krea'tor got together because of him, maybe he can make these two happy somehow.

In the meantime, the girl named Amerlee walked in. She looked taller now as he was sitting. He could barely notice where her left arm ended being real. Truly nice job—he summarized. Her brown eyes caught his attention along with the makeup she wore to enhance the effect. Although it was not his thing, too much makeup that is, she looked stunning, and the lips were just too gorgeous to say anything else about it.

"Ma'am, here is the file you requested!" she stopped by Emma's desk and since she did not dismiss her, she waited patiently.

"How do you like your job, miss?" Smith asked from the corner.

"You talking to me?" she turned her attention to him.

"Yes." Smith tried to be as innocent sounding as he could be.

"I love every minute of it, but let me ask you, do you like to work for your mom, doing her errands?" she pointed her right index finger at him.

"Mom?" Smith was sure he misunderstood something.

"Oh," she smiled, brushed her lightly colored brown hair behind her right ear, "We mean Diana on the Sky Riders."

"She is the mother?" Smith was still recovering from the earlier mockery. He was sure it was a mockery with some hidden agenda he could not quite pinpoint his finger on.

"Mother of all souls of the mighty bucket!" she winked at him.

It was so sexy it threw him off completely. Even with her smirks, he was lost in her eyes and pink lips.

"Mighty bucket, huh? She would be so pleased to hear you say that." he managed to reply.

"Look at you!" Amerlee flirted with him. "The errand boy is offended! I saw you here before!" she added.

"Oh?"

"You come by every week, are you here to check up on the girls?"

"Um." Smith's face flushed.

"Or am I wrong and you into boys?"

"What?!" Smith turned solid red while Miss Thorne was laughing in the back.

"Perhaps not . . ." Amerlee rewarded him with a smile, and Smith was mesmerized again. After he recovered, he decided to go for the offensive, "I heard you have boyfriend problems."

"Not me. Not anymore!" she giggled.

Something coy in her eyes caught Smith's attention.

"Oh, so Lou is taken, huh?"

"I mean, I feeling thirsty for a hot chocolate and I thought you could buy me one!"

Smith stared at her speechless while Miss Thorne continued to laugh in the background. He turned to her and was about to say something, but Emma reached for her purse and

threw some coins on her desk. "To the happy couple!"

"Coins . . . They still make them!" Smith stared at the corner of her desk.

"I finance this trip errand boy." Miss Thorne kept laughing.

"You going to get it!" Smith warned her while he scooped up the coins.

"Have fun!" she waved after them, hoping she did not overstep her boundary.

"So, errand boy, you have a name?" she looked at him from top to toe, like a prize.

"Evan. Evan Smith." Smith inserted the coins after he made sure the damn machine did not accept charge cards at all. He gave her the first cup while he held the second for himself.

"So does your boss allow you to have a private life at all?" she gulped from the cup minutes later.

"Yes, why?"

She did this thing of shaking her head, while looking away, but still smiling. "I was wondering whether you would want to put that charge card of yours into good use tonight."

"What you have on your mind?" Smith was not about to let her go at all.

Dinner. It was a bit new to him. They met at one of the mid to upscale restaurants in Super City. Strictly indoors, he was sitting across her in the warmly lit corner. She browsed thru the menu, and he had the chance to watch her making decisions. He could've read her mind but opted out of it instead. It was cheating, and he was just happy to be with someone new he did not know. She frowned for a moment - Smith thought it was probably a food she tried to imagine. His vision slipped below her entertaining face and into the V-neck of her blouse. Suddenly he felt he was being watched. Her eyes laughed, she smiled, shook her head: "What makes you think you gonna get there?"

"Um, where?" Smith pretended to be innocent.

"Stop playing with me, you stared at my chest!"

"Your blouse . . ." he tried to save himself.

"You like it?"

"I'm gonna wear it!" He uttered, but she heard it, laughed, "Funny guy!"

"Trying to be . . ."

"So, mister funny, can I order a wine?"

"Sure thing!"

"I love Stalingrad blend, do you?"

"I'm going to have to try it myself!" Smith never drank their wine, only their liquor.

She pretended to browse the menu. "It's expensive."

Smith tried to be as loose as he could be. "So, what?"

"Over five credits . . ." she held the menu in front of her mouth, most likely hiding her smile. That was the only regret Smith had. He was in love with her lips.

"Anything for you."

"Anything?" she dropped the menu, revealing her coy smile.

"Well . . . within reasonable thoughts." Smith tried to backpedal.

Serving was relatively fast, and the wine was great. Smith tasted a bit, but she got her glass full.

"What?" she placed her glass on the table, rather meticulously, amid his disapproving look.

"You like drinking," he said.

". . . And I see you don't. Why if I may ask?"

"Who is going to drive you home if I do too?"

"Oh, ho-ho!" she dismissed him with a single hand move. "What makes you think you can drive my car?"

"I saw you came with a sleek looking one, I took Pub myself." he referred to public transportation.

"Boy, I've got a limited edition NightCrawler. You'll touch me before I'll let you touch it!"

"Hm." Smith fired up his brain cells.

"Do you know it's a 470S." she tried to poke him with the numbers. "They don't make anything higher in series. Its maroon and chrome grills, sills and the whole shebang! I've got nano layer covers against smudges and scratches. Its auto healing and fully tuneable!"

"How do you know so much about cars?" Smith was mesmerized. She was anything he ever imagined she would be; a whole new chapter in his life.

"I used to race . . ." she laughed.

"What?!"

"Really. When I was a teen, I had my first boyfriend. You know, during the Chaotic Years. The war was over, Super City was partially built, but still lots of ruins, shot down alien vessels. I was fourteen. He was seventeen. Badass. He had this messed up NightCrawler. Two-seventy-Five S. I lost my virginity in the back seat between two repulsor enhancers and the power inverter was beneath my arched back. I remember watching the raindrops on the cracked back window as I got high after . . ."

"Nice!" Smith was salivating, trying to imagine it.

"What, you never raced?" she recovered from her memories.

"Not exactly. I mean later when I needed a fast car, I requested one from the KFT, but no. No racing cars. Knowing what I know now, I wish I would have been in the night scene."

"Do you like motorcycles?" she inquired further.

"Not really. I mean, if it's spokeless, or it's something exotic, I'll watch it go by, but I rather drive cars."

"Not into motorcycles, not into cars. What were you doing as you grew up?" she tried to figure him out.

"I was drafted into the service . . ." Smith looked away.

"Shit . . ." now it was her time to look away.

"Why do you say that?" Smith frowned.

"Because my parents worked really hard not to let me get drafted. I think they even paid off someone."

"You a bit younger than me, I don't think a six years old child would've been a good fighter." Smith replied.

"Don't patronize me, I'm a big girl and I do my penance by working for the PR Department!" she shot back.

"Hey," Smith held up his hands. "Don't need to be so defensive, honey!" he added.

She made a quick smile, then with her good hand she pondered the table: "So tell me, what was like. I mean in the service. You had a hobby?"

"Yeah, I was a fighter pilot. A good one at that. Reckless and daring." he laughed, remembering some stupid things he had done. All the talk backs to his superiors whom worried about his and their safety.

“How many kills? You killed, right?” she added after thinking of something.

“Yes, I did.” Smith became hesitant.

“So, how many?”

“I don’t know, I lost count after four hundred and seventy. But then I moved on to be . . . What?” he stopped as she was staring at him, her brown eyes ever so big, her lips twitching and a tear running down just below her left eye.

“I’m so sorry!” she said emphatically.

“Of what?”

“As a kid . . .”

“I was a teenager!” he shot back angrily.

“Still. I feel guilty, skipping service.”

“It was not your calling.” Smith shrugged casually.

“Was it yours?” she asked him as he used a napkin to dry up her tear.

“I had no other choice back then. I guess it was my calling. They picked me out of the orphanage with others. But I did not remain fighter pilot forever. After Kabnul they promoted me to . . .”

“You were at Kabnul and survived?” she seemed to be amazed.

Smith lightly smiled. “Many of us survived. The Unified Command Center did not, but lots of us did. Crazy times.” he shook his head.

“I heard it was a slaughterhouse . . . I mean, I saw a war movie with this douche bag investment guy about three years ago at the holo movie theater. It was really entertaining. Like the most important battle humans ever fought!”

“Publicly . . .” Smith responded cynically.

“Te. . . T. . .”

“Te’lek” Smith helped her out.

“I heard something in the radio about that. Scholars were debating the validity of that claim the Emperor made few years back that it was very important.”

"The pivotal moment of mankind's history. Were we not won; I wouldn't sit here with you today!" he gently touched her hands.

It did not elude her. Her coy smile softened, then something shot across her mind: "Were you there too?"

"Not as a pilot. I was a Captain by then."

"Shit, a Captain!" she shook her head, feeling even more depressed.

"Hey, it ended a long time ago." he tried to reassure her for whatever reason.

"So, was Te'lek as important as the Emperor said it was? As you said it?"

"Yes. I remember to the Emperor's speech at the University of Founders couple years ago."

"I went there to study!" she interrupted him.

"I did not . . ." he shook his head, the sad face returned, and he continued, "There were two battles, just as he said. A conventional that we lost and an unconventional that we later learned we won."

"What was it like?"

"You know, space is cold and dark. A ragtag fleet of UNHL and AOCP battle cruisers, the Emperor's own battle-damaged Trimaran, and a bunch of PODs. We lost almost thirty percent of the forces at the first battle. We knew it was bad. Very bad . . ." Smith drowned in his memories, trying to recount it from a different view. He pressed his lips. "Disaster was an arms-length away. There was a reorganization, lasting for couple hours and then we, ranking officers were called to the main deck of the Emperor's Trimaran where he made an emotional speech of how he failed, but there is another option, a last-ditch effort to win, but it would be bad, morally unacceptable." his face was twitching. He tried to cover his sadness, but he could not control the tears. He had to wipe them off before continuing, amid the intently watching Amerlee. "See, he said it would be a strictly volunteer mission, that he would have us sign the nondisclosure forms and that he is so sorry for failing us, the citizens. I volunteered just like all of us. We all signed the forms and returned to our ships waiting for the order. When it came, my job was to protect the fighters storming the replicator ship. The enemy did not immediately catch up with our true intent, but once they figured out our endgame, they became suicidal. They would just ram us even if it took them out or blow their ships up. The Emperor lost his Trimaran and my ship picked him up. We collected our few surviving people and withdrawn." His lips twitched as he added: "And the war was over six months later . . ."

"But what happened? What did the Emperor do?"

"I will never tell that." Smith shook his head. "Be enough that the reason they selected him was fulfilled, his deed would be never forgotten where it counts the most!" he said passionately.

"What does it mean? I never heard anyone speaking of this in that much detail before!"

"Not many of us survived. And the mental scars would remain there forever." he gulped up his wine entirely.

"You got those scares too?"

"All of us whom survived have those, because we know what truly happened there. He told us all openly what he was planning to do, and we stepped forward as one man to support him, because we knew that the decision will stay with him forever and him as an immortal would live very long. He would have to face the mirror every day, knowing what he had to do to preserve

humanity . . ."

"But what was that?" Amerlee was intrigued by the riddle.

"It was something he wowed to never do. For someone who doesn't have consciousness it wouldn't matter, but for someone who was a good man, who vowed to fight clean and honorably that decision was a suicide." he sighed. "I really don't know why I told this in our first date. I never really told this to any of my past girlfriends."

"Whoa, who said it was a date?" her good mood returned. "By the way, how many girlfriends did you have until me?"

"Oh, after the war I was dating with a radar operator girl, but it did not end well. I took a recess, then I was messing with a girl from the northern mountains. Then, as they asked me to work for the organization run by the Emperor, I was assigned to Upper Earth where I met a singer. I dated with a spy and a hacker. She was amazing, but really cold."

"You have no idea how hot I could be!" the coy smile in the corner of her eyes returned.

"I live day and night to learn that!" he flirted with her.

"Good puppy!" she finished her dinner.

Smith paid the bill and escorted her to the garage. The maroon NightCrawler was there. Just as she said, it was spotless, clean and shiny. She did something and the doors slowly opened.

"Nice!" Smith admired the chrome front.

"Hop in!"

He had to hurry up to see her land in the leather seat. She looked so sexy, so delicate, he just could not take his eyes off of her.

"I'm not a candy bar, Smith!"

"Why not?" he pretended to be upset.

"I promise you one day you will lick me from toe to . . ." she giggled, cutting it off. "All the way up . . ."

"I can't wait!"

"I know!" she glanced at him, laughing.

The ride was of course short. Five minutes to get to Future Street, where Smith pointed out the towering skyscraper as his home.

"You live alone?"

"Presently."

"I've got to work tomorrow morning, but why don't we meet at lunchtime?" she offered him scraps, and he practically yanked it away, "Bet!"

"You did not even ask what time." she reminded him.

"What time?" Smith cleared his throat.

"One PM!"

"I'll be there! Where do you live?" he asked her as she pulled to the curb.

"Oh, I'm in party city!"

"Hyper City, nice!"

"Not far."

"This car kick ass!" Smith tried to complement her, but missed the mark. She frowned, so he quickly added, "You too!"

"What?" she watched him as he remained in his seat, despite the slowly opening door.

"Give me a kiss!" Smith gulped air.

"Don't you think it's a lot to ask at first date?"

"So, it is a first date, then!" Smith realized.

She kissed him and he kissed her back.

"Whoa!" Smith said once their lips parted.

"Not bad . . ." Amerlee had to pull herself back from him or she would do more than just a kiss.

"See you tomorrow!" Smith jumped out of the car. He heard the whining of a repulsor and as he turned around, he saw the mighty NightCrawler doing some impressive maneuvers before disappearing in the late-night traffic. He kept grinning all the way home.

Chapter Four

Love is in the Air

"You look particularly happy, almost glowing!" Miss Thorne said once she finally approached Amerlee around ten AM on the floor. She was by the secure copier, authorizing archiving, a Letter of Support to a Senator.

"Yes, Ma'am!" she almost laughed, with a smirk smile on her face.

"So how did it go?"

"Go, what?" she pretended.

"With the guy, the errand boy?" Miss Thorne licked her lips.

"Well, he was amazing!" Her face went serious all of a sudden: "I never realized that while I was goofing around with guys and such, he was in the service . . ."

"He is a guy all right." Nodded Emma, wondering about that conversation. Whatever the two of them talked about, it made a deep impression in Amerlee.

"I mean, we women were also in the service, fought alongside, but now I feel guilty that I blew my chances to do the real deed. You know, being a patriot to serve my country. I never thought about it this way before."

"Well, you are here instead of being a housewife to some wealthy guy or woman, so I think you're doing your deed now!" Miss Thorne reminded her. It seemingly worked for a moment, then the dark clouds returned to her face: "He was at Kabnul and survived as a pilot. I mean, I never came across anyone . . ."

"Millions survived there." Miss Thorne replied, trying to downplay the presumed significance. And she knew it was true. She wrote countless LR to heroic pilots over the years.

"And Te'lek. He told me as much as he could. I think it deeply affected and changed him!"

"It did . . ." Emma answered darkly, fully agreeing with her assessment.

"You talked with him about that before?" Amerlee felt the hesitation in Emma's voice.

"Yes. When I met him, we talked extensively about that too. You don't know, but my father was a spaceship builder, and he used to talk about it and take me to the job site. He used to tell me stories about them, about the battles, about the manning soldier's heroic sacrifices so we could live a normal life. We would never find out of their true sacrifice, he used to say. . ."

"I guess your father was right!" Amerlee put a lot of emphasis on that, while frowning, then chuckled, "I'm just glad he lived thru so we could meet!"

"I'm delighted about that myself!" Emma nodded too.

"Do you like him too?" Amerlee became suspicious.

"Strictly as a coworker." she was quick to say that.

"You sure there is no enviousness there?"

"No. I could've made a move on him, but we both decided it would be a mistake." Emma tried to be vague. She remembered of the song, the now mainstream pop song from Ugrughughau; Midnight Magic, and their involvement in it.

"Yes, it would've been a colossal mistake! He is mine!" she announced, doing a poor job hiding her joy.

"Um, did you ask him if he has a girlfriend now?" Emma was not sure she should ask or mention that at all, but liked Amerlee. She shouldn't get hurt that way. The girl's response however surprised her: "Girlfriends come and go and personally I don't mind sharing until it becomes a deciding factor!" she shrugged.

"You mean it?" Emma was not sure she was joking or not.

"Yeah. I'm progressive." she stopped pounding the machine's holo screen and turned to her boss: "I somehow love that song,

Midnight Magic, it's so hot and romantic. And it's the loss of the girl she did not recognize the man to be the Emperor . . ." She bobbed her head to the star hit rhythm.

"Be careful so you don't fall into the same trap!" Emma uttered as she was about to turn around.

"What, why?"

"Your special friend, did he mention he met the Emperor, that he knew him before he became it, that they kept in touch over the years?" It was obvious he did not say it, because Amerlee dropped her papers and just stood there with her yaw hanging.

"What?" Emma shook her head.

"That nasty bastard did not say that! I'm gonna get him today!"

"So, how was the kiss?" Emma asked candidly.

"It was good. Really good. Not stellar, but good! I suddenly felt a deep connection with him. I do not like to kiss on the first date, but I let my guards down."

"First date, huh?"

"Oh, come on, boss!" Amerlee tried to hide her laugh and went back to her work.

"So, I had to find out from my boss today that you're practically the Emperor's friend!" Amerlee boasted at lunch. She and Smith met at the restaurant across the street from the firm.

Smith stopped chewing. "So?"

"So? It is a big deal, my friend!" Amerlee tried to joke with the tone.

"I'm sure you have interesting friends too." Smith tried to brush aside her concern.

"Oh, but meeting the Emperor before he became so inaccessible. I bet you go to his house every morning to eat breakfast!"

"No. I haven't done that yet . . ." Smith trailed off.

"Then I must do that with you. I was with my parents about a decade ago in his old estate, eating from his breakfast table, just past nine AM! I felt so proud."

Smith did not entirely get why that was so special, but the good host in him emerged instantly:

"How was the food?"

"Fresh!"

"Ha-ha. Good!" Smith was really happy to hear that.

She did not have that much time, so she ate and talked between bites, often humming a beat. Smith found it familiar, and he asked her about it.

"Oh," she blushed, "It's a pop song, a disco hit, called Midnight Magic from a famous singer-composer chick, Shoroska from Ugrughughau."

"Really?" Smith grinned warmly, mumbling something to himself.

"Yeah, why?" she stopped chewing.

"Is the song about a girl who blows off a guy who gave her a present, she brushes him off and he says something about never meeting again?"

"Yeah, he is the Emperor, and she founds out after his spaceship left the port at exactly midnight! So, you do know the song?" She poked him with her index finger.

"I'm so glad the prediction came thru!" Smith was full of happiness, almost slipping about his past involvement.

"What do you mean?"

"Did not Miss Thorne say she was there?"

"Where?"

"When Miss Atok met her and the Emperor at her apartment in Ugrughughau that particular night? When she told them never to be bothered at her apartment and the Emperor gave her the Letter of Support, I think, and told her they would never meet again?" Smith had to stop, because Amerlee looked at him like she saw a ghost. "What?" he asked her.

"That shit was real?!"

Smith grinned. "Yeah! I heard it was epic. I also heard the Emperor took Miss Thorne there to teach her how he operates."

"Man, you have to tell me all these stories! If the media would blow the lid off of

these . . ." Amerlee wondered aloud.

"Don't!" Smith became serious.

"Okay, okay, but why?" she knew it would be a bad thing.

"It's magic for a reason. You make it public and now the parties are all hurt. That isn't how magic operates!"

"So, you call him magic? Is that his codename?" she grinned, hoped she had learned something she did not supposed to be.

"I don't think so." he shook his head.

"Your answers disappointing me today!" she made a goofy face, then turned serious: "I heard you have a girlfriend!"

He stopped eating and looked her in the eye. For a moment he wanted to lie and say no, but emotions took over. Azure wouldn't be happy, and it was not fair to Amerlee either.

Resigned, he nodded: "Yes I do, but we're apart at the moment."

"Good! You're all mine!" she poked his legs beneath the table.

Smith was not sure he heard it correctly, "What?"

"I'm progressive. It isn't a big deal until marriage kicks in. It's obvious you two have some problems. It's fair game to me!"

"Hm . . ." Smith wondered about her. She was light on this, at least now, but later . . . The sudden thought emerged: "Hey, how many boyfriends do you have?"

She laughed, tried to jinx him with her eyes: "Who said you can ask me that?"

"After you just did." Smith was taken back.

"No honey, I'm all alone. Had a boyfriend, but we ended it."

"He did or you?"

"Why is that important?"

"So, it was you . . ." Smith was pleasantly surprised.

"How did you figure it out?"

"Something about you and your strong personality. I like it. But what about Lou?"

Her smile turned bad, like she just ate a bad apple: "He is just a friend, don't even mention him."

"He would like to be more than just that."

"No. He is weak. I need a strong one like you!"

"I feel bad now. Lou seems to be a nice person."

"Let's concentrate ABOUT US, OKAY?" she suddenly grabbed his arm and kissed it.

That caught him off guard. "Am I so special?"

"To me, yes. We need to meet again, say an early dinner on Friday?"

"Okay!"

"Hey, do you ever have to go off world to do business for your boss?"

"I do."

"So how come you available every time I want to see you?"

"Maybe . . . Maybe because the feeling is mutual?" Smith tried to joke with her.

"Give me a kiss!" she asked with a shallow voice.

Smith leaned over the table and this time when they kissed, he spiced it with a little mental joy. She was very receptive to that. She played with her hair afterward, covering her weakness. She bit her lips: "I better go or I just do something really stupid."

"Like what?" Smith did not get it at first, but when she shot a longing look, he caught himself. "

Oh!" he grinned as he took her tray to the trashcan, then escorted her across the street.

Amerlee knocked on her boss's door.

Emma was organizing her desk for tomorrow morning. "What's up, Amerlee?"

"Do you have a minute?"

"Just about. I'm leavin and so should you, so, what's up?"

"Um, I talked with Smith and he said you were there when the Midnight Magic was born. Is that really true? Why did not you tell me before?"

Emma had to stop. She straightened her back and nodded. “Yes, I was.”

“You never told me that!” Amerlee gasped for air.

“It’s personal. It was on the day I got promoted. The Emperor did that and wanted to show me what he said, how he makes deeds to society.”

“That must’ve been amazing!” Amerlee could not even imagine how it must’ve been gone down.

Emma played with her sharp fingernails on her desk for a second, before the emotions took over her: “You know what was the most incredible thing that night?”

Amerlee shook her head, eager to hear anything related to the story.

“We walked back to the Toxic, his spaceship in a hurry, and I asked him why are we running. He said she must not catch up with us. And I did not get it. He said she must see the spaceship leaving Ugrughughau and teleporting out of the domed city and it has to be midnight for a magical song to be born and floor the airways by the next year. He said to be really proud that I am one of the three people in the entire universe to know what really happened on that night. And you know what? It all came true! He foresaw it! And he allowed me to witness that moment!” she had to wipe her eyes as the emotions took over.

“Whoa! That’s something!” Amerlee digested the story.

“Good night!” Miss Thorne turned diplomatic and Amerlee got the message. She was leaving too.

She was tossing and turning; she was sleepless. She dreamed about Smith and his girlfriend. She was utterly jealous of her for some reason. Smith pretended not to care about the restaurant bill, but now she felt guilty for a moment. Perhaps she set the bar too high. She needed to give in a bit to him, so he would feel better. She knew she would. She had to laugh. Alone in her pristine and meticulously designed private apartment, where she spent so much time hoping to meet the right person and just now, she realized she would leave this place and never return if she could be with the man she truly loved. That realization frightened her and decided to turn in her bed and try to get some sleep.

*

Smith spent some time onboard the Sky Riders, checking on Azure's progress. She was coming along nicely. Diana pulled a protective curtain around her developing waist and was adamant about keeping it there. Smith had to laugh. He noticed the first time she was being replicated she acted this protective, perhaps it was a mother thing. He suddenly realized the parallels Amerlee drew days earlier. He left it at that and returned to the Villa-Castle to clean up.

Henry asked whether he would want a dinner, but he had to excuse himself, but then the previous conversation with Amerlee emerged in his mind: "I'm trying to date at the moment and the girl might come by one time. Please try to act as if you don't know me!"

"Of course, My Lord!" Henry nodded politely, then asked: "Although, if she comes by to see you sir, then she will know who you are."

"I see you keeping your brain sharp, Henry," Smith tried to joke with the old servant. "Look, I did not explain myself, we might come by together to eat and then . . ." He left the sentence open for him to pick up on. He seemingly did.

Smith stared at his car pool options. "Not that . . ." he uttered under his breath, standing front of an older Chevy pickup. "Definitely can't explain this one . . ." He moved on to the yellow Corvette he liked so much. He stopped front of the silver-gray model. "ProcessAutomatic." he shook his head. "It looks like a piece of shit compared to a NightCrawler." He frowned and grabbed the key. Of course, the car started without a problem. Low mileage, but its age showed. It was old, over eighteen years now since he got it. "Damn, I going to get it!" he walked back to the estate.

Henry was waiting at the doorway. "Is there anything I can do for you, My Lord?"

"Where is the Master Gardner?" Smith frowned.

"He is in town to get us a new . . ."

"Tell him I want flowers!" he snapped.

"But you're allergic to most, sir!"

"Just get nice flowers. I want a nicely organized garden!"

"I'll get right on it!" Henry got the cue, turned around and left. That left Smith alone with the keys to the ProcessAutomatic. Amid heavy frowning, he drove into the city. He supposed to pick up Amerlee from work, and so he parked beside her car. He winced as he locked it. "It's not going to go down well. . ." he mustered the obvious differences. As he took the elevator up, he called the KFT and left a VM for Mrs. G to get a pamphlet from the maker of NightCrawlers. He going to get something good, he decided. He knew in the back of his head it was an impulse buy he hated so much, but after all he could afford it. "I know it's not the point!" He was pissed at himself for some unknown reason. Aa had her own NightCrawler, a mythical 517S, parked at his house. Now he wanted one too!

Amerlee looked stunning in her deep blue one-piece dress, her long earrings and neat, black purse beneath her hand. She smiled upon noticing him in a sharp, gray suit. "Hey, I'm almost ready!" she greeted him.

"You wore this all day?" Smith asked skeptically.

"No, silly boy, I changed in the bathroom!" she giggled.

"Oh, the bathroom . . ." He nodded and turned toward Miss Thorne's office.

"She left already, something about a date." Amerlee uttered as she grabbed his arm. "So, where are you going to take me?" she probed him.

"Surprise, baby!" he walked her to the elevator.

“Not in this . . .” ‘Piece of shit’ She added as an afterthought. The ProcessAutomatic lie low beside her bigger and more luxury car, like a mouse in slippers.

“Oh, come on!” Smith upbraided beside her.

“Do I really have to?” She asked, nudging him toward her car.

“I mean, if I take you out to a place I choose, why can’t we go with mine?” Smith got pissed. He knew he would get it, and now that he got it, he was not happy at all.

“Please, please, please! I don’t need to know the place, it could be still a surprise from you, just not in that small car!” She cuddled up to him.

“It’s not that small, just low.” Smith lied. It was a small car and one of the reasons he no longer drove it. He caved and let her open the doors to her NightCrawler.

Once inside, she intentionally looked away as Smith turned toward the holo screen. He was about to touch the device when he realized something. “You told me I can touch you before I can touch your car, what’s up with that?”

“You touched me when you kissed me, remember?” she laughed.

“You know what?” Smith was still in a bad mood. He dismissed the whole thing with a single wave of a hand, “just drive to the Entrepreneur’s Club!”

She turned to him, observed him, his dissipating anger, and swiftly kissed him on the cheek. “Oh, are you really mean it?”

“What?” Smith was caught off guard.

“Really, to the Club? I know it has a thirty-five-credit nonrefundable reservation fee.”

“Now, how do you know about that?” Smith’s eyes narrowed. “You’ve been there before, huh?”

Amerlee tried her best to look apologetic. “Sorry . . .”

“Fuck me!” Smith spit it with passion.

“Don’t be mad, I love to go with you there. We’ll just split the check, okay?”

“I’ve got money!” Smith became defensive as he pulled out his fat wallet. It was full of lone ones as he bought lunch yesterday at Sam’s hot-dog cart.

“All right, hubby, don’t be upset now!”

“Okay . . .” Smith’s anger dissipated as he watched her making expert moves around traffic. They were there in no time. As a bonus she did not run over anyone, despite the opposite appearance.

Smith offered his hand to her, and she accepted with her gorgeous smile.

“First floor?” she uttered as he transmitted the reservation info from his phone to the desk clerk.

“But it’s a cozy corner!” he winked as someone escorted them away.

“Can I order something I like?” she worried what his budget looked like.

“Please, help yourself!” Smith browsed thru the menu. He was leaning toward a stuffed schnitzel from off world. It was premium, from Alkov-7, another extra twenty credits, but he knew that was good. He had no idea what she was ordering until the last minute. She had multiple selections, each in the price range of twenty to thirty credits. She tried to be as easygoing as she could; all the while she tried to measure his reactions. She got no response out of him. “Smith, I need to decide.”

“Decide then, honey. I told you I’ve got the money!” he became defensive.

“Are you sure?”

“I am!” he tried to be most convincing.

She battled with her emotions, but eventually she decided over the most expensive offering.

Smith explained to the waiter how he wanted the meat to be done, then turned to the girl. She watched him intently. “I would make a haphazard guess and say you’ve ordered from here before!”

“Yes, I did!” Smith cracked a smile to ease her tensions.

"Sheesh!" she added numbers together in her head.

"What?"

"Do you realize we're going to spend about hundred credits here, tonight? I mean including vine too. Even if we split it . . ."

"Hey, hey, I've got it!" Smith patted her real hand.

"How could you? I barely make over one fifty-five a month."

"Oh, now you're telling me your financial secrets?" Smith had to laugh. "I'm being paid handsomely and . . ." he purposefully cut the end of the sentence. It worked because she asked: "And?"

"And since I'm here with the most beautiful lips, I ever seen, I don't mind showing off!"

"Most beautiful lips? Smith, nobody ever told me that!" she seemed happy.

"Of course. Your lips are gorgeous, not to mention everything else around them!"

She blushed. "So, fifty-fifty?" she made her offer.

"No. I'm going to pay all of it. It's my thing since I'm the gentleman here." With a coy smile he leaned over the table. "I used to spend a ton of money here, but I stopped. Do you know why?"

She shook her head. Personally, she had doubts he spent a ton of money here. It did not seem to be his kind of establishment. Never less his game was pretty convincing, and she liked to be entertained, especially by him.

"So, it's because," he continued, like she was dying to know. "There is a restaurant down the street called the Restorante Balkanian where the reservation is only one credit and we can purchase the same meal for all of us for twenty credits! Check it out if you don't believe it!" he nodded amid seeing her doubting face. "Go there on Monday. Check it out!" He urged her.

"Were you going to be on Monday?" she picked up on his absence.

"Um, I have to run an errand for my boss. But I'll be back Thursday, I hope." he neglected to mention he has to go to SWEi Prime to meet with the Ancient Man to discuss some strategic measures since the decapitated Admiralty needed to be propped up.

"Do you plan anything special for the weekend?" she hoped he would.

"For us?"

"Yeah!"

"Bet!" Smith was about to kiss her over the table when somebody clapped his hand nearby. The mirage was gone and Smith seemed to be upset once again.

Amerlee recognized the man standing by their booth: "Amaron . . . Oh, so nice to see you again!"

Smith observed them both. The tall and good-looking man wore an expensive suit, definitely a show-up, but she seemed to be worried about something. He was intrigued. *What could go wrong*?

"Is it, Amerlee?" the man shot back. "I try to call you over and over again, but I see you no longer want to hang with a real man like me, you're in the boys' club with this looser, huh?" he made a disapproving look at him.

Smith decided not to respond to the words. Amerlee did it for him: "Amaron, this is my boyfriend, Evan Smith!" she hoped he would quit attacking him, but she was wrong.

"So, what's up, are you in some government business?" he nodded without a handshake.

Perhaps it's for the better of it, wondered Smith. "We can say that." he responded diplomatically.

"Look honey, if you want me back, all you have to do is holler, you know my number!" he winked. "Oh, by the way, I'm regional manager now for Super City! I make over a grand a month, not including benefits!"

"Are you a banker?" Smith tried to decipher it from his mumbo jumbo.

"Investment banker, and that's a huge difference! My company is one of the ten largest in this planet! We've got holdings in seventeen planets!" he boasted.

"Would you be working for Carlston CC?" Smith was not sure. He hated investment bankers, but he knew how the world was running.

"Now that's a smart looser!" Amaron acknowledged Smith's question. He was about to say something when Smith added, half way laughing: "How did the Wattzen investment played out for you guys? Not so great, huh?" he laughed openly now.

The man got pissed. "So, what, I supposed to be impressed you know these things?"

Quietly, Amerlee was impressed; Smith was willing to go against someone like Amaron, who was a known corporate tycoon. It was partially why she fell in love with him in the first place. Then again, it was partially why she broke up with him. And his unwillingness of being humble was another. Arrogance was a third.

"Do what you must." Smith shrugged.

"Let me ask you, how do you plan to support her highness from your honest job?" he was openly cynical.

"I think we can work it out. Love knows no boundaries!"

"What a bullshit line that is!" Amaron laughed, pointing at Amerlee. "You buying this bs?"

"I do!" she announced firm.

It shocked both Smith and Amaron.

"Reality will set in soon, lovebirds!"

Smith had enough. "There is a reason why I am here with her. It's because I am willing to walk the extra mile." Smith turned his attention to Amaron. "I mean instead of lifting her skirt like you've done; I'm actually entertaining her!"

"Yeah, but no money, no entertainment!" Amaron pointed it out. He did not even acknowledge Smith's accusation. Mostly because it was true. With money came respect and girls. He viewed it as a perk, a bonus, and nothing more. He saw Smith was a guy who earned things instead of being given things. Money always rules. That was the supreme secret. "So, what's your endgame Smith? How are you going to support her and yourself from your miserable handout pay?"

"Leave it, Smith!" Amerlee saw Smith getting angry. Knowing Smith's service record, she could imagine him killing Amaron right in front of everyone. It would ruin him and her too.

She would have to go to the prison to see him every day. The thought frightened her. That's why Smith's reply avoided her ears at first.

"What?" she heard Amaron, sounding like an unbeliever as ever.

"I said I own a planet!" Smith responded calmly, hands across his chest.

Amerlee became curious. He never said that to her.

"And how did you acquire that shithole? I'm guessing it is a shit-hole . . ."

"It's a desert planet, but its habitants live fairly good beneath my guidance. I even get a yearly stipend from it that I usually just reinvest!"

"Pathetic! What do you buy, let me guess, more sand?" he laughed at his own joke.

"Water if you must know."

Amaron stopped laughing. "Okay, say that you smart enough to make a good investment. How did you acquire the asset?"

"Easy, I won on a bet!" Smith shrugged calmly.

"Bet?" echoed Amerlee with big eyes.

Smith nodded at both of them. "As Mr. Amaron pointed out, I work for the government, so I've been in the service too, fighting the Klons as a pilot. I was a reckless one, and after the war I allowed to keep my fighter. A CX version. Modified and upgraded. Whistles and bells, you name it, I had it!" he stopped to give time to Amaron, who was a tiny bit impressed by him mentioning the service. Amerlee already knew that, so that was not important. "I was cocky enough to help some of my friends at a bar fight on a faraway planet in the Amur region. Turned out it was owned by a local gangster and the way he settled the bar fight pissed me off. We made a bet to do certain maneuvers as a fighter pilot on a range. I went first, and I did it. He backed out of the deal and instead of offered me a planet. He was impressed with my skills. He honored the bet, and that was it! Forty grand I keep a year from the dividends. It helps me go by."

“See, I know some hotshot pilots, Smith. What’s that maneuver you referring to?” Amaron asked, boasting about his knowledge.

Smith perceived as a direct response to his poking. He put on his poker face: “Do you know the stuff the Honor Guards has to do to pass? I mean the laser bar at one hundred feet high. They have couple miles to line up and descend. Pass it beneath and you’re made it.”

“So?”

“So, to be in the Elite Honor Guards, they lowered this bar to fifty feet.” Smith added. It did not elude his attention that Amerlee’s mouth began to hang.

“You did this to win a planet?”

“No. I had two bars, one mile apart over a lakebed.”

“It’s doable . . .” Amaron imagined the feat.

“At the speed of the sound. And of course, upside down!” Smith casually added.

“Impossible!” Amaron shook his head in disbelief.

Smith half shrugged. “I own the planet and I am here tonight. So how is that so impossible?”

Amaron yawned. “Well, it’s nice to bump into you guys. Enjoy the dinner. Amerlee, my offer stands!” he waved goodbye and went upstairs to the galley.

“You really did that?” Amerlee was more than impressed.

“I did say I used to be reckless.” Smith winced.

She turned serious and boxed into his shoulder: “If you do something like that, I’m going to kill you!”

“And how is that exactly supposed to help our relationship to move forward?” Smith joked.

She looked away, complained something stuck in her eye, but she just had to wipe off the tear of worry. She believed every word of him, unlike Amaron, who kept pointing toward them from upstairs with two of his buddies around.

“Is he still bothering you?” Smith did not look up.

“He is an asshole! Do you really, really own a planet?”

“I do.”

"What's the name?"

"I'll tell you one day, I promise!" Smith excused himself while the dinner was served and went upstairs.

"Look at the self-made millionaire!" Amaron grinned while holding an SWEi Sunset Colada.

"Mr. Amaron, if I would have a word with you!" Smith grabbed his arm and pushed him away from his people. The man frowned, turned angry, then laughed: "So you do love her!"

"It would serve you good were you to keep your distance from Amerlee and possibly from me as well!" he spoke softly.

No more hesitation, no more embarrassing anecdotes, Amaron noticed the changed man. "Why would I do that?" he asked somewhat cautiously.

"If you want to keep your body intact, that is . . ." Smith continued.

"Is that a threat? Cause I broke bigger man's balls like you!" he raged instantly.

"We never discussed the name of my first planet!" Smith spoke again.

"Do I supposed to be scared of you?" Amaron took a step back. He noticed something of a calculated measure coming from his opponent.

"Normally no, but in this case, you angered me. I don't like to be angered or annoyed. I have enough problems without you around! Make no mistake I am here with Amerlee because I choose to, not because I have to!"

"Is that supposed to make me cautious?"

"You decide. The word of my planet has only four letters. It starts with the letter 'G' and continues with an 'n' . . ." Smith retrieved a lone business card from his pocket amid Amaron's transformation, whose hands began to tremble. He licked his dry lips and took the card like a robot.

"Do you know the number?" the piercing eyes asked him. Amaron glanced below, recognized a direct line to the KFT, wholly owned by the Emperor.

“Are you.. . . ?” he was afraid to ask, to continue.

“I’m an immortal; unlike you I would survive a fight. Don’t bother Amerlee ever again!” Smith’s voice was cold and mean, edgy and meant to intimidate.

“I won’t!” he mumbled.

“See that you live up to that promise! Now go and don’t come back tonight!” Smith pointed toward the door.

Amerlee wanted to slice the food, but Smith hadn’t returned yet. She glanced around and noticed him with Amaron. They were at a distance, so she could not fully ascertain what was going on, but saw as Amaron held up his hands and he backed away from Smith, then turned around and practically ran away. She caught his eyes as he turned around and noted pure fear. Amaron did not back down from anyone. She was intrigued and as soon as Smith took his seat she asked while tasting the exceptional food: “What did you tell him? I saw you two upstairs!”

Smith smiled, cut into the schnitzel. “I told you I know the Emperor. He told me to use his influence freely, so I gave a card to your ex to call in case he has doubts. It’s a direct line to Mrs. G, at the KFT. She would tear him to pieces!” Smith had to laugh.

Amerlee watched him quietly. She was not sure he was joking or not. He shouldn’t joke with or in the name of the Emperor, but then again who he met the man before he became the leader might just do.

They talked about his planet and about her work before calling it quits. Just as Smith promised, he paid the entire bill with cash that basically emptied his wallet, making Amerlee feel really guilty. He tried to give her a great evening and first the car, then the food and that asshole Amaron . . .

They were standing by her car. She bit her lips as she kissed him, bit him gently on the neck: “We have such a special chemistry! I feel electrified around you!”

“I feel the same way.” Smith uttered into her ear.

She looked into his longing eyes and he caught a wicked smile in hers. “What?”

"How 'bout you're going to show me your apartment tonight?"

"I don't think it's a good idea." Smith frowned. He did not want to rush things.

"Just the place and I would leave . . ."

"Would you?"

"If you are going to be the perfect gentleman you calling yourself, I wouldn't have to worry, right?" she giggled.

"I will be that!" Responded Smith, wondering whether she meant any of it.

"Come on!" she hopped into the beast.

Smith took the role of the satisfied passenger. He felt she was getting too close to the other cars and constantly looked into the sleek mirrors. He often glanced at the internal camera mirror as well.

"I see you checking my driving skills!" she did not turn to him.

Smith focused straight ahead. He was made, and he knew it.

"I'm a professional, see!" she switched to autopilot, and the turbo powered down.

"I still don't think it's a good idea!" Smith waved his ID card at the door handle.

"So, your girlfriend is inside?"

"No, I told you she is . . ."

"Relax. If she wears a sleazy dress, I can match and we could have a threesome, only that I'm a dominator!" she winked amid giggling.

"She won't like that." Smith was sure of it. Azure was a dominator herself.

Amerlee decided not to answer to that, instead with great attention she surveyed the living room. The nicely done pictures on the wall did not elude her at all: "Interesting. Movie posters?"

"From my childhood."

"Ah, the minimalistic bathroom and an equally rustic work room!" she glanced inside, opened one of the built-in cabinets; "No female panties. Is she normally wearing one?" she turned around to confront him. He was standing right beside her.

"I love sateen panties!" Smith grinned. "Her stuff isn't here. She doesn't like to be here. She likes bigger places." He trailed off.

"So, is that mean you have another place to live, sir?"

"Ah, yes . . ." he replied while she pushed Smith aside to check out the bedroom. "Double bed, mmm . . . Would the other place to be onboard the Sky Riders? And I did see your fascination with the Starship, there is a picture of it hanging on the wall!" she added.

"I'm in love with it, but you also had to notice the historical spaceship picture on the bedroom wall!"

"Galaktika 4!" she nodded as she glanced around the kitchen. "I would say you have a good housekeeper robot or you full of bs!"

"Why do you say that?" Smith felt a trap being sprung.

"It's too clean for a guy!"

"I, we are living on the Sky Riders, this is a work home. When I have to run errands between the KFT and other places."

"I heard the Sky Riders have a city inside. Is that true?"

"Yes."

"What do you think if I really want to see it, you can arrange it for me?"

"I can certainly do that!" Smith promised.

"And I won't get disappointed, huh?" she danced around him. Smith attempted to turn with her. She was playing with him; he was sure of it.

"So, are you going to be a perfect gentleman or a nasty one?" she inched forward.

"I said I would be a good one!" Smith was not sure which way she wanted to play it. Intricate web of female doings . . .

She moved even closer until their noses touched. Smith practically melted. She hugged him tight and giggled. "I can feel you. It doesn't want to be a perfect gentleman at all!"

"All right, let's go back to the PR, so I can pick up my car!" Smith pushed himself away from her.

"Are you sure?" she seemed disappointed.

"Salivate for me for a bit longer. I have a perfect gift for you next week if you still like exotic cars." Smith grinned.

She locked elbows with him and tried to appear satisfied. She was not. She wanted him to make the move on her in the apartment. "A car, you own it?"

"No, I don't, but let's just say I have access to it . . ." Smith lied.

Once at home Amerlee just took a bath, cleaned her long hair and with a sip of a sparkling wine she headed to her bed. She was hoping to get laid by Smith, but somehow, he decided against it. She was willing, but maybe Amaron's appearance had something to do with his mood. She wanted to satisfy Smith too, but he rejected it. *Perhaps I offended him*? She wondered. More she thought about it the more she was convinced she should've let him drive that piece of shit car of his. "Stupid, stupid me!" The realization hit her. He wanted nothing but to show his world to her. "I've messed up again!" She concluded. Now she had to wait for almost a week to see him again.

Work was brutal. She kept thinking of him. By Tuesday she went to the restaurant, the one Smith recommended. To her shock everything was true: the prices, the taste, the food, even the waiters and waitresses. Smith knew his shit! She often reminded herself to be nicer to him next time he is around. She had to wait for couple more days for that to happen. By that time, she had a conversation with her mother too. She asked her to visit their estate while they were going off world for a seminar. Her mother had the guts to ask about Amaron and she was brave enough to mention her new boyfriend, Evan Smith, to her. Naturally, she grilled her about his background. It was no secret her mother and Amaron understood each other well. Probably their hawkish nature was the root cause. Her mother was more than dismayed when she found out Smith was not rich and was in the service. She lectured her about meeting the rich man, so she could turn out to be a money spending like her own mother was. She hated the idea. She wanted to be in love to marry someone. Her mother pointed out her age and being single, still. It pissed her off so bad that they scheduled a dinner together so she can show up with him two weeks from now. Once she hung up with her, did she realize what she had done. She had to fix him up for the dinner or their parents would rip him apart!

Wednesday she was called into her boss's office. Miss Thorne asked for updates and reviews than when she explained her work, she inquired about the dinner from last week.

"How do you know about that?" was the first thing Amerlee asked.

"Smith told me, raving about you, your dress and that how it seemed nothing worked for him. You know he is trying hard to impress you with things!"

"I know . . ." Her head went down, knowing she came to the same conclusion on her own.

"Evan, I mean Smith is a complicated person. Broken inside, so he is looking for the few things that make him happy. That he found you is perhaps a good thing for him." Miss Thorne summarized.

"Does a woman make him happy?" Amerlee was not sure she understood her boss correctly.

Emma laughed. "Men usually interested in women. Yes, he is. He has many work secrets he can't share. Those he can share it with know him and look up to him, so he is looking to meet women who don't know him, the real him. He I think fears that once his secret is out the woman, he is with isn't going to stay around."

"Oh, so that's why his girlfriend and him are apart?" Amerlee thought she connected the dots.

"No. Az . . . I mean they're apart, but like Bonnie and Clyde, they will always stick together. She doesn't have any other choice. It's like it's hard wired into her."

"What is that mean?" Amerlee did not want to hear that. Her heart was sinking.

"His girlfriend is . . . how to say it nicely? Aggressive. Not with him." she frowned, then shook her head. "Never with him, but she broke quite few bones and jaws just because guys thought she was a sex toy. I think, secretly he enjoys that in her."

"Is she a sex toy?" Amerlee stared at her boss with big eyes.

"To him, perhaps. She won't let anyone else touch her, and if he says to her to break a bone, she is the happiest person to carry out his orders. She was a soldier too. From a different time . . ."

"Not the Klon wars?"

Emma frowned. "Not exactly. But to credit her courage, when Smith was captured on a routine mission and thrown into jail several years back, she was the one who rescued him against all odds. Smith had many friends, others whom owed him their rise, but this girl, this lone girl on a single spaceship sent away by him, found a way to save him. It takes courage to do something like that." Emma bit her lips.

"So, they depend on each other?" It upset Amerlee. She was hurt inside. Insurmountable, that was her quest.

"Yes, but Smith will never marry her."

"So, I have hope?" Amerlee's voice was shallower than she hoped for.

"Perhaps. He definitely has feelings for you. Thing of it is, he is really nervous about his secrets. I told him many times you wouldn't care. I think . . . But if he feels insecure about it . . ." She shrugged, not finishing the sentence.

"I would love him the same way!" Amerlee jumped right in.

Emma seemingly understood her and nodded once: "Smith is a kind of person who forged good relationships with people. He knows everyone who matters, he can even ask for favors and although he rarely promises anything, once he does, he would move Heaven and Down Earth just to make it happen."

"You admire him!" Amerlee realized all of a sudden.

"I know who he is; what he had done for the Monarch and I wish I could tell you, but I just can't. Only he can tell you." she seemed to be sad, but a sudden thought appeared in her face: "Tell me, did someone piss him off that night? I think he was upset about someone."

"Shit, he met my ex . . ." Amerlee cursed out loud.

"Your ex-hotshot banker?" Emma remembered to a tall guy in suit courting her when the PR Department came to life.

"Yes, that's the one. He called Smith a looser and a fool. I thought he would jump on him and beat him up."

Emma nodded thoughtfully, then smiled.

"What is it?"

"You know he could've killed him on the spot?"

"What? How?"

"Smith knows all the moves. He knows how to kill someone without touching him or her, without pulling a gun. Did you ever hear of the reverse heart beat?"

"Yeah. But it's just a myth, right?"

"No, it isn't! So, it's obvious Evan did not kill the poor guy. What happened next?"

"Smith excused himself. I thought he went to the bathroom, but actually he must've gone upstairs to the galley to meet the guy 'cause they were arguing about something."

"Did your ex leave in a hurry?"

"How did you know?"

"I had a haunch." Emma grinned.

"I saw pure fear in his eyes and I never seen that before. I still wonder what he said to him. He said to me that he gave him a card with a direct line to Mrs. G's office."

"Do you doubt what he said?"

"No, but he said he could threat people like that, 'cause the Emperor allowed him to do. I think he should be more cautious."

"Are you opposing his attitude?" Emma was curious.

"I'm worried for him, for his safety." Amerlee automatically touched her chest.

Emma saw the gesture and tried to reassure her: "Trust me, he can do that. He and the Emperor were like buddies. The Emperor did not forget about Smith and once the war was over, after the Chaotic Years, he made him his courier. Smith can and could get away with far more than an ordinary human would! And I think he learned from our master, because he stays in the shadow and only comes out when no one expects him. Does that sound familiar?"

"Should I fear him?"

"Definitely not. I think you should embrace his knick-knacks and love him. I know he is in love with you. Even if he did not say it yet."

"He turned me down." Amerlee was not sure she should say that to anyone.

"Why would you say that?"

"I gave him the opportunity to make a move, and he declined. We joked before whether he is a gentleman or a dirty guy and now, I think, I might have pushed him to the wrong side of the fence."

Emma frowned. "You probably did. If you accuse him of being not a gentleman, he will do everything in his power to look like a gentleman. Even if it goes against his own wishful thinking."

"So, you're saying he wants me?" Amerlee sounded hopeful.

"Oh, he does, but he said to me before leaving for his errand that you sent him mixed signals, so he backed down. He attributed that to female witchcraft, which by the way he thinks you are a master of and left it at that."

"I should've raped him!" Amerlee slipped.

"He would've liked it . . ." Emma giggled.

"I have to make it up to him!" Amerlee sworn. "What do you mean secrets' of him?"

"He works closely with the Emperor. He is powerful in some sense. Some take it the wrong way. Don't take it the wrong way! He is happy with you and cares for you more than you'll ever know!" Emma opened the door for her. It was time to leave.

Wednesday slipped by relatively quick for her and as an added bonus she got an IM, Interactive Mail from Smith. He allegedly thought of her a lot (she felt the same way), his work was busy and hectic, but he would stop by to have lunch with her the next day around one pm. She felt electrified. Later in the day, she often caught herself thinking about what to wear the next day. She dreamed of him, but he remained elusive. From the morning tea, she imagined him sitting beside her, watching her moves, even her robotic arm. She noticed early on he tried to downplay the fact she has the birth defect, but it had to be obvious. Her wardrobe lacked the Tee version of clothing, as something always had to cover her arm where the extension hooked to her bone and skin. She wondered before how he would take it where she would show her the arm. She was more insecure about it now than when she met him, probably because she was bonding to him and did not want to lose him. She shelved the idea for the moment and concentrated on the electronic clock on the wall. It wanted to be her enemy today by seemingly slowing to a crawl! She practically flew thru the doors as her brake time came.

"Smith!" she was truly happy to see him by the entrance. She jumped into his arms.

"Somebody missed me!" he recovered by kissing her on the cheeks than on her lips.

"So, how was your trip?" she asked once inside.

"It was productive. We laid down some ground rules." Smith remained vague about his mission. She did not like it. "You must say things in better detail!" she lectured him.

"National security, honey!"

"I'm practically working for the same company, definitely for the same entity as you. Why can your trip be a secret?"

"Because I can't discuss it, but I promised you for entertainment and I got the perfect place to be with you! Bring a day's worth of recreation clothes with you tomorrow! I'll pick you up from work and we off to go!"

"Where?" she tried to decipher him.

"To the Thousand Islands! I rented a cabin on a private island!" Smith announced.

"Are you serious?" she could barely believe in her ears.

"I ordered a beautiful sunset for us to watch it!" he added after pausing to admire her.

"You can't order a sunset!" she frowned.

"I just did!"

"Do you always get what you want?" the coy smile reappeared on her face, to Smith's biggest delight.

"Mostly!" he hid his smile, but his good mood was really apparent. She attributed that to herself. *He probably missed me—* she thought. That made her happy too. She wanted to share the bad news to meet her parents, but decided there was plenty of time for that later.

Unfortunately, time appeared to fly too fast. Smith said he had to go, but kissed her passionately, after which she watched him leaving with passionate eyes. She felt warm inside. He truly missed her!

Smith had formulated a plan to help Amerlee regain her full herself for some time now, but was not sure how to approach the subject. He watched her cells, her brain; how it works together and came to the conclusion he would need Aa's expert advice and her blessing as well. That was one problem, the how to travel to see her with Amerlee without too much suspicion from the girl was another entirely. He called Miss Fontana and Tata for a group conference call from his office in the KFT to request graduate Honor Guards to fill up empty posts on the Prince and its escort ships. Tata gladly delegated the task to Fontana, who was proud to work on something important. She promised to fill up all empty positions by the beginning of the next week. Smith intended to use one of the support ships to reach Captain Aa if he decides to go with the plan. Of course, it also mattered whether she would want to have a real arm. He would have to reveal himself to her, and that nagged him. He ended up calling Tata back and asking for a favor. The old man was happy to throw in some support and promised to have his granddaughter nearby shall the need arise to have that particular talk, to make another person a true believer. In a way, it helped Tata to bond with Elise too.

Smith admired the Alfa Romeo of the PR department's garage. He could not find Amerlee's car anywhere, so the girl was either sick, or more likely she heeded his advice and took a cab or

Pub to get to work. He tried not to get there too early, but against his best estimate, he got there fifteen minutes early. He decided to talk with Miss Thorne and sneaked by the open offices without detection.

"What's up, boss?" It baffled Miss Thorne to see Smith in jeans quietly closing her door.

"Hi, what's the situation?"

"What situation? Are we at war again?" she was not sure what he was referring to.

"Does Amerlee was useful today?"

"Oh." Emma released a half smile. "She was often lost in her thoughts."

"Oh, she'll get what's coming, but I want you to draw up two LRs for me next week. One for Josh and one for Captain Aa. Send the one to Josh via an official courier, let him feel special!"

"How about Captain Aa's?"

"I'll take that to her in person when the time is right!" Smith responded.

"Okay. I'll take care of them first thing Monday morning. Is Amerlee coming back to work too?"

"Why wouldn't she?" Smith was dumbfounded.

"If she finds out who you are, maybe she lives off your stipend . . ."

"That will not likely to happen!" Smith shook his head. "For one she isn't that kind and for two I like to delay the truth as long as I can."

"Don't do that, boss. The longer you delay it, the worse it gets for her. She has feelings for you!" Miss Thorne disagreed with him on that.

"I think about that!" Smith brushed her concerns away with his good byes and walked with a straight back to see his love.

"What is it? Is something wrong with my dress?" Amerlee looked down at her clothing as much as she could. Smith mustered her like something was off with the secretary style beige, two-piece.

"I don't think a skirt is the right thing for where we are going." He said it loud, but inside he thought Azure never wore them and he actually did not miss it on her ever!

"You know we have to look professional. Especially in case the Emperor would drop by!"

"The Emperor likes what he sees!" Smith responded, salivating.

"Now how do you know? Or you two discuss that too?"

"Okay, okay, just give me your bag." Smith gave up. She looked stunning in the dress, but he thought it would be easier to drive in pants. "Oh, have you ever drove a stick shift car before?" he asked her in the elevator.

She stared at him, and he was not sure she was surprised or angry. But as soon as she replied with her fierce attitude, he knew he should've kept his mouth closed.

"Of course, I do. Do I look like a housewife to you?" she calmed down, gave a moment and continued: "I haven't been driving stick in a while, but I'm in love with the idea of being in control!"

"Now why is that doesn't surprise me at all?" Smith mustered her before letting her out of the elevator.

She walked to her reserved parking space than stopped upon seeing the bronze car.

"What kind of beast is this?" she scrutinized the vehicle.

"Upper Earth made; it's called an Alfa Romeo. They heavily modified it when it was acquired by the KFT about twenty years ago."

"I can see the fine dust." she touched the big hood. "Key entry?" she dismayed the lock on the car.

"Original interior, minus the additives."

"Analog?" she hopped into the leather seat, while fixated on the dashboard.

"Mostly."

"Car, turn on!" she commanded.

"As I said, honey, its analog, here is the key." he gave it to her to her biggest dismay.

She placed the key to the ignition and turned it with an awkward move. The car came to alive.

"Pretty quiet for an internal combustion engine, huh?"

"It goes with gas?" she winced.

"Yes. Don't worry, I had it filled! It has an extra-large tank and we won't need it on the highway, anyway." Smith elaborated.

"Why?" she clutched to first and floored the pedal. The car took off like a bat.

"Oh, where is the seatbelt?" she almost fell out of the chair.

"Manual!" Smith pointed to his seatbelt, already around him.

"So where to?" Amerlee enjoyed the stick shift in traffic.

"To the Central Super Highway!"

"Are we really going to the Thousand Islands?" she gave a half look of attention. He was grinning.

"I said so, but we're going to pull into the dirt lot before the underpass." Smith pointed to the right. The big lot was empty, minus a lone tractor trailer. Its owner was checking the fifth wheel assembly. Smith presumed he was headed thru the desert to North.

"Okay, so it's not so ordinary!" he walked to the rear and showed her the cutout where the bumper should have been.

"A black hole . . ." She bent forward as she did not want to mess up neither the knees nor her skirt. A vague warning surfaced in her mind regarding to Smith's wish not to wear a skirt, then straightened out: "So what is it for?" she asked, but Smith was fiddling with something inside the car. She walked behind him and slapped his behind.

"Aww!" Smith jumped and hit his head in the low ceiling. "What's that for?" He was not sure why she had done it.

"You think only guys do that?" She giggled.

"All while I try to impress you!" he sputtered.

"Bending forward?"

"No! By activating the system!" he pulled a lever, flipped couple switches and the side stabilizers extended from the main body.

"It's going to be a nice day!" she glanced up to the azure blue sky.

"With a perfect sunset!" Smith doubled up.

"I told you, you would never know it for sure!" Amerlee frowned. *He was overconfident.*

Smith battled with his insecurities about whether to let her drive at all. Eventually his better self won and showed her a bigger lever to the right of the steering column.

"So, I just pull it down?" she asked.

"Gently!" Smith hissed as he heard the metallic sound coming from the rear.

"What was that?"

"I said to do gently. You probably dropped it, but it usually comes back up . . ." Smith ran to the back with suspicion.

"Hey, what the heck is that?"

"It's a small airplane engine!" Smith opened the trunk, revealing the digital switchboard. "I have to initialize the system."

"Amazing, hey it's a souped-up energy cell! Two of them!" she realized seconds later. "I want to drive!" she announced. Her hand suddenly itching.

Smith pretended not to hear her.

"Can I? Please, please!" she leaned on his shoulder.

"Just hold the steering wheel tight! The onboard computer will help you out once the system is active!"

"So, we can go to the fourth level, right? I want to do over two hundred miles per hour!" she already imagined driving.

"Actually . . ." he produced a card and threw at her.

"What's that?"

"Take her all the way up!" he commanded.

"You can't take it to the ninth floor!" she frowned.

"Let's go!" Smith put on the seatbelt. She pulled out of the lot, beneath the colossal and ancient highway system, then took the ramp. They watched the entrances go by as they climbed to the fifth level. There, she stopped front of the metal gates and waved the card front of the reader. It beeped affirmatively and the electronic board lit up: Race Time! The metal gate pulled aside, revealing the green arrows built into the concrete floor.

"Oh, that's so cool!" she forgot to cover her excitement.

"When you reach two thousand RPM at sixth gear, put it to neutral and activate the afterburner!"

"Afterburner?" she turned to him, looking confused.

"Don't stop below four hundred!"

"MPH?" she screamed as the car hopped on the ramp to the restricted ninth floor and began to accelerate.

"The car is murder!" she shook her head later once they took the ramp off the top floor and merged with the afternoon traffic. Soon another off ramp appeared and upon Smith's insistence she took it.

"You seemed to be really nervous over three hundred MPH."

"One sneeze and we could've been dead!" she shuddered. "Wait, how fast did you drive it?"

"A bit over four hundred in the desert. But that was many years ago."

"Don't do that ever again!" she seemed upset.

"Why?"

"Not if you want to be with me!" she added.

"Okay!" Smith dropped the subject.

The same card opened the gates for the private road leading to a hilltop where a modern architect house stood; its balcony overlooking the Ocean.

"That's so romantic!" she hugged him, while he first kissed her forehead, then as she looked at him with her big brown eyes, he kissed her.

"That's better!" the good mood of her returned. "Do you have a key to the inside?"

"I believe I have!" Smith grinned while searched his side pocket.

Amerlee quickly checked the rooms. Everything was meticulously prepared, even the vase on the glass table was in the dead center. So, there were no humans, only robots. She dropped her guard down and relaxed; she walked to the glass windows. "That's nice!" she mustered the view, then turned around. Smith lurked behind her and now, being made, he raised his hands to grab her head instead of her hips.

She smiled, knowing exactly what was on his mind. "What do you want?"

"Just a kiss." Smith lied.

"A-ha!" she did not believe a word he said.

To ensure his sincere intentions, Smith kissed her again.

"Liar!" she said between kisses.

"I'm trying. . ." he uttered.

"Stop trying!" she spun around, away from him.

Smith pushed against her as his hands worked their way from her hip up to her shapely breasts. She leaned back on him, then quickly turned around and began to unbutton his shirt.

He tried his best not to rip her blouse apart as they succumbed to joy.

*

She was drinking a wine, watching the spectacular sunset thru the windows.

Smith disappeared into the bathroom and she just noticed then, the opened wine, the one she said she liked the first time they went out. Things were perfect! She hoped to be up better part of the night with him. She even forgot about her conversation with her mother. Later on, in the bed, she promised herself Smith has to do her on her mother's desk for complete satisfaction!

In the morning she woke up before he did. She slipped out of the bed in her undies to make some breakfast, but to her shock a complete breakfast table was waiting for her. She quickly covered her naked breasts and glanced around. There was nobody around;

she was alone. Upon closer inspection, the meticulous nature of the food made her realize it was all robot work. High end, no doubt. She pushed the levitating table back to the upstairs room where she found Smith smelling her side of the bed.

"What are you doing?"

"I miss you!" he announced, then smiled: "Breasts on the table, yummy!"

"Hey!" she pushed the table aside and jumped on his lap. They kissed softly, then with passion.

"What is on your mind?" Smith sensed her insecurity.

"What if somebody is watching us?"

"Nobody is watching!" Smith shook his head, sounding pretty serious.

"But you can't be sure! Do you know the person who owns this house?"

"Along with the island . . ." Smith corrected her.

"Who is it? Do I know?"

"He is a public figure. Lyahim promised me there would be absolutely no recordings of any kind. He said there are robots onl . . ."

"Lyahim, who?"

"The President."

"Yeah, right!" Amerlee laughed. "Stop playing with me!"

"I assure you, if you stick with me, I'll introduce you to him one day!"

"My father got an official letter from him a couple years ago. It's his near centerpiece of egoism ever since! Uh, by the way my parents going away for a week."

"So?"

"I need to check on their estate. Do you know where it is?"

"No."

"Road of the Bound! I know you want to come with me!" she winked.

"Every day and every time!" Smith kissed her chest amid her laugh.

Amerlee was sipping on a tea, looking out the window with only a white underwear and a long shirt she found in the bottom of her bag. She turned around to see what Smith was doing. With his dreamy eyes, he watched her. She blushed. "What?"

"Have you ever wondered what were you doing if you would be set for life?" he asked her, thinking about something.

"Set?" she echoed the word like she did not like how it sounded.

"Set. I mean if you were to live in a communion with someone and have a house staffed with robots and your significant one would have enough money so you wouldn't have to work. What were you doing then?" Smith asked, more specifically this time.

Amerlee had to frown. "I would be bored. No. I need to do something. Maybe not full time, but still. I think I would find a cause to fight for. There is just so much injustice in this world!" she sipped from her tea, then with her big, brown eyes she turned on Smith's: "Why?"

"Nothing in particular."

"Not like I ever going to be in that position."

"Why? You never know!"

"Come on, Smith! Even with a planet, you still work and me, I have to . . ."

"Why?"

"I like it to be independent, self-made!"

"I can dig that!" Smith hoped it would sound believable.

"Dig? Where did you come up with such a word?" she cozied up to him. He threw his hand around her shoulder and kissed her neck, trying to forget about Azure. She had hip talk.

"I need to save a lot of money for my arm. I've been meaning to show you." she said shyly.

"Show me!" Smith took up interest in the new subject.

"I'm actually nervous . . . Amaron was not interested, but you might be."

"Don't even speak of that bastard's name again!" snorted Smith, and she kissed in return, then showed her left arm, did something in the inner linings where a previously hidden cover popped up.

"What's that?"

"My Interactive Device controls the temperature and the skin tone, my embedded neuro transmitters control the movement, but I usually have to take it off for recharging and breathing. You know, so the skin can heal overnight. The disarming is manual." she placed her right thumb for authentication. Smith heard a faint hiss. The arm began to dangle, and she grabbed, twisted with a decisive move to separate it.

Smith admired the girl's mental strength.

"See!" she licked her lips, feeling nervous about it.

Smith touched her arm, gently, and then kissed it lightly.

She closed her eyes and kept her eyelids closed to wipe her tears away. "Do you take me as a whole?"

"Of course!" Smith replied, mystified by the event.

"I love you!" she turned to him for a kiss. "I love you so much! You see, when I turned twenty my father gave me this arm, but it won't last forever. Wear and tear and eventually I already feel it I will need an overhaul. You know doctors; they will try to sell me a new one. So . . . That's why I work." she shunted her eyes.

Smith tried to sound utterly gentle: "What if . . . say you would have your very own arm?"

"What?" she seemed hurt.

"I mean, if it were to grow. Not immediately; it takes time and antibiotics and supervision, but say I were to find someone who can make it happen. Would you consider it?" Smith was shy to ask.

"Smith, that's utterly kind, but it's a birth defect. My parents could not make it happen when I was a child, so now I'm an adult. It's too late for me!" she shook her head.

"Would you consider a professional opinion for me?" he pushed the subject.

"What do you mean?" she gouged him from up close, trying to measure his sincerity.

"I mean, I can arrange a trip next week to see someone who owes me big. Hear her opinion, before you turn me down!"

"Is that important to you?" she realized something.

"You have everything. You've been most of the places I try to take you, let me do something good for you!" he seemed to be unrelenting in his quest.

"But. It's priceless. It's impossible . . ." she finally took a moment to think it thru.

"Please, just listen to her. See what she as to say!" Smith asked her so gentle she was about to cry.

"Who is that woman?" Amerlee became suspicious.

"Colleague of mine. She is in the service, on active duty so we would have to catch a ride and I happen to know that a spaceship is going to meet her next Thursday."

"I don't know if my boss would let me go on such a short notice." she frowned as realities set in.

"Don't you worry! Miss Thorne recently had to draft a LR to her. We can deliver it in style!"

"What's her name?" Amerlee poked his side.

Smith had to move amid laughing: "It's a surprise."

"I have to check on my parent's estate. I was hoping to do it on Tuesday morning. I got the morning off from Miss Thorne. I don't have to be in until ten."

"Okay." Smith was not sure what she was getting at.

"I want you to escort me there! Road of the Bound!" she winked.

"I love when you wink!" Smith kissed her, throwing her off guard.

"So, what do you say I pick you up seven AM sharp?"

"So early?" Smith yawned.

"Well, we would stay busy until ten!" she kissed him back.

"Oh, okay!" he grinned.

In the afternoon, Amerlee drove the car with Smith back to the city. He seemingly enjoyed the passenger's role, but inside he was hoping she wouldn't hit a boulder every time they turned. She was right; it was difficult to give up control. She even invited into her apartment. Smith was genuinely surprised of her tastefulness and even mentioned he would need her decorative taste to finish his house. She was up for a grab, but suggested he should talk it over with his girlfriend first.

Smith spent an entire lone Sunday in the Villa-Castle. Possibly, the only good thing came out as he was able to catch up with the ever-elusive Master Gardner. He gave him marching orders, and that satisfied him. Toxic's holographic emitter came by later and she was open about Amerlee. Toxic was not hostile, but seemed to be interested in Smith's emotions.

"I know you like Azure better!" Smith told her while he drank tea with her. Of course, she only imitated the whole thing, but it was still a nice and appreciated gesture.

"Whether I like her better or not isn't a question. Amerlee is a great person, and it changes you, ways you can't comprehend yet!" she said enigmatically.

"So, what do you know of her?" Smith frowned.

"I know enough!" she responded.

"Did you talk to Diana about this?" Smith realized she would love to talk about it with someone in her class.

"Why is that important?" she dismissed his suspicion.

"I knew it!" Smith shot back, feeling his suspicion been rightful.

"Have a nice stride in the pool or something, boss!" The hologram mimicked frowning.

"Okay. I guess you can't swim with me!" Smith was about to leave.

"By the way, what did you bring to her as a gift from SWEi Prime this week?"

Smith turned around with a shock on his face, "What?"

"Don't tell me you forgot to bring anything to someone who is craving for your presence in every moment of her life?" The holo Aa lookalike was laughing.

"Of course not!" Smith lied and jumped into the pool. There, he had ample time to think about it. He forgot to bring present that was for sure. He forgot to be nice to her, and that was eating him up. He did not sleep right and was up early in the morning. He decided to drive into the city, to a flower shop and grab a dozen of white Cimbers, then headed to the PR department. It was around eight thirty. He hoped to drop off the flowers to Amerlee and leave, but to his surprise neither her girl nor Miss Thorne was at their desk. He ended up wondering around, then with a swift choice he patted Lou's shoulder. The man turned to face him: "Sir?"

"Lou, where is Amerlee?" Smith felt like a fool.

"Uh, she was sent home by Miss Thorne."

"Is she sick?"

"I . . . I don't know." The man in his late twenties hard pressed his lips. Smith saw the doubts and signaled: "Come with me to the lunchroom!"

Lou parked his hands on his flat stomach as he tried to appear relaxed. He was nervous; Amerlee's new boyfriend was asking him questions. He was torn between telling as much as he knew, versus what he really wanted to say to him. Smith sat across him, his hands flat on the gray, round table. They were alone.

"So where is your boss lady?"

"Miss Thorne had to meet someone from the fourth floor, sir." he replied, then asked, his eyes fixated on the spare card reader in the corner: "Do you honestly love her?"

"Yes, Lou." Smith wanted to apologize to him for such a long time.

"You know she was drawn to you for a long time! She spoke of you before you two met."

"Really?" This was news to him.

"She joked she would ask you out. I did not like that." he flinched.

"Listen, Lou . . ." Smith was trying to calm him, but he threw his hands in the air: "Sir, I know she doesn't want me the way she wants you, but please, don't hurt her!" he pleaded.

"You're a good friend of her. She told me that!" Smith tried to please him, but he phewed: "Please! I know. I'm her best friend, wish it would be more, but . . . now I know it never will be more."

"Probably not." Smith pulled his mouth. "Listen, to be honest I heard of you two and that day I met her Miss Thorne called Amerlee into the office so I could get you two together. I did not know she already had other ideas." Smith shrugged.

"She was staring that damned banana basket!" Lou nodded toward it.

Smith made a face. "So?"

"So, I think she is in heat . . ."

"What?!"

"And I'm an apple person." Lou snorted, angry.

Smith stared at the banana basket, imagined her holding one, and knew he should be by her side. The urge to leave crept up. One extra look at Lou, the young man with his sad face, and he flinched. "Lou. I'm gonna tell you a secret, okay?"

"What secret?" he glanced at Smith, looking hurt.

"Do you like apple, huh?" Smith disregarded his question. "Do you want one?"

"I left mine at home. Feel so utterly lost today!" he blurted all of a sudden.

"Okay. I'll make you powerful, but you can't spill this secret to anyone, okay?" Smith offered his hand to him.

Lou accepted the hand and shook on it, half-hearted. Smith grabbed his wallet and began to shuffle thru his various ID cards.

Lou watched him, fixated on the different addresses with identities.

"Are you a spy, sir?" he sounded utterly humbled.

"Worse . . ." Smith uttered, found the one he was looking for, tucked the rest back to the valet and opened his palm where a red-skinned apple formed to Lou's biggest amazement. "Eat it!" Smith tried to reassure him. Lou took the apple and carefully bit into it. "It's really good!"

"That's great, 'cause I've been doing this trick since my mentor showed me a long, long time ago. It was before I went into the service in the war. Now, this ID, take it to that reader and use it!" he tossed the card across the table.

Lou picked it up, glanced at the address, and his face went pale: “Is that true?”

“Use the machine!” Smith commanded him, and Lou walked on his wobbly legs to the card reader. The machine beeped affirmatively and whatever shot across its tiny screen put a deep impression on Lou, because he fainted on the spot.

“Damn it!” Smith helped him up from the floor amid Lou’s deepest apologies.

“I’m so sorry for my outburst, My Lord!” he almost begged at him.

“Don’t do it, Lou. See, I’m madly in love with Amerlee and she doesn’t know who I am. I feel nervous about it. My life isn’t as easy as you were thinking it a moment ago. And yes, I read your mind.” Smith responded amid kind words.

“D . . . Does my boss know it?” Lou was shaking.

“Miss Thorne? Yes, she does. She knows how to keep a secret too. Now, be proud that you shook hands with an immortal, Lou, and keep it to yourself!” Smith spotted Emma returning to her office.

“I am grateful forever!” he deeply bobbed his head as he consumed the rest of the apple.

“So, what happened to my girl?” Smith popped up moments later in Miss Thorne’s office.

“Amerlee?” Emma frowned. She had to explain her actions to Smith, and that made her insecure.

“Yes. I heard from Lou she was staring at the banana basket?” he laughed.

“What did you do to Lou?” Emma became alarmed.

“I told him who I am, but he’ll keep that as a secret because now he is proud of himself, the man who shook hands with the Emperor.” Smith winked.

“Whatever!” Emma shook her head, then nodded: “Yes, Amerlee was fixated on the bananas and I know exactly why, so before she would make a fool of herself, I sent her home.”

“Good.”

"You aren't mad?" she tested the waters.

"No. You did what you had to do. I'll disappear to find her, but before I do, I need you to find out something."

"Sure, what?"

"Say if I would like to part from an object that has been with me for a number of years. A car. And if we would put it up to an auction and give the money to charity, where would we market it or auction it off?"

"Oh, so now you are embarrassed of your ProcessAutomatic?" Miss Thorne laughed.

"How do you know about that? Oh, that damn Amerlee!" Smith realized amid huffing and puffing.

"She was kind of disappointed." Emma honestly responded.

"I already ordered a luxury model from EEG, makers of the NightCrawler. I'm going to get an 517S!" Smith reacted.

"Does she know it?" Emma tried to hide her amusement.

"Not yet. Of course not, hey!"

"I just thought of something!" Emma wondered. "The Museum of the Emperors by the ocean beach is always interested in personal artifacts. Should I get in touch with them, see if they would offer a number?"

"I want a five-digit number!" Smith reminded her before leaving the office.

Smith felt to be sixteen, holding the flowers and knocking on Amerlee's door. It took him a set of knocking for her to open it.

"Aw!" she was delighted to see Smith and the flowers.

"I see they sent you home." Smith kissed her. She barely let him go. "Okay!" he said once their lips parted. "I see I rocked your world!"

"Now wait a minute. Perhaps I rocked yours and it just feels that way!" she scoffed.

"I can leave . . ." Smith pointed at the door.

"Don't!" she was quick to say it.

"I think I told you before how nice your home looks like!" Smith glanced around. The double bed did not go unnoticed for him either. He turned around, felt a poking eye on his back. She was standing five feet apart from him in a white dress, high heels, and her hair neatly on her shoulders, and he finally noticed her eyelashes: “Blue, eh?” he pointed out.

She blushed.

Another point for Smith . . . –he thought. Happy in the first place that he noticed it.

“Why are you so nice to me?” she asked, looking at him like a candy bar.

“I was worried for you when I did not see you in the office!” he replied honestly, while thinking *No wonder Miss Thorne sent her home.*

“A little hiccup, but now I’m fine. I really wanted to surprise you tomorrow with the stuff, but hey I’m feeling happy now, let’s go and eat something. Are you hungry?”

“Hungry for you, my love!” he uttered into her ears as she shut her eyes happily.

Smith played the content passenger on the seat beside the hottest girl he had seen awhile. She was definitely good with cars. “Couda’ ‘been a getaway chick for a heist!” He chewed the words.

She grinned. “It’s sometimes so arousing what you say, Smith!” she concentrated on the road.

“Yeah.” Smith decided to shut his mouth before her mind wanders away from driving. “Hey, where are we g . . . ?” He glanced thru the sedan’s window. They just passed the first checkpoint to the Road of the Bound. “Oh, your parent’s house!” he said amid realizing her plans.

“No, we just passed that!” she continued to grin.

Smith noticed how her nails gently sank into the steering wheel.

“Are you going to rape me?” he asked, giving her a thoughtful look.

She glanced at him, with a who-knows in her eyes: “Do you want me to?”

"Perhaps another time." Smith felt he was going too far with name callings.

"I can tie you to my car. . ." she added with a wild thought in her mind.

"I don't do well being tied to anything!" he disagreed.

"You have no idea what do you miss out on then." she giggled.

"Uh, oh!" Smith's frown and discomfort deepened as they slowed down by the second checkpoint.

The girl flashed her ID, then an actual e-paper, and the guard scanned it. "Have a good breakfast, Ma'am!" he saluted.

"Where are we going?" he tried to decipher.

"I was hoping to hold on to the request 'till tomorrow, but I just could not do it!" she swiftly kissed him before turning right at the old iron gates. "Welcome to the Villa-Castle, my love!" she spoke.

"Nice!" Smith mustered the gleaming flower beds. The Master Gardner was given a marching order just yesterday. And the results were definitely pleasing!

"Look at those beautiful flower beds! I so love his taste!" she practically sang.

"I'm delighted!" Smith felt relieved for some reason.

As soon as they exited the car, Smith had to sneeze.

"Don't tell me you are allergic?" she locked elbows with him as they walked up on the steps. She turned to the right, stopped for a second to give a good look at the DSR: "The Emperor's personal Deep Space Reconnaissance ship!"

"Toxic . . ."

"That's right! A beauty herself!"

"So, it's a she?" Smith hurried after her.

"Definitely. The Emperor needs a good and trusting friend. He has to call her, her!" she replied, like it was obvious.

He tried to look amazed by his own estate, looking at it like an outsider. He glanced around the atrium when he noticed that droid, what's its name, he was thinking. "PNG-9 . . ." he uttered. It was steering at their direction.

"What?" she turned to him.

"Nothing!" Smith watched the droid scurried away amid high-pitched noises.

"I don't think we supposed to alert the locals!" she glanced at the huge, wooden clock. "Good, nine forty! We still have a bit of time to eat from his table!" she led him to the grand table.

It was practically untouched.

"I wonder where is he . . . ?" she grabbed a plate.

"He who?" Smith was clueless.

"The Emperor. And I know you know, but on every planet, he owns, there is a breakfast table served from six to nine every day, local time! Isn't it amazing?"

"Pretty much." he grabbed a sandwich. Suddenly he felt he was being watched. He turned to his right and noticed Henry from the corner. He instantly frowned and Henry scurried away.

Smith turned back and just watched her assembling a plate. He could watch her doing that every morning. He was so lost he did not realize she was putting it together for him! He felt really humbled.

"Thank you!" he uttered.

"You welcome, love!" she licked the sour cream off her fingers.

Smith melted on the spot!

"Orange juice! Yummy!" Smith was happy she served him so good. Like she knew him already. They were sitting beside the big breakfast table. Amerlee was amazed by the decoration, the lavish ornaments. From her exciting explanation, Smith realized she believed they were coated with gold. He will have to correct her; they were made from solid gold!

Suddenly somebody stopped beside them.

"He . . . llo!" Smith, startled and shocked, glanced up at the arriving Henry. The loyal servant worked up his courage to bypass him entirely and directly ask Smith's companion: "Miss, do you find everything satisfactory?"

Amerlee jumped from her seat and offered her hand: "It is my great pleasure to meet one of the Emperor's house servants! My name is Zoon Amerlee, and this is my boyfriend here, Evan Smith! I still have the letter if that's a problem." she was about to produce the e-paper, but Henry dismissively waved in the air: "It won't be necessary miss! The guards informed me of your impending arrival!" he bowed a bit.

Smith frowned.

Amerlee stopped. "Oh. I'm a bit surprised there is no one here beside us. I would've thought there is nothing left for us, as we are so late!"

"Miss, there is always something left. It's true that some days all the food is gone by the time we supposed to pack it up for the city shelter, but there were only two visitors and they came nine oh five. People usually don't sit around for a long time." Henry took his time to explain.

"Smith, we're in luck, you hear this?" Amerlee was happy she could please him. Smith was likewise happy.

"If there is anything you two would need, just yell and we will try to accommodate your needs!" he bowed at both of them as he left.

"He is so nice to us! I wonder why the special treatment!" she uttered as soon as the servant got outside of an earshot.

"Yeah . . ." Smith wondered himself.

"So how is the food? I think it's really fresh and delicious!" Amerlee watched him eating another sandwich. She even poured more juice to his glass, and she was so into perfection she missed the entity's arrival. She noticed Smith's shaking head. "You don't want more?" she was a bit disappointed.

"Nah, I am . . ." Smith felt he was being made. "I was just looking at that!" he pointed at the green hovering disc with the hologram beneath it. The hover disc activated a tractor beam and pulled out a chair to Amerlee's biggest shock.

"Who are you?" she asked from the hologram.

"I'm Toxic!" the hologram frowned amid producing a holographic plate with equally fake food.

"Look, the ship must have an AI!" Amerlee drew the most logical conclusion.

"Hah!" the hologram turned toward the girl and the inconveniently shifting Smith in his chair.

"That is a neat feature!" Amerlee pointed at the hovering disc.

"Inconvenience at the moment . . ." The hologram brushed her off. The hologram grabbed some food from her holo tray and imitated eating it, before turning its attention to the mesmerized girl: "It's so nice to finally meet you," she paused before revealing, she knew her name: "Amerlee!"

"How? How do you know my name?" she was shocked.

"I know everybody's name. Think of me as a loyal guard dog of the Emperor. It's my job to know everyone; I just normally don't show myself. For example, the male human beside you are called Evan Smith!" Toxic pointed out.

Amerlee turned to Smith for encouragement, and as she did that, Toxic winked at her Master. Smith was less than thrilled. He already sent a mental communication to her, and he made it clear he wants her gone. Instead, the reply was that she would be gone soon. Not the way he imagined for sure!

"So, why did you show yourself?" Amerlee was intrigued by the entity. "Does my man that special?" she pointed toward the shrinking Smith.

"He is special, of course, but the focus is on you, my darling! I waited for so long to finally meet you!" the hologram replied imitating to drinking from a teacup, rendering Amerlee outright speechless. "Me? How so?"

"I like to meet strong and confident woman like yourself!" the hologram continued. "Someone so beautiful and smart! Some of the Emperor's past girlfriends aren't such. I mean they are beautiful or they're smart, but to be raw and humble at the same time is so far a rarity!"

Smith frowned. Azure was not dumb. Neither was Tri'ng. But then again, she was cold as ice. He got bogged down by the comparisons, completely missing out on the continuing thread between the two of them.

"I'm sure the Emperor can choose the beauty queens of virtually any planets." Amerlee responded.

That threw off the hologram for a second. "Is that what people think of him?"

"I mean no disrespect!" Amerlee tried to back out of it.

"None taken. You know how to dress . . ." The hologram wondered away. "A real woman. Let the man chase after you if he feels like it. Smart. Wickedly smart!" she concluded.

"That's me!" Amerlee felt awkward amid forcing a smile on her face.

"As I said, I'm glad we met!" the hologram pretended to stand up.

"Likewise," Amerlee was not sure what to say. She looked down at the hologram's vibrating hand. Slowly, she took it and felt the warmth of the air molecules forming the fingers wrapped around hers. It was a strange moment to shake hands with a hologram. She felt it was a really special moment. "Um. Did you meet my man, Evan before?" she just realized.

"Once or twice." The hologram did not elaborate further. "But the focus is on you. My focus is solely on you! We'll be good friends!" she clarified.

"I'm sure . . ." Amerlee could not imagine why she would see her ever again, but whatever.

"Really?" Smith stared suddenly at the hologram. Knowing she came from the future, this unexpected drop by constituted as a revelation to him.

"Really!" the hologram dissipated into the air and the hovering disc lit up as it teleported away.

"Creepy!" Amerlee summarized in one word. Smith could not agree more. But at the same time, he felt energetic. It would mean Amerlee would stay with him for a long time! That made him really happy and confident. Amerlee of course mistook it for her doing. She flirted with him, trying to lure him back with her, but he excused himself as he allegedly had tons of work to do.

Somewhat disappointed, she reminded him to be ready seven AM sharp the next day. Smith asked whether they could meet perhaps eight o'clock, but Amerlee remained adamant and he caved.

After Amerlee left him near the PR Department, he headed to the Sky Riders to see Azure's progress, but Toxic's speech bothered him so much he called for a limo and asked Deril to pull up beside the DSR on his estate. He marched up on the ramp to see the hologram who formed as soon as he stepped onboard.

"What the fuck was that all about?" Smith directed his anger at her. "I did not reveal her existence to you! What's this all about?"

"Relax, boss!" Toxic tried to dismiss his worries.

"No. I'm not relaxed. Don't mess with her. She'll think about this for a long time and ask questions. If it's true and you two will become friends that I seriously doubt, then why could not you hold back until such time?" Smith barely contained his anger.

The hologram looked at him, mimicked the gesture, then nodded. "You're right. I just could not wait; I had to greet her!"

"Not to mention that you are from an alternative future. How the hell are you supposed to know about her?"

"I just know," the hologram shrugged. "She is your first! The most important person for you and she is likewise feeling the same way about you!"

"First? What first? She isn't virgin and neither I am!" Smith fumed.

"Not like that . . ." Toxic shook her head. "Look. She is strong willed. She doesn't care how the world looks at her; she is content about herself, because she knows she is a good person."

"Azure . . ." Smith started, but Toxic shot him down: "She isn't a per se a human. They programmed her to be such."

"Okay, how about Aa?" Smith shot back.

"Aa is smart and hot and wicked and confident about herself, but . . ."

"But what?" Smith glared at her.

"Aa wants you. She is only dressing hot to please you. You would never see Aa in a skirt unless you order her to dress in it."

"That's not the measure of a true woman!" Smith disagreed.

"Go now. Leave me by myself!" Toxic practically threw him out. She was cursing too.

The first. . . "You would never forget your first . . . real . . . wife!" She reminded/contemplated herself.

*

Amerlee was eating at her kitchen table. The food was good, but her mind was far away. She missed Smith every minute. Come to think of it, every instance. "That's so horrible!" she said at the empty house. "I'm not the one who supposed to fall in love!" she lied to herself. She caught him many times before actually asking him out. She even mentioned him to Lou. He seemed to be understanding that way.

"Aw!" she took a quick shower with the thin water film casket running up and down twice and hopped into her bed, but it seemed empty without his presence. No naked, hairy chest to touch, no sweet smile to look at and definitely no sexy eyes . . . She grabbed a pillow and pulled close to her chest. She had a crazy dream about him being at a table and writing a paper letter.

"What's that?" she asked, vaguely remembering they just had a fight.

Smith seemed to be her man, but at the same time another notion lurked in the back of her mind; he was somebody else too . . .

"A choice!" He was still angry.

What exactly about, she could not remember.

"What choice?" She asked; her heart beating with heavy thuds. She was so nervous.

"If you so into money I can make it happen!" He responded angrily and hurt.

"No, I . . ." Her nervousness took over her senses.

"Amerlee, here is a check, a million space credits, so it's ten million credits. Take it with Lou, marry him for ten years to please Lou and your parents or . . . or take me and my long-lasting true love!" he tossed both the paper and the check across the table.

Amerlee stared at the many zeroes: her mother would just take it. Her father would think of her as being a cunning girl! She was about to cry. She felt losing him and it hurt. It physically hurt her! It felt like somebody was twisting a sword into her heart. She was about to fall into two separate pieces, but to lose him, she gasped for air. Unspeakable pain shot across her mind and she felt drowning.

The next moment she woke up amid screaming.

She stopped.

She wiped off her sweat, but felt her entire back being wet.

"Stupid dream!" she cursed, but she knew she wouldn't survive losing him. It horrified her. "Stupid, stupid dream!" she took up a new position, trying to calm herself. Money meant nothing long as she had him. She smiled as she went back to sleep.

Smith just finished taking a short shower when the doorbell rang. "It must be Amerlee!"

He opened the door.

The slender, athletic woman practically attacked him.

"What . . . ?" Smith grabbed the doorframe as the girl kissed him with such a ferocious force he almost fell backward.

"I missed you!" she uttered sensually.

"I . . . um, we saw one each other yesterday, you know?" Smith was not sure what got into her. Her skinny fingers were still attached to his arm, holding him surprisingly firm.

"I had a bad dream! Come!"

Whatever she was thinking, the darkness evaporated, replaced by elevated joy and happiness as she pulled him after her.

"Okay, okay!" Smith yanked the door shut and followed her. "Honey, I can reassure you that . . ." he could not finish as she pulled him closer and instead of kissing, she bit into his lips: “You’re mine!”

“Okay . . .” Smith decided to play along. He touched his swollen lips. She was a madwoman today!

Couple more kisses later, he found himself in her car as she zipped across town. Her moves were rawer, angrier this time. He watched her silently from the side, trying to figure out what changed. He wanted her for sure, but decided to take it easy, take it slow, to salivate after each other. This was just a mountain of emotions, dumped on top of him. Sometimes Azure would turn out to be such; almost mean and submissive at the same time, but it only happened to her three or four times during the years they’ve been together.

He expected a rough ride and was not disappointed in that regard. As soon as they walked thru the parent’s estate, she tossed her coat to the floor, kissed him passionately and proceeded to the terminal on the hall to disable all the recording devices. His weak, but logical step on *we should check on the logs* idea went completely unnoticed as she grabbed his ass and pulled closer to her.

Smith was uncomfortable, feeling his own growing erection, but she led him into a darker room, full of old looking furniture, jumped on the mahogany desk and locked her legs around his waist: “Take me!”

“Okay . . .” Smith was not sure whether it was a cleverly designed trap or she truly meant it. He hoped she would, but to have such a great luck with a girl, it was almost beyond his beliefs.

She unzipped his pants and grabbed him while he worked his fingers beneath her blouse.

“Rip it!” she demanded.

“Rip it, it is!” he obeyed. At the sound of the tear, she laughed with almost sinister joy: “Fuck me hard, baby!”

“I’m really good at following commands!” he grabbed her left breast and kissed it while the girl beneath him moved to an ancient rhythm.

"Fuck me harder!" she twisted around with a certain kinkiness in her eye; her hair all messed up, but she seemingly did not care.

He grabbed her hands and pushed her hard against the table.

"That's the way, baby!" she yelled with joy.

"Would you care to tell me what this was all about?" Smith lay beside her on the floor. Their clothes were thrown all over them.

She laughed, kissed his sweaty chest amid blowing a chewing gum, laced with chemicals; a smoother version than a drug laced cigarette.

"Did not you like me?" she smiled sensually.

"Oh, I never had such a good time, but I just feel this isn't like you . . ." Smith was sure of it.

"I want it rough, with lots of passion, that's all!" She lied, glancing toward her mother's work desk.

"That's all?" Smith echoed her.

"From you, baby, of course! I want you to remember how good you had it with me, so you never leave!" she voiced her insecurities.

"You're very special to me! God, I feel like falling in love!" he exhaled.

"God? A man who works for the Emperor, yet worships God himself?" she had to concentrate hard to the thoughts, as the drug was taking over her senses.

"It's a slip of a thought." Smith caught himself. He was truly relaxed with her, to allow such a deep, old outcry to surface.

"I won't tell anyone, but . . ." she began to circle her fingers on his chest.

"But . . . ?" Smith felt a trap being sprung around his manhood.

"But you have to work for it, hard!"

"That won't be a problem!" Smith twisted and got on top of her to kiss her lips.

She turned her head amid laughing: "What you think I just let you rape my lips like that?"

“I can do better!” he promised, kissing her flat belly and promised her again as he worked himself lower.

“Right there!” she giggled with joy. He was hers as far as anyone should consider.

While later on they exchanged short messages, Wednesday was a cool off period, a recollection of thoughts. Amerlee decided not to call him, see what he was going to do. Apparently not much. Angry at him, she grabbed her IC bar (Interactive Computer) as she sent a mental message to his address. The return message was almost instantaneous. As she absorbed the mental note, she smiled with happiness. He did miss her!

“Was that Mr. Smith?” Lou took a nervous peek across the divider.

“Oh!” Amerlee realized he must feel awful. He had no intention to hurt him. “Yes. He is a nice guy!” she covered her feelings.

“I bet! He is really special!” he added.

“What do you mean?”

“I mean to you!” Lou had to watch his mouth or the wrath of the Emperor would certainly reach him.

“Oh, yes!” Amerlee had to smile again. Later on, her boss called her into the office. She presented her a letter in a box to be delivered to Captain Aa the next day. Of course, that she did not know as the box was to be opened by Smith. “A nice way to get paid while also enjoying yourself!” Miss Thorne took the official receipt from Amerlee.

“What do you mean?”

“The spaceship Atlantis is really nicely decorated. Just got done couple months ago and now a full complement of fresh IHG graduates is onboard too!” Miss Thorne replied.

“Oh. I did not know!”

“Every space ship in the fleet of the Prince looks almost the same, so if you know one, you almost know all of them! They’re leisure ships, almost never used by the Emperor.” she added.

“What does the Emperor use then, the 26th fleet?”

"Almost exclusively." her boss nodded. "Before all this madness with the X-Force he occasionally took them out, mainly the flagship, the Prince. I like that spaceship!" she added, before Amerlee could ask.

"Don't be late tomorrow!" she added to Amerlee.

"I'm not even sure we'll be back on Thursday or not." Amerlee responded. That never even surfaced in her mind until now.

"No, you won't. Smith already signed you out, so nothing to report back until Monday!"

"The trip takes two days?"

"One day there and another back. Presumably . . ." Miss Thorne replied.

"Presumably?"

"With Smith, one would never know." Emma enigmatically responded.

Amerlee thought she implied he might stretch it out or the military would for some obscure safety related reason never to be explained to the passengers onboard, but her boss thought all that from a different perspective. A sudden incursion, one unapproved shoot out, and Smith might have to delay returning to the planet. What would he do with Amerlee was a question she had no answer for. Never less, all she had to do is to pay Amerlee the courier rate above her day pay. That was Smith's order, and she would do that to the letter.

Chapter Five

Heroes

"You're late!" Smith concluded as Amerlee grabbed her purse from the car.

"I think I've got everything . . ." she mumbled.

"I know you've got everything!" Smith replied, looking at her like a candy bar.

She blushed and pushed a stray hair out of her eyes.

They were standing on the tarmac, deep inside the military portion of the International Spaceport. A military car took them from the parking lot where she left her own car behind.

"The box!" She shouted.

"I got it!" Smith grabbed her arm hurriedly as she seemed nervous about the elevator taking them high up to the purple/blue spaceship towering above them.

"This thing is huge!" She glanced around.

"Not that big, but it's definitely impressive!" Smith agreed.

"Over eight hundred meters. The thing IS huge!" She brushed him off. "By the way, Miss Thorne did not say who the box is for." She hoped Smith would slip or tell her their destination, but she was out of luck. Smith remained tight-lipped about it, revealing only that the person lives high in the food chain.

"So, the person is in the military for a while, huh?" she kept poking him.

"Yes. She is a Captain in the Space Navy operating near hostile territory. I don't even know whether we would be back by Friday night or it will be pushed into Saturday!" Smith replied.

“Is the person a she?” she grinned upon extracting something meaningful from him.

“Yes.” Smith replied reluctantly.

“I get paid either way!” she chirped happily.

“Yeah, I know . . . I don’t get paid like you.” he admitted, sounding sad.

“What? You need a loan or something?”

“Nope. Just that I got a reservation at the Gaff for both of us if you like chill out and club music.”

“Gaff?”

“Yeah. It’s the high-end clubbing scene on the Sky
Riders . . .” Smith winked.

“Clubbing?” She seemed surprised. Her expressions changed to Smith’s biggest delight, who observed her stray freckles moving around her nose.

“I keep telling you, people have deep misconceptions about the Starship!” Smith shook his head, winking.

The Captain of the Atlantis greeted them personally. Amerlee felt special to shake hands with the grumpy male, working so closely with the Emperor.

“I don’t think he ever saw the bastard!” Smith swayed his head as they were being escorted to their quarters.

“Bastard, you mean the Emperor?” She seemed mortified.

“Yeah . . .” Smith did not even look up. He was searching his belongings until he found his swimming gears.

“Where are you going?”

“Swimming. Their pools are pretty awesome! I’ve been planning to do that!” he said and left her alone.

“Damn. No swimming set!” She tossed the contents of her traveling bag across the double bed. She began to grin as she found what she was after. Second choice was . . . She quickly changed up and after utilizing the kiosk at the room for directions, she went after Smith.

Smith was swimming alone when he heard the splash. He stopped and wiggled himself around just in time to see Amerlee resurfacing nearby. He washed the drops out of his eyes and luckily it did not betray him as she swam closer.

"You look breathtaking!" Smith was out of breath.

The owner of the pink, wet bra barely hid her smile. "I can swim too!" she swam around him, so he can muster her equally wet undies.

With one big whoosh, he practically galloped after her.

A good fifteen minutes later, Smith, being exhausted, pulled himself to the edge of the pool. A low resonance shook the water's surface and reverberated from end to end.

"What was that?" Amerlee looked around, concerned.

"We just jumped to light speed . . ." Smith explained.

"So, who is your hero in the Space Navy, Smith?" She playfully splashed him.

"Um. Maybe Admiral Tarbuk or Jandailh . . ." He contemplated; then it dawned on him she wanted to tell her side, so he asked: "Who is yours?"

"My hero is Captain Aa!" She popped her chest.

At the mention of her name, Smith pulled his mouth.

"What? I think she is gorgeous, and she definitely knows how to dress!"

"You know how to dress too!" Smith was quick to point it out, sensing a trap nearby.

"Yeah, but she is more beautiful than me!"

"I disagree!" Smith responded strongly, and it made her blush.

"Thank you, but I think she is more ideal. She definitely dresses provocatively. Rumor has it she and the Emperor are good friends!"

"Maybe." Smith felt quicksand forming beneath his legs.

"I mean deep friends . . ." she laughed.

"What do you mean?" he pretended to be clueless.

"Lovers!" she uttered into his ear.

Smith adamantly shook his head. "I don't think so . . ."

"Come on, Smith! She lost her ship couple years ago in a space battle and what does the Emperor do? Gives her an SPD. I mean, nobody gets an SPD! It's rare as hell. I often wonder whether she greased his balls to get that SPD!"

"Eww. That's nasty!" Smith repelled the idea.

"Come on; don't tell me you never thought of it!"

"Never!" Smith was certain of. "By the way, why it has to be sexual all the time? Why can't it be honor and respect?" he asked her.

"She is probably the hottest person in the service nowadays, and she rarely expresses how good she looks. Mostly only when she is around him. I saw a couple of holo pics of her. She is stunning. Expensive clothing. All for one person, I'm certain! But don't get me wrong, she is my hero forever! Girl's rules!"

"This trip's going to be really interesting . . ." Smith uttered under his breath.

Captain Aa paced back and forth in the Ready Room behind the DU's bridge. She quietly contemplated the reasons of her required presence at the docking. She received the news thru official channels about the protocol ship's arrival the next day. While it was unusual and she assigned Commander Danek to meet with the Atlantis's Captain she now learned her presence was also required. She asked Victor to confirm the communique and after the answer she only got more curious.

"Captain, it's almost time!" Commander Danek stepped beside her.

"Four thirty in the afternoon already?" she glanced thru the composite glass windows.

"Four ten to be exact." Danek turned to a specific spot where a small lightning strike against the darkness of space; a vessel returned to normal space. He turned around and the Lieutenant running the navigations department confirmed it was the Atlantis.

"Do you know what this is all about?" Aa finally decided to ask her Commander's opinion. First, she thought it would be a weakness from her part to ask, but how better way to gauge his XO's thoughts?

"I have no clue!" Danek responded.

"You always think of something!" She began to walk to the exit as his loyal second in command followed.

"It might be irrelevant. Actually, I think it has nothing to do with it, but . . ."

"But what? Tell me!" She demanded. They stepped into the turbo lift and Commander Danek asked for midlevel exit. The platform moved with a hiss and he opened his mouth: "The Emperor's push into reestablishing the once proud and abundant members of the Honor Guards might take effect."

"How so?" she turned to him. Smith told her no such thing.

Commander Danek shrugged: "We received seventy-five cadets."

"And I had to send back five of them . . ." Captain Aa frowned. She and Tata had a long discussion about it.

"It's not inconceivable to imagine the Emperor sent newer cadets to the Prince and its support ships like the Atlantis. Each space ship supposed to carry twenty-five to thirty Space Fighters. I would guess that at least thirty cadets were transferred as most of those pilot seats became vacant over the years."

"It's all interesting, but how does that relate to our situation?" Aa hurried to the airlock.

"Well, two things. For one I received a note from Tata Crubon that the Emperor appointed a new liaison who supposed to relay information between us and Tata."

"Let me guess, she is a female." Aa frowned. Tata loved hot, young chicks.

"Well, allegedly the Emperor was also involved of appointing her to the post, but yes, she is a female. Also, a pilot update pushed thru the fleet suggested over a hundred new pilots took up respectable positions on Down Earth. Since the Prince and its support ships are berthed there, and since no new space-based station got commissioned, I decided it would be a relevant solution. And if there are new pilots, the Emperor, knowing how much he is fond of the DU might send them here to do some shake down, an exercise."

"Amazing!" Captain Aa followed his logic.

Commander Danek uncharacteristically grinned. "And knowing the Emperor how much he loves us and how seriously does he think of the importance of the new generations of IHG graduates, he might ask you to meet the Captain in person."

Captain Aa looked like someone who just swallowed a lemon. "Great, just great!" She waited as the crew equalized the airlock, then the double blast door slid aside, revealing a male and a female human.

At first, Captain Aa was not sure it was a joke or a dream, then recognizing Smith, she smiled with happiness: "Smith, how nice to drop by!" Soon a frown followed her joyful outcry. "But I would've thought you travel on the Tox . . ."

"The toxicology report, you mean?" Smith seemed to work hard to push the girl standing beside him and constantly glancing at the floor forward into the light.

"Toxicology report?" Captain Aa echoed his words, totally confused. She and Commander Danek glanced at each other briefly. From the looks of it she was sure that this time the XO was also clueless.

"Ma'am it is a pleasure to finally meet you in person!" The woman, slightly older than Aa, offered her hand as she stepped into the hallway.

Commander Danek frowned, wondering about this surreal situation and the following of the complete lack of protocols.

Smith recognized the root of the confusion and he jumped beside Amerlee. He gently touched her shoulder to gain her attention: "Honey, these are military people. They live for protocols. Here, we have to ask permission to get to their spaceship first!"

Amerlee turned red, mumbled something apologetic and worked hard to look small, returning partially behind Smith.

"Like this!" he attempted to smile and saluted strong: "Captain Aa, permission to get aboard the Destination Unknown!"

"Permission granted!" she returned the salute along with the three soldiers behind Commander Danek, who recognizing the awkwardness ordered them to leave. He figured the fewer eyes the better. The beauty and the closeness of how Smith shepherded the woman who was with him made it clear this was a girlfriend situation, but the woman was definitely no Azure, neither Tri'ng, so he was eager to learn the details.

"You should do it!" Smith opened the beige box, and the woman picked up the letter inside. With great humbleness she presented it to the speechless Captain of the DU: "Captain Aa, in the name of the Emperor, please take this Letter of Recognition, prepared by the PR department, blessed by our great leader who recognized your continued exceptional service to the Monarch!"

"Thank, you?" It visibly moved Aa. She shook hands with the woman, who took a quick glance at her, then back at the floor.

Smith grinned in the background and pointed at the woman with both of his hands, while encouraging both the Captain and the Commander to get more interactive with her.

"What's your name, hon'?" Captain Aa turned with great interest at Smith's companion. She recently learned of Azure's passing and was surprised Smith seemingly moved on so quick. She hoped she could spend more time with him, but it was apparent that was definitely not be the case now. Pushing aside her anger, she figured she better learn who the girl was.

"Oh . . ." she seemed humbled to be spoken to. "My name is Zoon Amerlee and uhm, he is my associate Evan Smith, but it seemed you two already knew each other . . ." her eyes were about to return to steering at the floor, but Aa gently lifted her chin: "We are both women. There is no need to look away!"

"You are my living hero!" she blurted.

Aa blushed. "Thank you, but I'm just a lucky girl from Delta City's streets, who got the chance to meet the Emperor years ago! There is nothing special about me, I think . . ." she added with some hesitancy.

Smith cleared his throat in the background and as Amerlee turned to him, he called her to come closer.

"Yes?"

Smith moved even closer and uttered: "Do you want me to ask her about that greasing business we discussed earlier?"

Suddenly she looked meaner than mean and horrified.

"You look so hot when you are mean!" Smith concluded while laughing.

"Greasing business?" Aa frowned. She was seeing/feeling the situation in another frequency. As usual, Smith was perfectly composed, but the woman seemed elevated, almost too excited until she realized she was in love; she saw the white mental outbursts as strong waves encompassing her. It was no secret to Aa who she was in love with either. She seemed sad and annoyed at the same time. Now she understood why her presence was required, although on a personal note, the woman's presence made her feelings hurt.

Smith nodded, acknowledging Commander Danek, then turned back at Aa: "Captain Aa, while our official business was just the letter I came because I need a favor from you!"

"I'm listening." Aa changed posture.

"Look at my girlfriend, Amerlee . . ." Smith commanded, and Danek swallowed hard in the background. This was serious after all!

"She looks special." Aa was not sure what Smith was implying, other than the fact the woman obviously did not know who he was.

"Yes, she is! She was born with a birth defect. I need your second opinion about that!"

To Aa, who she was learning from him every time they met, this request sounded astonishing. *Her expertise was required?* She even asked for clarification.

"I need to know for certain that it can be fixed, by growing it!" he admitted, his mouth narrowing, his eyes tightening.

"I see. This is important to you!" she suddenly realized.

"Most important!" he replied seriously.

"But . . . you know the answer already!" She tilted her head. Amerlee was born with the defect. She saw her fake, motorized arm as a crude substitute for the real thing. She also knew that those whom neither Emperors nor healers the technology worn by the girl was beyond sophisticated.

"I need to be sure!" Smith's voice changed.

"Let me talk with her alone! Do you . . . ?" she left open the end of the sentence. She wanted to say 'allow' but was not sure Smith would let her say it.

Smith nodded, offered his handshake to the Commander: "Mr. Danek if you don't mind, please take me to the hangar bay! I want to see the new pilots in action!"

"This way, sir!" Danek took the hand and walked away with him.

Amerlee bit her lips. He left her alone in this magnificent piece of human engineering with the hero of her most secret dreams. Smith was seemingly interested in pilots and knowing he was one in the service for a while, she could relate to that. She glanced at the slender woman, slightly taller than she was. Captain Aa was less than thirty years old, that was certain. Her uniform just like her young face was spotless and devoid of any wrinkle.

"What is it, Amerlee?" Aa asked her gingerly.

"Captain?" Amerlee looked most uncomfortable.

"Please, ease up. I told you we both are women. Tell me, how did you meet Mr. Smith?"

"Oh, I worked up my courage and asked him out!" she giggled.

"Nice!" Aa nodded, recognizing her strong personality.

"I know!" she smiled and brushed her hair aside.

"Amerlee, walk with me!" her tone changed, became commanding. She moved her hands behind her ramrod straight back and began to walk. She noticed however her guest remained couple steps behind, looking hurt or perhaps displeased. "Please!" she added kindly. Amerlee eased up and joined her.

"I'm sorry about this awkwardness . . ." Aa apologized.

"It sounded harsh to my ears. I'm not a soldier. I have never been in the service." she admitted.

"Never?" Aa glanced at her, looking surprised. That was news. Smith loved girls from the military, so Aa felt the need to clarify herself: "When the Emperor lifted me out of poverty, but before I became a Captain, he often asked me to follow him to somewhere. He used to say mean and strong: "Walk with me!" It was more like a command and never a request. I give him homage, trying to mimic him in his absence." Aa explained.

"Nice work secret!" Amerlee felt a special connection brewing between the two of them.

"Do you know why you are here, then?" Aa asked. They were walking down the deserted hallway; headed to the hydroponics gardens.

Amerlee nodded. "Smith told me you owe him and he needs your second opinion."

At the mentioning of owing him, Aa's face got longer. Amerlee noticed the change. "What's wrong?"

"You're right. I do owe him!" The realization hit her like a lightning strike. It was different than she would imagine. She hoped to fight side by side with him, but this, this was unexpected. Smith most likely wanted to avoid an argument, so he never told her about Amerlee. He was smart. She suddenly stopped and turned to the woman: "Were it not for Smith I would most likely be dead in Delta City. So, you're right, I owe him my life!" she sounded serious.

"Do you think Smith would ever tell me that story?" Amerlee was hoping.

"Perhaps . . ." Aa had to look away and wipe the tears out of her eyes. Smith should've been with her, not with a civilian!

They continued to walk.

"I feel this heavy wall around him sometimes. Like he is hiding a great secret and it poisoning him." Amerlee admitted.

"He has many secrets indeed. He walked with the immortals for so long it poisoned him." Aa responded.

"I love him!" she suddenly admitted to her.

"I know!" she nodded like a teacher.

"How? he told you?"

"No need to tell me. I can see it!" Aa replied, trying hard to mute her yelling internal thoughts of jealousy.

"See it?"

"Amerlee, do you know what does it mean to touch, to shake hands with an immortal?"

The woman shyly shook her head. "No." She replied honestly.

"You suddenly realize how small you are, how big the universe is. That beyond the curtain is another room and beyond there is another curtain and yet another room and that endless cycle reach into infinity . . . Do you understand me?"

"I would be a fool to say I do. I work at the PR department hoping that one day I might see him, perhaps I hold a conversation with him." Amerlee had to swallow hard. She became emotional too.

"I totally understand you!" Aa nodded emphatically. "When I was a young chick, fending for myself, I, just like everyone else, sought the blessing of an old woman when I needed to. She was so old; her face was full of wrinkles. She seemed ugly too. Legend had it; her father shook hands with the Ancient Man once. See, a personal touch goes a long way. It generates legends that travel from generations to generations. Just by knowing that story being true gave her immense powers. And to come to think of it, she had nothing to do with it. After all, she did not touch the immortal's hand. Imagine me kissing him, touching him like another human. And I only tell you this because of my special powers. For you to understand what I have as a result of being around him. Once, several years ago, I did something. . ." She bit her lips and stopped for a second before continuing: "I was weak, and he felt he needed to encourage me. So, he gave me a gift. It was a special thing. It represented in his palm as pills. Two pills in two hands, but I could only take one, he said. I took one and now I'm a healer. I can see your body like no machine can see it. I can feel you like no one except an immortal can! That's why Smith brought you here. He is so worried about you, that something would go wrong that he needs a reassurance from me to go thru with his plan, assuming you would agree to it."

"Why do you say it that way?" Amerlee became nervous.

"Because you have something special; love. And I know him. He would never do any change to you unless you agree. His principles about personal freedom are commendable. I won't deny, I tried to make a move on him many times."

"On my Smith?" her eyes grew big.

Aa smiled gently. "Yes, Amerlee, on your Smith. It never worked. Partially because of his code of honor. Ah, here we are!" she led her inside the garden.

"It feels humid." Amerlee practically bit into the air.

"I brought you here to show you something. If I do this while others present, they think I'm a goddess, but I just want to show you, so someday, you might understand what I want to say . . ."

"To?"

"To you . . . of course!" Aa smiled gently and began to draw the sign of infiniteness into the air. "You know, when I first saw this trick from the Emperor, I did not get it. I was stoned, petrified, and did not understand how he had done it. He told me, he showed that to me, so one day I would draw my own conclusion about certain things. And he was right, in time I did. So now I show and teach you, and it makes me feel really good. I hope that one day you will understand it too!"

Amerlee watched her doings and began to shudder: suddenly she felt cold. To her biggest amazement, the water molecules in the air froze up as Aa touched them: swirled her fingers around and around. The frozen icicles fell to the ground, forming the symbol of infinity to Amerlee's biggest amazement. She kneeled to the floor and watched the gently fallen frozen water. Aa locked eyes with her while continuing her miracle. As the ground turned frosty and white, she kneeled beside her, stopped her weavings and tilted her head. The snow particles began to move closer to each other while melting the same time. Within minutes it took up the shape of a small dog. The white, frozen water melted and the skin texture changed to something that was looking glassy. Then the small dog shook and began to bark. Aa smiled and stopped, hovering her hand over the fake animal. As a result, it collapsed into a puddle of water.

Amerlee was crying. She did not know why, but she was.

"I was touched by the Emperor, Amerlee. I became more than a human, yet essentially I will always remain human." she stood up. Amerlee followed her with awe; "You are an Empress to me!"

"You can learn it too . . ." She shrugged casually, downplaying the significance of what just happened.

"I would never be able to do it." she was sure of it.

"No. You are wrong on that one!" she said with genuine belief that scared Amerlee to her core. Aa continued: "One day I asked the Emperor what is it mean to be? To be an Emperor, an immortal. Do you know what he answered?"

Amerlee shook her head, soaking in every word she said.

"He said to be an Emperor is to feel everyone, to know everything; know all the perturbations off all the actions in the Universe ever made and will ever to be made. To know how will it all end, but allowing the constituents to make their own mistakes, to tumble, to get up and walk again; to give them the illusion of freedom!"

"Amazing!" Amerlee was ecstatic about it. When she calmed down on their way back to the airlock, she asked: "Why did you show me all this? Why did you tell me what you told me?"

"Because one day, one day when there will be no more secrets between the two of you, you will understand exactly why did I show this to you! Why we had this long conversation."

"You're cryptic like an Emperor!" Amerlee scoffed.

"Thank you!" Aa took it as a complement.

Back at the airlock, Smith and Commander Danek was still talking. Aa broke their chitchat: "I see why did you choose her over others."

Amerlee was sure she meant herself, but seemingly, Smith did not take it personally. For her, it was less clear. Aa was an amazing woman; touched by the Emperor himself. She can do magic like they could! A man would be happy beside her. Why Smith did not choose her was a mystery, but one action of his she was completely satisfied with. It was clear for her; Aa thought of her as of someone special, better than she was. Amerlee quietly disagreed, but kept it to herself. She would not be the one who breaks the illusion, ever!

"Hold my hand!" Captain Aa offered it to Smith, who took it. They both closed their eyes and became still.

Amerlee glanced at Commander Danek, who felt obligated to explain it to her: "She is somewhat telepathic. She will show to him what she chooses to show about you."

Amerlee felt humbled, standing in the quiet.

The ritual lasted less than a minute.

When it was over Smith slightly bowed at the Captain: "Thank you!" he said with humbleness in his voice.

"You're welcome!" she hugged him emotionally.

Smith smiled at Amerlee and offered his hand: "We can go now!"

Chapter Six

Twin Cities

Amerlee spent the afternoon in their cabin without Smith. First, she thought he was busy with something, but the room's computer located him on one of the upper-level hallways, near the communications array. She wondered whether his past had something to do with the gigantic dish or was he doing something important. She trekked across the spaceship as it was en route to Tau Ceti where the gigantic Parallels would let them thru to another Universe; final destination: Down Earth! She was on a spaceship before; a passenger space ship. Matter of facts, several times in the past, but this was unlike anything she experienced before. His parents took her once to SWEi Prime on first class. It cost a fortune. She was seventeen. They tried to please her so she would give up racing. She told them she did. She lied.

"Why did it surface now?" She asked herself, sitting on her bed. Ever since they returned from the warship, Smith seemed to be withdrawn. She always thought there were luxury space yachts out there, where the seats aren't cramped, the walkways not like a miner's worst nightmare and the person doesn't feel akin to can food beans. Now she realized the power and wealth the government had. It had to come from tax money, she contemplated. She was not sure. She decided to find Smith and bug him for a while. He was where the computer said he would be: standing alone, watching the blue and red streaks around them; each a star in normal space.

She gently touched his shoulder: "What's wrong, my love?"

"Nothing!" Smith shook his head, thinking of how to tell her his secret.

"You look heroic!" she took a step back to admire him.

"Really?" Smith's bad mood evaporated.

"Why have you stared the window so intently?" she felt he should rest his brain.

"I was thinking of you and I . . ."

"Oh? In what context?" she hoped it would be romantic at the least, something decidedly hotter than the most.

"I was thinking of what the Captain said!" Smith referred to Aa's statement.

Amerlee's face changed. It became cloudy: "She said you already know the answer you came for, is that it?"

"Yes . . ."

"What was the answer?"

"That I knew it was possible to re grow your arm even before we embarked on this journey."

"Then why have we done it?" her eyes grew bigger.

"Perhaps all I was doing is to ask permission from her." Smith contemplated. He was not sure himself.

Amerlee remembered what the Captain told her about making a move on Smith before. She felt there was something deeper amiss there, but she did not know what.

"I never told you, but I had a crush on her before." He finally admitted.

"I see." She was relieved he said so. She already knew.

"It never evolved beyond that." He kissed her lips. She fought it before giving in. When their lips parted, she watched him intently: "I understand. She is powerful."

"She is growing more and more powerful by the day." Smith admitted, misunderstanding Amerlee's suggestion.

"Is she going to drive a wedge between us?"

"No. She wouldn't do that. I know her enough!" He suddenly and vehemently disagreed.

"But if she is close to the immortals, she could ask them to lure you away from me!" she sounded nervous, her lips twitching.

"Oh, silly girl, it isn't like that!" Smith had to laugh. "She will be never as powerful as I am!" he added, slipping his tongue, but luckily Amerlee never realized it.

"She drew magic in the air for me. I think she was trying to tell me something." Amerlee then explained to Smith, Captain Aa's doing in the hydroponic garden.

Smith nodded. "She is learning. Good. But she can't convert molecules yet." he seemed pleased, almost satisfied. Amerlee watched him and wondered why that was.

"One day I will reveal my secrets to you, but not yet!" Smith knew what was on her mind even without looking into.

She seemed upset. "Why do I have to wait? I don't have secrets I withhold from you!" she sounded upset.

"My case is different." Smith looked away.

"Captain Aa said you walked with the immortals and that it poisoned you!" she grabbed his arm, looking all too worried.

"Really?" Smith probed her. "That's interesting, knowing how she keeps walks with them, still!" He sounded cynical, and Amerlee defended her without realizing it was not her job to do; "She is a living hero!"

"Oh, so that's supposed to make it all normal? Did you know she even has a past Emperor showing up occasionally on her? I think they have a love affair."

"No way!" Amerlee did not believe a word he said.

"Let's relax honey!" Smith waved in the air dismissively: "Soon we'll be on Down Earth and you going to get drunk tonight I promise!"

Amerlee felt drunk the moment Smith opened the last triple blast doors to the Sky Riders's inner city called Twin Cities. It was breathtaking. Gigantic skyscrapers towered above them; some even morphed into their own mirror like image until Smith pointed out the existence of the second city looking down from over their heads. It was truly mind bogging! So as the antigravity limo ride to the bow of the otherwise immensely large alien Starship. The Gaff was a bizarre outcropping among the shorter buildings; glass floors and walls to the dance floor below where beautiful girls and guys danced to catchy tunes. Smith apparently rented a booth, and she loved to lay back on the lush sofa with him.

"This is so erotic!" she giggled. She already had three or four drinks.

Smith frowned. "Perhaps you want to dance below? I would watch you!" he promised.

"I can do that in your house!"

"The feeling isn't the same.

"You mean the vibe?"

"Yeah . . ."

"But if I were to strip for you . . ." she winked.

"Oh, man!" Smith tried to imagine, and she burst into laughing: "Honey, I can see what you think!"

"Oh, well." Smith tried to cover his embarrassment.

"Look who it is! The love couple!" Diana gyrated by on black high heels.

"Boss?" Smith sat up on the sofa, suddenly alarmed. Amerlee sensed utter uneasiness from his direction.

"Boss?" Diana seemed surprised by Smith's greet. "May I?" she pointed to one of the two chairs on the other side of the oval table.

"Sure!" Amerlee played with her hair as she put herself into an upright position. She grabbed Smith's hand and held it strong, apparently, she was not sure what to make out of the meet, but he just smiled toward her.

Smith understood her and nodded in Diana's general direction: "Knowing that nothing is by mistake coming from you, may I ask; were you spying on me?"

Diana sucked on the green lollipop; her lips almost kissed the top of the teddy bear shape sugarcoat. She smiled: "Of course I did. I'm the representation of the Starship's AI. My business to know all the visitors coming onboard!"

Smith turned to the pale Amerlee and tried to reassure her it was all okay. He failed miserably.

"It's a pleasure to meet you, Amerlee!" Diana offered her tiny hand.

"I don't know right now whether it's likewise from me or not." she shook the hand, unsure of herself.

"Relax, you aren't in trouble at all. I just wanted to meet you. I heard so much about you!" Diana explained.

Smith bit his lips and tried to move into the dark. His ears were on fire!

"Toxic also mentioned you and Smith visited the Villa-Castle the other day and we are always keen to that kind of gossip!" she elaborated further.

"Is Smith in trouble because of me?" Amerlee made the wrong conclusion.

"Far from it, but I do have to yank him away from your full attention for a minute or two!" she apologized in advance.

"Let's go!" Smith jumped from the sofa and as soon as they got outside of Amerlee's hearing, Smith pushed her chest; "What are you doing?"

"I wanted to meet your first!" she seemed upset.

"Here we go again with this first bullshit. I'm not a virg . . ." Smith was shut as Diana pressed her fingers on his lips: "Sss! I meant what I told her. There is a reason I came by. May I ask where have you entered into the Starship?"

"Why?"

"Just answer, please!" her voice seemed tense, unusual for her.

"Two thirds, the end of the inner city, why?"

"Our resident disliked her closeness to you . . ."

"Azure?" Smith's eyes grew wide.

"Yes. Her body was twitching in the pod. I suggest both of you to be present when we open the pod, that way she won't harm her, ever!"

"So, she can already sense me and that I'm with someone else?" Smith had to understand this.

"It would appear so . . ." Diana looked the floor.

Smith scratched his eyelids. "Boy, this going to be something I'm not looking forward to!" he admitted.

"Thing of it is, she seems to be calm now. But she'll be ready within a month, so you are going to have to make some decisions by then. Whatever they will be, we're standing with you!" she reminded him.

"Where are you going?" Smith watched her eyeing a tall male at the bar.

"Who said you can have fun, but not me?" she laughed and left toward the bar.

Smith returned to Amerlee.

"So, did she call you by names?" she kissed his shoulder.

"No, but reminded me that like everyone else, I also have a deadline!" Smith's eyes twitched.

"Work?"

"Its work all right, but not the kind you would think."

"Since you already seem unhappy, I have to tell you something . . ." Amerlee seemed to become shy all of a sudden. With apologetic looks she turned to him: "I sort of agreed to my parents to introduce you to them over dinner!"

"What?!" Smith felt the walls falling onto him.

"Calm down! I can get you ready for the onslaught!"

"I don't think that was a good idea at all!" Smith shook his head.

"Just don't take it personal. My father is a businessman. He approaches life from his point of view and my mom while in heart a good person as I was growing up, she let me know mean ways what she thought I should do to catch my man."

"Meaning?" Smith watched her. She seemed hurt all of a sudden.

"She thinks the only way to have a good life is to put love aside and marry someone for the money," she winced.

"I see. That should be interesting!" he disliked the dinner already.

"I'm not like that. I love you who you are!" she quickly kissed him.

"Well . . ." Smith was not sure he should say something like who he was right about now.

Amerlee pushed her face against his: "You know me! I'm an independent woman because I reject my parent's ideas! I am who I am and I ask no pity and I carry myself with pride!"

"I love you for that!" Smith kissed her.

"Then just be a nice guy, don't take their inquisition too personal and we'll be thru with this, I promise!"

"Just so we're clear. I won't get mad at them, but I will not sit by idly if they mock you. You are my everything and I will stand with you in the rain if I have to, but I won't yield!"

"Aw! I so love you!" she kissed him again, feeling warmth inside.

Chapter Seven

Dinner with the Parents

"So, tell me boss," Miss Thorne took her sweet time to walk around Smith, who dropped by the PR department Monday morning. "You have no other things to do but to screw with my employee?"

"Literally?" The devilish smile appeared in the corner of Smith's mouth.

She gave him a mean look. "I mean as our dear leader. Seemingly all you do is pester around Amerlee. Efficiency is down more than three and a half percent!"

"Ah, you're trying to mimic Tri'ng, aren't you?" Smith was still trying to figure her out. He was not sure she was joking or telling him her true concerns.

"Perhaps. Perhaps I'm really curious about your long vacation on Down Earth."

"Okay, let's be serious here. Azure is out of commission. It was on my watch, even if I was not there on her side of the mission. I had to protect others, but never less her body is dead and I'm waiting for her to be reborn. It's true, she shouldn't get my entire devotion, but she isn't. And about being occupied, I'm working on multiple cases as we speak. For one, two weeks ago at the Heinar region in the Marazza quadrangle a megacorporation decided that instead of the two centuries and well worked space shipping route they would cut across the Heinar region. As soon as the Monarch got wind of it, they advised the Furtelo corporation to back down. They ignored the warning and contracted an explorer VII type of high accuracy mapping vessel. It entered into the region two weeks ago and promptly lost contact with the outside world. The Furtelo corp then decided to contract two security company vessels. They entered the region a week ago. Guess what happened to them?"

"Disappeared?" Miss Thorne was not sure.

"Lost contact!" Smith shrugged. "So, two days ago, they bought and commissioned themselves a probe. It's a multi spectral spherical analysis capable device. Extremely sophisticated. Point two light years into the Heinar region, it blew apart. Seemingly no data indicate it was being attacked. So now I have to tell the bad news to the Furtelo's managing board and it won't be pretty. I pretty much think I know what happened, but I'm still looking for evidence in the Temple of Knowledge about the original warnings regarding to that region about a thousand years ago. The books were written in AED, (Ancient Earth Dialect) so it takes a considerable amount of time to find what I'm looking for. Case number two is a bit less complicated, running a joint mission with the Ancient man on the reorganization of the Admiralty on SWEi Prime. That nearing to its end. Door number three hides an anomaly in the Forrest of Darkness, adjacent to Delvon-17, a gas giant with multiple mining colonies. The gravitational shear from the Forrest of Darkness, a swath roughly two light years long, began to randomly change. The scientist on the science vessels has no answer to that. If they can't predict the change people will lose their life and the companies might go bankrupt faster than case number two would be solved! Would my explanation satisfy your curiosity, My Lady?" Smith finished his rap.

"I mean no disrespect, sir!" she recovered after digesting the load of information.

"Of course not. You're a mortal. You can't understand that. Even when I appear to relax, I'm working!" Smith was a bit annoyed by Emma's questions. He was about to leave when she asked: "Aren't you stopping to see Amerlee?"

"Let her think you ringed me out. It would make my position more solid for tonight!" his annoyance disappeared, replaced by a hollow smile.

"Wait . . ." Emma was not sure whether Smith played her as part of his problem number four or it just came as a spur of the moment. Nevertheless, Amerlee dropped by less than thirty minutes later and tried to sniff around inconspicuously. She had to come up with something plausible or she would begin to think about it. Emma knew that was the main thing Smith wanted to avoid, so she decided to play along.

By ten AM Smith knew all about it because Amerlee sent him a message titled 'so sorry about my boss'. He replied with a don't worry about it, for what she replied with 'don't forget about six PM tonight'.

Not only he had to call Mrs. G to have his suit prepared, he also had to calm himself by using old techniques he learned from his fellow past emperor; Comon. He ended up staying in the KFT all day long, working on his company's dealings to Mrs. G's biggest delight, although he was unable to have her say that out in the open.

Shortly after five PM he received a message from Amerlee asking if he would be at home. After a short contemplation, he let her know about his work at the KFT. Even though it was just an interactive message, her surprise and shock were almost touchable by him.

Amerlee pulled front of the towering skyscraper. Smith's message that he was there shocked her at first, then she became proud of him. Her man was working in the Emperor's building. It was a strong coming! She could certainly use it during dinner, she wondered. The policeman told her not to leave the car alone for more than ten minutes and she nodded; she had no problem keeping the time limit front of the iconic building. She walked thru the glass front door into the pleasantly decorated lobby and stepped to the receptionist. The middle-aged woman glanced up from her workstation: "Can I help you with something?"

"Um. I don't know whether he is here or not, but I'm looking for Evan Smith!"

At the mention of the name, the woman shook, and it did not avoid her attention. Perhaps she knew Smith personally? She never found that out, because the receptionist called someone, talked to the other end of the line, then gave her the old-fashioned phone handle.

"Thank you!" she took the crude device.

The woman's voice coming from the other end was old, but firm: "Mr. Smith is on his way to you, my darling!" and she hung up.

Amerlee frowned. All these theatrics for nothing? Soon she heard her beloved Smith's voice, coming from the elevators. Apparently, he was having a heated conversation with someone. She took a peek from the lobby and noticed a much younger, round-faced guy really trying to explain something to him:

"Listen Del, it's not that I don't trust in your design improvements, but we should really see it in a simulation world before we commit to build it." Smith reasoned.

"Yes, Mr. Smith, but I just thought that if we . . ."

"Listen, just hold your horses, input the parameters into the company's server and . . ." he could not finish as Del suddenly grabbed his right arm and said, "Am I dreaming?"

"Why?" Smith turned to his friend, observing him a bit worried.

"Because I see this hot woman in the lobby steering at us! I'm not kidding, look!" he pointed straight at Amerlee.

"Shit!" Smith smiled awkwardly. "Del, I've got to go now!" he pulled his suit together.

"Do you know her?" Del began to sweat.

"Yeah . . . My date for tonight!"

"Ho-ho-ho! And she isn't Az . . ." He could not say what he wanted to say because Smith grabbed him by his neck. Del froze up. "Perhaps I should turn around!" He shrieked.

"Perhaps!" Uttered Smith and slapped him on the back. The young man turned around and pushed the button for the elevator, but he took his time watching the classy woman in a sexy blue dress giving a kiss to Smith. He even looked back from the elevators, shaking his head. The woman was indeed something!

"Who was that young guy?" Amerlee glanced at Smith as they got into her car.

"Oh, a protégé of the Emperor, Mr. Del. He is an engineer now at the firm."

"The Emperor talks to that kind of people?" Amerlee frowned instantly.

"He is the protector of the people; how could he not engage with an ordinary face?" Smith asked in return, albeit playfully.

"That guy was big."

"Del is short." Smith disagreed.

"I mean, he needs to lose weight!" she clarified.

"Oh. I don't think he will ever be going to do that." Smith was sure of it. "You should see his best friend, Mr. Jott. Now that's the total opposite of him! Tall and so skinny if you put a lamp at his stomach, you can see sunlight just staring his back!" Smith laughed.

"How do you know them, Smith?" she tried to learn people around him.

"Oh, I ran into Mr. Jott once when he was at the Temple of Knowledge with Mr. Del. They needed some help to read books written on AED."

"You can read Ancient Earth Dialect?" Amerlee was doubtful of that.

"Yeah! I'm that guy!" Smith nodded, pointing to himself for encouragement.

"Really?" Amerlee could not believe it.

"Really! I had time when I was growing up and I learned. Ask anyone, they tell you. That I'm good at!" Smith replied proudly.

"What else do you good at?" she asked, eyes glowing, portraying her big, happy smile with it. "By the way, you are looking good in a suit!" she admired him.

"I don't think we should go there now. Just right before dinner with your parents would suffice!" he replied timidly.

"How 'bout I pull over, darken the glass and we go to the back seat . . ." She did her best to arouse him.

"No!" Smith shot back. He was sure it would turn out to be a disaster.

She grabbed his manhood. "He disagrees!"

"You know we love you!" Smith blushed.

"And you?"

"Me too!" Smith reassured her.

"Better tell that to them! I keep telling them how lovely and good-hearted you are. That's your strongest point!" she nodded amid driving.

"Oh, I'm so doomed!" Smith shook his head, anxiously sipping on his fingernail.

After driving along the Road of the Bound, Amerlee pulled into the driveway on the left. The house was a three-story villa, with a nicely done lawn where the flowers were just in their prime. Smith kicked the yellow flower, hoping it would be just a cheap hologram, but it was not. It swayed!

"Hey, hey!" Amerlee scolded him.

"Sorry. I just had to check!" Smith pulled his feet. "How 'bout we turn around, you tie me to whatever and I tell my secret to you?" He did not want to face the parents at all!

"Now you the one backing out? I can't do that to my parents whether you tell me your secret or not." she scoffed, then added, pointing at the flowers: "The flowerbed's symmetry is always pronounceable!"

"Oh, I feel like a high school nightmare comes to life . . ." he choked on the air, while shaking his head.

"Relax, baby!" Amerlee grinned upon seeing her parents.

The tall man and equally well-maintained woman in their late fifties were standing in the hallway, past two humanoid like droid and a human servant.

"Look at these adoring people!" Smith hissed as Amerlee kicked his ankle.

Smith absorbed the visuals. The house was like a museum; everything had a predetermined place. The floors were hardwood, the side wall had a deep green trimming, and the wallpaper had an intricate pattern. He shook hands with Zoon Magol, Amerlee's father. He noted the daughter got the cute nose from her father. He had no idea what she got from her mother, Zoon Melonie, but as soon as she began to babble, he hoped she got nil. Amerlee's mother wore nice amethyst-zephyr necklaces with a platinum hookup. Plentiful of jewelry hung from her arms and fingers, and Smith was absolutely delighted Amerlee lacked that sort of creative habit!

They gathered around the dinner table.

The human servant announced the menu, then droids began the serving.

"So, Mr. Evan," Magol turned to Smith, "How do you like my humble retreat?"

Amerlee quizzed Smith earlier about these not oh-so-routine questions and now she was eagerly waiting for his response, giving looks akin to a schoolteacher's.

Smith tried to smile and be humble and not kill anyone tonight. Toxic sent a mental note earlier that their early departure from the living would make things more difficult for him, so he opted out of that plan: "I am really impressed, sir! Your daughter never told me how you came upon acquiring the license to live on the Road of the Bound!"

"Oh, yes!" Magol gently patted his wife's hand. She smiled in return, revealing her perfect teeth.

Amerlee diplomatically smiled. She knew the story as it was his father's centerpiece storyline.

"My dear grandfather, let the emperors bless his poor soul, he came across the Ancient Man once, early in the war. His merchant ship helped secure the Emperor's passage and in return he was awarded with this land. The fame that he was allowed to exploit helped him to expand his fleet of ships and reinvest the profit into construction equipment. The family still, to this day, owns Launch Pad 37C at the half way transfer station on the manmade island!

You know, the artificial island between the continents." he said proudly.

"Nice!" Smith knew exactly what the father was talking about.

"And you, Mr. Smith, do you know personally anyone who owns a land or a house on the Road of the Bound?" he asked in return.

Smith began to count it in his head: his Villa-Castle, the Limos' and the drivers' home, the modeling agency's estate, Josh's clan's up the other way in the mountains, the Ancient Man's huge estate, Claire's his next-door neighbor's, countless of friend's houses from the war. He glanced up. "Nah . . ." he shook his head with a sour smile.

"Well then, how does it feel to be so close to the immortals?" Zoon Magol asked.

"Makes me really humble!" Smith forced a smile on his face.

As they served the main dish, the best and freshest meat Smith ate in a long time, he was reminded again and again what kind of credentials he should get to stay with Magol's only daughter. Mostly he let it go, as he felt too tired to go up against the parents. He also reminded himself he would only make it hard for Amerlee.

"Smith works on board the Sky Riders, and just today I picked him up at the KFT!" Amerlee could not withhold the secret any longer.

"Is that true?" The father asked, his eyes poked Smith like thousand needles.

"Yes."

"A courier . . ." Melonie made a not so kind face.

"A courier perhaps, but never less I took your daughter to the stars last week on one of my business trips and she meet Captain Aa onboard her Super Planet Destroyer. A protégé of the Emperor! I let them introduce to each other. It should help her . . ." Smith trailed off. Amerlee was not too happy, and he wondered why when Magol snorted with obvious disgust: "Protégé?"

"More like a mistress!" Melonie finished his sentence.

Cute. Smith made a mental note to remain quiet.

"Mom, she was spectacular! She showed me stuff I never knew was possible!" Amerlee blurted, defending her hero.

"We know you like her!" Her father tried to establish defense lines, but his daughter smashed them: "She isn't a mistress! I spoke to her, and I saw what she is capable in my own eyes!" she said defensively.

Smith was glad he opted out of this conversation, but it was nice to hear somebody defending Aa so passionately!

Cake was served, laced with chocolate RB-2, a rare ingredient, grown only in off Down Earth environment. Smith liked it. The food was top-notch; the servants were professional, and the estate was magnificent. But the parents? He did not like them at all. They were both egoists.

"So, tell me son, why would I even allow you to keep seeing my one and only daughter? After all, you're nothing but a courier."

"I work for the Emperor, shouldn't that count?" Smith shrugged, trying not to take it personally.

"Sure, it counts, but at the same time my daughter already works for the PR department, works for the Emperor just the same. In my view, men should take care of the woman of their choosing!"

"Um, see . . ." Smith tried to get around the problem, rather unsuccessfully.

"Look, son, you are already a couple of years older than my daughter. She, although not always with my best interest in her mind, made good choices. You already made it and if that's all you can show that you share your life between the Emperor's Starship and the KFT than your track record is extremely weak."

"At least I'm not a truck driver!" Said Smith, trying to upend his case.

"Nasty!" Amerlee's mother shook her head in disgust.

"So how did you ask her out, if I may ask?" The father asked.

"Well . . . I did not. She did." Smith sadly admitted.

Amerlee's parents looked at each other. It was a telltale of struggle of the absent, unspoken words. Akin to two destroyers shooting over each other's bow. Smith did not have to wait for long for the blowback.

"What?!" Amerlee's mother yelled with passion.

"I wanted him mom and I'm not going to apologize for my actions!" Amerlee, losing her patience, said it with passion. She glanced at Smith, who appeared to enjoy the moment, but as he caught her look, he changed posture.

That bastard! She thought.

"See Mr. Evan Smith," Magol started a new thread, "people like me, who have influence, money and wealth, we pick up hobbies, like collecting real books. Paperbacks of all kinds!" he stepped to his long shelves, touching some: "This is a second edition SWEi book on the magnificent Piper Halo, this is an even more rare one from the Central Trade Planet, all poems of the incredibly talented Mimi Noel. This and the home planet's own offerings are plenty for me."

"I see you have The Origin's at hand!" Smith stepped to an eight-book series, old, golden framed paperbacks.

"Lucky guess from your side Mr. Evan as they are five hundred seventy plus years old, written on AED. Do you know what that means?"

"Ancient Earth Dialect . . ." Smith pulled out one of them and hit it up somewhere in the middle. He glanced around the page, reading it carefully as the sentences could be really tricky to translate. Magol took a peek over his shoulder.

"Centerpiece of the entire opera!" he thoughtfully nodded.

"The baby offerings? Please!" Smith shook his head acerbic.

"You can read?" Zoon Magol frowned.

Amerlee pressed her lips hard to squash her triumphing smile. Smith was good at something that earned the frown of her father! That was better than expected!

"Of course, I can!" Smith closed the book and carefully returned to its place. "But it's still a sad thing!"

"Scholars believe The Origin is authentic in every way!" Magol misunderstood him.

"Oh, I don't doubt that at all. The fact that generations after Bristol's fall took their newborns to the rooftops to offer it to gods is that I dislike. I really don't know who started that bullshit ritual, but we know it carried on for a long time." Smith spitted the words with clear anger.

"You know history. That's commendable!" Magol nodded, satisfied with that part of the inquisition. "But that is unfortunately not enough. This is a material life. One must procure wealth and influence to make it. Tell me, how do you intend to provide for my daughter?" he turned around, grinning at Smith.

"Tell me something in return. Since when does the parent decide who their children should marry?" Smith shot back.

Amerlee tried to signal to Smith from the background. Her father's logic was perfect; Smith would never win that way. But then again, it was not the objective. She already decided, and she wanted to be with Smith. No amount of anger or threat coming from her parents would change that.

"Since parents can be powerful!" Melonie spoke defiantly.

"Oh!" Smith glanced at Amerlee and seeing her face, he promptly cooled off. Things got out of hand. He had to honor Amerlee's request, so he shut up again.

"Mr. Evan, you must know by now that our daughter was born with a birth defect, that causing certain emotional, mental and monetary hardship for her." Magol began yet another thread.

"I'm aware." Smith nodded thoughtfully.

"Do you know or aware that the motorized hand needs an overhaul or a complete replacement in the near future?"

"I am."

"Good. Now do you know what the price is for one hand such as hers?"

"Irrelevant." Smith shook his head.

"Oh? How so?" Magol glanced at his wife, seemingly surprised.

"Sir, I love your daughter!" Smith spoke with passion. More passion than ever before in his life. He did not realize that until just weeks later.

"So?"

"Love knows no boundaries. See, I presumed you love your daughter, but money gets her a new motorized arm. Love will get her arm back, by growing tissue at the cell level!" Smith boasted.

"Was that a mockery?" Magol turned red to contain his anger.

Amerlee was not sure how she could intervene, but suddenly felt a compelling reason to do so!

"No, just plain truth! Let's make a bet! I promise, your daughter will have her own arm, bone and muscle and blood in three months. She will be able to use it like her own other arm!"

"And if you fail?" Magol grinned with satisfaction. Nobody can do that.

"Or you will never see me again! Deal?" Smith offered his hand.

Magol's grin widened: "Deal!" he grabbed Smith's younger hand, but Smith wouldn't let it go: "Oh, a clause." His eyes narrowed like a hawk's: "If she gets her hand, you won't be able to use me or this story to advance yourself. Ever!"

"Okay." Magol laughed.

"I will remind you to this when the time comes!" Smith looked straight into Zoon Magol's eyes, then with a totally innocent voice he announced: "Good night!" he turned to the pale Amerlee. "What's wrong?"

"Are . . . you . . . lost your mind?" she did not fully recover from the moment.

"No. I just found it!" Smith laughed while feeling relieved.

"We need to talk!" she stormed out of the estate. Smith tried to keep up with her. She opened the car's door and barked with anger: "Get in!"

"Okay, so what's wrong?" He was nervous. She should've been proud of him, standing up to her parents, but as soon as the car came to life and she put it on automatic, she began to pound on the steering wheel and cry.

"What's wrong?"

"You stupid fool! My father will make your life hell if you not deliver!"

"I will!" Smith shrugged casually.

"How?"

"I get your arm re grown." Smith replied like it was a normal thing. "It already

began . . ." he uttered quietly.

"Nobody can do that!" she shook her head.

"There are races who can!" Smith disagreed.

"My father tried and tried so hard before! Now we have three months left. What am I going to do without you?" she turned to him; her face contorted from pain.

"Why would you lose me?" Smith did not get it.

"I can't live without you, don't you get it that I'm in love with you, you fool?" she fell into his arms, still crying.

"Okay, I think we need to talk seriously. I take you to someone tomorrow who can explain something to you!" Smith tried his best.

"I don't want to! I so want to go back in time and undo this nightmare!" she cried beneath his arms.

"It will be fine!" Smith used his powers the first time on her. She stopped crying and said: "I feel so tired suddenly!"

"Sleep!" Smith kissed her nose, and the girl was asleep the next moment.

The NightCrawler took them to Amerlee's apartment building, where Smith grabbed her body and carried her to her apartment. He put her to bed, then pulled out his old-fashioned smartphone and dialed a number. "Tata, I will need that favor from you tomorrow." he walked back to her bedroom and exhausted, he sat down in the chair opposite to the bed. He did not even realize when he fell asleep.

Chapter Eight

A Favor from Tata

Amerlee slowly opened her eyes. Judging by the light and the direction of the sunrays, she was late from work. She sat up on the bed and noted Smith sitting across the room, still sleeping in an awkward, slumped position.

"What happened last night?" she mumbled, holding her head.

"Oh, you are up!" Smith's back straightened, and he practically jumped from his seat to close his arm around her.

"Smith?" His emotional out-pour surprised her.

"I've got breakfast for you. Just wait a lone second!" he disappeared into the kitchen only to return with a big plate.

"I've got everything here I saw you had before!" he grinned.

"What? Why are you doing this?" His actions baffled her.

"Last night you seemed really upset." Smith looked sincere.

"Shit!" she remembered all of a sudden. Her mood crashed. She tasted the food; ate like she was not sure of herself.

"What is done is done." She glanced around nervously, "You put me to bed last night?"

"Yes."

"Why have you stayed, Smith?" she watched him with her big, brown eyes Smith was so fond of.

"What kind of boyfriend would I be if I were not taking care of the woman I intend to be with?" he asked in return.

She watched her food intently, not looking at the man who spoke the words she craved for so long.

"You know, just looking at you, I can run away from my life and be with you. Work in a piss poor little town, perhaps as a truck driver, home every weekend just to hope you would smile at me!"

"It's so nice for you to say that, Smith!" she patted his shoulder, trying hard to avoid the emotional down spiral and eventual cry again.

"Irresponsible as hell, but the thought did occur to me." he nodded couple times.

"Why is it irresponsible?"

"Because I have obligations. Truth of it is, for this, between us for this to work, you need to change too and I'm afraid if it would shatter the glass . . ."

"What do you say?"

"I love you!" he turned and kissed her.

"I love you too!" she was relieved. They said it, both! It was so difficult to coerce a man into admission. And especially now that things went to literally shit . . . Then she remembered Smith saying something about meeting someone today, and the sudden thought materialized: "Work!" she shouted.

"Relax," Smith patted her real arm. "Miss Thorne is a truly understanding person."

"She is okay if I don't go in to work?" she thought she was hallucinating.

"Yes, she is!" Smith did not elaborate she had no other choice than to comply after they had a heated conversation about how long does he intend to hide his secret from her.

"Let me take a quick shower and dress up." she was staring at the floor to see where her slippers gone.

"I'll take care the remnants" Smith pointed at the tray.

Twenty minutes later they were in Amerlee's car. She still felt stoned from last night, activated the automatics to have the car navigate out of the city.

"Where?"

"Toward Styx, take the main highway, then take exit 78 to East!" Smith laid back in the formfitting chair to relax.

Amerlee also relaxed after a while. She glanced at Smith, who had his eyes closed. Seemingly he was thinking hard. She knew he was trying something very hard. What exactly that was she was in the dark about, but the curious part of her decided to speak up and ask: "Who will we meet today?"

"A girl. Well, a young woman. She is on her way to her grandpa's property. We will meet them there." Smith's eyes popped open.

"Do I know them?"

"Have you ever heard of Tata Crubon?"

At the mention of the name, Amerlee's eyes grew wider. "Appointed by the Emperor!"

"Bingo!"

"What?" Amerlee did not get the word.

Smith smiled warmly. "Yes. You will talk to her granddaughter. I won't be there, because Tata and I will go over couple things, but mainly because what you two will discuss should remain between the two of you."

"Is she special like Captain Aa?"

"No!" he closed his eyes, nodded couple times. "Not yet. She is smart she knows some secrets."

"What kind?"

"You'll find out soon enough!" Smith turned away from the interior. It was a signal to Amerlee, and she understood.

The car galloped beneath the Central Super Highway and began its accelerated ride thru the flat land.

Smith made a face, still glancing thru the car's windows: "She feels that there is something wrong with this world. What is wrong she doesn't comprehend, but she feels it!"

"Is something wrong with this world?" she asked concerned.

"Yes," Smith nodded quietly. "I know all the secrets. And if there is one I don't, I know the tools to unlock it. You studied at the University of Founders, have you ever heard of a student named Helan? She finished perhaps five years ago." Smith dug deep into some painful memories.

Amerlee was thinking hard. She finished school over a decade ago. Something did come up about a witch girl messing with guy's brains. Heartbreaker. She was way too beautiful. She frowned.

"Helan? Was she a beautiful sissy girl, playing with people's mind and then she became an archeologist in Bristol? Did not she die there?" she added, watching Smith's changing expression.

Smith nodded. "The parents buried an empty casket. She is still alive, but she can't come back. So yes, she is dead to this world. She also knew that something was very wrong with this world, but was mistaken in thinking it was the doing of the Emperors. I was tasked to either silence her at campus or turn her. That is how I met Mr. Del and Mr. Jott. In connection with her. I succeeded by sending her to Bristol, to become an archeologist. She supposed to discover great things, create a buzz about them in the media, and then the Emperors would've confirmed her thesis." Smith's lips curled downward. The past was past.

"Never happened, huh?" Amerlee was a quick study.

"No. She dug a little too deep . . ." Smith said sadly.

Amerlee who enjoyed driving under any circumstances let the car drive itself as she was more interested in lies, secrets and everything Smith had to say today. She felt she needed to pour strength into his faltering emotions: "Your knowledge of Down Earth's history impressed My father, you know."

Smith's mouth twitched. "It is a lie . . ."

Amerlee could not say anything to that. Inside she was fighting; wanted to tell him he is mistaken, but by now she felt she should also trust him. She shelved the idea of fighting and they just sat in silence as the NightCrawler accelerated past a hundred and sixty kilometers per hour.

"So, we got three months?" she finally asked, anxious and nervous at the same time. Smith's sad face turned even more sour:

"More like four weeks. Diana told me my girlfriend will wake up by then."

"Diana has your girlfriend in hostage?"

The first time since the ride began, Smith laughed. "No, but in a way, she acts like a caring mother. She was gravely injured in our last mission. Her body, I mean, not her mind." he trailed off then added with deep certainty: "You must be present with me when she wakes up to set the record straight!"

To Amerlee it was a horrible idea: "I think she would be emotionally unbalanced. We should wait."

"No!"

"Why?"

"Because how she was programmed . . . genetically, you know? To obey to the first person, she sees . . ."

"I don't understand!" It did not make sense to her at all. Of course -she just realized- Smith never elaborated whether she was a humanoid. Or perhaps the girl was sent by the Emperors to keep a check on him and he has no way out of that arrangement. She had no idea, and the more she thought about it, the more confused she got.

"You will. In time you will!" he reassured her in the meantime.

She had to shelve that thought too. It was pointless to think of it until it happens. Suddenly another memory fragment popped up in her brain: "So why were you so disappointed about the baby sacrifices?"

"Because they were pointless. Lots of things are pointless." he flinched. "The opera, the Origins . . . Do you know where does it play out?" Smith sounded melancholic.

"Mainly in Bristol city?" she was unsure.

"Yes." he exhaled deeply. "Bristol is a dreaming city. It's like hiding the loot in plain sight. All those scholars and archeologist working there, working day and night, wasting their life because they're unwilling to admit to themselves that something is very wrong with this world, with humanity, with history to the point of . . ." he trailed off, then as a reassurance mostly to himself he added: "But then again it's all part of the experiment!"

"So, Helan learned of the experiment, whatever it is?" Amerlee seemingly connected the dots.

"Yes. She used the gateways to travel instead of waiting for the Emperors to go there."

"Gateways?!"

"I'm sure you remember the old saying about the Ancestors whom allegedly planted the seed of humanity in a thousand worlds?"

"I do."

"What do you think of it?" Smith suddenly became curious about her and her mind.

"It's like the opera, The Origins, I think." Amerlee shied out. "It has a basis, but I don't think we have to take it literally."

"You, just like everyone else, are so wrong about that!" Smith seemed disappointed.

"But Bristol isn't the answer. I heard the buildings have no windows and no doors!"

"True. But the buildings are dormant. They're in deep sleep." Smith nodded once.

"Come on Evan, how would you know that?" Amerlee could not keep her mouth shut on that. He said things nobody ever said, not even her professors back in school. Truly intriguing theories, worth spending a lecture on, yet nobody ever said a word, so it had to be false. Or a secret—an annoying voice said in the back of her mind.

"Remember? I know all the secrets!" Smith lifted his chin proudly. "The experimenters don't allow humanity from this planet or from anywhere else to come to the right conclusion, that's why the last two Emperors were practically abducted from Upper Earth. They fall outside of the puppeteers and the experiment. They and of course the anomalies."

"Anomalies?" she let the puppeteer's comments go as it bordered insanity!

"People with abilities they not supposed to have. Or people who have birth defects. They're anomalies, not supposed to happen. That's why I willing to tell you this and not worry too much about the consequences." Smith took her hands in his and began to play with.

Amerlee swallowed hard. "Not even little?"

"Always, but if you stay by my side, you will see all these secrets sooner or later. So, if after today, after the conversation with Elise, you say okay Smith good bye I will understand, but if you decide to stay, you'll have a hell of an exciting life. Of course, you'll have to make many decisions about what you want to do with your life or how do you want to live, but that will be your choice. I just hope that the girl can shed light on things you did not look into. All you need to know in advance that no matter what, I am standing by you. Hopefully, you'll stay, but if you go, I will survive. Don't know how, but I will. I have no other choice. I will always remember you and knowing myself that's a hell of a long time!" Smith looked utterly sad.

"I'll stay with you, no matter what!" she kissed him empathetically as the car took the exit and began to climb the gentle, grassy hills.

Soon Amerlee caught something high above the hills. First, she dismissed as a hallucination, but the sleek, dark object connected to an even larger object, standing on the ground. She realized this as the car climbed the last hill. "Is that a spaceship?"

"A ZON Starship; a key to all secrets surrounding Down Earth, the Ancestors and Humanity!" Smith nodded, his hands itching for action.

Tata Crubon was a tall man, some wrinkles on his exposed, pale skin, but seemingly life dealt rather generously with him—noted Amerlee as she offered her hand. He kissed it instead of shaking, making her blush.

"The pleasure is all mine, lovely Amerlee!" he boasted a wide smile. "I'm humbled to meet Smith's most precious!" he added. She felt uncomfortable. It was obvious; he was flirting with her!

"Hi there, Elise!" Smith smiled as he spotted the young girl in a white dress standing by a table with four chairs. A lone, rusty droid served refreshments in the background.

"Mr. Smith! I am humbled to be in your presence!" she was visibly shocked. She shook on his hand shyly, then glanced at him: "I won't wash my hands for a week!" she promised.

Smith's eyes narrowed, but he smiled. He licked his dry lips before answering, rather diplomatically: "It won't serve you no good once you return to Styx." he winked. "They don't know and they can't feel. You're almost alone in this world. A pity, I may say!"

"I'm proud to stand alone, having to know you sir!" she responded, amazing Amerlee. She saw nothing but defiance in her adolescent eyes!

"Thank you, but pledge of allegiance isn't required . . ." he trailed off, talking exclusively to her, shutting out everybody else in their private conversation in the open.

Elise thought she understood him and continued his thread: ". . . Except believe, and you have mine for the rest of my life, My L . . ." she continued, but Smith cut her off, before she would spell out something, he wanted to convey to Amerlee different. Elise realized herself too, because her eyes got big and covered her mouth. "Sorry!" she stared at the ground and blushed.

"Tata!" Smith turned to the grandpa: "Show me your progress!" He then turned to Amerlee: "Be good!" he smiled at her and left.

"Something to drink, perhaps?" Elise offered refreshments from the table.

"Water will be fine!" Amerlee was polite. Smith was right, the girl was special. She carried herself in a certain way, talked with Smith so revered it was borderline of insanity!

Elise poured the drink into a glass cup and presented it.

Amerlee drank from it and was glad that the old-fashioned sunshade was large enough to cover the bright sun hovering on the blue sky with the artificial meteor cloud in the background occasionally casting shadows on the ground.

"It's a beautiful day." Elise spoke, watching her. "Kind of like hopeful, you don't know whether it's going to rain or it will be just the most beautiful sunset you ever witness!"

Amerlee frowned. "I was told you are special."

"I am not special, although somebody found something in me years ago. The Emperor required my mother's brother's help. He sent his agents thru the PR department whom made contact. My uncle is a businessman, very material type and money loving. He took the help in hope they would present him with a Letter of Support."

"Very interesting!" Amerlee took in the information like water.

"Well, he was. The Emperor was engaged in solving a serious problem across the old Wall, In the City of Bristol. He did not care too much about my uncle or me. I was miserable at that time, having shattered the bones in my left arm so bad it required me to have a stasis chamber around it. My uncle wanted all of us to meet the Emperor's representatives over dinner at a membership only club. He hoped the meeting would forge us, and especially him, to be seen as well connected. The agents agreed, and the exchange took place. There was a man and a woman sitting across our table, seemingly quiet, well composed. My uncle introduced them to us only as the will carriers of the Emperor. My mom instantly recognized the man, having been always intrigued by the UNHL Space Navy. He was Mr. Josh Kulighan, the war hero. My brother was also ecstatic, completely missed the quiet hottie sitting beside him. She was a captain, Captain Aa!" Elise noted the changes on Amerlee's face. "You know her?" she asked, stopping the recollection.

"My hero! Smith took me to the stars, and we met her onboard her SPD!" she replied, tears in her eyes.

"Mr. Josh Kulighan shared a story of how he lost the grace of the Emperor and his title as Admiral, because he defied the Emperor. I think it was a covered warning to my uncle not to get too cocky . . ."

"Man, the dinner had to be something!" Amerlee tried to imagine it all.

"Very memorable." Elise agreed. "Having learned an amazing story from him, my mom turned to Captain Aa and asked whether her life was equally challenging and amazing. She immediately deflected the question and instead asked what happened to me. My mom told her the facts; that I broke it in school, that I severed it for a while and that most likely I would never regain all motor functions. I think she was already interested in me at that moment, but as the dinner went on my brother, who was also love space Navy stuff recited all the Admirals from memory, wondering about how come the 26th UNHL fleet has two SPD and that sort of things. At that moment, our guests revealed they both serve in that fleet. That not just impressed my uncle. I could tell he became uncomfortable. I think he realized he got snotty with the wrong kind of people. My brother Janos kept pressing them for tidbits, details. How they work and from their answers I gained insight into a family like organization with utterly professional members. They also liked each other and I think they were happy to work together. While Janos was impressed with Mr. Josh Kulighan's resume of leading the auxiliary fleet, he began to ask Captain Aa whether she has an equally impressive list of accomplished tasks. She smiled, shook her head and remained in the background. I was intrigued by her, because I already sensed she could be really deadly. Everything she showed was just a pleasant cover, and it all blew up in my uncle's face when his son went too far. It was magnificently eloquent. So smooth, to this day I kept wondering about." Elise got lost in the memories.

"So, what happened?" It piqued Amerlee's interest.

"Mr. Kulighan stopped her and reminded that while it might be true, that she was not as magnificent as he was, she still delivered her promise of fighting with the Emperor side by side of the battle at the Central Trade Planet despite her Planet Destroyer being destroyed. I was certainly impressed. My brother asked her about the future of the 26th fleet now that there were two SPDs serving and my uncle's son, Tobol laughed about the funny name of the SPD, Destination Unknown, like as if even the military wouldn't know where to go next. And right there and then, when the Captain was already over my arm, intrigued by the metal cast spun around so eloquently like a ballerina, eyes locked with Tobol, fire in her eyes and she said: '*Look at my eyes boy, I am the extended will of the Emperor! You never see me coming and when I arrive it's too late because my enemies are dead already. And when I disappear in deep space, I'll be going somewhere else to lay wasteland to those whom disagree with my master, hence the name of my SPD, Destination Unknown*!' That was the most awesome response I ever heard! She was sound, strong and direct; fire in her eyes like hell. No weakness and no regrets! She was a woman who knew who she was, what she was capable of! She called the Emperor her master and at that moment I realized they have a bond like no other human has. She believed in him and that belief, that unconditional loyalty to him gave her strength beyond anything. I wanted the same, no doubt. I wanted a fix point in my life. Something I can always fall back to as a last resort. To gain strength when I need. I craved for something like that for so long and I wanted to learn. I think she sensed that. She immediately disregarded everyone around her and asked me about the healing process. She gauged me for some reason only she would know than she said: "*I was a street girl once upon a time, rich people and the Emperor as distant as the Zenin-Kron Empire. I used to steal, rob people to feed myself; I was not concerned with the how of the universe. In my thoughts I supported the Emperor, but in reality, I did not really care. . . . until I met him face to face. He carried me under his wings, he lifted me when I fell, he showed me my potential and he made me a believer! I'll do this out of my own will, but I wish I could make you a believer!*" And with that she touched my cast, I felt warm from beneath, my hand was glowing and the cast fell to the ground. She fixed my arm and I don't even feel the change of the weather!" Elise looked at Amerlee, face straight, her eyes wet, dry cry. "Do you understand what she had done? Instead of asking me to believe in her, in him, she has done something out of her heart; a goodwill to change my mind, forge me and she did!"

"Incredible!" Amerlee was crying with her. Captain Aa was a true hero!

"There is more, of course, as I was only swayed but not changed. Over two years have passed when my uncle got into some deep trouble. I still was not told what exactly happened, but my grandpa sought out at us, having lost my parents when they were just children. He hired a private investigator who died under mysterious circumstances, putting him into trouble, so he contacted the Emperor's PR department. The Emperor assigned Mr. Josh Kulighan and Captain Aa to the case just because he already saw the threads. He suspected my mom and my uncle were Tata's lost children. So, during the course of my uncle's problem somebody sent a thug to our home, to abduct my mom, to put pressure on my uncle, but she killed the person. It was a sudden decision by my mom. Captain Aa came to the rescue and cleaned everything up. She was a professional, like how I first met her. Days later she called my mom and asked her to bring us, children to a street corner in Styx. My uncle had to bring his son, too. And I already sensed this will be something unscripted! We met at the iconic bridge on 85th Ave at the corner of the park. My uncle was angry for some reason. I think he was still worried for his life. Miss Aa was there, waiting for us with an umbrella. My uncle, the mean attitude, he asked what's that for and Captain Aa responded plainly that exactly at eight pm, rain will pour down on the city. Tobol laughed, saying weather service mentioned nothing like that."

"And . . . ?" Amerlee leaned forward on the table.

"And Miss Aa responded that her employer loves clichés, therefore it will rain. As my uncle began to laugh, it began. First just drops, then torrential rain. We cuddled together, Miss Aa opened her umbrella and from beneath her looks swept across the running people and I saw her eyes. It was most telling! She knew it would rain, but nobody else did. She looked down at the ordinary citizens, because she knew they don't believe in the one who they should. They don't follow the one they should! Then at exactly eight pm a black limousine arrived. Came out of nowhere and we all got inside. Creepy stuff. There was a man inside, but he remained in the dark. He . . ." she stopped, swallowing hard amid recollecting the memory. "He asked me to show my palm so he would do a reading, to tell my life. It looked so theatrics. But to my uncle it was childish. Captain Aa was mesmerized. She believed what the man said will be my future. He looked at me from a distance and said Aa did a great job fixing me. Then he said he can tell I was having memory problems. He nodded and said he fixed me, and that I'm mnemonic now. It took me couple days to realize he really did that to me, but back to that car that night . . . My uncle was thinking of something, and the man in the car spoke of it. My uncle got scared, I could tell he was spot on. Mariol asked how does he know what does he thinks and the man turned cynical. He said: "*Do you really think if I can make the rain fall from the sky, I would have trouble reading a human mind?"* That was powerful stuff! He also talked about the ZONs and their connection to early human history. I never knew our history was so intertwined with theirs. I never understood ZON's history to begin with. Now I love it. And I do hang with my grandpa and learn every day about the Starships!" she pointed to the towering monument. "In ten minutes, that man shed light on one of the greatest mysteries in the universe. It was really something!"

"What happened after?"

"Not much. More secrets, I don't think I supposed to tell you. Mr. Smith will if he feels like it. Or if you crave for it."

"Captain Aa is truly a heroic person, but how does this anecdote help me to explain Smith?" Amerlee was still under the story's spell.

Elise leaned forward, laughing, her chin resting on her joined hands: "How does it feel to be so lucky like you are?"

Amerlee startled; "Excuse me?"

“I so envy you!” she looked at her, observing everything before she spoke again: “And it took me a long time to

understand . . .”

“Understand what?”

“That the man in the limousine was not the Admiral!”

Elise watched Amerlee. She did not get it. A bit sad of that, she nodded: “Go home and think of what I said, then ask Mr. Smith tomorrow to take you out to breakfast. Make sure it’s before nine o’clock!”

“Sure . . .” Amerlee sounded confused.

“Oh, one more thing. Haven’t your Smith promised you something?”

“Like what?” Amerlee frowned.

“I don’t know. A new hand or a beautiful sunset?” she glanced toward the sun.

“Why?”

“Did nobody ever tell you that he rarely promises, but whatever he does, it always happens?” Elise tilted her head, gestured and formed a kiss with her lips: “Go home and think and ask him for breakfast!”

Chapter Nine

Breakfast

"So how was the girl talk?" Smith glanced at her on their way back to the city.

"I have lots of things on my mind, Smith!" Amerlee shot back. She was still confused. She had to think about what Elise said. It was obvious the pronunciation was not on Captain Aa, no matter how much she talked about her. It made no sense! Then something flashed in her mind: "Elise told me to tell you to take me out for breakfast in the morning!"

Smith began to grin.

She noticed. "What's the smile for?"

"Nothing!" Smith suddenly kissed her.

"She said to do it before nine. I guess you know a special place?" she inquired.

"As a matter of fact, I do!" Smith became happy. It did not matter that Amerlee remained sad and angry. She did not understand why the change, but Smith got out of the car as soon as she pulled over and left. He even whistled!

She got home and did her laundry, thinking of the conversation with Elise. All she could think of was Captain Aa. She even sent a message late at night to Smith that she will cancel the breakfast, because she can't miss more time from work. She timed it after ten PM, hoping Smith would not get it until the morning. She needed to distill the information she got from Elise. Her mind however remained preoccupied, feeling missing out on something as she somehow arrived to work. It was not even eight in the morning, but Miss Thorne was already in. A bit nervous, but impatient, she approached her: "What are you doing in?"

"I came to work?" Amerlee did not get her boss's concerns.

"No. You supposed to have breakfast with . . ." She could not finish as her personal communicator received a message. She read it thru her special contact lenses: "ah, of course he thought of everything!" she turned to Amerlee. "There is a car waiting for you! Come, I walk you to the car!"

"Why? How do you know of my breakfast plans?" Amerlee looked at her, baffled.

"Smith just sent me a message. The limousine is already here!"

"Limousine? He paid for a driver to pick me up?"

"Silly girl!" Miss Thorne shook her head. "You don't get it, do you?" she escorted her thru the lobby.

Amerlee spotted the all black, Upper Earth made limousine with a huge, towering black man as the chauffeur waiting outside. "Ah, the princess!" he grinned and opened the door for her.

"What's this all about? I did not argue with Smith last night!" Amerlee felt she was not let in on the joke.

"No, and I hope you never will, but in case I never see you again, I wish you a prosperous life!" Miss Thorne hugged her passionately.

"I'll be back . . ." Amerlee stepped into the limousine, confused.

Miss Thorne turned around as she sent a message to Smith: '*package is on the way!*'

Amerlee became inpatient as the limo turned left and arrived to the Road of the Bound's main gate. It did not even slow down! The gate lifted, the soldiers saluted, and they were thru! She moved around uncomfortably as the limo zipped by her parent's villa.

"Where are we going, sir?" she asked from the driver.

"To the Villa-Castle, My Lady!"

That shut her up. She glanced at the floor until she came up with a reasonable conclusion: Smith must've used his bribery and influence to have the Emperor see her arm. Perhaps even Captain Aa would be there. Perhaps she is the Emperor in disguise? It was also a possibility. The limousine pulled thru the gates, into the front where the entire personnel was outside, lined up to mimic a wall from the car to the building's stone entrance.

"Are you sure I supposed to be here?" she asked shyly from the driver who nodded and opened the door for her. There was an older man, gray hair, waiting, smiling nicely. She saw him when she took Smith here for breakfast.

"My Lady!" he bowed. "You have been expected!" he showed her the way. Amerlee walked across the gravel circle to the marble steps with heavy legs. She was alone and was truly nervous. Not even Smith was there to greet her! Anxious to see anyone, she headed toward the morning table and she stopped. There was somebody standing by the table, eating a chicken finger. The man dipped it into the sauce and upon hearing her arrival, turned around.

He was her Smith!

Amerlee was petrified.

Smith boasted his biggest smile: "My Lady, I expected you!" he opened his hand to her.

"Smith?"

"Yes?" Smith slowed down. She supposed to either run away or cry from joy. Since neither happened, she did not get it yet.

"Why are you eating from the table?!"

"Because I just could not wait. You know I love to eat . . ." he made an apologetic look at her then made a sweeping gesture: "Tell me what you want and I gladly place it on your table!" he pointed at a smaller table with two chairs.

"Where is the Emperor? It's before nine o'clock. Only he can touch the table!" she frowned.

"Correct!" Smith turned back to the table to grab another one. They were truly good this morning. His hand was reaching for the nearest one, but Amerlee yelled: "No!"

"What?" Smith became annoyed as he touched the piece and bit into it.

Amerlee saw something from the corner of her eyes the moment she yelled. It was the marble statue. It opened its eyes than closed it! She gasped for air.

"My Lady, I can touch whatever I want on this table as opposed to you. Well, at least until nine o'clock, but I wanted you to have the privilege to eat with me before others would show!" he smiled gently.

"I . . . I don't get this." Amerlee's head got lighter.

"Well, did not Elise tell you yesterday she thought the man in the car was not the Admiral, yet Aa kept referring to him as her employer?"

"So?" Amerlee knew that was a solid fact. She grabbed it with her mind. Solid ground.

"So, you have to know by now that there is truly only one person who she obeys, and that's the Emperor?" he stepped closer to her.

Amerlee felt the solid ground just turned into quicksand. The weakness traveled from her legs into her arms. She was gasping for air. She glanced at Smith, who kissed her passionately.

She kissed back.

"Your friendly Emperor, My Lady!" he kissed her again.

She kissed him back again, this time with more passion, more forceful.

"Are you, really?" her eyes were glowing.

"At your service!" Smith felt delighted and like a huge weight rolled off his shoulder.

"So, I can have anything from the table?"

"Sure!" Nodded Smith.

"What if I want something not on it?"

"Like what?"

"An apple!"

"Yes, My Lady!" Smith opened his palm, and an apple formed in his hand.

Amerlee smelled, then bit into the apple. She felt a heat wave touching, encompassing her. She was almost flying; she was full of happiness. She tossed the apple to the breakfast table: "Take me upstairs!"

"I live to satisfy your request, My Lady!" Smith offered his arm playfully, covering his smile.

Amerlee stopped. "So, then your girlfriend who is sick is Azure, huh?" The realization hit her in waves; "The girl who defied the galaxy and saved you?"

"Yes. She was killed in action, but luckily, I had her memories updated just before her death. It takes six months to grow a new body. Diana is supervising the efforts!"

Amerlee nodded. "Nothing I can't handle for the right man!" she smiled at him and he smiled back: "I think you are dying to go upstairs!"

"Something like that!" The coy smile Smith loved so much returned to her face.

Chapter Ten

A New Beginning

TWO WEEKS LATER

"Let me see it!"

"Nooo . . ."

"Come on!" Smith's voice hardened and Amerlee let her boyfriend see her arm. They were in the Villa-Castle, where Amerlee took up residence for the better part of her days. She worked from there, did not quit, and Smith was proud of her for that.

"It's coming along nicely!" Smith observed the miniature hand.

"It looks as if I'm a circus girl!" Amerlee disliked her situation.

"What did Mr. Chengen say?"

"The Delvonian doctor?"

"Yes."

"He said the same thing . . ." she grumbled. "That it's coming along nicely!" she added in a calmer tone.

"Good! I had to give him clearance to leave the Sky Riders daily. Now, next week, Captain Aa will drop by to check up on you. I am supposed to do some mental exercises with her while they will reload her ship with stuff and hopefully everybody will be happy." Smith explained.

"Two weeks and Azure will come out of her chamber!" she reminded him.

"We must be there together, showing unity. She will leave you alone after that." Smith caressed her face. She closed her eyes. She loved his affection for her. "I know!" she nodded lightly, opening her eyes.

"What is it?" Smith looked at her, seeing the changes as she was thinking of something important.

"I think you should invite my parents to dinner."

Smith's head slouched. "That's a bad idea!"

"Why?" she asked him, emotional.

"Because I am who I am. This is my house and I won't take shit from nobody!" Smith replied, then when she gave her a frown he added: "It's not fair to you. I love you. I don't want to cause hardship to you!"

"I'm fine, and you know it!" she empathetically touched her blouse. That could completely sidetrack Smith she found out earlier, especially when she coupled it with a similar understanding, apologetic look. It worked. He watched her longer than he should have, then he looked away. "Do you want to piss them off?"

"I want them to be scared from you and from me!" she revealed the truth.

"Your father is just a businessman." Smith tried to ease the situation.

"Let me worry about that . . . Let's involve Azure too!"

Smith's eyes narrowed. "Why?"

"She would kill me if she loves you just a bit. I think she will be jealous of us, so she could channel that anger into meeting my parents!

"You witch!" Smith shook his head, thinking it over, and began to sneer. He liked it. "I will have to remind him of not using my name for his advance. Is that okay with you?"

"Yes, my darling!" she happily kissed him on his forehead.

"Okay. Then I have Miss Thorne to draw up the letter."

"Why can't I do it?" she inclined to help.

"No. It's not professional. We can go in to the office together, but I need to talk to her."

"Okay, boss!" she saluted, drawing smile onto his face. That's all she cared for at the moment. To be happy with him!

Breakfast became an elaborate scheme. The first week they went thru the same ritual every day: having a smaller table beside the big one. She would point out what she wanted, then Evan would pick it and place it to the second table. Then he would sit with her and fill up the belly. This method seemed awkward for him; she suspected it made him feel like she was just a second-class citizen. She tried to get up earlier than he was and she just asked the ever so loyal Henry to prepare something for him. That did not work either, as he became worried for her. Smith revealed he thought she would try to outsmart the guards around the Emperor's breakfast table. As he said they would cut her arm, Smith shook just thinking of it. It was obvious to her he imagined the entire scenario, and it horrified him. He loved her and cared for her; she knew that from day two. She found that weakness of him utterly adoring, so to ease further tensions now they ate together in the Winter Wing. The better part of the wing was a gigantic hall; ball room, ready for any kind of event or activity. There, Henry readied the huge, oval table every morning and the staff dutifully prepared a second set of food for both of them to consume. It was a partially mirrored smaller selection of the main breakfast table.

She and Smith just began to eat when she spotted his emerging annoyance.

"What's wrong?" she uttered sensually, just to play with him. She had to giggle as he froze.

"Can I help you with something?" she used her left leg to poke between his.

Smith swallowed hard. "I forgot what annoyed me." he admitted.

"Then it could not be as important, now, could it?" she seemed delighted.

"Oh, yes!" Smith instantly realized as he was grabbing another warm doughnut. "That this is a waste of food!" he referred to the double breakfast table situation.

"The mighty Emperor . . ." she snickered, while withdrawing her leg from below the table. "Who would've thought he is so worried about wasteful practices?"

"It's not funny!" he seemed to be annoyed.

"You can't get around this problem and it is eating you away? Tell me, does President Guvojan worry about that sort of problem?"

"I don't know. I'm not him!" Smith's annoyance grew steadily.

"I know he got breakfast tables too!" she winked.

"Sexy." Smith got sidetracked by it.

"So . . ."

"So?" He frowned, suspecting a mockery in disguise coming from her.

"So, let's see your options. You could forgo with tradition and abolish this."

"Can't do!" Smith shook his head vehemently. For her quizzical looks he responded apologetically: "Other past Emperor's estates exhibit this tradition too. I can't change this!"

"So even fewer options for my mighty man of the morning!" she tried hard not to laugh.

Smith frowned. "Snotty girl!" But gestured for her to continue.

"Spank me daddy!" she leaned forward so she could almost utter it to his ears and for him to see beyond her cleavage. She loved messing with him. It was really entertaining! He tried his best not to misplace his attention, and she continued: "We can go back to the first week, when you thought I was just a visitor, a second-class citizen, a mortal and you had to pick from the table." She saw his boiling anger, so she playfully patted his hand. "We can also stop eating together. I ask for a grab from Henry and be done with it or . . ." She left it open. Smith's expression changed upon realizing this was the best solution. "You witch!"

"But I'm a pretty one!" she rebuffed the critique.

He shook his head. "Not the one. But you should be the one who says it!" he wanted her to form the word, and she gladly did: "Sexy!" she pronounced as sexually as she could.

"That's the one!" he grabbed her head and kissed it. "Yummy bread!" he stated when he let her go.

She almost choked on the food as she laughed hard. "You're a funny guy!"

"But I think I am yours!" he teased her.

"Yes!" she responded way too quickly.

"I am driving!" she grabbed her sunglasses on her way out.

"What about me?" Smith tried to catch up to her.

"My car!" she took the side door to the outside where a couple of cars parked on the gravel.

"You just hate me for having the 517S, do you?"

"No . . ." she looked the other way.

"Maybe we could go with the Scania truck, no?" Smith pointed to the metal gray extended cab tractor, gleaming beneath the sun.

"I don't drive those!" she lifted her chin.

"I had to get another car after donating the ProcessAutomatic to the museum!" he tried to find a valid reason why he acquired the maroon car sitting at the corner.

"You've got great money for it, so don't get feisty about it!" Amerlee reminded him while she continued not to acknowledge Smith's NightCrawler.

Smith was about to say something, but then decided to just shake his head and get into Amerlee's ride.

"I can have a little chat, face to face with others too?" She aimed at his eyes in the elevator.

"Do your thing, my talk will be a bit longer." Smith said.

Her eyes narrowed, then she let it go. At least Smith thought of that until she stormed out the opening doors.

“Feisty, must be in love!” Smith smirked after her. He knocked on Miss Thorne’s door and got admitted to the office where he explained his reason being there.

Amerlee grabbed a few things off her old desk, then decided to use the secure connection from her terminal to upload her work. She glanced around, but if people noticed something, they did not point it out. Suddenly an approving finger appeared by her face.

“Lou?” she was not sure.

“Yeah, Amee! So how is the rich girl’s life?”

“You know?” she frowned.

“Yeah. Mr. Smith had a very revealing conversation with me couple weeks ago.” The young man grinned. “I am happy for you!”

“Thanks!” she looked a bit sad.

“Hey, no regrets, right? Have you tried his car pool yet?” Lou thought how much does she like to drive.

Amerlee had to grin. “First thing!”

“Just remember, I think he is a guy who likes to be in control sometimes.”

“I let him win occasionally!” she laughed, glowing like a Christmas tree.

“I mean driving . . .”

“That too!” she smiled. Lou was always nice.

“So boss, how does she fit into your picture?”

“What do you mean?” Smith glanced thru the window. He found her immediately. Miss Thorne watched his face easing up.

“In love, huh?”

“Something like that.”

She could tell he did not like the personal admission, so they moved on, working on the Letter of Invitation. Smith was ready to sign however she was phrasing it.

“Boss, I don’t like to intrude, but maybe it should be a less formal lunch instead of dinner, don’t you think?”

“You think I would go overboard?” Smith thought about it.

"Well, if the point is to piss them off, then you shouldn't waste your time for a dinner with them." Miss Thorne tried to read between the lines and figuring his true intentions. Amerlee told her before she was having issues with her mother. Especially when she broke up with Amaron.

"You're right. Let's have lunch instead and move the date to a Tuesday?" Smith worked his etiquette magic.

"Inconspicuous day, huh?"

"Trying."

"Is this going to be a force projection?" Secretly Miss Thorne wanted to be present when this happens.

"Maybe . . ." Smith liked the idea.

"May I suggest moving the date further up when Azure would be present?"

"Why?" he asked while thinking, why does Emma think the same way as his Amerlee?

"She will have anger toward both of you. Maybe you could talk to her and channel her anger into a nice projection of force. After all, she has the title of Personal Family Bodyguard!"

"Excellent idea!" Smith ecstatically clapped his hands and noticed the approaching Amerlee. "She walks in a very peculiar way!" Smith watched her making a stride across the floor.

"How?"

"Damned sexy!" He licked his lips, whistling afterward.

"You did not have to buy the entire collection!" Smith rolled his eyes upon seeing Amerlee leaving one of the boutiques, her hands full of big bags. It was after they left the PR department and ate at the nearby restaurant.

"You gave me some money to spend, so I spent it. You not supposed to critique a woman about how much does she spend on dresses!" she reminded him, trying to keep her face straight. It was difficult as Smith began to think about that.

"Um, well, I just . . ." he could not finish as she kissed him and as his arms wrapped around her arched back, she slipped some bags onto it.

"What the . . . ?"

She laughed. "Come on, two hundred credits aren't the end of the world if you love me.

"No, definitely not."

"Especially when you see this lovely two piece black and dark green lingerie set!" she winked. "Maybe early as tomorrow morning."

"Yeah, I love mornings . . ." Smith's mind raced ahead in time.

"But before that I got a nice leather corset for you to adore me in tonight!" She acted silly.

"Need more money?" Smith salivated standing beside her.

Chapter Eleven

Going Down on Memory Lane

Just as Smith expected, the evening was busy, and the night ended in spectacular fireworks. He slept in the morning so they could both eat breakfast after nine o'clock. Nine oh one, and they raided the table, then withdrew to the Winter Wing so no one could bother them.

"You never told me what Miss Thorne told you?" she asked for the butter and Smith gently gave her the spread.

"Nothing much. We do a lot of business that is military related. I don't think you would be interested in knowing it." Smith frowned.

"You are my business. I need to know everything about you, so that I could relate to your problems!"

"Honey, that's a lot of messy business." Smith was tired, even in the morning, to tell her everything. He saw her face darkened, so on a positive side he shared something relating to her: "Oh, she advised me, us, to have a launch with your parents instead of dinner. She said dinners were reserved to truly important guests."

"Okay, I can relate to that!"

"She also mentioned having it when Azure is around."

"I told you so!" she reminded him, while playfully poking his stomach.

"Yes, and both of you are right. We'll going to do it two weeks down the road. That would give plenty of time for your parents to get ready for the big event!"

"I can't wait!" she snickered.

Smith frowned. Hatred or wishing bad luck was beyond his regular features.

Upon seeing his reaction to her statement, she shyly added: "To see my mom's face!"

"Okay, okay." Smith let it go, but it was too late. Amerlee was thinking about something hard that bothered her for real.

"What is it?" he tried to uplift her mood.

She paused for a moment, before asking: "How did you and Azure meet?"

"Oh, boy . . ." Smith shook his head.

"Did she ask you out, or you two hooked up before you went to prison? Weren't you with Commander Tri'ng at that time?" she tried to remember to the newscasts.

"This just gets worse by the minute." Smith held his head in his hands.

"What?"

"Your questions!"

"So, what? I need to know you. I need to know the history between the two of you. I don't think it's such a long reach to ask these questions!"

Smith scratched his head, thinking how to tell her and what to tell her. She thought along the same lines, 'cause she warned him: "No lies!"

"No. Definitely not!" he vehemently agreed.

"So? Did she ask you out?"

"No."

"So how did the two of you meet?"

"That's a difficult question." Smith was trying to figure out how much should he tell her about the truth, about the past. His hesitation pissed her off. "Don't get cagey with me!" she looked angry.

"No." he sighed. "Okay, so I met her kind, the Maximus line on Mars, before the fall of Earth." He could tell it rattled the cage.

"Excuse me?" she looked at him with big eyes.

"I said . . ."

"I heard what you said, but it doesn't make any sense! Mars is deserted now, and only present in Upper Earth's solar system!"

"Yes. And I did say it was before the fall of Earth. I meant before 9732."

"How is that possible?" she glared at him.

"Tame traveling is possible!" Smith opened his hands.

"No, it's not!"

"Come on! Think about it. Did not the newscasts say I practically live on the Trixec, that I always travel with the 26th UNHL Fleet? Did you ever wonder why?"

Smith watched Amerlee's face. She was shifting her weight, deep into thinking, so to help speed up the process Smith asked:

"Okay, so tell me an example, something linear?" He decided to go for a different approach.

"Time. I was born, now I live and I will die. Its linear and I can't go back in time to talk myself out of anything."

"Aha. Great example. There is only one problem with

that . . ." Smith began to nod.

"What?"

"It's not true."

"What do you mean not true? I mean . . . But then." Akin somebody struck by lightning Amerlee frowned, the frown disappeared and she placed her right index finger just below her lips and looked into Smith's eyes: "So, then somebody could go back and undo me meeting you and then I would never find true love!" she became nervous all of a sudden.

"It's nice looking it from a personal perspective!" Smith smiled, but deep inside he heard every word of hers, especially about true love.

"No, it's serious!" she pressed on.

"I know." Smith agreed. "So be enough that before this Cold War type of scenario with the AOCP we, I mean I and my lunatic friends fought a six years long Time Wars where the enemies of the Monarch kept changing mostly the past. I was at the founding of the UNHL, the time the Klons attacked the Outer Planets, when Mars made a stand so Earth could escape. I was there! I got stuck in the past once . . . I spent six months fighting for my life in a civil war torn planet. Oh, it was a mess!" Smith shook his head as Amerlee just listened, her eyes as big as a melon. Nobody ever heard of these things! She never heard of this in the newscasts.

"So, Azure . . ." she tried to fit her into this madness.

"Yes." Smith found the lost thread. "Let's stick with the subject, you're absolutely right. So, I was on Mars with Aa, Baby Haas, Josh and a bunch of others and we got wind of the AOCP agents trying to locate and destroy someone, but their history was inaccurate and they blew a luxury liner before the person of their interest could make it there. Nevertheless, his girlfriend was blown to shreds. So, this young and cocky boy, he would only mess with chicks, have sex, get high and drink all night. This fellow would become a very iconic person during the war with the Klons, as we learned. I sent Aa to mess with his head. Naturally, it worked. Aa could be very cunning and sexy when she needs to be!" Smith wondered away.

Amerlee grabbed his head: "Focus!" she was sure Smith's long-time crush on Captain Aa was still ongoing.

"Oh, yeah. We saved his ass and delivered to Mars under disguise. There, he learned that Earth agents abducted his father. Earth was a nasty, messy place back then. Wildly rich people lived there; population control was around five hundred million." Smith stopped. He wondered whether he should tell her the reason he firmly believed Earthers had fallen during the Klon attack, whether to even tell how unlucky Earth was to come upon the Klons in the first place. Then he decided that this was not the time and continued nonchalantly: "A civil war just ended couple decades ago. This iconic fellow's father, Mr. Karalan, he had his hand in every kind of business. Weapon's design, city building, space ship building. You name it. Rich stuff. He even spent considerable time to devise a human form, hardened bones beneath the blood and skin. It was meant to be a pleasure model, to satisfy rich Earthers. Nice ass, sweet talking, you know what I mean?" Smith cut it off as she began to make ugly faces.

"Continue!" she waved in the air with hardly covered annoyance.

"I liked Maximus. Her line was redesigned because after the civil war, this form of pleasure seeking became banned. He injected more soldier ideas, re-formed the brain pathways, but five hundred models were already made and they were in deep sleep state. We used Maximus and a dozen of her kind to bust Mr. Karalan out of prison. Thirty years later, at the end of the war in 9732, we showed up again. By this time the iconic fellow had a wife." Smith left the chair as he finished breakfast. Amerlee finished long time ago. He opened his arms, and she shunted her eyes.

"What?" Smith did not get it.

"Out in the open?"

"I am taking you somewhere to finish the story!" he said as their hands locked.

"Where?"

Smith smiled, and he teleported away with her.

"Hey, how did you do that?" she turned around. They wound up in the Central Supercomputer's parking lot.

"Your boyfriend is a powerful one!" Smith winked and led her thru the glass doors.

"I see! This was amazing!" she played with her hair as they got into the elevator. "Where do you take me?" she asked as the curiosity got the better of her.

"To a special chamber. We aren't staying there. It's too early for you to do what the chamber is supposed to do, but there is someone who you must meet if you love history!"

"I love history!" she bobbed her head.

"Good, then tell me what was the name of the man who supervised the building of the all Earth encompassing sarcophagus?"

"Hm . . ." she imitated thinking hard. "The Doctor!"

"Good job, honey!" he gave her a wet one. She was longing for more, he could tell. He loved seeing his power over her. "So, the Doctor, what was his wish?"

"Oh, everybody knows what his wish was, Smith!" she shrugged, like it was a nonstarter.

He insisted: "Tell me!"

"He wanted to get a stasis pod to live to eternity!"

"Again, good job!" he kissed her again, then the door opened and Amerlee's yaw dropped. They were in an immensely huge underground chamber. The floor was black and yellow, pyramids of more yellow and black surface rose in the distance. Some were couple hundred meters tall.

"What is this place?" she looked around, still floored from the view.

"A very important one. It's a simulation chamber. Later, perhaps I can show it to you, but you must mature before I let you use one of the pyramids." Smith led her thru a maze of yellow and black cubes.

"What do you mean more mature?" she snorted, disliking his reply.

"Look up!" he demanded, and she glanced toward the ceiling. Again, her jaw dropped.

"Is that . . . ?" She tiptoed beneath the huge, golden cylinder, suspended from the ceiling. The cutout was on the wrong side of her, so she inched around to get a better view.

"Is that what, or who?" Smith pushed the envelope.

"The Doctor?" she recognized the middle-aged, bald-headed man with his eyes closed in the cylinder.

"Yes, he is! And he had a name before he became the man, as history would know the Doctor. Do you know what was his name?"

"No." She shook her head sadly.

"Of course not. It is not public. He wanted it to be forgotten. My good friend, Johnny." his voice faltered: "Johnny Karalan . . ."

"He was the boy . . . ?" she spun around, keeping her eyes on Smith, who triumphantly nodded: "Yes, he was. He is here, because the man, the genius who saved human kind, had only one wish; to live forever. And for someone who saved an entire race, that wish was granted!" Smith theatrically bowed before the cylinder than locked elbows with Amerlee.

"Where are we going?"

"To the surface where I teleport us back to the Villa-Castle!"

"This is amazing! So, he owned the Maximus line, huh?"

"Yes. He had lots of play with the original Maximus line. He tweaked it, removed lots of the sultry background of the model, gave even more soldiers traits, and he remembered that it mesmerized me. He gave me a data crystal and said it was his personal version, and that it was listening to her name best as Azure. At that point her soul, her design, was locked away. But we had a visitor that day. Her name was Rebecca. She was a former prisoner of the Planetary Defense Forces. She escaped, seemingly she knew exactly who I was and why I was there, at that time frame!"

"Who was this Rebecca person?"

"She was a human, albeit not your ordinary one. Back then, they called her kind a Super Human. Our history has a different name for her kind. An Ancestor. At that moment I realized the Ancestors could travel between time and all the anomalies in our life we have, the missing toys when nobody touches them; the nightgown you place on the chair but in the morning is on the floor. Those sorts of things are happening because they can walk around us undetected. They can slow down time, travel in time and travel between Universes, realms freely. They seemingly don't even use technology, so it's must've been an evolutionary trait."

"That's unbelievable!" she shook her head, trying to accept what he just told her.

"You are going to learn a lot of things, my darling!" Smith grabbed her hands, and they teleported themselves back to the Villa-Castle. They sat down onto the cool marble steps in the shade before Smith continued: "So, this Rebecca held the data crystal in her hand, glanced at us and said that she could see her DNA from where she was standing, then she blinked and said she added immense mental capacity to her because I would need it. I swear to the past Emperors, honey!" he said after Amerlee gave him a crazy look.

"I returned to my present with my crew and the crystal, and by that time my relationship with Tri'ng went to hell. I tasked Diana to develop Azure. She did, and the only direction I've got from Johnny was that she has to open her eye to her master when she was born or else. I was present. She was sixteen and a half, and I was petrified of it and from her in general. I had Aa teach her for tricks, Diana taught her other tricks. Unfortunately, we were running out of time and soon President Guvojan had us cornered; I was with the Ancient Man. We and our closest friends went to prison with us and I had Azure leave with the Toxic. I sent her away, because we never had the chance to get acquainted the way I wanted to. She was crying. I honestly hoped Josh Kulighan would rescue me with Captain Aa, but as faith would have it, it was Azure. She contacted Josh Kulighan, who brought her and the Toxic before Admiral Tarbuk, and then they mounted a daring attack with the help of Tata Crubon. But I did stay in prison for over a year and a half. The only way Azure was able to locate me was due to her telepathic abilities. In her quest, I suspect she somewhat harmed Tri'ng's sensitive mind, but none of us could prove it. President Guvojan did a nasty trick to her mind thou. Basically, she had to choose between me or telling me the reason why did we, the Emperors gave up our freedom and went to prison. Turned out we volunteered because otherwise SWEi Prime would have turned into a wasteland as Guvojan's people poisoned the water supply. Guvojan knew she would have this moral dilemma; to choose to save the entire population of a planet or go back to me, who loved her, but cheated on her. She loved me, but she had to let me go. Guvojan's mental gate ran havoc in her eloquent mind; she forgot all the emotional attachment she made to me over the years." Smith wept silently.

Amerlee never knew this horrible story. She just stood beside him, rubbed his shoulder in silence.

Smith wiped the tears off and continued: "Fucking motherfucker knew she would save the planet. He wanted me to feel like shit! She looks at me now, with her eyes empty, and I can tell she doesn't remember a thing. We had a great run together. She is a gorgeous woman with an elite, an explicitly focused mind when it comes to hacking. She was also cold as ice, but I still found love with her. Not anymore. I saw it in her eyes and decided to step aside. I always mourn when I see her, when I pay special attention to her, but she doesn't understand. She knows now that we lived together, we were lovers, but she doesn't feel anything toward me beside some form of loyalty." Smith's fingers bent with anger. He formed a knuckle. "Damned you, Guvojan! But a good thing came out of this after all. The leader of the X-Force, the Kre'ator who fell in love with her almost two hundred years ago when he was just a teenager and she was back in time with me to set certain historical anomalies straight, finally got together. I am happy for them. Truly. Azure saved me, and in return I owe my life to her. That is how it is, and that is how it must be. Plain as that. She will be around me as long as she wants to, but because she was programmed to like me, she always will. I still love you though!" he turned to her.

She was weeping too. She understood that beyond the money, power and gleam there is nothing but tortured souls.

"I'm so sorry what you went thru!" she leaned on him.

"Don't be! Past is past. I live for the moment!" he playfully grabbed her ass as she glanced at him. Her down curled lips moved upward and soon they were in each other's hands.

Chapter Twelve

Girl Talk

"Hi, can I come in?" Amerlee timidly knocked on the DSR's green hull. She was not sure what exactly the ship would do. Smith was vague about her, revealing only that she supposed to be pretty sophisticated. She was here to check out the clothes, his and bring in fresh ones for herself; essentially to do laundry. Smith hinted Aa was too busy to sail to Down Earth henceforth they would meet her close to Danal IV. That was fine by her. What was less fine is his state of wardrobe. He admitted he relaxed on that one, and since Amerlee was very adamant, he gave her full permission to check out his belongings on the Toxic. So now there she was, knocking shyly, hoping something would happen. There was a muted ping and slowly the green ramp lowered so she could march up on it. There was definitely cold coming from within the ship. It felt strange.

"Hello?" she rolled her eyes, feeling utterly insecure.

Soon a vortex of light particles converged near her position, and Captain Aa formed before her own eyes. "Hi Amerlee, I've been watching you . . ."

"Oh. Then why did I have to knock on the outside hull?" Amerlee asked once she recovered from her surprise.

"I wanted to see what would you do. I know you are here for the wardrobe situation, please follow me!" she led her down the hallway.

Amerlee felt the need to strike a conversation: "I don't hear any noise onboard. Is that mean they have powered you down?"

The hologram turned around, and it seemingly scrutinized her.

It was very disconcerting for Amerlee, who was a bit afraid she would disappear forever. Smith would never find her. She would end up in a dark hole and die lonely, endlessly crying for help.

The hologram tilted her head as the door slid aside, revealing a low ceiling room with four bunk beds.

Amerlee stepped inside. The hologram followed her, pointing out Smith's wardrobe. "I would never do that . . ." she added, or rather the voice came from the walls as there was no green emitter around.

"Do what, ever?" she opened the doors to Smith's clothing situation. It was lethargic, just as she suspected: half the clothes were disorganized; the other half was too worn for her taste. Evan should have neat clothes for all occasions! Smith said they would spend couple days off world. That meant seven sets of clothes for every occasion. He was seriously underdressed.

"So?" she scooped up the thrown in shorts and Tees and collected them into a black bag.

"So . . . ?" The hologram watched her doing.

"So, you said you would never do that, but you did not explain yourself." she picked up a black-sleeved shirt, turned it around and frowned. *Funny taste.*

"You thought I would lock you up somewhere. That you would cry and die without Smith coming to rescue you!"

"How do you know that?" Amerlee snapped, mostly to cover her exponentially skyrocketing insecurity.

"I can read your mind." the hologram casually shrugged.

"Get out of here! Smith too?" she was not really believing in her, but the thought Evan would do, did emerge.

"He can if he wants to. I think he won't do that with you, saying something about discovering your feelings thru communications if I remember correctly." Toxic admitted.

"Please don't do that, reading someone's mind is not nice at all!"

"I'm not really reading it, you, just like everyone else isn't trained to hide it, so basically you are broadcasting it. The more intensified a feeling is, the louder you scream. I am really well tuned for that sort of things." the hologram frowned.

"How can an AI be tuned for human brainwave readings?"

"Who said I was an AI?"

"What?" Amerlee felt this conversation was utterly weird and embarrassing. She heard of AIs that were convinced they were humans. Nobody was supposed to tell them they weren't. *Perhaps this is a similar case*? She wondered.

"No, it isn't. I am not an AI!" Toxic shook her head avidly, watching Amerlee.

"So, what are you then?" Amerlee lost patience.

"Come with me!" Toxic imitated grabbing her arm and pulling thru the hallway. They passed Smith's favorite room; the small galley and went to the rear, next to the storage rooms. The hologram instructed her to turn a latch and pull up a cover.

Amerlee's lips formed an 'oh' and she actually took a step backward. What she saw was too out of this world.

"So, what do you think?" The hologram scratched her virtual chin, watching part of her own self; muscles, blood vessels and arteries pumping fluids across the openings. It was like a skinned human body part.

"Is this a joke?" Amerlee was about to vomit.

"I said I was not an AI. I showed you, so you would believe me when I said it. I am organic. I am a living spaceship; another entity!"

Amerlee took a step back and closed the hatch. "Who built you?"

"They did not build me." The hologram shook her head, her voice coming across to Amerlee as someone being utterly annoyed. "I grew up on Tahhaul High Ponds. Seventh, to be exact! The Prophet came by to touch me, to tell me stories and to upload Captain Aa's consciousness as his first wife was in the alternate future I came from, about a thousand years from today. Are my answers satisfying enough?"

"Who is this Prophet you talk of, so highly if I may add?"

"Evan Smith, of course!" Toxic replied while escorting Amerlee back to the cabin.

"So, in this alternate future Captain Aa became his wife? How come?"

"I see you understood that part." The hologram spoke with a sinister voice, but continued more sincerely: "Well, Tri'ng sacrificed herself, so during a long journey Aa and Smith became cozy, you know how I mean?" the hologram winked hard.

Amerlee frowned in disbelief. "This is crazy!"

"Aa eventually died, but they uploaded her consciousness into my mind, so I could understand her emotions, her life and her reasonings." The hologram imitated watching Amerlee, who suddenly turned quiet.

"I see you love him!" Toxic realized.

"You are a quick learner!" Amerlee snorted, still angry. Mostly that somebody can read her so well.

"Don't worry, now that you are in the picture, Smith won't marry Aa for sure."

"Great, so who do I have to fight with? Azure?"

"No, Azure is a different situation all together. Don't feel resentment toward me, I hope we could be like best girlfriends!"

"I don't know about that . . ." Amerlee grimaced, feeling weird.

"I know you will replace Smith's wardrobe, well most of it. He needs it. But Azure would never do that. She was limited in that regard. Her talents lied elsewhere."

"Yeah, killing right?"

"That too. She could be very stupidly sensual with him." the hologram frowned. "At least I think that was the objective."

"I could do that! I could be so stupidly sensual with him he passes out before foreplay ends." Amerlee was sure of it. "What does stupidly sensual mean?" she stopped all of a sudden.

"Damned if I know it." Toxic shrugged, then laughed with Amerlee. When they stopped, Toxic's hologram brushed her long hair aside. "You will find out more of her once she comes out of the chamber. She is shorter, so I guess she will hate you by being almost as tall as Smith."

"I think there will be a lot of things she will hate me for."

"Yes, and no. She is different. You are different. You more like Aa. Sweet cherry pie, but classy too. Azure is more playful, but there was definitely a drift between the two of them lately."

"Do tell me!" Amerlee dropped the black bag onto the floor.

"Azure like to party, I think. Party and silly stuff . . . Smith would watch her but not get involved. I think that pissed her off."

"He needs a serious woman. Do you think I could fulfill the void?"

"His void?"

"What are we talking about?" Amerlee lost track.

"I definitely think you are sophisticated enough. Just wear more classy stuff like you already do along with leather."

"He loves leather." she blushed.

"He has an Amerlee in leather fetish, huh?" Toxic tried to joke. *Aa would joke like that.*

"Yes, he does!" Amerlee giggled as she was leaving with Smith's clothing on her back.

Soon she returned with two bags, one held by her awkwardly short and tiny, still developing left hand. Toxic watched her placing his clothes into the cabinets with great care. She felt nervousness coming from her at the same time. It would send mixed signals to Smith if he would care to touch the imprint she unintentionally left behind . . .

After a while she decided to ask: "Amerlee, why the hesitation while you arrange his clothing?"

"You can feel that too?" She spun around.

"Yes."

"I just thought about my insurmountable quest to keep his heart."

"What do you mean?" the DSR was clueless.

"I mean, Smith got Azure on the side. Now I know how they met and what bonds them together. They will remain friends forever. While I don't know how he and Captain Aa met, I presume it's some similarly exotic way. She is a strong woman; she knows what she wants, and it was obvious she wants him." she winced from emotional pain. "I don't know how to keep him around me! I'm not a soldier; I never handled a gun before, or a sword. I don't know too many fancy moves, street fights beyond basic stuff. I don't know anything about tactics, how to fight a battle in space. I'm worthless!" she began crying.

"Hey, hey!" the hologram tried to hug her.

"I feel warm!" she glanced around the swarm of the light practices.

"I can excite the light and create warmth. I know you feel tiny, but you made it so far. Listen!" The hologram retraced her steps, so Amerlee can see her as a whole.

"Yes?" she wiped off her tears.

"I think you could be indispensable to him, just have to find that something!" she winked.

"He is the Emperor, fighting wars with the enemy of the Monarch. His girlfriends are either spies, killers, or emerging tacticians! And I'm neither of them!"

"What did I tell you a moment ago?" the ship sounded akin to reprimanding a child.

"Find a weakness . . ."

"Exactly. So, what he isn't good at and you think he should improve upon? Or rather you should improve him?"

"I don't know," she shook her head.

"I know you have a degree in Intergalactic Business Relations. I even know you worked for a corporation doing marketing for a bit." The hologram added.

"So?"

"Find how his image or branding could improve and he will look up to you!" Toxic gave her advice.

"That's a great idea, but doesn't he have advisers? I heard Diana run his business along with Mrs. G . . ."

"Find something that can be improved upon and ask him to give you authority. How hard is it to ask?" the hologram opened her arms.

"But then I have to succeed!" she realized, flinching.

"You're a businesswoman, a strong personality. You'll find your way!" Toxic reassured her.

Chapter Thirteen

Galaxy Qbe

By the time Smith arrived at the Villa-Castle, Amerlee already wrote down a bunch of questions. He asked her if she was ready for a multi-day trip and since she nodded; he grabbed a sandwich and locked elbows with her as they walked up on the Toxic's ramp.

"Toxic, baby, teleport to the Qbe! I need to talk to Hunter and Melissa, get a haircut from Enzo and perhaps spend a night at my house."

"Qbe? What's that?" Amerlee never heard of that.

"Another planet I have a base on it." Smith turned to her hesitantly, kissed her on her lips as the DSR teleported away.

Amerlee learned it was a two stepper, something of a security measure. From the DSR's bridge she watched as they sailed between two SPDs, the gateway to a small solar system with only two large planets and a sun.

"What's this place?" she inquired.

"Yeah, tell her, what's this place?" Toxic laughed from no particular place.

Smith winced. "Not funny!" he then turned to Amerlee, who sat at the navigation's control: "A private retreat. It is one of eighty-six planetary systems that were designated as a fallback position shall the Klons overtake the galaxy. The special property of these planetary systems were the facts that they removed their locations from every star chart. Basically, these systems don't exist unless you know where to look for. I used Galaxy Qbe after the war to pick up military equipment from its vast storage shelters to fight a multi cloned villain. There were surprises along the way, and I decided to keep a presence here. There is a domed city, called Paradise City, but we have neighbors who don't like to be disturbed, so we honor that agreement." He pointed beyond a gigantic bubble. Toxic helped out Amerlee by zooming in to where Smith was pointing, revealing about a dozen of aging Tri-Maran hulls, half suppressed by the jungle.

"What is that? Are those wrecks?"

"Yeah. After Kabnul Admiral Vroxen and others brought their people to this planet where they crash landed with the intention of never returning. Last I've heard about four million humans lived across the planet in seventeen colonies just like this. They don't want to be found and for them this is a perfect place!"

"There are statues of Admiral Vroxen everywhere as a war hero!" Amerlee was quick to point it out.

"Yes. They think he died. He did not. I was actually able to snatch him from here, thou. He runs our Upper Earth sailing navy fleet for couple years now. Tata used to do that, but it's obvious he has a new job now." Smith explained.

"Nobody found it out?" Amerlee was sure somebody knows by now.

"Not yet . . ." Smith's eyebrows rolled.

"This is nice . . ." she carefully walked beneath the sign hanging, seemingly in the middle in the air.

"Yeah, watch, so you don't get fall into the water!" Smith pointed out the miniature creek running across the property.

"Outside pool, here too?" she was surprised.

"What can I say, I love water!" Smith excused himself.

"Can we get into it later?" she fondled his hand.

"Sure!" he glanced up to the evening sky and frowned: "That's disappointing . . ."

"What is?"

"Not a fiery red sunset as I hoped for!" he shook his head.

"Something not as you hoped for?" she giggled as she disappeared into the house.

“Not bad!” she came back out a while later just to find Smith in the swimming pool.

“I’m glad you like it. It’s not a big house, but well maintained by the Mayor.”

“Melissa?”

“Yes. Her husband is Hunter Paradise. He is my friend. I only call him out of this retirement when I really need him. I scheduled a tour tomorrow to see the production facilities.”

“For what?”

“Oh, they make the outer hull of the Vertigo class Starships here, out of sight!”

“Ah, production facilities, here we go!” she flinched as it was not her field and disappeared into the house to change up.

The facility was extensive, as she learned the next day. They cooked some of the materials up on the other moon from where they were transported here. She got the feeling that they preserved this planet and they did the dirty work either in space or on the moon. She was bored by the grim choice of transportation; her choice of race car was not available, only the same looking green and yellow cabs. Although Smith did say he has a cab reserved any time he visited, she was not thrilled by the ‘special’ treatment at all. She was more impressed by the design factory and the endless warehouses where they stored the parts for the Starships before being assembled in orbit. Smith said sometimes workers did it on the planet, but the mysterious locals don not particularly liked that option, so the majority of the work was done in low orbit. She still has not recovered from the fact that eighty-six such small solar systems exist in the galaxy, where military treasure is hidden in plain sight. It was so unbelievable she kept thinking he was just joking. She briefly met a young girl named Sasha who worked in the factory. Seemingly Smith had some sort of convoluted history with her. It did not avoid her attention that the girl had an old-fashioned metallic arm extension and she even asked him later, en route to a villa by the ocean, why she never got a better replacement. His answer shocked her:

"Agent Sasha is learning that her actions have consequences. You must never speak of her name out in public as the Ancient Man ordered her to be killed, and I promised my mentor that I personally carried out his order. I have offered her a place to live out her life. Albeit she is a prisoner, I still consider her penance to be brutal. She had a good life, recruited by the Admiralty to be an agent. She was set up and used as a scapegoat and there was not much I could do about that, except to offer her seclusion from the world. You will notice that there are many who live in exile here. They cannot return to the real world or the outside world thinks they are dead. Most of the Sky Riders' original crew and inhabitants were and are refugees. Mainly political, but just like Sasha, there are ex agents as well. There is a well thought out plan in place, maintained by Diana to rotate refugees between the planet and my Starship. Some even earn their permanent relocation to the Qbe. It is like prison, I know, but better than to be dead . . ." he shrugged.

"So, you trust Agent Sasha that she is here?"

"I have to. Although I have leverage on her."

"What is that?"

"Sasha has relatives living on Down Earth. She understood very well what would happen to them, where she would try to

escape . . . In a way, I feel sorry for her to be in the position she became. She was the sacrificial lamb, and it was too late for me to change anything in a meaningful way. I said that earlier." Smith made a face.

"You have a complicated life . . ." Amerlee admitted.

"Yeah, but now I have you!" he hugged her passionately.

"Is that a winner's team?"

"I really hope so!" he kissed her while the cab zipped toward its destination by the ocean.

Melissa and Hunter Paradise came by the evening to join for a dinner.

Smith introduced them to Amerlee and droids began to serve the food.

"It's nice to see you here again, boss!" Melissa complemented him.

"Oh, I know. Bad memories."

"Couple years now, isn't it? Since the last time you spent time here." Hunter stopped chewing.

"Yeah. Azure and I spent some time here, but it will always remind me to . . . Tri'ng." Smith was hesitant and Amerlee felt his emotions thru his voice. He sounded sad, almost hurt.

"Come on, Smith, it was not all bad!" Hunter tried to cheer him up. "I mean, you met Toxic . . ."

At the hearing of the DSR's name, Smith grinned. "Yeah, I even bit into the ball shape not knowing what the heck it was!"

"See!" Hunter smiled.

Amerlee frowned. She had no idea what they were talking about, but it was entertaining. Secrets and all!

"So boss," Melissa spoke and Amerlee noticed she always call him the boss. Not like he was not, but still it was interesting.

"Yeah?"

"I know you mentioned Sally to your guest, right?"

"Ah, Agent Sasha. Yes. I keep forgetting her private name. I should start to call her Sally myself!"

Hunter began to laugh and Smith stopped eating. "Is something funny?"

"Yes, she finally chose a full name to go with her and she wanted to be Sally Sasha . . ."

"Great." Smith sounded bitter.

"After your last talk with her, she seemingly changed a lot. She no longer tries to escape and even purchased a motorcycle. I think she is into modifications . . ." Hunter added.

"I never knew to pay so much attention to a lone immigrant." Smith frowned.

"She is a special case. High profile and personal!"

"Indeed, she is both to me. Yes, I had a talk with her the last time. I told her I would not want to meet with her again, telling her she did bad things. I guess she got a job, huh?"

"She is still a secretary." Melissa added.

"But she was at the factory." Smith disagreed.

"Yeah, four days in the office, Wednesdays are on the field for supervising. She seemingly likes the job we offered up to her!" Melissa continued.

"Any boyfriend yet?" Smith tried to get the scoop.

"Maybe. There is guy at the factory who is a supervisor now, but used to be a worker; big biceps and a broad smile. She maybe developing something there!" Melissa barely hid her smile.

"I would not want to be the poor guy once she lifts him up." Smith shook his head, trying to imagine the situation.

"Why would she do that?"

"To toss him onto the bed . . . By analytics she should be as strong as Azure!"

"Boy, we saw the results of her! Broken jaws!" Melissa and Hunter looked at each other.

Amerlee heard that Azure was breaking some bones before. She thought Toxic was exaggerating. Maybe she was not.

"Keep an eye on her just in case . . ." Smith rummaged thru his plate.

"Of course!" Melissa's seriousness returned.

"So, is Sasha really that close to your heart?" Amerlee sipped from a cold charblin while she was lounging beside Smith, watching the starry but clear night, while the ocean waves licked the sandy beach.

"In a way. I feel sorry for her and her family she left behind." Smith nodded, drinking from his own glass.

"Why?" she tried to take a peek into his brain.

"Because she was trying to do the job, they ordered her to. During the execution phrase she felt it was morally wrong to do the killing and sought for confirmation. For that, she was labeled a traitor, and they sent killers after her to execute her. She was innocent, but the planet where she was plunged into chaos, civil war as the results of her actions, and it was utterly inconvenient for the Admiralty to pull her out in light of her traitor like mindset. The only person who could shed light on the Admiralty's plan was her, and for that she had to die. My mentor and I were onto the Admiralty, cleaning ranks, but they sent the kill order out weeks earlier. My mentor disliked her for not carrying out the order whether it was right or wrong. I offered her hand to him as a sign of being killed. That way she can live. It's a complicated case peripherally involving Tata Crubon and his family, Josh Kulighan and even Captain Aa. Simply put, too many people were at risk if I fight for her life. After all, she did refuse the order . . ." Smith gulped from the cup again. "It was a no-win situation. But I guess I admired her courage to defy the Admiralty."

"When you were away for four days when we met, you said you were on SWEi Prime, you were taking care of this matter?"

Smith looked away, feeling guilty: "The back end of it, yes."

"Complicated man!" she gulped the rest of her drink before getting up.

"Retire already?" Smith turned toward her, just in time to see her shedding the clothes.

"What?"

"Honey!" she jumped into his lap and caressed his face under the bright moonlight. "I so love you!" she kissed him passionately.

"So, do I . . ." Smith tried to say, but she kissed him again, muting his answer.

"What's next?" Amerlee beamed with joy as the Toxic landed on the sandy beach to pick them up after breakfast. She pointed it out that mysterious servers did serve a thirty-six-menu breakfast table in the lounge.

"We're going to the planet that frightened your ex . . ." Smith glanced around, waving mental goodbye to the peaceful place.

"What?" she did not understand him.

“Destination Gnem, my first planet!” he hooked into her elbow as they walked across the sand dunes to reach the Toxic’s ramp.

Chapter Fourteen

Destination Gnem

"The place is anything I ever imagined it would look!" Amerlee turned around on her heels. She was standing in one of the Presidential Palace's balconies, watching the towering obelisks, some still being worked on. She already met President Joel, who warmly welcomed them upon their arrival. The milk bath was refreshing. Smith skipped it for a ride to the city. He even had a personal driver, albeit when the dusty old yellow cab pulled up, she got nervous; it resembled to a kidnapping. Smith waved goodbye to her and two hours later he reappeared, after shaking hand with the cab driver.

"What was that all about?" Amerlee felt peace around her like never before. The bath was truly exotic, even for her. She learned Azure always took it whenever Smith and she visited the planet.

"I visited his family. It's a long story, hon . . ."

"Tell me!" she demanded.

"I . . . You'll meet the Death Squad members. The girls from different ruling Clans fighting for me. When I was rescued from prison by Azure, I was beyond angry as my memory was suppressed just like the Ancient Man's and everybody else's who was with us on the prison ship. I wanted to see blood and so as my mentor. I devised a plan with the than renegade Admiral Tarbuk who defied the Admiralty to . . ." he suddenly stopped as tears appeared in Amerlee's eyes. "What?"

"I just shocked how much the general public doesn't know about you. About your true life! I would worry myself to death!" she closed her fingers.

"I see," he smiled gently.

"Please, continue. How is this tie to the yellow cab?" she was beyond interested.

"Okay, so I formulated a plan to punch thru the body of the AOCP. It was the time Captain Aa lost her PD, the Executor and gained command of the Destination Unknown. When under my supervision, we attacked shipyards near the TCP. For the plan to work, somebody had to pilot the prison ship to keep it moving or AOCP would learn something went wrong. I asked for a volunteer and one of the Death Squad members stepped forward. I promised her to bring her personal remains back to the planet, to present it to her Clan. After the attack Azure and I came and me, well, you don't know me like that, but I wanted to grab a local cabbie to do the transportation. The guy tried to rob us at gunpoint. Azure of course offered her services, but I declined. Turned out the cab driver's daughter was terminally ill, bitten by a stray animal. I asked him to take me to her where I fixed her, healed her. The driver was so astonished that he pledged to be my transportation guy whenever I'm here. So, I do!"

"That's amazing!" she shook her head. "So, there WAS a robbery involved!" she mumbled it for her own reassurance, but Smith heard it; "What?"

"I saw you getting into that dusty cab and I instantly thought of gunpoint and getting kidnapped!"

"You were worrying. Sweet!" he kissed her.

"President Joel has some surprises for you!" she glided down the steps with him beside her.

"Oh?"

"Come!" she pushed open the big doors into one of the conference rooms, where a row of nicely dressed tables housed all his canned fish line-ups.

"Nice!" he patted a couple. "I ate this. It's actually pretty good! Um, what's that?" he pointed to a green table with about fifteen tiny dark plates.

"Caviar!" President Joel appeared out of nowhere, personally catering to his guests.

"I thought I said quite clearly, I want canned food for the poor!" Smith frowned.

"Well, it's long been not the case, My Lord!"

"What are you saying?" Smith mimicked Amerlee's trained moves as she dipped a piece of toast into one and took a bite.

She bobbed her head. "Delicious!"

"Yuck!" Smith forced it down his throat. He did not like it at all.

President Joel nervously clapped his hands. "So?"

"Don't waste time converting the fisheries to this . . ." Smith hated his original ideas being twisted this way.

"Okay . . ." Joel became timid.

"How much did you guys already make?" Smith suddenly had an emerging bad feeling about it.

"Projections for this year looks out to be something of a hundred ton . . ."

"What a waste!" Smith shook his head, cutting his sentence in half.

"So . . ." The President needed directions.

"Chop it!" Smith was mildly frustrated. "You know my ideas. From the get go. I said I would have fisheries on a desert planet. And that I want the poor to have a chance to eat from it's results. Good protein . . ."

"We export to over fifty-seven planets and seventeen space communities, but this is increasingly for the middle class." Joel pointed at the silver-colored canned food without a label.

"I hate to hear it . . ." Smith disliked the situation.

"What about the existing batch of caviar?" President Joel pushed for clarification.

"Market it under a special onetime deal and forget about it!"

"Okay!"

"Honey . . ." Amerlee saw an opportunity in this. A problem, something she could surely solve!

"Yes?" Smith turned to her.

"Let me deal with the existing caviar . . ."

"You want to eat it all?" Smith misunderstood her. She had to laugh. "No, silly man. Let me deal with the existing batch. All of it!"

Smith frowned. He contemplated for a second, then shrugged, like he just wanted to forget all about it. "Be it."

"Can we take home some?" she brushed over his shoulder.

Smith rolled his eyes. "Joel, how much do you get here, on the premises?"

"Well, about a ton . . . We got more in the warehouses across the planet." he added, earning a wary look from Smith.

"Can somebody take it to the Toxic?" Amerlee swallowed hard before asking out loud.

"Make it happen, Joel!" Smith ordered, and the President nodded. "Immediately." And he scurried away.

"What are your plans?" Smith turned to Amerlee, feeling a plan being hatched by her active brain.

"I'll make myself indispensable to you!" she winked amid smiling.

"You already are!" he grabbed her fingers.

She blushed, shook her head. "No. You never asked what I did before working for the PR department."

"You're right. I'm a guy who doesn't poke into the past. Only the present and the future matters!" Smith shared his philosophy.

"Well, I did marketing in Super City and across the ocean in Delta City! Big time marketing!" she winked. "Product developing and all that . . . I think we can create a niche with the caviar. I already see the design on the boxes saying something like 'Emperor Brand' or blend. First, we would introduce it in coolers in your limos. Let the elite enjoy it first. Free samples. Then if the reception is good, we can begin to make exclusivity agreements with chains or the Entrepreneurs Club. You could sell it fifty times what it worth to make it and reinvest the money into whatever you want!"

"Amazing!" Smith shook his head. "You know what, I let you be in charge of it. I would've never thought of it that way. If any positive comes in, I mean anyone willing to pay for this caviar thingy I let you keep fifty percent of the profit. The other fifty goes back to Gnem. Deal?"

"Bet!" she grinned from ear to ear. *She was in*!

Chapter Fifteen

Trouble on the Horizon

"Shit!" Smith almost fell, kicking the box in the hallway with his leg. "Fucking caviar . . . Should just dump it all!" His toe was aching. He returned to the Toxic as he had to communicate with Josh Kulighan and Toxic's military uplink was the only secure connection from the surface he could think of. Amerlee was still in the Palace, under the watchful eye of four Death Squad members she gouged from a distance. Smith tried to reassure her, they would die before they would give in, but Amerlee viewed the whole thing as backward and detrimental to women as a whole. As Smith had to talk to Josh regarding to the escalating situation near the Green Void—he never learned why it was called as such, as it was black, he returned to his beloved DSR.

"Hey-hey!" Toxic formed the hologram to greet him in person.

"Is Josh on line yet?" he gently patted his aching toe.

"Couple more minutes. Listen, um, boss . . ." she wanted to talk to him.

"Yeah?" Smith swiftly glanced up, still caressing his toe.

"About the canned food . . ."

"Joel said it was almost seven hundred fifty buarak for one small can of caviar." he yanked the paper out of his pocket and turned around to drop it to Amerlee's bed. "Aw . . ." he limped away. "Fucking caviar . . ."

"I . . ." the hologram stared after him.

Smith returned a minute later, not limping anymore. "You wanted something?"

"Yes!" she regained her confidence. "Into my office, please!"

"Office?" Smith followed her suspiciously. "Oh, you mean the bridge!" he hurried after the hologram.

Once the doors closed, the hologram turned around: "I want to talk to you about this caviar business!"

"You want to taste it?"

"Silly boy!" the hologram imitated to slap his face.

"What?" Smith tried to duck from the virtual slap. "Is Josh on line?"

"I wouldn't know and we won't know until you listen to me!"

"Insubordinate ship!" Smith shook his head. "Okay, let's hear it!" he caved in.

"Let her handle this and shut up!"

"What?"

"She is insecure and needs to prove herself to you!"

"Amerlee? What is she insecure about?" Smith scratched his head.

"Her worthiness!"

"What? You sure you got your facts straight? She loves me and I love her!"

"But she increasingly sees Aa's and Azure's talent. She is a civilian, and she knows she can't compete, so she is trying to find something else. I think the caviar will do it!" Toxic explained.

Smith wanted to dismiss it, but the more he heard, the more he found it realistic. "So, you're saying I should let the runaway train roll out of the station?"

"Exactly!"

"But if this becomes a failure, she'll be very disappointed. Should I form a shell company to buy up the stuff? But then what the hell I'm going to do with it?" Smith contemplated his options.

"Fool, don't you dare to get involved that way!" the hologram shouted at him.

Smith backed down. "Okay, got it!"

"Follow her plan and assist her. I'm sure opportunity will presents itself. Make sure you're there and grab it for her!"

"I will!" Smith reassured her, not knowing what else he should say. "Now about Josh . . ."

"He is eager to listen to you, boss!" Toxic dissolved the hologram and Smith hopped into his chair.

The Captain of the Auxiliary fleet seemed to vary.

"Talk to me!"

"Smith, we have an issue with this situation." Josh seemed to be unsure of himself.

"So, you're involved now? Directly?"

"The locals don't have the will or the capacities to keep investigate and pick up all the debris littering the busy shipping corridor."

"How long is this so-called Void?"

"Almost two light years long, but only the AOCP side of it is flat; the rest is a maze of holes and bumps."

"I thought the AOCP side has a ding in it." Smith decided to entertain himself with the new issue.

"Oh, yes. It's a curved ding the ship captains use to accelerate their ship. Like a slingshot."

"It deflects matter even there?" Smith frowned.

"Yes. Most aim just before the ding and red line the reactors. The resulting repelling force so strong that it hurls any object beyond safety."

"You sure this misery did not start with the two weeks old incident when a freighter exploded for some unknown reason and three of the four freighters hit the debris blowing up as well?"

"I feel there is more." Josh swayed his head.

Smith winced. "What does the Admiral say?"

"Admiral Tarbuk would welcome your guidance . . ."

Smith frowned. "Listen. I looked up this Green Void in the databanks. Nothing special. It supposed to be harmless besides the aspect of repelling objects. Nobody ever reported any kind of altered behavior."

"It has to start somewhere!" Josh disagreed. "Look Smith, Denna-7, the travel point . . . Most of the freighters had sent a ship to collect the debris of the first incident. Then there is the second incident. There were four barges. The lead ship accelerated faster than the others, left them by two clicks and just before hitting the ding as you eloquently put it, he had a massive electronic failure. Radar went whack and the power drainage was so massive he had to shut down the core."

"But he survived, right?" Smith shook his head.

"I think he survived because of the unscheduled acceleration!"

"There is no known weapon of any kind, even under development that would produce something like that as a result." Smith scratched his head.

"I insist . . ." Josh clenched into the subject.

Smith winced. "Send some of your men after this freighter captain and have it investigated. Board his ship and ask for telemetry. Save everything. Thank him for cooperation."

"Denna-7 will start to send its pocket cruiser on the return trip."

"Good. Keep an asset in the area and monitor it!"

"I can't cover two light years and you know that!"

"Okay. Just the inbound and the outbound of the Void. If you would get the news of another unexpected explosion than realign your assets for a closer monitoring and keep me posted!"

"Yes, Smith!" Josh said his byes.

"Captain Aa is concerned . . ." Toxic said.

"Don't tell me, she is nearby this too?"

"Admiral Tarbuk had her realign just outside of this zone, the far side at Orus-17. They have a Ring, an Accelerator. Most freighter captains pay for the initial boost, then use your so-called ding to get the real deal."

"Interesting . . ."

"What I try to say is that the Accelerator goes by a schedule. Due to the nature of the Ring, the initial vector is set."

"And the Green Void limits the vectors, right?" Smith was catching on.

"Right. Most freighter captains choose to slip by the border and use the ding as opposed to navigate thru the maze on the other side." Toxic added.

"So, you share Josh's suspicion of AOCP involvement?"

"It could go either way, boss. I suspect we'll be visiting this subject again!"

"Great!" Smith shook his head, dismayed by the prospects, and left.

*

"Your arm is almost complete!" Smith probed Amerlee's left hand.

"It feels as if just dangling sometimes . . ." she felt embarrassed.

"Aa will double check my work. Do you still take the pills?"

"My hair grows wilder as a result, I think." she frowned.

"Side effect . . ." Smith brushed aside her concern.

"How long do I take it?"

"Dwindle it down by the end of the week. Do you have a supply?"

"Yes."

"Good. Smith twisted it, but it barely made any sense as he was watching it at the molecular level, checking on accelerated muscle and bone growth. It was more of a reassurance toward her.

"The entertainment was really interesting last night." she referred to the exotic dancers and the flame barfing guy. "But I think you stole the night!" she remembered to the moment when Smith stepped off his high seat and restarted the flame for the poor guy, just by opening his palm.

"Yeah . . ." Smith grinned.

Amerlee's expressions changed. "Captain Aa said even I can do some of your tricks. Was she correct?"

"She is right, of course. All I would have to do is change some of your neurotransmitters, pathways and flip a DNA and you would be very receptive to my teaching."

"Why not then?"

"I don't think it's always a blessing. Perhaps . . ." Smith felt a lesson was in order.

"Perhaps what?"

"What is constant in the universe?"

"Time?"

"Good!" Smith was pleasantly surprised of her answer.

"What better way to observe the world around you?"

"But it's at a constant speed." she protested.

"Come with me!" Smith had a sudden idea. He led her thru the side door to outside of the garden, into the sculpture's workshops. People stopped chiseling until the work leader yelled at them, then turned to Smith and Amerlee, bowing deeply.

"I don't want to disrupt the workshop. Please tell your men to continue!" Smith ordered him, then noted the bird cages in the middle. "Perfect!" He stepped closer and asked for a clean cloth. Three workers rushed with materials. Smith placed one onto an unused workbench and helped Amerlee up. Then he himself jumped.

"What now?" Amerlee glanced around. She had to look downward to see the workers with their primitive hand tools working tirelessly.

"Sit down, comfortably, legs crossed over!"

"Close my eyes too?" she obeyed to his requests.

"No. Not this time!" he did the same, then opened his hands to her. She placed it in his palm and looked into his eyes.

"Breathe in and out, slowly, and relax. I will guide you!"

"To what?" she watched him, perplexed.

Smith smiled and closed his eyes. It was the first time he touched her mind as he began to create a bubble and slow down time. The sounds, voices changed. That was the first Amerlee noticed. Then she turned to her left. The worker hit the chiseler with a hammer and it went slower than slow motion. She somehow zoomed in and noted the sweat drips, rolling gently on his bare arm into a puddle, finally dropping into the ground. As her view was guided, she saw the initial cloud bubble as the water drop hit the sand. She saw the tiny dirt pieces stuck on the bubble's outside surface, before they sank in, and then the bubble burst and swallowed by the sand. It was mesmerizing until she gazed at the birds. They flapped their feathers so slow; she could see their body flexing. Then her mind began to see the muscles beneath the feathers, beneath the muscles, the bones and the molecules, the atoms that made up the cells of the bird. She had to shout, but it was more of a yawn. Then with a snap, normal time returned.

"Do you see now that there is more to life than just work?" Smith glanced down at her, offering his hand.

She was still dazed by the flow of information, but took the strong hand and allowed her body to kiss up to his. "Amazing!" she whispered, looking at him passionately.

"Good. This was lesson one!" Smith kissed her.

"Amazing talent!" she whispered again.

Smith had to smile as he escorted her back to the palace.

"Where now, my prince?"

"We're unfortunately leaving tomorrow morning. We have a celebratory show up, a rare occasion I allowed for Joel. We're going to the military base where they train pilots and space ship captains for hauling freight as Gnem slowly becoming an economical centerpiece of my worlds."

"Me to?"

"You too."

"Tomorrow?"

"Tomorrow will be another day. I have a growing matter on my hand. Not pretty, I'm afraid. At least Josh insists."

"Josh, who?"

"Kulighan." Smith replied, then continued his hasty explanation: "So we're meeting Captain Aa. Her ship is better equipped than Josh's. I want to oversee this mission before we return to Down Earth. Remember, Azure is coming on line next week!" At the mentioning of her, Amerlee turned serious.

"Then a lunch with your parents will be in order . . ." Smith added more candidly.

"Smash day!" Amerlee grinned.

“Be careful with that. They’re still your parents.” he warned her.

“I want them to accept me and my choices!”

“But if you crush them, it will cause forever bitterness!” he shared his thoughts.

“You seem more worry for them than I am. Why?” she turned to him.

“I try to be fair here. It will mortify them they might upset me before. And Miss Thorne will be there personally, to have them sign the agreement . . .” Smith reminded her.

“I don’t see the problem with it.”

“Ah. Good.” Smith let it go. He had to worry about the Green Void and all else.

*

Captain Aa was partially dismayed while she watched Toxic docking with her Super Planet Destroyer. She hated the idea Smith had a girlfriend he presumably shared everything with. She wanted to be in that place. She should’ve been in that position! She nodded at the helm controls while her holo display showed the feed near the docking port where Commander Danek patiently waited for the guests to arrive. She hoped to send a clear message to him; she was displeased!

As Smith disembarked, the obvious absence of Aa was hard to miss. He stopped, turned around, nodded for no apparent reason, and spoke to Commander Danek, who was waiting patiently at the bottom of the ramp: “I see Aa is angry . . .”

“I would not know, sir!” Commander Danek was pushed between a rock and a hard place. His loyalty stayed with his Captain he must cover for, yet he was speaking with the Emperor. He also tried to remember that.

“Funny. Okay, I can see her point.” Smith rummaged around, still holding Amerlee’s hand. “Commander Danek, please clear the main hangar bay for me and have all non-essential crew show up there!”

“Are you punishing my Captain?” was the first he could say.

“No. I am actually giving her a chance to evolve! I feel generous today . . .” Smith turned around and left toward the bridge with Amerlee practically running beside him: “It was amazing! People responded to your authority!”

Smith scoffed. “I am supposed to be some kind of mighty fellow, you know!”

“Now you are joking!” she stopped at the elevator.

“Yes, I am! Captain Aa showed her woman's side by not showing up to greet us. Let’s see, how does she manage to evade us next.”

“So, she was insubordinate?”

Smith sighed. “Yes, in a true sense as this is a blatant display of disrespect for a uniformed, but she is a special case for me, so she knows I won’t punish her.”

“Unless some wicked way she wants you to punish her . . .” she added quietly.

“She does have a personality like that, but I just can’t.”

“Why?”

“I owe my life to her father . . .” he looked straight, so Amerlee wouldn’t see weakness and remorse in his eye.

Once on the huge bridge, Amerlee noted the military was trying to please the Emperor. The show was visible, and since it was the first time for her to step onto the bridge of an SPD, it was also memorable. Captain Aa greeted them at the Ready Room behind the bridge, where she dutifully examined Amerlee and gave a favorable outlook on her hand’s progress. Amerlee tried to read her, but beyond the unusual rigidness of her posture and looks, she barely detected any hostility. Perhaps the woman thought Amerlee wouldn’t last that long. She was not sure. Or perhaps she was hit with the realities she would stay with Smith and it angered her. Anyway, after the discussion of hers, the two of them moved to the trouble of the week. As she listened in, a bigger and deeper problem unfolded before her eyes. Upon Smith’s insistence, the 26th UNHL Fleet sent a dredger, a specially modified vessel to comb thru space and pick up debris so this horrific accident would never happen. It seemed for Amerlee Captain Aa increasingly shared the war hero, Josh Kulighan's view of this being an obscure ploy by the AOCP, but as to what outcome it would serve eluded her. Apparently, it eluded her Smith as well, who opted for an unfortunate coincidence as an explanation.

"We will see soon . . ." Captain Aa swayed her head, visually opposing Smith's explanation.

"So, you think the dredger will be gone before it could finish the operation?"

"No. To the contrary I think it's the safest vessel as its moving pattern keeps changing. I think AOCP may use an exotic weapon here and somehow they're getting precise information from the Accelerating Ring!" she replied.

"While I cannot discount this option, I don't think it's real. I mean, what's on the other side of the border? Anything?" Smith glanced up at the holo screen depicting the region. The Green Void hung like an abstract design of some sort, the border hung like a curtain, and about a quarter light year beyond a lone moon and two smaller moons rotated endlessly.

"Meet the guy behind door number two!" Aa pointed at the larger moon.

"Funny!" Smith recognized his own wording coming from her.

"Thanks!" she quickly moved on, but Amerlee caught the episode. "It has three settlements. A scientific community as far as we know."

"Okay, so our information is presumably current just before the border closure, right?" Smith asked without blinking.

"Yes."

"Get with the Admiralty and ask them to re send all pertinent information. Analyze it and then contact your Admiral and ask him to contact Admiral Qaw to see if he got anything exciting about them."

"So, we won't mount an attack now?" she seemed disappointed.

"No. I don't see anything beyond suspicion here." Smith disagreed. "But better be cautious!" he glanced up at the holo screen again. Aa had a point.

"What's up with the main hangar, boss?" she added after Smith seemed to be upset.

Amerlee tried her best to stay and look invisible.

"Your next lecture from me. It's time for you to start practicing more advanced things than having a dog made of water bark at the wrong tree . . ."

"Are you upset with me?"

"Not as a professional." he frowned in return. "You're still my apprentice. It's time for me to show you who is behind door number three!" he quickly winked, earning a relieved, pleasant smile from the Captain and a mean look coming from Amerlee's direction.

Amerlee watched as about eight hundred men and women gathered in the main hangar. Her man turned to the audience, telling those whom here to cause trouble to move on. Nobody did. Apparently, everybody who showed up wanted to see whatever he decided to show. He said something along the lines of mostly nobody will understand, so he will guide them to recognize the act. Up until she felt the pleasant nudge in her brain, a flicker in front of her eyes, she did not realize what true guidance meant. Smith, or rather the Emperor connected with everybody's brain, linked up to show something. He briefly spoke of this trick being heard and even displayed at the Museum of the Emperors, then he produced a funky-looking glass bottle. It took her a minute to realize the neck of it was melted back to itself. There was a candle inside. Then he turned to the humble-looking Captain Aa, who blushed as he mentioned to her people. He saw her trying to light the candle inside the bottle years ago, but as far as he knew it ended disastrously.

She nodded, then spoke loudly that indeed it was. Amerlee heard stories of this bottle, where the goal was to light the candle than sustain it, but she never understood how could that be possible. She barely listened to him stating what people thought of this; that since the Emperors knew how to teleport, they just teleported air inside the candle, so as the initial light.

"That's not how it's done!" His statement was mockingly unpleasant to her ear.

"People tend to be presumptuous, and so that usually is their downfall . . ." he added.

Amerlee frowned. Smith was harsh, but then she reminded herself, he was the Emperor here. It was his right to be harsh if he chooses to be.

"I know what some of you were looking for. That I might create a jar of water and sand, then create something from it. Well, let me tell you something; since this is a spaceship, I won't waste your precious oxygen. That's right! You can't create something from nothing. I need atoms, so let there be light!" he changed tone and extended his left arm that suddenly glowed, then a tiny fire lit up in the middle of that light.

Amerlee's jaw opened half way.

Smith continued: "Now let's zoom in on the bottle!"

She heard his voice in her brain. It was mind bogging. Somehow the bottle encompassed her mind, zoomed into the atomic level, to see gaps. The voice in her head like a humble teacher spoke again: 'All we have to do is enlarge the sub atomic gap, like this . . .' The atoms moved aside, revealing a dark void.

'Then we just push the air molecules across to fill up the void and excite the light to spew a piece of itself across and . . .'

Amerlee closed her mental eyes and opened her real's and her eyes got bigger as she noted the flickering light in the bottle.

"Easy as pie!" Smith glanced around. The crowd was speechless.

"Can I . . . Can I have that particular bottle?" Captain Aa opened her hand toward it.

"Sure!" Smith smiled and gently gave to her, then turned to the crowd: "That's all it takes. So that's why I connected to all of your brains, to show. No camera can show what you've seen. Take it in and think about it!" he nodded toward them then said his byes to the Captain before he grabbed Amerlee's hand: "Off we go!"

"You're so powerful!" she clenched his hand hard.

"You're making me blush!" he turned to her, but he felt elevated too.

*

Amerlee had dinner with her parents. Smith was not invited, and in a way she was relieved. After returning from space, they spent the day at the KFT where he introduced her to the no nonsense Mrs. G; his secretary. Apparently, he was serious about the caviar business and made her a business associate. For now, she had a basic idea what the cover should look like, so Smith said the KFT owns a smaller printing shop where they could print the labels. All she had to do was design them. Then of course she retained her job at the PR department, a part-time job now. She had a busy day and now a busy evening. Smith claimed he had a business meeting to attend. She would've canceled hers to go with him, but as it turned out, it was with his mentor. From the hearsay she got, he was an extremely dangerous entity, so she was happy she did not have to go. Now that she was staring at the Prenuptial Agreement her father drew up, she was not so sure anymore . . .

"Daddy?"

"Your mother told me you are still in love with that boy, so I think we should secure the heritage!"

"You mean your heritage?" she shot back across the dinner table.

"All I try to do is to protect you!" his father replied, resting his heavy eyes on her.

"You haven't said a word about my arm!" she complained.

"I'm still assessing the outcome of that gift." he said cryptically.

"What do you mean?"

"If that is true," he pointed at her daughter's real looking arm, "then he had to sell his soul to someone and then it's more important than ever to sign this."

"We aren't getting married, dad!"

"Then what the hell are you doing, goofing with him?" her mother asked, since she could not withhold her anger anymore.

"You should be happy, mom!" Amerlee thought she would be happy; he did not become an exclusive thing for her.

"I would be if you would marry a rich guy. You are pretty enough to browse thru the catalog!" she reminded her.

She made a dirty face at her, then returned her attention to her father: "He did not have to sell his soul for that!"

"Never less, I have my reservations. The Prenup is there to stay. Take it home to show it to him. If he is so sincere, it shouldn't matter to him."

"Oh, dad!" she was between tears.

"Did I mention we got an invitation to the Villa-Castle for next week?" he almost grinned from excitement.

"The Emperor!" her mother added proudly.

"Nice!" Amerlee pretended to give proper complement.

"Sorry that we can't take you, but it's for us only." her father said, adding: "Of course it's for lunch only. I guess we will be done in about an hour. I can't imagine what got into the Emperor to support us in such a way."

"What way?" Amerlee scrutinized him.

"My company's stocks are up four percent!"

"You've made it public?" she could not believe in her ears.

"Of course! It's a big thing. If you ever get an invitation, you will understand too! We got the letter thru an official courier. It was epic!"

"Just like your arm, honey!" her mother added warmly to encourage her. She stared at her left arm from the moment she stepped thru the door. At first Amerlee thought Smith's doing made a lasting impression on her, but as it turned out she was just checking how she looked with a real arm, to increase her chances now to be married.

Typical mother stuff, and it bored and angered to her core at the same time.

"Are you planning to take a picture with him?" she asked without thinking. By the looks on his face, it was the wrong question.

"Out of the question!" he shouted. "I don't wish to anger the Emperor, so I won't even dare to ask!" he closed his eyes. "Perhaps a selfie with your mother in his front steps . . ." he dreamed of it.

"What's with the transportation?"

"We got it covered. Reputable company, but not the Emperors. Your mother and I thought of it for long-long time. We want to avoid looking like a desperate couple, sucking up to him!"

"Interesting choice." Amerlee responded, drinking the wine.

"So, your mother tells me you cut back working for the Emperor's PR department, but she did not say why? I hope it isn't because of your boyfriend." her father asked with a slight warning in his voice.

"Not exactly. They gave me an assignment. Well, actually I requested it. It's marketing. A new product from a rich guy who doesn't know he could be even richer by selling stuff at a premium price!"

"Dashing rich guy?" her mother asked, earning a frown from her. Then she thought about it. "Maybe . . ."

"Is there any way we can help?" her father thought she might change and go for the dashing rich guy.

"No. I want to do this on my own dad. I want him to see I'm not just a pretty girl!"

"You have my blessing!" his father winked at her mother, who nodded approvingly in return.

Amerlee shook her head. If they would know that was also Smith . . .

By the time she got home, it was so late Smith was actually asleep. She slipped into the bed beside him and fell asleep too.

When she woke up, Smith stared at her from the windows.

"What's wrong?" she realized with a slight relief it was after nine o'clock.

"Many things are wrong. For one, this thing at the Green Void is pissing into my soup!"

"Complications?" she grabbed her sateen panties.

"We can say that . . . Another incident happened overnight. A lone ship blew apart. I had ordered Josh Kulighan to personally take charge of the cleanup. He has to grab the debris and try to reconstruct the vessel. Something doesn't add up, just as Aa said." he pulled his mouth for emphasis.

"She is your apprentice, right?"

"What's that supposed to mean?" he leaned forward.

"Nothing!" Amerlee realized she stepped onto his toes with that one.

Smith shook his head. "I see your father wants to be protective . . ." he waved the Prenuptial Agreement in his hand.

"Oh, you not supposed to see that!" Amerlee bit her lips, cursing at herself.

"Not a big deal. We aren't married yet, but if that's make him happy, sure, I sign it!"

"Married?" Amerlee echoed the word.

"Sure. You aren't getting any younger and it would be a great legacy!" Smith shrugged.

"You aren't against marriage?" her eyes got big.

"I am on the grounds that I'm an immortal, but hey love is love. I do love you. At this point we aren't there yet, but I'm certainly open to the suggestion. I will give it to your father at the luncheon. Hey, you did not slip the details to him, right?" he asked, but she was already in his arms: "My own Empy!" she kissed him all over.

"Now you are turning into Azure. By the way. Diana left me a message. Today is the big day!"

Amerlee got upset and worried the same time. "She'll hate me!"

"That maybe, but never less you knew the day would come!" he reminded her.

"Do we have to?"

"Hey. I don't want to hear that kind of talk from anyone! She saved me. Long as she wants to live in a human form, she got it!" Smith shook his head. "Okay. Before we do go, however, we're going to visit the KFT. Do you have a preliminary sketch of what you thought to be on the caviar label?"

"Yes. There are seven varieties of caviars and each should have a different color as a divider. The back side already have Type I thru VII, so I figured we just leave it as such."

"You're the boss!" Smith let it go.

"Call the limo, boss!" she joked, then kissed him and disappeared into the shower.

Chapter Sixteen

She is Not Just a Pretty Face

"It's totally different now!" she exclaimed as they stepped thru the entrance. The receptionist smiled and nodded toward them as they walked by. Smith did not even slow down. It was natural for him, she observed, which was good.

Amerlee had a dream. She was a piss poor girl in a dirty town who met a con man who pretended to be this wealthy guy. Eventually the walls crumbled, but it was too late; she was married to him.

To draw confidence, she looked at him as he pushed the elevator button. He scanned the lobby, shook as the chime reported the elevator's arrival. He turned around and walked inside with her.

"Eighty-sixth floor . . ." she uttered nervously, and he began to smile. "What. . . ?" she tried to hide her momentary confusion.

"Nothing . . ." he kissed her lightly, but longingly, giving her all kinds of ideas.

It was less romantic as Mrs. G gave looks akin to shots across the bow of an eighteen century Upper Earth ships sailing across the Oceans.

Smith stopped to have a short talk with her while Amerlee walked into his spacious office. She loved the view! The city laid before her eyes and the Sky Riders' gigantic and dark body blocked most of the view to the far left, giving her a headache. Smith told her on the way in to brace for Azure's awakening. She was hoping this day would never come. As soon as Smith was supposed to be done with a small paperwork issue and her introduction to a young guy named Del, they were off to the Starship; he said. Drawing the conclusion from his earlier pep talk, she was sure this Del guy was somebody either very important for the company or for him or

both . . . Could even be the same guy they discussed weeks earlier just before she discovered her Smith could read AED. Her daydreaming was cut short as he strolled in, sat on his chair and brought the holo display to alive.

"I just going to sit around . . ." she played with her hands, not knowing what to do.

"Okay . . ." Smith was seemingly already immersed in his work.

Amerlee found a chair opposite to his desk and took up residence there. Whatever her love had to do; he was doing it. Suddenly Mrs. G's voice interrupted the quietness: "There was a call earlier from Josh Kulighan . . ."

Smith suddenly stopped doing whatever he was doing and his morning bad mood reappeared. "Do you know what his message was?"

"No, sir. He was repeatedly trying to reach you without explanation."

It did not go unnoticed for Amerlee she never once used his titles, just a respectful 'sir'.

"Thank you." Smith glanced toward Amerlee amid mild head shaking: "I told you this will be a problem!"

"The Green Void?" she asked in return.

"Not just a pretty face, huh?"

"I hope not." she tried to smile to lighten the mood.

"Yeah, the Green Void. I will be ending up in space again. This time longer, I

suppose . . ." he rummaged across his desk.

"I wanna go too!" she said suddenly surprising even herself.

"You?" It seemed Smith himself was surprised.

"Yes, me!" she was upset. He would go with Azure and they two would hit it off like nothing happened! *Can't happen under my watch!*

"But you hate space and military and such." he mulled over it.

"You tell me I'm useless?" she moved for a defensive position.

"No . . ." he bit into his lips too late.

"Good. It's settled then. I'm coming with you!" she hoped her stance conveyed a strong response.

"How 'bout you pick up some moves and learn how to discharge a gun?" Smith also revealed his own worries.

She shook her head: "I'm not that violent person."

"We'll see . . ." he returned to his previous work, then fiddled with the holo keyboard for a moment while she asked: "Why haven't you hooked your IC to the company network?"

"What?"

"I mean hi-tech companies nowadays use neuro transmitters to do work. They just sit in chairs, nice and comfy while their brain works directly in a VR type of environment in a much better way than you now."

"I hate technology!" Smith manufactured an orange in his hand than levitated toward Amerlee who grabbed it, peeled it and promptly ate it.

"See!"

"But . . ."

"Not under my watch!" he shot back, then added in a softer tone: "I guess I don't want to become like Kalen . . ."

"Who?"

"Opposite of the Bristolians." Smith referred to the Ancestors. She recognized that, because her eyes got bigger: "You must've seen things!"

"You have no idea!"

She made a face and remained quiet for the remainder of the time. Fifteen minutes later they were on the thirty-fourth floor where Smith was seemingly was either lost or was looking for someone he could not find.

After Smith scouted practically the entire floor, he told her to stay put while he disappeared into the men's room. At the first corner, near the faucets, he spotted Del, his back firmly against the wall.

"Hey!" he was relieved to see him.

"Hey, Smith!" The young man lit up, apparently also happy to see him.

Smith cautiously approached him: "What are you doing? I thought you would be receiving congrats in the main auditorium." he tilted his head, pointing toward the exit.

"See, I had this miniscule problem . . ." Del scratched his head. That was the moment Smith noticed he was still holding the wall. Literally!

"What did you do?" he asked him suspiciously.

"I was trying to convince my supervisor about the composite materials being used in industrial buildings with a live demonstration, but unfortunately the separator gave away behind me. I called my personal robot to find some high strength glue in a jiffy . . ." he seemed nervous, constantly looking around.

"To?"

"To glue this damn fake wall back!" Del seemed upset as precious moments passed without his personal assistant at sight. "Can you hold this while I take a peek?" he asked nervously.

"Sure!" Smith helpfully jumped into place while Del ran out of the men's room. He was back moments later with a sad face. "The robot is having difficulty finding a maintenance worker!"

Amerlee, while trying to appear pleasant, not the least bothered by approving male looks, wondered around. It was a typical unimaginative layout and decoration she came to use to; darker carpet on the floor, the walls having a brown plastic cover up to the neck. Ceiling was white as usual and on the plus side the occasional flower baskets on the hallway seemed to be real, not just a fake plastic or a disappointing hologram. A young man showed up from the men's room and practically ran past her. He was short, but round not just around the waist but his face too. He mumbled something like sorry and he was past the corner. She barely recovered from the event when he came back, running again; his face full of worry as he disappeared into the opening. Somehow, he was the kind of person Smith would befriend for some strange reason and since the last time she saw him was thru the same opening; she decided to look inside. She was not scared or nervous. If it would turn out to be a bunch of guys inside, she would just be pretending to be lost. Plenty would offer her help; she was sure of it. Interestingly, inside the men's room the carpet was replaced by a shiny slim marble floor. The dark feeling remained, but the matte bricks on the walls reached until her shoulder, replacing by a gray to white painted wall until she turned in the corner and walked into the men's room, that was covered by a fancy plastic wrap. And by the looks of it, Smith was right there with his round sidekick holding the wall . . .

"Maybe I can do something here?" Smith turned around awkwardly to observe the off peeled section of the wall covering when Del began to continuously tap his shoulder.

"What is it?" he asked, clearly annoyed, then still holding the big sheet he turned back while explaining himself: "Look, I think I can use my power, but if you keep bugging me I just . . . Hi!" he suddenly noticed Amerlee standing at the corner mustering them.

"Who is that chick? I saw you two together before . . ." Del was floored by her presence.

"The chick has a name . . ." Amerlee took a step forward.

"She is hot!" Del uttered to Smith, who began to sweat. This was not how he intended to introduce her to him. "Well, you see she is Amerlee, my . . ."

"His girlfriend." she finished his sentence, freezing both men dead in their tracks. "What were you two cohorts doing together in the men's room?" she scrutinized them both.

"Well . . ." Smith pointed at the wall.

"I have a perfectly good explanation!" Del recomposed himself while his right arm still held the decorative element.

"Smith, have you trying to cover for him?" she smiled a bit upon recognizing the rare motive behind his love's actions.

"Yes . . ." Smith gave up, seeing no real alternative to hide that from her.

Del was seemingly upset, because it painted him to be the troublemaker. Right at the first time he met her.

"So, you did something to the decorative element and now trying to hide the mess from your boss, is that it?" she asked Del directly.

He rapidly nodded: "Yes. Can you help too?" he misunderstood her.

"So, you're trying to cover up your mess from your supervisor who no doubt has to report to his boss, who reports to his one, and the summary goes all the way up to the owner of this building and company?" her index finger slowly moved from Del toward Smith.

"Shit!" The realization hit Del hard. He began to sweat uncontrollably.

"She is not just a pretty face, I meant to say that!" Smith was impressed by her handling the situation. He finally found the moment to 'see' at the molecular bonding level and make the permanent bond to literally fuse the decorative element to the underlying wall. A second later, the covering snapped into place. Del frowned: "Intelligent walls?"

"No. Intelligent woman!" Smith shook his head, then turned to Del: "Amerlee needs the printing business I know you are a master accountant. We need a rather quick print of a small batch of stuff for her."

"Okay, sure. I can make that happen right now!" Del tried to be as helpful as he could be after the realization of Smith being the ultimate owner hit him like a lightning! And the possible repercussions shall he decide to exercise his powers.

"Good!" Smith liked what he heard.

"I have the files on my IC, shall we?" Amerlee offered him the exit and Del flew past him like she was the devil. Once outside in the spacious hallway, his approaching boss bowed toward Smith: "My Lord! I am happy and grateful to see you on our floor!"

"Good. Um, Mr. Shaw . . ." Smith read his title card before continuing: "I will commandeer Mr. Del here for a side business I need him to be on. I hope it won't cause permanent delay on any project you charge of, right?"

"No. Not at all! How does My Lord know of him if I may ask?" his nosiness crept up.

Smith had to smile. *If he would only know*. "Let's just say we know each other pretty well, isn't that true, Del?" he turned toward the still sweating man.

"Yes, oh yes . . . Sir?"

"Call me Smith!" Smith dismissed his concerns, earning envy looks from Del's superior.

Suddenly his videophone went off. Smith frowned and activated the device: "Yes?" he listened for a second, then hung up.

"Mister Shaw, I'm apparently a busy man. Mrs. G just informed me that the President wants to speak to me, so I must go. It was nice to meet you!" he offered his hand and he could tell it was a parting gift Mr. Shaw was looking for. He accepted it with a deep bow and scurried away.

"Is the President really was looking for you?" Del uttered not looking toward him.

"Yes. Chibab wanted something, but I just did not want him around. Take me to your office or wherever you reside so I can call him back, please!"

"Oh, yesss!" Del tightened his fist and led them down the hallway full of cubicles where his co-workers worked, then into the corner where his cubicle was. Del's roaming space was a bit bigger and offered walls on two sides and a window to boast about.

"Your humor makes me laugh!" Smith sat down at his desk while Del ceremoniously gave full access to his workstation, hoping his co-workers saw his special guests.

"So, is this going to elevate you to stardom?" Amerlee noticed the meticulous nature Del was handling the matter.

"I hope so . . ."

"Do you have a girlfriend?"

"Yes!"

"Amazing!" she shook her head.

"Oh, so you like it, huh?" Smith talked to a mirror like device, a company vidphone.

While neither Amerlee nor Del could hear the full conversation as the speakers were directional, they could hear Smith's surprised voice. The man was delighted: "And you missed it yesterday? . . . ran out already? Well, I think we can remedy that. How bout I send a full product portfolio to your office via a courier from my PR department today? I don't have much but I promise you can get a sample from all of it!" Smith listened intently, then nodded: "So If I have an extra Type II, can I send that too? Okay. No problem, Ylahim!" he disconnected the call and glanced up to Amerlee. He impressively nodded: "Bravo honey. Your idea taking off despite my skepticism!"

"Was that about the caviar?" Amerlee hoped it was.

"Yes. He takes my limousine most of the time for official business and noticed that the complementary caviar was gone. He loved it and wanted to know if I have more. He loves it so much he wants to buy some if it becomes available!"

"Premium price, of course . . ." Amerlee began to calculate things.

"Well, the complementary line up is free of course!" Smith tried to sweeten the deal as he believed it needed ample of that.

"Of course. It's a good promotion. Del, my dear . . ." she turned to the melting young man beside her.

"Yes, Ma'am?" he whispered at her.

"We need to print some labels a.s.a.p!"

"Let's go!" Del turned around and began to practically run across the floor toward the main lobby.

"I guess your smile made him motivated!" Smith glanced up from Del's desk.

"Guess so!" she giggled.

"My smile doesn't make him that motivated, I wonder why . . ." Smith joked as they went after him.

Chapter Seventeen

Azure 2.0

While Amerlee amazed Del with her ideas and subsequent resourcefulness, Smith called Miss Thorne about sending someone to the Villa-Castle to pick up the caviar samples, then to deliver it to the President's personal residence. In a way, he was most impressed by Amerlee and her optimistic outlook on the caviar business. Thirty minutes later they parted with a bag of labels. More were on the way, as Del promised to print over a thousand overnight and deliver it to the Villa-Castle by the morning.

Being done with that business, he pushed her toward the elevators. She was fighting it mildly, knowing exactly where they were headed. The limo with Deril at the helm took them to the Sky Riders, a short ride within the city limits. A hovercraft picked them up and moments later landed in Dock E2 in the rear. Diana was waiting for them. She slightly bowed front of her while still sucking on a green lollipop. Smith seemingly did not care or did not notice it as out of the ordinary, so she pretended not to notice it either. Weird as Diana was, she acted surprisingly as a human, especially after apologizing for the scene when she was with her Smith in the high end clubbing, the Gaff, and back then she had to act as Smith's boss.

As Smith constantly walked faster, leaving her behind, Diana licked the swiftly disappearing lollipop and turned to her at a sudden moment: "I love lollipops. Smith programmed that into me before Plan B was activated . . ."

Amerlee squinted: "You are plan B, right?"

"Yes, this body. As you probably know, an AI is limited to do business and forbidden to give kill orders, all this stupid human made laws, so being created a human form he circumvented them. Pretty neat idea isn't it, especially from a human, huh?"

Amerlee was not sure she should be grateful for Smith's resourcefulness or be mortified.

Amerlee arrived with Diana to the room; two rooms down the hall from the so-called Control Room, she had no idea what it was. She had a vague idea they were above the Twin Cities, but also behind it. Since she did not see anyone on the empty corridors, she deducted this was not open to the public. Two battle droids held the door, and she walked past them rather shyly, having heard of their fearsome capabilities. None of them moved. Diana stayed to her left, while Smith cautiously approached the clear tube, holding a delicate female body inside of it. There was a breathing tube attached to the mouth as the body was suspended into some kind of gooey emulsion. Amerlee spotted movement, but Smith grabbed her hand: "Hold my hand tight. She has to see we are together, in unity, as soon as she opens her eyes!"

"Okay . . ." she was unsure of it. She was unsure of herself too. The female body was naked and surprisingly beautiful for her taste. It was awkward, to say the least . . .

"Go ahead!" Smith nodded toward Diana, who just watched them. But something did happen. The tubing opened, releasing the emulsion and the naked body onto the tile floor. The liquid quickly disappeared into the small holes in the floor. Smith helpfully held a towel toward the coughing and wet girl.

She coughed relentlessly. She fought her own senses hard to open her eyes as she sensed something strange: there were three humans in the room! One of them walked away, but two remained. One of them was her Smith, her eternal lover, but there was another female and her mental signature was unknown to her. She brushed aside her wet hair, smiled to greet Smith, but her smile froze to her face as she noticed the tall, slender woman beside him. And to her shock, they were holding each other's hands! She was gasping for air; he had a woman already! Things like how long she was under flashed thru her mind.

"Breathe!" she heard Smith's commanding voice, and she gave in to him. The coughing stopped, and he gently gave her a big towel. She accepted it. She felt naked, beyond the fact that she was indeed naked. She was embarrassed as Smith introduced her to Amerlee.

She gouged her like she was about to kill her.

Smith saw that, and the mental onslaught almost knocked her to the ground: 'NO!'

"So . . . Sorry." Azure held her head, as the pressure wanted to spit her brain in half.

"What's wrong with her?" The girl beside him seemed to worry about her state. *Nice* . . . She thought.

"I'm fine!" Azure winced. The pain was gone. "Who are you?"

"I'm Amerlee Zoon. Smith's girlfriend . . ." she seemed uncomfortable upon saying. Azure almost smiled. Amerlee must've heard of her talent. *Good*!

"That's right Azure, she is mine, just like you!" Smith stepped closer.

The devastation inside her brain muted. "What?" It instantly turned into swirling madness; madness directed toward Smith.

"I need you. I need you as a friend, as a worker, my Personal Family Bodyguard and as a girlfriend!" Smith hoped to clarify everything in one sentence.

"You never liked multiple relationships . . ." It dawned on Azure.

"You dealt with Aa before!" he reminded her and with that her bad mood reappeared.

Smith saw or felt that about her because he continued with a gentler tone: "Let us escort you to the observation room. You only have forty-eight hours and after that you on a mission with me!" Smith added as he offered his hand.

She made the physical connection to him and immediately felt stronger.

It however did not go unnoticed for Amerlee, who scoffed upon seeing those two holding hands. She quietly followed them down the hall, to the left and into a small bedroom. The walls were oval at certain corners; the ceiling was not flat, and it irked Amerlee for some unknown reason.

Azure laughed, knowing exactly what she found so alien. “Honey, those whom built this weren’t humans, just appeared to be. These Starships were their own domains, built to their specifications. It’s useless to try to make sense of it. Your human logic would never get the satisfaction out of that brainstorm!”

Amerlee just stared at the girl, knowing she was right. Smith, being tight-lipped, told all about it to her.

“Azure . . .” Smith finally spoke and Azure turned to him instantly: “Yes?” she asked with a honey voice.

“Listen, it’s been couple months since you were killed in action. About four, to be precise. Your body is eighteen years old, but otherwise everything should be the same. Diana will be in later to do all those torturing tests she had done the first time you were here, okay?”

Azure nodded obediently as she got into the bed. She even pulled the sheets up to her neck.

“Azure, Amerlee is about to stay, you better get used to it! I’ll be back later to talk to you alone!” Smith left with Amerlee in his hands.

Azure was quietly weeping. *Perhaps I have done something horrible that he gave up on me . . .*

“Are you really going back to her room alone?” Amerlee was not sure she heard that right. As far as she was concerned, they could be already hooking up behind her back! The fact that Smith was supposed to take her to some fancy restaurant did not make a dent in her gut feeling.

“Look at you!” Smith frowned after shaking his head, thinking about her jealousy. “I have to talk to her alone.”

"About me?"

"About herself. It is between her and me."

"Why?"

"Because . . ." Smith left it at that. It became too complicated to explain her. Azure and he had history. Long, deep, convoluted history . . .

*

Smith slowly walked up to her bed. She appeared to be in sleep. Her eyes were closed; her skin soft and clean like a baby's. But as he hovered over her, Azure eyes snapped open. She pulled up herself, letting the sheet uncover her shapely breasts: "Yes, my master?"

Smith flinched and pulled up her sheet. As he was doing it, she pushed it down to her chest, rubbing it along the way. She tried to observe him both mentally and visually. Both feelings were there; yearning for lust and anger, but the later one seemed to be the stronger one, so she discontinued the exercise.

"I said earlier, four months" Smith began like a teacher, "Amerlee is my girlfriend now."

"But you said I am yours too . . ." she was openly disappointed.

"Awkward, I know. It was not how I imagined it would be."

"Both of us in your bed?" she glanced into his face, ready to kiss him.

"Not that." he frowned. "Rather that I would hook up with Amerlee. It was not supposed to happen, but oh well . . ." he smiled, "I'm so glad I did. She is an amazing woman!"

Azure felt akin to be stabbed in the heart. It was painful for her to listen, but understood he developed serious feelings toward Amerlee. "How long was I . . . ?" She asked to break the silence.

"Four months. I'm glad Diana uploaded your memories to the data crystal just before the . . ."

"Yes, it was a great idea. I still remember my anger toward you as you hung with Captain Aa while I was back on training."

"Ah . . ." Smith would rather forget that.

"Okay, I see that isn't making you happy. We had a slight rift than."

"You wanted too much party. I was busy!" Smith replied bluntly, and it felt good.

"I felt it too."

"But you don't remember what happened after, do you?"

"No. Just blank . . ." she realized.

"I tried to make up to you. We hung out on a hillside facing an empty beach and the Ocean, right on Down Earth. We made love in the open." he smiled.

Azure giggled.

"Then I left you in charge of a mission."

"A real mission?" Azure became all ears.

"That's right. It was heavily organized, dealing with the Trust or rather its loose end."

"Oh, that's right. Tata?"

"He got reunited with his children. It partially tied to that and to the Aragon Corp. We found out of their true misbehaving and while the Ancient Man was cleaning ranks at the Admiralty, I was tasked to bring back the funds. I had to take personal command of the operation on the CTP, to thwart off telepaths, keeping Josh and Aa safe, but that could only happen once Commander Tri'ng retrieved the necessary information from the AOCP banking network. You, my darling, were in charge of another retrieving operation on an AOCP planet. Agent Sasha was your captive!"

"Was Nyikha there?" she slipped.

Smith smiled. "Yes. You requested her presence. Hunter Paradise was there too . . ." he observed her face, but she did not bite down, no expression changes, nothing that would indicate her devotion toward him. "Well, you must talk to him, because I told him he would see you again, and he did not get it."

Azure laughed. "Imagine his scared boyish face!"

"Imagine that . . ." Smith was less enthusiastic.

"So, what happened to me?"

"You were killed in action. You guys got the money and transferred the funds, but there were some complications and AOCP forces were onto you and your team. It was a partial setup from the bank administrator who had some complicated side dealings with Agent Sasha. Bullets were flying, and you saw something that did not catch Hunter's eyes. You jumped to protect him and died in his hands!"

"Aw. It was so sweat from me. I must have had a momentary lapse of judgment." she referred to her kindness of protecting someone other than Smith.

"Perhaps . . ." Smith thought entirely different.

"What's our assignment?" she was ready for battle.

"Hold your horses! Diana has to okay your leave first. Then before we would embark to the Green Void, not far from Danal IV to deal with something inherently fishy, I need you on something!"

"Anything, my darling!" her sweet smile reappeared.

"Diana will give you all pertinent information regarding to the Green Void and Josh's involvement there so far. I need you to brainstorm with me on that one . . ."

"Does Amerlee suiting up for this too? What's her specialty? Sword fights?" she was mentally already getting ready for any fight Smith was willing to bring her in on.

Smith's frown deepened with every question she asked. Eventually she noticed it; "What?"

"Amerlee will come, but won't engage directly with us. I plan to keep her with Captain Aa on the sideline . . ."

"That won't go well."

"No. Aa already met Amerlee when I needed her help to repair Amerlee's arm. Unfortunately, or not, Aa seems to be Amerlee's hero!"

Azure shook her hair: "Oh, boy!"

"Captain Aa already showed her some interesting Emperorish stuff. I guess they're bonding well . . ." Smith shrugged.

"Is that a directive from you?"

"Could be . . ."

"Great. So, Captain Aa is still in the picture, huh?"

"Definitely! She is my apprentice!"

Azure made a pig face, expressing her dislike. "What's Amerlee's specialty?" she realized Smith never answered to her.

"She is a businesswoman I guess with an underground car racing background."

"Is that a joke?" Azure was not sure he meant it or not.

"No. Not a joke." he shook his head. "So, before we go to space, I need you on one very important event and you can't mess this up!" he lifted his index finger as a warning to her.

"I'm all ears!" she responded immediately.

That same evening Del dropped by the Villa-Castle where Henry desperately tried to figure out where to put Azure and her belongings once she would arrive the next day.

Amerlee accompanied Smith to the Toxic, sitting beside the estate where Del was offloading crates after crates of printed cover labels and some boxing samples for the seven types of caviar. Amerlee liked two of them and told him to go ahead and make five hundred copies right away.

She was still checking the labels when Del pulled Smith aside: "Um, can I ask you a personal favor?"

"I am all ears!" Smith replied naively.

"It's about Jott . . ."

"What about him?" Smith's mood darkened.

"Is there a way you could employ him somewhere after all?"

"Del . . ." Smith sighed. "I told you both that there was one last chance left to work for me. He declined. Now if I offer him a job, I just backtracked on my words. How does that look coming from the Emperor?" he leaned forward for added emphasis, scaring Del.

"Well . . . I don't know?" he pulled his mouth.

"Me either."

"They're having money problems and I can't help as Tilla and I are looking to start a family." he blushed.

"Great!" Smith slapped his back so hard Amerlee turned toward them. She was intrigued by Del's continued presence. She walked closer to listen into their conversation. What she understood shocked her:

"Tell you what. There might be a low-level position opening as an assistant engineering for your department, as you have to do more work for me in the foreseeable future."

"I do? I mean, I do!" he nodded upon realizing what that meant.

"It doesn't pay that well as yours and it's a part-time job, but it will go on the board tomorrow. I'll make arrangements from the Villa-Castle. Have his resume turned in first thing tomorrow morning!"

"I'm so thank you and in your debt!" Del hugged him unexpectedly, then to cover his embarrassment he added: "You know ever since Adele lost her sister, Sally . . . She is still reeling from the loss of her sister and it's taking a toll on their relationship."

Smith emphatically nodded.

Amerlee just stood there, barely breathing upon hearing of Sally's name. So that was the connection! Agent Sasha was the sister of Jott's girlfriend who had dealings with her Smith! It was also obvious to her; Smith did not tell the entire truth about Agent Sasha's fake demise to Del either.

*

"Are you ready for tomorrow?" Smith asked Amerlee over their late breakfast. They were back to the routine of eating after nine o'clock together.

Clouds emerged on Amerlee's smooth forehead as she reminded herself of the 'event'.

Smith read her face. "Good. Remember, no matter how hard will I try to be empathetic, I am the Emperor!"

"I know . . ." she shunted her eyes, then she remembered to something: "Does Azure is in the loop?"

“She is now! She is working from her observation room to get the show rolling. You should check your e-mail she had some horrific ideas about dressing both of you the same way to floor your parents!” he winked.

Amerlee became uncomfortable in her chair. “What do you mean horrific ideas?”

“All I had to do is tell her your parents acted not nice when I was invited to their house to re-channel her anger toward them. This way you are off the hook and she will be the most professional body guard you’ve ever seen. She already asked for the best senior cadets via Miss Fontana for the gig.”

Amerlee rolled her eyes. “Is that show really necessary?”

“I am the dreaded Emperor. I have to look mean when mean is necessary . . .” Smith tried to be funny, but by the next day upon seeing both of the girls in matching deep cherry red evening dress, he began to have other ideas as well.

Chapter Eighteen

Payback Time

Magol helped his wife Melonie out of the sleek limousine. He expected a deserted front yard to the Emperor's Villa-Castle, but as it turned out, his deep wish to take a photograph of it was shot down. He swallowed hard upon seeing the meticulously neat row of military men and women standing on their sides, lined up from their car to the steps where an awful young girl in a stunningly vowed deep red dress welcomed them. In a way, he had the distinct feeling, the girl gazed past them even when she addressed Zoon Magol: "Welcome to the estate. My name is Azure; rescuer, and bodyguard of our beloved Emperor! Please follow me inside!" she escorted them up on the steps, inside the towering building. "Toilets and bathrooms are to your right!" she turned around and pointed to her left.

Magol and Melonie glanced at each other, then Melonie quietly disappeared behind the ladies' door.

Zoon Magol waited in silence, and while waiting he spotted a limousine's arrival thru the big windows. Another stunning young woman in a lovely deep blue dress stepped out of it.

Zoon admired her beautifully shaped ankles when Azure stepped forward and uttered: "She is Miss Emma Thorne, the Emperor's personal liaison in the PR department."

"Does the Emperor have a business to conduct before our lunch?" Zoon tried to decipher something here.

"Oh, absolutely not! She is here upon My Lord's request. She is serving papers to you, sir!" Azure tried to act like it was normal, but Zoon Magol scoffed: "Business papers?"

"I was told it was about something you and him agreed before." she added, trying to be as innocent as she could.

"Must be mistaken, dear, I have never met the Emperor before today!" Magol was sure of that.

Azure quietly smiled, but it turned into a sinister one. She patiently waited until the wife emerged from the bathroom and let Magol's wife take his husband's hand then added before turning around to lead them to the Winter Wing: "The Emperor never mistaken; only mortals do . . ."

"What was that about, my darling?" she uttered into his ears, but he never responded.

Something was never right from the beginning. He felt it before, and now the same feelings crept up again. He barely took notice of the solid golden ornaments along their path to the wing that was redressed for the occasion. They moved the tables to the side and placed a massive wooden table in the middle. It was old and dark, meticulously aged to look like a few hundred years old. In reality, it was barely twenty and Magol knew the designer firm well; he ordered his wife's work desk from them. It cost a fortune. There was a gracefully aged butler to their left, standing by the table's corner. Across the long table, beyond the candles and the lunch baskets, a man and a woman stood facing away from them, according to tradition. What caught Magol's attention was the fact that the Emperor's bodyguard, Miss Azure, had the same stunning dress as the Emperor's female companionship. He barely had time to point that out to his wife when the two women and the man in the middle turned around.

"Shit . . ." Magol blinked hard, suppressing his thoughts.

His wife went so pale he was seriously worried she would faint.

"Welcome to my humble estate!" The Emperor offered their seats without the customary smile. "My butler, Henry will accommodate your needs thru out the lunch!" he pointed at the man standing at the corner. He bowed slightly.

"Hello Daddy!" Amerlee smiled shyly, standing by Smith's right.

Magol swallowed hard.

"Before they would serve the appetizer and the soup, I would just like to point out that your daughter's arm was regrown just as I promised some time ago!"

Melonie clenched her husband's fingers. She knew this was a payback lunch . . . There was nothing to do but to endure the show now. She glanced up at him and she could tell the same thoughts flashed across his mind.

Amerlee lifted her left arm, showing the smooth skin and the tight muscles beneath it. She rubbed her right hand from her palm to her shoulder. "All in one. It is real. Captain Aa from the XXVI UNHL Fleet and Smith initiated my dormant stem cells to work and created my arm along with the pathways so I can command them at my will!" she explained, calling the Emperor on his human name, a privilege only a few could get away with.

Her father stood so stiff he could pass to be a tree in the forest. Her mother was equally frightened, but managed to say: "I am delighted, Amerlee!"

"Now about our business!" The Emperor signaled to Miss Thorne to step out of the shadows with two pieces of smart paper. She walked to Zoon Magol and presented them. The Emperor spoke instead of her: "Sing it, place it to your eyes and fingerprint it at the bottom of each page. One copy is yours, the other is going to the National Archive as an official document between me and you. As I said when we shook hands that night, less than three months ago, you will not be able to use the fame of your daughter's miraculous recovery to your own advantage. You will not gain anything from her wellbeing!"

Zoon authenticated the documents, then cleared his throat: "I stand corrected, My Lord!"

“So, do I! My Lord!” His wife chirped all of a sudden. It was Amerlee and not the Emperor who reprimanded her; “No one asked your opinion, mom!”

“Now, that we conclude the business part . . .” The Emperor waited until Miss Thorne hurried away with the papers, then continued: “The lunch shall begin with a toast to the majestic Monarch!”

They waited until Henry poured from the single bottle, he preciously placed in front of the guests, then lifted their special glasses, with the pale green more like yellowish, sparkling delicacy, and toasted for the health of the UNHL as well.

Amerlee tried to taste every molecule of the wildly expensive Deghna. She of course drank it before, shared a glass with her then boyfriend. Ten thousand credits for a bottle. It was meant as a way to spend insane amounts of money. She often wondered whether Smith ever drank it, but from the looks of it, he was familiar with its mildly hallucinogen properties. He offered the remainder of the bottle for her parents to drink from as they please, adding that there was plenty more in the basement. She knew they would never ask, and that it was nothing but a cleverly addressed insult. Just as Smith said to her before, he would go out of his way to show his might and he did!

The five-course lunch was magnificent, the cakes were equally stunning, but she felt nothing but anger toward her parents. They must’ve felt awful, but tried hard not to show it.

When it was time to leave, it was the Emperor who walked up to them and offered his hand: “I hope you enjoyed this quick lunch as much as we did; it was time we were both acquainted with each other the proper way!”

“Yes, My Lord!” Magol replied akin to someone who saw a ghost.

“The pleasure was mine, ma’am!” The Emperor kissed his wife’s hand. Smith saw the fear in her eyes, the trembling lips, the crisscrossing thoughts in her brain. He had to mute some of those fears, otherwise she would’ve collapsed right in front of him on the floor.

"It was all so picturesque!" Amerlee said afterwards.

"You think so?" Smith and Azure asked the same time, then Smith added: "My ladies, you both look so stunning in this dress!"

Amerlee smiled and Azure seemed relieved, but within their brains they were both thinking about the first night . . . A little worried and a little excited at the same time. The bed was big enough for four people, but they both wondered how to address the question. It turned out to be addressed by no other than Smith himself, who ordered them into his bed around ten o'clock. Azure slept on his left while Amerlee was on his right. Azure was up before both of them, grabbing a bacon and egg sandwich from the kitchen when she ran into Henry and into his arms.

"Mistress Azure . . ." Henry managed to say.

"Yes?" she smiled at him warmly.

"Nothing," he managed to catch himself. "How was the night?"

"Disappointing one might would say, but at least I slept well!" she imitated yawning.

Henry seemingly took the hints and smiled along with her.

Azure bit into her lips, "Hey Henry, what's the customs say about a girl sleeping in the significant left or right side?"

"Mistress Azure, just like at the table, the arrangement was specific. Only the more significant one can stand on the right from the man . . ." he shut up upon realizing it demoted Azure's standing with Smith. He quickly added, "I hope you will stay with us

forever . . ."

"I hope so too!" Azure was not so sure anymore, but for the time being she would do anything to please Smith.

Chapter Nineteen

A Minor Detail

Azure was watching them from the corner. They were all sitting in various seats on the Toxic's bridge. Smith brought four Death Squad members, possibly thinking along of something bad, worrisome she imagined. He seemed to be relaxed, even joked with her, but she deflected it, paid him no mind. It was obvious he considered Amerlee's presence more of an annoyance than pleasantries, but he did his best to hide it. She wondered whether he actually knew what he was doing or was that all his sub consciousness doing it. He remained vague about Amerlee's past beyond the fact the two hooked up via his PR department. She found it annoying. Now she had to share! She sought for a one on one with Toxic to discuss this annoying matter, but as so far that chance eluded her.

Suddenly they dropped out of light speed, the selected choice of traveling from Smith today, and amid the twinkling of the stars she spotted an SPD with couple Planet Destroyers around it. She zoomed in with her enhanced eyes, but to her surprise it was not the DU, it was the Trixec! She turned toward Smith, who saw her reaction and nodded, "Yes, it's the Trixec. I have something to do first . . ."

Azure wondered about, then realized he would find Aa's companionship most embarrassing under the circumstances provided by the Trixec in regard to the Toxic and just had to smile.

"What?" Smith sensed something coming from her.

"I guess you want no groupies from look-alike twins, huh?" she winked. It must have hit a bull's eye, because he blushed.

The conversation did not go unnoticed by Amerlee, who suspected something was going on between them. She frowned, wanted to ask something, but then Azure shot her down: "Yeah, that would really throw a switch in your brain!"

Amerlee's frown deepened. "What does Azure mean by?" she asked from Smith, who tried to downplay the significance of the entire conversation. "Nothing," he said.

Amerlee was about to let it all go, but then Toxic's hologram formed to Smith's right, flexing her holo fingers: "I can't wait to step onboard! How long do you need to do your thing, honey?" she pretended to massage Smith's back.

"Hey!" he brushed off his shoulder. "Dunno. Maybe half a day . . . I need the Trixec's special capabilities to do a couple of things."

Upon hearing it, Toxic's mood darkened. "You better physically dock then!"

"I planned to!" he responded amid questioning looks from Amerlee. While she got no direct response, she watched Smith navigating the DSR himself as they landed inside the Super Planet Destroyer's Starboard POD.

Upon landing, Smith grabbed his utterly slim briefcase and made physical contact with Amerlee. "We're here to do business with the Admiral of the XXVI UNHL Fleet. His name is Admiral Tarbuk. While he is a polite and cunning character, I would exercise caution around him . . ." he uttered into her ear, but of course both Toxic and Azure heard it. As he walked out of the bridge Azure walked by and uttered into her ears amid laughing; "Yeah, his family has many sex parlors back at their home planet!"

"Come on, frightened sister!" Toxic's hologram encouraged her by continuously brushing her hologram hands over her shoulder.

"Was Azure telling the truth?" Amerlee asked while walking on wobbly legs.

"I can hear that!" Azure chimed in from the distance.

"Hear what?" Apparently, Smith was deep in his thoughts, unable to assess the girl's talk.

"Yes, my dear, but there are multiple surprises awaiting you!" The hologram added.

"Like what?" Amerlee stepped out into the pristine environment. The dock was deserted, apparently was not much traffic there at the moment. Still, the view had to sink in for her, so she did not notice how Toxic's hologram changed into a solid skin and bone type of entity. Smith squinted, apparently scanning for any welcoming party, but they were absent. The next moment somebody forcefully kissed him.

"What, the?!" he pushed the face off of his face to get a better look at who the person was.

"Captain Aa?!" Amerlee looked at Smith with her big eyes, seemingly startled, a bit angered.

"Not, honey!" Toxic smiled and withdrawn, apparently reached her goal already. It upset Smith on the other hand: "Hold your horses, Toxic!"

"Toxic?" Amerlee was confused.

"Party time!" Azure glimmered, remembering past times.

"Toxic is right, Amerlee!" The woman walked back to her and began to play with Amerlee's long hair until she swayed her head, apparently annoyed by the displayed overenthusiasm.

"But how?" Amerlee asked.

"The makers of this fine ship allowed me to exist in a fully human form!" Toxic shrugged.

"Down Earth?" Amerlee was confused. Smith was about to tell her something when an overly enthusiastic young man ran up to them, saluted hard, then bowed: "My Lord! I am Commander Delhun, I oversee the pilots on the Trixec. I just want to let you know that the Admiral is on his way. He did not expect your presence and as such it caught him off guard!"

"It's okay Commander, just tell him we are waiting for him at the . . ." he pointed across the wide deck, toward the forward corridor into the body of the Trixec.

"Got it, My Lord! Again, welcome onboard!" he ran away, presumably to notify the Admiral. Amerlee watched the scene, trying to remember every piece of it.

"Let's get to the nearest terminal!" Smith began to trek across the hangar deck, Azure right behind him.

Amerlee and Toxic walked a bit farther back.

"You can exist like a human, flesh and bone?" Amerlee asked from her, drawing the conclusion.

"Yeah. I am planning to get permission from Smith, to visit the galley. I love to consume food!" She already dreamed of it, Amerlee could tell.

"Wait, now when you return to your ship . . ."

"Yeah, the bugger is, I return to be as a hologram only!" Toxic finished the sentence.

"What about the food?"

"Well, that's a great question, one that if I were to explain, you would need a bachelor's degree from advanced robotics-genetics, a field of study, not yet invented!"

"A what?"

"Amerlee, my darling!" Smith finally stopped as they reached the other end of the flight deck.

"Yes?"

"Look at this terminal, would you?" he pointed beside him. Amerlee swiped her hand over the terminal and it came to life. "Nice product, apparently a 3D version!" she began to utilize. "Great response, better than what I expected!"

"That's because . . ."

"Sssh!" Smith muted the overeager Azure before she could spill the beans.

"So, you have been on the Destination Unknown recently and also on the Atlantis. Have you seen this technology anywhere?" Smith questioned the brunette.

"Well, come to think of it, I only saw that on the DU's bridge . . ." Amerlee wondered aloud.

"Bingo!" Smith nodded.

"So?" Amerlee was still in the dark.

"The DU was recently launched. The Trixec is twenty years older, yet if you go on and observe, every kiosk is 3D on this

ship . . ." Smith admitted.

"Maybe because if they did right after the war; her keel was laid during the chaos, at the last six months, and perhaps the order was mixed up, no?"

"Come on, honey! They operated things in emergency mode; payment was highly uncertain. You would think they were skipping on things, wouldn't you?"

Amerlee frowned. "But the kiosks all 3D, maybe

because . . ."

"I see you are one of the less out of the box kind of thinkers, aren't you?"

"What's that supposed to mean?!" Amerlee jumped on the defensive.

"It means you don't know jack!" Azure giggled from the background.

"Hey!" Smith shouted at her, then continued nicer, turning back at Amerlee; "This ship, while it bears the name of Trixec, is not the same that was manufactured after the war!"

"What? Wait, a minute . . ." Amerlee seemed lost, then shook her head. "Nobody can re manufacture an entire SPD unnoticed. I heard the Valencia took almost five years to build!"

"True, but never less this Super Planet Destroyer is a re-manufactured one. The original blew up in a battle some years ago, but it was a very important space ship, so important that the powers to be decided that it was necessary to recreate it for me to use it again. However, these powers to be lived so far in the future, they forgot that in this time frame the 3D kiosks were practically nonexistent."

"What? Wait . . . The future linear bullshit again? Are you out of your mind?" Amerlee remained skeptical or rather confused, remembering her recent conversation about Azure's emergence into his love's life.

It did not help that Azure along the Toxic had a blast of amusements.

Amerlee could not protest any longer as Admiral Tarbuk showed up, bowing deeply.

After the short introduction when the shocked Tarbuk learned the brunette beside Smith was his girlfriend and not his secretary, Smith told him of his real reason to be here: "We need to make a quick jump, four to five months into the past preferably. I will take care of the calculations. All I need from you is to make the necessary preparations!"

"Are we looking for trouble?"

Smith had to smile. He asked his question many times involving time jumps, and he used to answer something along the line that 'don't we always', but this time he seriously doubted it.

Admiral Tarbuk recommended sailing with the Trinity and the new Executor only. Smith agreed.

"So Tarbuk, how is the new Executor?"

"Captain Murdoch took command of the ship. He is happy he no longer does power shares! It's an even more modified Victory IV.2D, with beefed up weapons around its bridge. They're hologram based. Very effective if I may add! It also has rail guns!"

"Good. Glad to hear it. Tell it to my Amerlee this ship isn't the same as the original, would you?"

"Oh, of course!" The pale blue humanoid bowed toward Amerlee. "This is a re-manufactured Trixec. The original perished about seven years ago in a battle against the AOCP."

"But we've been at a standoff less than five years!" Amerlee disagreed.

"Well, honey, the Emperor has some interesting bed time stories than . . ." Admiral Tarbuk shrugged and was about to leave. He paused for a moment, then turned back: "The most noticeable modifications are the 3D holo kiosks, but the galley's protein generators are equally interesting. They contain recipes for foods from races I never heard of. And according to their data banks, they belong to the UNHL. So, I would look behind every panel for a surprise if I were you." he turned around and left.

As soon as he got outside of earshot, Toxic began to inch toward Smith: “Can I? Please, I just want to go to the . . .”

“Go and eat food!” Smith shook his head, then grabbed Azure’s and Amerlee’s hand. “Let’s get to the BASEMENT!”

“What is the basement? Does a spaceship have one?” Amerlee naively asked, but was floored once inside the central elevator shaft. Then they arrived at a place she never heard of. Her amazement reached new heights once she was told they were no longer onboard the SPD! Her mouth hung wide as Smith and Azure jumped into their seats in the big room, full of holo-screens. It took Smith couple seconds to initialize the entire system, while Admiral Tarbuk executed a mini jump about fifty light years. All they needed to do is get out of the prying eyes. Then Smith began the countdown from two minutes as the Temporal Time Displacement Generator spun up and the SPD’s two side gondolas revealed the stunning Christmas tree looking engines. When the clock vibrated with all zeroes, a black hole kind of anomaly formed directly across the SPD’s path. The trio sailed across and moments later Azure reported that they were back in time, about five months.

Smith wasted no time and first called Diana, told her to begin forming a new Azure as Diana affirmed the girl was there just the other day to save her memories on a data crystal.

As soon as that was done, Smith made an encrypted call to Admiral Qaw and told him a date and a request to send the two usual DSRs to Captain Aa’s location. Once he finished with it, he withdrew, thinking of what else he should accomplish while in the past, then as nothing else came to his mind, he revved up the TTDG once more.

Chapter Twenty

The Green Void

"It was amazing, simply amazing!" Amerlee swayed her head as she walked beside Smith. Azure giggled from the background, then abruptly stopped: "Hey, honey, that isn't the way to the Toxic!"

Smith stopped, then said, "No. I decided to eat in the galley!"

"Galley?" Echoed Amerlee, sounding disappointed.

"Mass kitchen . . ." Azure flinched, then added, "Officers only, though!" she tried to sound with ample upbeat.

Amerlee frowned. "We eat with the officers?"

"Got to eat somewhere . . ." Smith hopped into the Pearl Train, the exclusive feature of the newer SPDs. A train running along it's keel to deliver humans and life forms to the destination in no time. Once inside the pearl shaped car, he shrugged: "Besides, I need to beat some time before Baby and her crew arrives."

"They're coming too?" Azure seemed to be surprised.

"I presume I will need all the professional help I could get!" Smith explained.

"More than we can provide?" Amerlee frowned.

Upon hearing her question, Smith's mood became gloomy. Azure felt his mental eruption. It was more than she expected. *So, Smith really won't take her* . . . Azure realized. In a way she was relieved; a job with Smith alone. And in a way she was also relieved: Amerlee won't be in harm's way. The next moment, she caught herself. *Shit, now I like her too!* She made a face and decided to stay out of the upcoming fight.

Smith got out the pearl train first, then turned around to help Amerlee get out.

"I'm fine!" Azure hopped out. She waved into the air, "Love birds first!"

Smith scoffed, but never less obeyed. He put his arm around Amerlee's shoulder: "I so want to talk to you about this mission!"

"How can I help?" She glanced up at him, hoping he would say something she could reply to.

"Oh, boy . . ." Azure began to slow down to give them ample space.

"You seem to be upset!" Smith watched Amerlee eating from a tray. The food was not bad; she was actually delightedly surprised of its quality. She stopped eating and placed the fork beside the tray before looking into Smith's eyes. "You never intended to take me with you, do you?"

"Not this time, sadly, no . . ." Smith shook his head, trying to look apologetic. Luckily, the galley was practically deserted, and somehow Azure decided to take up the northern corner all by herself. He lowered his voice: "Azure comes with me because she is a soldier girl. She has been in rough situations before." he saw she wanted to say something, so he quieted himself.

Her voice was shaky, probably from all kinds of emotions: "I love you. I can't be a soul mate unless I go with you wherever you go! I want to stand with you!"

"It's nice, but . . ." he stopped, thinking about how to form the words. He seemingly found the right thread, because when he continued, he hit a different tone. ". . . but I have to protect you. You don't know how to respond to various threatening situations, you don't know how to fight back, heck, you don't even know how to shoot!"

"So, is that it? If I learn how to shoot, I can go with you the next time?"

"I like your persistence, but see Azure is replaceable, you aren't!" he shook his head.

"I want to go with you the next time! I will learn!" she was adamant to the point he nodded, apparently giving in. "Captain Aa will teach you all she can. If you can pass her tests and she vouch for you, then yes, you can!"

Amerlee stared at him, eyes big, thinking if it will ever happen. Her hero was both a professional and the Emperor's apprentice. It was highly unlikely she would learn as much as to pass her undoubtedly rigorous tests. She won't tell that to Smith, that was for sure!

"Look . . ." Smith softened his tone. "I'm worried of you. I don't want to see you get hurt, that's all!"

"Do you love me?" she asked shyly.

"I do!" Smith uttered.

Amerlee smiled and moved over to the table to kiss him.

The fork in Azure hand just popped as her muscles folded than broke it in half.

*

Captain Aa took a sweeping look across her bridge. The officers worked diligently, fluently, and mostly without her direct guidance. It was her time! She fought hard for this twenty-four-hour off period. Her SPD, the Destination Unknown, encircled Danal IV, along with her support ships of two SCCs from Captain Josh Kulighan's forces; a pocket frigate and a resupply ship. She heard nothing further from Josh regarding to his troubles in the Green Void. She assumed he was cycling thru his theories after the latest loss . . . Admiral Tarbuk okayed her request just yesterday. She was hoping she wouldn't have to postpone the exercise. It supposed to help her learn more about human capabilities of the extreme. There was this exercise she hoped to master, but to keep herself in shape, she had to repeat it every so often. Commander Danek rigorously watched her officers, then without turning to his commanding officer, he said, "It will be fine, Captain! We will keep your ship in one piece!"

"What can go wrong, huh?" she half joked, then the two of them retreated to the Ready Room in the rear, where she transferred her powers to him. Commander Danek ceremoniously turned to a holo display in the left corner. A giant red clock began to tick back from 24:00. "The clock is running, Ma'am!" He saluted ceremoniously. That was her cue to leave. She was about to turn around when the Communications Officer reported, "Two DSRs from the XXXII UNHL Fleet just came out of hyperspace. They request to speak to Captain Aa!"

At the mentioning of her name, Aa's face turned longer. She squinted, took a hesitant half step toward the door before signaling with her hand: "Put me up on the screen!" she spoke to Commander Danek, "I don't think this is going according to the script!"

"Not yet . . ." The Commander hoped this misunder-standing could be cleared in a timely manner, but as soon as the DSR's commanding officer showed up on a personal screen, his Captain's face went thru a transformation, and not the best one either, Danek observed.

"What can I do for you, Colonel Re'kl?" Aa defiantly crossed hands on her chest.

"We were ordered by Admiral Qaw to report to you for further instructions!"

The reply so shocked Aa, she glanced at Commander Danek, before asking: "Your companion is Captain Mya?"

"That would be correct, Ma'am!" The Colonel nodded, a shade of relief on his face.

"Do you know if the Emperor made the request to send you guys here?" she asked.

"Yes, about six months ago!"

Aa had to gulp for air. This was bad . . . Something must've happened for Smith to travel back in time! This was definitely unscheduled. But then again, why only two small DSRs if he was aware of something horribly bad? She reasoned Smith wouldn't be far behind, but she had to hand over the situation to her XO. She ought to, before it would get out of hand and she would have to postpone her exercise. They prepared the ice slabs for tonight's workout, and she hated the idea of sacrificing it all. "Commander Danek will take care of you, as I am on leave for the next twenty-four hours!"

"Understood!" Re'kl responded, then added: "We just wanted to check in, Ma'am!"

"I appreciate it!" Aa signaled the Communications Officer to cut the feed.

"Go! I will take care of this!" Commander Danek felt he needed to encourage the wavering Captain. He could tell she was contemplating really hard to forget about her exercise. Amid encouraging looks he stated, "You told me yourself you want to make the Emperor proud!"

"The Emperor might need me, in light of this . . . whatever is this is?" she pointed toward the holo screen.

"You have an adept crew. There isn't a thing they wouldn't be able to handle!" he responded as any XO would have. Apparently, she thought along the same lines because she left the bridge in a hurry.

*

Commander Danek wished he would've not said those encouraging words to his superior half an hour earlier. He was on his way to the Starboard POD, where the Emperor's spaceship the Toxic was about to land. He gathered couple of deck officers in a hurry to greet him, lined them up by the rear of the DSR and waited impatiently.

As soon as the ramp opened and the Emperor appeared, along with the now familiar face of Miss Amerlee and Azure, he and his staff saluted hard.

The Emperor glanced around, noted the droid workforce's tireless movements around the hangar, the pulled aside heavy fighter jets, then his gaze slipped back onto him.

“Where is Captain Aa?” he inquired.

Commander Danek hoped this question would never come up. Unfortunately, the Emperor was growing impatient, so he had to respond, “She took twenty-four hours off.”

The Emperor frowned. “What a bugger!”

“Pardon?” Commander Danek hoped to sound extremely polite.

“Is she off the ship?” he asked him a moment later, apparently thinking of something.

“No. She is doing some exercises.”

“Exercises?”

“Yes, My Lord, the kind of you would do.” he pulled his mouth, unable to ascertain whether he should’ve said that, but the Emperor lightened up upon hearing it. “Great! That is good news for me! Now, as you must be aware now, this lady beside me is Zoon Amerlee!”

“Yes, My Lord . . .” Danek thought it would be best to acknowledge the woman swiftly.

“She needs some training, and I think I really should talk to Captain Aa about it. I, as you probably know, am here due to the escalating situation at the Green Void so I to assist to Josh

Kulighan . . .” he wondered around, slowly walking toward the hangar’s edge, dragging along Danek and his officers. “Did two DSRs from Admiral Qaw’s fleet arrive yet?”

“Yes, My Lord!” Danek was happy to report something positive.

“Good. I will take them with me; now lead the way to the Captain’s quarters!” The Emperor instructed Danek, who felt pity for his superior, then again, he realized, he should feel pity for himself too . . . Captain Aa will not take the intrusion into her private life too lightly!

Along the way the Emperor asked, “Did a high-speed transport ship arrive yet?”

“Um, excuse me, My Lord?” Danek was dumbfounded. He heard of no such thing.

"Once they arrive, have them land on the Starboard POD and allow the occupants to get onboard the Toxic!"

"Whom would they be?"

"Baby Haas and perhaps some Honor Guards." The Emperor responded, then as they had to stop by the elevator he asked, "How does life treat you, Commander Danek?"

"Fairly, I guess!"

"Hang in there ol' buddy!" The Emperor patted his shoulder, then let it go as the circular door flipped aside.

Danek thought he might forgo with the cleaning procedure of this piece of clothing for weeks, to have his imprint linger around longer than shelved the idea as he pushed the button for the officer's deck.

Smith lightly smiled and gave encouraging look toward the seemingly still upset Amerlee.

Captain Aa woke up. For a second, she thought her nap did more harm than good, as she had a mild headache, than the chime repeated itself. She became angry. Whoever was on the other side will be going to get it from her! She tightened her blue silk robe and snorted, still fuming: "I'm going to kill whoever woke me up!"

"You should rethink your statement, princess!" she heard Victor's polite voice.

"What, you have an opinion? You not even supposed to listen in!"

"I'm always listening in once the Emperor is on board . . . You know, to secure his majesty!" he added.

"Smith?" Aa almost tripped and stopped. "Is he on the other side?" she asked, but Victor decided not to answer.

"I see . . ." she gulped air and attempted to smile as she opened the door.

"Hi! I heard you are doing some exercises!" Smith pushed Amerlee in before he stepped into the room himself.

"Amerlee!" Aa noted the shy-looking woman standing couple feet away from her.

"Captain Aa!" Amerlee saluted, but of course with the wrong hand. She forgave that to her. It was alright. After all, Smith used to say the thought of what counts!

"What do I owe the pleasure?" Aa still was not sure what it was all about. If Colonel Re'kl was waiting for the Emperor, his wait should be over. Why was he on board, she could not figure that out. Something in the back of her mind spoke along the lines of trouble for her, but she muted the persistent thoughts and forced on an even bigger smile. Smith must've seen it, because his good mood slowed to just a tad over great: "I really don't want to intrude, so I'm leaving, but I wanted to tell you in person that I am dropping Amerlee off on your ship. Treat her nicely while I'm in the combat zone. Also try to teach her to some basics, please?" he gave a quick kiss onto her cheek, then a longer kiss went to the upset looking Amerlee and Smith lit up in a fireball, teleporting back to the Toxic.

"That was quick . . ." Aa flinched. She glanced over to Amerlee, who seemed to be surprised. To encourage her, she said, "Men, they all leave us as soon as the next hunt is on, eh?"

"What was that?" she pointed at Smith's earlier, but now empty spot beside her.

"That was my darling, how Emperors move from one place to another. He teleported away. Rude for us, perfectly normal for them. Come, have a seat!" she offered her some refreshments. While she was mildly offended, she had to share her personal space with Smith's girlfriend, hospitality took over. Amerlee accepted the juice and the seat. She cleared her throat: "Smith said he was worried for me, so he dropped me off. He said I should learn from you!"

It was pretty obvious to Aa why Amerlee ended up on her ship now. She would presumably slow him down. In a way she would, she realized. But now she had to babysit her. "So how good are you with guns?"

"I never fired one." Amerlee admitted, looking at the glass.

"I see . . ." Said Aa, but she was cursing inside along, feeling pity for her at the same time. Pretty crazy and conflicting thoughts.

"Would you teach me?" she asked, shy as a feather.

"You need basic lessons, but don't feel bad. All Smith was doing is to protect you by dropping you off on my ship!"

"I want to be with him!" she replied longingly.

"Yeah, but you would be excess baggage for him. This could get dicey, cause . . . Did he tell you what the Green Void was about?" The Captain realized she might don't know a thing. After all, it was a military/intelligence matter.

"Yes. He explained it to me in great detail. He thinks AOCP is behind the space ship explosions."

"They have to be. Space ships just don't blow up by themselves." Aa admitted.

"I would just hang onboard the Toxic, you know?" she sounded sad and lonely.

"Yeah, but how would you react to a dangerous situation? You, yourself, don't know that!" Aa voiced her concern.

"I would remain cool!"

"Really?" she produced a gun from somewhere and suddenly aimed at her face.

Amerlee went pale and began to shake. "Is . . . Is it loaded?"

"Betcha!" Aa winked as she withdrew the gun, and with a slick move it disappeared from her hands.

"You scared me for a second!" she placed her left hand on her chest.

"Yeah, I see that. We need to work on your coolness. Let's go down to the shooting range to assess your limitations!" Aa dropped her robes and grabbed jeans and a T-shirt.

Amerlee looked away.

Aa saw that and laughed: "No need to be intimidated by me."

"Don't mind me saying, but you look gorgeous!"

"You are likewise!" Aa bobbed her head and grabbed her communicator while escorted Amerlee out of the room. She had to call her XO to get a VIP room for the guest.

"See . . ." Aa was holding the target practice paper in her hand. Amerlee pointed at the lower left corner: "See, I think it was me!" she sounded excited.

"Yeah, that was you all right, but the circles begin a half a foot to the right! This was fifty feet, the closest. What happens at seventy-five or one fifty?" Aa thought this was a disaster. She spoke loudly, "And you grabbed my instructions right; one leg forward than the other, elbows bent, so the recoil was absorbed by your muscles and you held the gun correctly in your hands!"

"Tell me how much a round cost?" Amerlee protested, her mind revolving around the idea of buying her own ammo.

Her question startled captain Aa: "What?"

"I mean, if I want to practice later?" Amerlee knew she was way behind.

"I don't think we can remedy this overnight. Rounds are free. They are blanks anyhow." Aa dismissed her concerns.

Amerlee bit her lips, then raised her eyebrow. "How good are you? Just for comparison, you know . . ."

"Oh, you don't want to know!" Aa shook her head. "I'm a gunslinger. Used to be for hire. Not a good comparison. No. Definitely not!" she kept shaking her head.

"But I do! I heard you're exceptional. What's an exceptional good look like?" she was adamant.

"That's a no-good comparison to your aim, Amerlee." Aa shook her head gently. "I mean I held a gun when I was five years old, I did contract killings by the time I was fifteen and I only got better than that since!"

"Show me!" she stomped the ground.

Aa took a deep breath, giving up. She shrugged, like she was done protesting and took the gun from Amerlee, replaced the clip and looked deep into her brown eyes: "See, I'm looking at you!"

Amerlee shook at the first pop, glanced around, ready to drop to the floor, but Captain Aa continued to look into her eyes and it made her uncomfortable. The pops died down, and the Captain turned around to have the paper reeled back. She unclipped and left it at the table as she walked away.

Amerlee was not sure what just happened.

"Have a happy evening, we'll discuss it tomorrow!" she heard it. She glanced down at the table and despite the happy face of Aa's gun marked on the target practice, she began to cry uncontrollably.

She was a failure! Captain Aa was truly a professional, better than good! She was sure she'll never going to be with Smith on a mission. He'll go out with Azure every time and chit-chat about their kills while she'll be relegated to cooking at best . . . She could see it all! She fell asleep in her assigned cabin, while a black robed Death Squad member watched her door on the hallway. Smith left two of them behind to make her feel comfortable. She was not feeling comfortable at all! She knew the Death Squad members were good at shooting, too. Seemingly, the world was out to get her!

Chapter Twenty One

Hypothesis

"I mean, the data doesn't support it!" Josh shook his head. He just finished disseminating the newly acquired information to the sitting parties. They were on board the Trixec as Smith asked everyone to meet there. He took Baby Haas and her companions with the Toxic to the Trixec as soon as the Honor Guard high speed transport ship left.

Colonel Re'kl and Captain Mya often glanced at each other. They were the only ones around whom had to play catch up.

Smith shook his head then searched Josh with his eyes. "I still say the Acceleration Ring and its computer systems are compromised . . ." he referred to the local route's gateway. The other end was near Danal IV. He cried out loud: "Why is that I want to forget Te'lek so bad and every goddamned time I end up here lately? Anyone?" he glanced around, but of course there was no answer.

"What do you want us to do?" Admiral Tarbuk asked after a moment of silence.

"I would leave capital ships as they are. You being here has a certain calming effect, and the DU is fine where he is. Captain Aa is close by. If we need her, she could be around in no time. She also has some nifty assets onboard. Would somebody call her and ask whoever is in control to lend us an Avrora7 and 9 spy craft? We have to coordinate here!"

"Considered it done!" Toxic nodded from the corner.

Smith acknowledged her nod and continued: "Captain Mya, I want to cut you lose as soon as this meeting is over. Not in that you leaving the zone, but you have a special role to play. Since your DSR is better equipped for electronic warfare, I task you to attack the Accelerator Ring's control station at this end. You must hack in as undetected as you can, filter thru data and give me a firm answer whether others planted malware already. If they did, what's its purpose and preferably who made it! It's an extremely important task. Despite everyone's assumption that I'm chasing a ghost, I believe their computer systems are compromised. Perhaps longer than even I think!"

"I will leave as soon as this meeting is over!" Captain Mya saluted from her chair.

"Good. Now, looking at the raw data, I must say it's always happening at the baffle region of the Green Void. Never before and never after. Always at the edge. It has to have significance!"

"Do you have an angle?" Captain Josh asked.

"I do. For now, let's set up our forces. I will join you with the Toxic at your position. Avrora9, the extreme duration spy craft must patrol at very close of the border!"

"The AOCP borders?" Colonel Re'kl asked for clarification.

"Yes. Can I have the holo map please!" The Emperor walked closer to the holographic display. He used a laser pen to draw an oval circle. "Avrora7 with its smaller but highly sensitive payload must patrol this region. At the same time, Colonel, I need you on the other side. Have your systems powered down as much as you can and guns pointed toward that planet on the AOCP side of the border!" He enlarged the map and pointed at the rouge mini planet, a moon. "I suspect the problem is coming from there. Have somebody contact Admiral Qaw and ask him all intelligence about that moon!"

"It's useless. The moon is dead!" Josh shook his head, disagreeing with the Emperor.

"Captain, the rouge planet has a gentle sway. Nobody knows why, but thirty years ago, and I remember quite clearly because I read the papers about it, there was a mission trying to learn its secrets. The scientific paper concluded that it has a partial hollow core with magma flowing inside. Apparently, its mass was tilting and it might have been causing the gentle sway. So, where I'm getting is that the sway is cyclical and we need to tie that to our hypothesis. See if the explosions occur when the rotational sway as at a certain point."

"What's this hypothesis of yours revolve around?" Josh was highly skeptical.

"That this is another sign of AOCP asymmetrical warfare. We need to figure it out fast and neutralize it if it's so because if we don't, we will start to see this coming to play at other areas!"

"The planet that is about two hundred thousand kilometers from the Green Void, some hundred and twenty thousand kilometers over the UNHL—AOCP border and has some kind of mysterious laser rays to kill the spaceships?" Josh shook his head, feeling highly skeptical.

"No, Josh. Look at the data. We assumed that they blew up. At least the first three times. So, let's have it. There had to be a bomb onboard in order to blow if we take out the death ray idea. How did they plant the bombs? It's risky. Too risky, but let's go with the bombs. Why would it always blow at a certain point?"

". . . To create confusion for you?" Josh felt quicksand forming beneath his feet.

"Yes. Definitely confusion . . ." Smith agreed, shaking his head. "So, the last explosion was special, right?"

"Oh, you mean that it was undercover?"

"Yes. Exactly."

"We had good telemetry!"

"And you must have received a report that nobody got onboard the space tug and the tug did not stop at the station."

"Yes . . ."

"What did the data suggest?" The Emperor tried to gesticulate to speed up his admission. Others in the room had a distinct feeling this little rivalry between the two of them was a special case. Not even Admiral Tarbuk would've dared to try the Emperor's patience so open, so vehemently.

"Weird data . . ."

"How so?" Admiral Tarbuk asked, growing interested in the subject.

"I had a live connection with them, telemetry beaming to me all the time. After the explosion I was able to grab most of the vessel's main structures and utilizing the Trixec's secondary AI we were able to reconstruct the explosion."

"And that was not right?" The Emperor lightly nodded, anticipating the answer.

Josh grimaced. "That's why I say the data doesn't make any sense of . . ."

"So, what was the data?" Azure leaned forward. She grew impatient with the run around the subject.

"It suggested an implosion style bomb."

"That's strange . . ." Tarbuk frowned. This had to be the Captain's latest report, the one he neglected to read in light of the Emperor's sudden appearance and their subsequent short time jump.

"We could not detect any residue of any type of explosives, but there are types that would disintegrate to other substances, so it's not completely unexpected." Josh tried to save face.

The Emperor studied the implosion's reconstructed 3D image. He re-winded the sequence, forwarded, tilted and pan the reconstruction, then left his chair and began to think. Occasionally he glanced up, glanced at the second holo projection of the AOCP moon and tried to make sense of it. Suddenly, he slammed his left fist into his right palm. "Gotcha!"

"What?" Josh frowned.

"Admiral, we desperately need a multipurpose space ship to be positioned around here!" he zoomed out and pointed to an area, a protrusion into AOCP space.

"Okay . . ."

"They have to observe the far side of the moon as best as they could! Set up another three automated decoys to come thru with uranium ore at the gate, with Danal IV as the final destination. We won't be able to catch them the first time . . . No, we don't . . ." he shook his head, glancing at the holo projections.

"What's in your mind?" Baby asked. She knew enough of his boss was already forming a response.

"Captain Josh, have a rather large scanning operation set up there!" The Emperor pointed to an area between the Green Void, the AOCP rouge moon and Danal IV.

"For . . . ?"

"Decoy. They undoubtedly observing us. We won't truly know their assets."

"Qaw's intel just came in!" Toxic announced with a voice it grabbed everybody's attention.

"See, I told you . . ." The Emperor softened his tone and nodded as Josh began to grapple the situation.

"Five scientific outposts . . . Who would've thought?" The hologram glanced at the Emperor.

"You could not find your bomb because there never

was . . ." The Emperor watched as they incorporated new data into the holo projection. It showed the rouge moon's positions every time the ship 'explosions' occurred.

"Every time it's at the same angle!" Jena exclaimed.

"Strange coincidence . . ." The Admiral glanced at the Emperor.

"That's no coincidence. I bet they have an underground chamber that releases the projectile."

"What projectile?" People around the room turned to the Emperor.

"It's a kinetic weapon!" The Emperor showed them his fist and palm, then smashed them into each other.

*

Amerlee woke up. It was four AM. She tossed and turned in her bed. The temperature was perfect; the bed was pretty good for a military space ship and her clothes supposed to comfort her, but they did not. Commander Danek promised her to share information regarding to Smith, although he called him the Emperor with deep and respectful voice. Her hair got messed up. Frustrated, she pounded on the pillows: "I got to get better!" she decided to dress up. Since most soldiers looked her funny in skirts, she decided to grab jeans, like miss professional Captain Aa did, and headed down to the gun range with a quiet Izim, the Death Squad leader. "Do you girls ever sleep?" she turned to her in the turbo lift.

Izim understood her master's request to treat the woman with full respect, but it felt she was betraying her oath to respond only to the Emperor. "We do." she replied.

"Not too chatty, are we?" Amerlee was trying hard to strike a conversation with her.

"Not really."

"Smith said you girls are excellent conversation partners . . ."

"To our master we are!"

"I thought he said to treat me like you treat him!"

"Yes, my bad miss Amerlee. We take twelve-hour shifts, but we could be flexible."

"So how skilled are you shooting wise?"

"Not as good as Captain Aa, but close . . ." Izim elaborated.

"Can you give me pointers?"

"Certainly, but you must not be hard with yourself. Up until today you haven not fired a gun. You can not expect to be a professional overnight!"

"I guess not, but I have to try . . ." Amerlee's jaw tightened.

To her surprise, the entry to the gun range was closed by two soldiers, whom exercised their authority and blocked their path.

"The gun range is closed until further notice!" They explained dryly.

"Is there another one?" Amerlee frowned.

"They are for training purposes for our troops. You can't enter them!" The soldier on the left responded.

"Funny, did not you say this one was closed?"

"Yes, Ma'am!"

“Do you know who my boyfriend is?” Amerlee got pissed.

“Irrelevant, Ma’am. Captain Aa herself closed the range due to its proximity to the chamber!”

“What chamber?”

“She is doing exercise in the camber . . .” One of the soldiers carefully pointed to the left.

“Great. I’m not here to see her, now let me in!” Amerlee was losing patience.

“We can’t!” he responded.

Amerlee was about to give up, but suddenly Izim stepped between them: “In the name of the Emperor, step aside!”

The soldiers glanced at each other, then the closer one shook his head: “The Captain ordere . . .”

“Do you want to die today, soldier?” Izim relaxed her muscles. The soldier must’ve noticed her pose changing, because he glanced at his buddy again. He nodded and said, “Don’t disturb our Captain!” And with that they stepped aside.

“That was nice!” Amerlee patted Izim’s shoulder.

“I’ve learned from the Emperor to bluff sometimes, so I was ready to fight with him, though I was not prepared to kill him.”

Amerlee was horrified upon hearing her. They walked down the hallway and they stopped at the junction. To the left was the gun range, to the right was the so-called chamber, an equally large room that was set up as a ring for boxing and another for fencing. Amerlee grew curious and took a peek in. Her breath could be seen in the cold.

“Freezing in there!” she uttered to Izim, who took the courage to defy orders and take a peek herself. “Freezing exactly. Thirty-two Fahrenheit, most likely.”

“Why the water?” Amerlee pointed at a pond beside a gigantic melting ice cube.

“Apprentice . . .” Izim uttered with respect and pulled Amerlee from the door.

“What?”

Izim escorted her to the gun range then explained, "The Emperor's apprentice was inside the gigantic cube. It's an exercise. She has to heat her body to melt the ice!"

"How can that be done?"

Izim responded thoughtfully: "By taking control of your body. It's a test even some of us, Death Squad members were forced to participate in. I hated it . . . The minutes feel hours and the radiating cold is unbearable. They taught us to shoot out that sensation or . . ."

"Or?" she caught the cliffhanger.

"Or die. I mean froze to death." She frowned, then added, "I've heard a story that somebody passed, but almost froze. Her heart beat dropped to like eight beats per minute. It took her a month to recover, but became a Death Member!"

"Die?" Amerlee repeated the word, sounding horrified.

"Yes, Ma'am. Captain Aa is the Emperor's apprentice. It's not just a word one speaks lightly. There is knowledge and practice behind it. She is practicing that knowledge. In your words, I think they would call her awesome."

"More than awesome!" Amerlee placed the tray on the table. First steps were assembling the hand gun. Izim was a great help in that. She stood beside her, guiding her moves, making the miniscule adjustments and two hours later she was able to hit the most outer circle with her blanks.

"You should rest!" Izim suggested.

"No. I just started to feel it." Amerlee disagreed.

"Sometimes it's just like a poker game. The day isn't yours." Izim explained.

"How would you know that?"

"I know many card games as part of my training!"

"Jack of all trades?"

"I leave now. I suggest that you take a break!" Izim left her alone. She decided that was the most prudent move. Her absence will force Amerlee to take a break whether she wants it or not. She had zero illusions. Without an expert's guidance, Amerlee wouldn't be able to better herself.

As Izim left, Amerlee began to gloat the gun, laying on the desk: "You fucker, you better shoot good or I going to throw you off the spaceship!" she talked to it angrily.

"Will that going to help?" she heard Captain Aa's tired voice. Amerlee spun around to face with the really exhausted looking woman. A towel was wrapped around her neck, while her entire body was gleaming with sweat and moisture. Even her usually meticulously kept hair was a mess. But it did not stop her from stopping by.

"You survived!" Amerlee exclaimed, relieved.

"It would seem so . . ." Aa tried to smile. She stepped closer and nodded upon seeing some used target papers. "You improved, quite a bit!"

"I am!" Amerlee hoped to convey strength in her reply.

"Who helped you?"

"Izim!" Amerlee bit her lips. Somehow, she felt it was a submission to admitting her failure.

"I see. You should rest . . ." she was about to turn around.

"Izim left, thinking I would just give up, but none of you know me! I will get better!" she sounded defiant.

"Good." Aa nodded, took couple steps toward the exit, then abruptly stopped as a stray thought flashed across her mind: "You should try it with your left hand." she suggested. Actually, she thought about her while doing the exercise, but viewed it as a form of multitasking as opposed to getting sloppy and not focusing on her body and the ice cube.

"I'm right-handed!" Amerlee frowned. "Anyway, that is how you showed me to shoot. Why the change?"

Captain Aa paused for a moment, then without explaining she shrugged, "I think you should try it with your left hand . . ." And with that advice, she left.

Amerlee held the gun in her hand. Its barrel was really hot. "Try it . . ." she sounded skeptical. "Try it with your left hand, huh?" she tried to hold the gun in her left hand, but her fingers got entangled. "Now, how should I do this?" she stood there, angry at her own incompetence. “Mother fucker!” she shook her left hand to loosen her stuck middle finger. The gun dropped to the floor. “Piece of shit!” she leaned forward to grab it and somehow her left hand got a firm grip on it. “Die, you incompetent pussy!” she shouted angrily while charged toward the range, emptying the clip, not even looking. When the blanks were away, she threw the gun at the desk, the earplugs away and stormed out.

Unknown to her, Commander Danek was thru a long night shift. It was relatively quiet, except that another SCC showed up briefly. It belonged to their auxiliary forces. He needed a long-range fighter with a missile extension and another extension for electronic countermeasure mission. The crew handled it with ease. Then another message came from Admiral Tarbuk to expect more ‘special’ request from the Emperor. At dawn he was notified of Amerlee and her assigned Death Squad member’s visit of the range. Since his Captain was about to finish her exercise, he paid some attention to the Emperor’s girlfriend and her workout. He saw her practicing relentlessly and although he was not entirely sure what it was all about, he could see she was partially determined, partially in despair. She was from the specimen Smith liked women from . . . His interest peaked once she left the gun range. Albeit tired at the end of his shift, he turned up at the gun range to grab the paper. “What’s so bad about this one?” he turned around. He could not find anything wrong with it, so he took it with himself and retired to his cabin for a short nap.

Captain Aa slept four hours. She could not afford more to herself as Smith reminded her before, don’t sleep too long after the exercise. She took another quick shower and left to find Amerlee. She found her at the rear looking galley reserved for high-ranking officers.

“A common place to meet!” Aa pulled out a chair opposite to Amerlee.

“How come?”

"Smith loves his stomach. Whenever we were on an extended voyage, he loved to hang out in the Trixec's galley. He hatched many great ideas there!" Aa admitted, feeling lightly jealous.

"I slept a bit; I think I'm ready for more!" Amerlee replied.

Aa laughed, then shut up as Amerlee looked rather upset. "I did not mean to hurt your feelings." she added apologetically.

"I'm not even sure I had the gun the right way in my left hand . . ."

"That could be tricky. I myself righthanded." Aa admitted, then glanced at the entrance. "Is something wrong Commander?" she noticed the tall man standing at the doorway, just

looking at them from the distance.

"Not really . . ." he held the folded paper in his hands. "May I?" he asked for the adjacent seat. Amerlee had no problem with it beyond actually feeling important at the moment. The mighty SPD's first two commanding officers shared the table with her!

Others thought along the same line as the neighboring officers quieted down pretty noticeably.

Captain Aa glanced at the paper, then asked her XO to give her the paper. She unfolded it and began to frown. "Did she do that?" she asked him, without looking at Amerlee.

"Yep . . ." Danek nodded rather proudly.

"Do what?" Asked Amerlee, but her mouth hang open as Captain Aa opened up the paper for her to see it.

"I did not do that." she sounded unsure of herself.

"Yes, you did!" Commander Danek rocked on the chair, feeling anxious all of a sudden.

"When?"

"When?" he echoed her question. "Right before you stormed out from the gun range. We've got cameras, you know!" he added to explain his knowledge on the subject.

"I did this?" Amerlee sounded utterly surprised.

"Left hand, huh?" Captain Aa began to nod while tilted her head. Unknown to Amerlee, she shifted her senses and 'saw' what she always suspected: Amerlee's left hand was quite superior compared to her right hand. Secretly, she injected some precision cocktail into her DNA when Smith asked her to look into the matter. Apparently, he did the same thing.

"All I was doing is aiming at the general direction." Amerlee explained. "I was not pointing it at the center, heck I was running, holding the gun in my left hand alone. You sure it was me who did this?"

"Yep!" Aa slapped her right hand on the table, scaring both Amerlee and Commander Danek at the same time.

"Where are you going, Captain?" she asked.

"You're coming too!" Captain Aa pointed back at her. "We're going back to the range. Let's see what your new arm is really capable of!"

"Should I come too?" Commander Danek was not sure until his commanding officer added: "You too! I need someone to guide her while I observe her movements!"

"What do you mean by that?" Commander Danek was not sure of her Captain's orders. Once on the range, he understood. A bit of nudging Amerlee, a more relaxed posture for her, a finger slightly off the angle, all he needed to correct while Captain Aa watched both of them from the side. She 'saw' Amerlee holding the gun, saw her reactions as they unfolded and adjusted her stance. She also 'saw' the impulses firing up in her brain to guide her left arm. It was magnitudes more orderly and precise than the right hand she tried just a day earlier.

Amerlee was really impressed with her upgrade and learning curve. She could almost claim a bull's eye out of five pages of papers. She repeatedly hit around the second circles.

"Let's relax a bit. Commander Danek, please return to the bridge!" Captain Aa announced.

"Ay-ay!" he left in a hurry, while Aa escorted her to the opposite room.

"It's empty." Amerlee glanced around. She was wrong, of course; she spotted a bunch of soldiers fencing. It was pretty surreal. For this time and age.

Aa followed her gaze. "Fencing really took off once I showed some moves to my officers. I require them to learn the basics. But the real reason we are here is the ring!" she pointed at the elevated podium. She helped her up there, then jumped into the ring herself. "I'm about to show you a couple of moves. It's good to watch somebody's movement, but if you are confident, you could split your focus between my body language and my face. I might try to trick you into a move, but watching my eyes, you could gain entry into my mind!" she loosened her muscles.

"So, we're off to fight now?" Amerlee frowned, then it dawned on her; she might learn new tricks. She was out of the game for so long!

"Yes!" Aa bobbed her head and began to advance. To her surprise, Amerlee charged at her full force, and before she could realize what's happening, they both ended on the floor. Amerlee on top of her, holding Aa's golden hair in her hands.

"You fight dirty, huh?" Aa responded, surprised at her opponent's move.

Amerlee grinned, but not for long. Aa used her long legs to wrap it around Amerlee's own, and with an incredibly twisted move she spun both of them around the floor. Now she was on top, using her left hand to apply pressure on Amerlee's throat.

To Aa's second surprise, in less than five minutes instead of Amerlee giving up, she pinched Aa's right hand, just above the joints. She lost her balance and began to lean to the left. Amerlee rolled away and as soon as she was out from Aa's immediate reach she kneeled down with one leg, ready to jump. By that time Aa let herself to fall, but twisted her body again and rolled onto her back, then thrusted into the air. Upon landing she was ready to attack too; hands in a fist formation.

"Shall we continue?" Aa asked, breathing fast.

"Perhaps later . . ." Amerlee realized they could only harm each other whatever comes next.

"Good call!" Aa let her hands drop. "I would hate to inflict pain on your delicious body!"

"Was that a flirt?" Amerlee stopped dead in her tracks.

"I'm flexible!" Aa grinned, but then her grin faded: "Needless to say, if I charge at you and you use your arms to block me, I would've used my legs to smash your pretty face and we wouldn't want that, do we?"

Amerlee's grin faded, too. "Yeah . . ." Realities set in pretty quickly.

"All right, so I won't bust you about your basic fight skills. You'll see amazing things from us or from even Evan!" she grabbed two towels while tossing one to Amerlee.

"Like that mythical reverse heart beat kill?"

"There is nothing mythical about that!" Aa casually shrugged as she took the lead.

After escorting Amerlee to her cabin, she changed up in hers, then headed to the bridge. Victor pushed a message to her that displayed on her left arm, temporarily muting her tattoo. Danek received a coded message from the Emperor. She was interested.

As Commander Danek explained later, the Emperor asked for two spy planes to be dispatched into the Green Void. One was an Avrora7, and the other was a 9 series plane. Of course, she did not even know they had those around. Luckily Commander Danek knew enough to amaze her with the spy plane's alleged specs, like the invisible hull, the passive radar system built into its leading wings and some other goodies.

Chapter Twenty Two

The Plan

"How is my order coming along?" Smith checked his station first. They were on board the Toxic, pretty darn close to the Green Void's bend, albeit 'upward' from the normal shipping routes. It gave them a great view of the busy region. Toxic used most of her passive radars to gather information, not to mention one of the active side radars that was aimed at the Void itself.

"We've just got the reply from SCC 26-54. Commander Rick reported the mine laying operation just began!" Azure told him, overly excited. She loved missions with Smith.

"Good!" Smith nodded, double checking the main holo projectors. It grew to be a rather convoluted operation, the so-called disinformation campaign aimed to confuse the AOCP spies. The multipurpose ship, along with another SCC from the auxiliary fleet, began to lay space based advanced mines. They were partially stealth by their nature. The idea was that a fast-sailing hostile space ship would get too close before realizing what was in the way. The mine laying operation was just past the Accelerator Ring, cutting off an old route from AOCP space. It was abandoned over five years ago, but it was a great show.

Another SCC conducted a different kind of disinformation by uploading grainy pictures and alleged sighting reports to the local social media. Smith jokingly called the ship the rumor mill . . .

Thru mediaries, he was able to persuade the Accelerator Ring's staff to rearrange traffic, to have one of the decoy cargos be placed with less important ships. He hoped the enemy would pay attention to that.

Suddenly Baby's report yanked him back to reality, "Second report of Avrora9!" she announced excitedly.

"Anything interesting?" Smith yawned. He was sleepy.

"Annotation from the Trixec's senior staff . . ."

"Show me!" The sleepiness evaporated. Next, he stared at the grainy picture. The optical sensors were really good at picking up the seemingly stationary space ship.

"What is that?" Asked Jena suspiciously.

"AB-62, an AOCP space ship used by any one of the Section agencies." Smith frowned. "An older model nonetheless." he added.

"We are well out of its range!" Toxic added thru the speakers as she was not 'present' at the moment.

"But not the minelaying operation!"

"Should we alert them?" Baby asked.

"No. Best let it go. Let them be. What the heck is that?" he suddenly noticed a long dark baffle beneath the spy ship, closely resembled a crossover between a XX century submarine and an airplane.

"Directional radar of some kind . . ." Toxic appeared out of thin air and frowned. She used her software to enhance the already enhanced picture.

"I don't like it!" Smith scratched his head.

"It looks to be a power-hungry device. Upon analyzing Avrora9's telemetry, there is some heat fluctuation there and there!" Toxic highlighted two other protrusions at the spy craft undercarriage.

"Advise the Eclipse to cloak themselves. We should do the same!" Smith glanced worriedly at Toxic.

"Transformation is already underway!" she answered.

"Send a directional message to Admiral Tarbuk and note our concerns!" Smith added.

"Done!" Toxic nodded.

“Our decoy is at the staging point!” Jena read her console. “Less than five minutes to jump!”

“Start recording!” Smith told Toxic, but she was already on it.

“Another detonation!” Josh watched the telemetry with deep dismay. As the decoy got to the Green Void’s bend, it blew to trillion little pieces. His orders were to slowly withdraw as emergency ships began to appear.

Thirty minutes later, Toxic docked with his ship and the Emperor greeted him at the airlock.

Josh was particularly dismayed: “We saw nothing!”

“We did. Come onboard!” Smith gestured, sounding excited.

Josh followed him onto the Toxic’s bridge where Jena and Baby worked the consoles. They were giving new orders to Avrora7 and some of the conventional, long range reconnaissance fighters at the border region.

“So, what did you guys see?” Josh was impatient.

“Just watch!” Smith pointed at the holo display, covering his grin the best he could.

They slowed the telemetry to one ten thousand of normal play. As the strange object appeared out of nowhere, Josh’s mouth began to drop. “What the hell is that?” he glanced at Smith, then he focused back at the object’s long, triple cylindrical nose as it hit the cargo square on, smashing it to the edge of the Green Void. Within milliseconds it recoiled, miniature rockets adjusted its position while at the same time the middle of the unit began to rotate around a centerline. Three pods emerged thru the openings and the next moment the object disappeared.

“What the hell is that?!” Josh repeated his question.

“Got me, but it’s essentially a projectile. The AOCP is now shooting at us, sir!” Smith responded with a hint of sarcasm.

“How the hell are we supposed to stop it?” Captain Josh exclaimed in pain.

Instead of answering directly, Smith asked Jena to put up another feed they got from the multipurpose warship spying directly at the planet.

Josh watched in amazement as the same object appeared out of nowhere and it slowed down to a standstill. Then it slowly began to fall toward the planet where huge, retractable doors opened, revealing a deep pit into the planet.

"How the hell is it going inside the planet?" Josh activated other layers of the captured image as his anxiousness crept up on him.

"My guess would be tractor beams." Smith replied. Jena nodded from the back.

"This isn't sci-fi!" he snapped suddenly. He was pissed mainly that Smith was right.

"No, but Toxic analyzed the cylindrical nose, and she is certain it's a form of steel inner structure with a very thick outer layer of Bi-Manadium4!"

"That's an artificial element, manmade . . ." Josh bit his lips.

"Indeed, it is. And it's also extremely heavy. And it is heavily ferromagnetic, so the modified tractor beams act as giant magnets to pull it back. Neat design and they also have an AR." he pointed at the screen.

"What?" Josh watched as the Accelerator Ring swallowed the object.

"So, its slingshots thru space?" he turned to Smith. "How the hell are we going to stop it?!"

"That's a good question . . ." Smith grimaced. He could not figure it out yet.

"We have what, like a minute before this thing repositions?" Josh asked.

"Like thirty seconds the most!" Jena replied, as calm as she could.

"We're so doomed!" Josh had to sit down. That Bi-Manadium4 was practically an indestructible material. To top it off, they had no time to take over the weapon.

"Toxic also certain it's all robotic, so there is no human element inside. Although there is a hollow core and a certain mechanism is inside suggesting that for test purposes, they could man it, but the immense G prohibits any kind of living creature to survive inside."

Josh suddenly became fatigued: "So how is that helps us?"

"They don't have time to adjust anything. Once they slingshot this thing thru the AR it's away and until it comes back, there isn't a thing they can do with it. That will be our only advantage!"

"You call that advantage?" Josh shook his head in disbelief.

"Yep." Smith nodded, then turned to Baby. "Send a sight to-sight message to Colonel Re'kl and tell him to head to the staging point. Then tell the mine layers to keep continue! When is the next decoy supposed to come?" he asked from Jena.

"Three days and sixteen hours."

"Good. Don't intervene, just let it happen!"

"So, what's the plan?"

"We need to act like there is nothing suspicious. Your already positioned SCCs going to aide recovery like the last time."

"And you?" Josh asked for information.

"I'm returning to the Trixec. We're going to make a very special order . . ." Smith wondered away. He slowly formulated a plan to counter the threat. Old memories surfaced from the war, the end, the guerilla warfare he waged . . . This was a special project from AOCP. It required special attention before they make a serial production of it.

"Of?"

"Three Songolar 7B tactical killer missiles . . ." Smith began to grin.

"Oh, my! How are we going to mate them to this misery object?"

"Let me worry about it now. I also have to make a payload modification."

"10 kiloton nukes aren't enough?"

"No, we need more. We gonna wipe those bases off the planet with some strong, but compact nukes. I know for a fact we developed them. The next time they aim that thing at us we are going to give them some present they can deliver it to home!"

"Instant sunshine!" Azure grinned in the background.

"I hope you can mount them on time!" Josh clapped his hands. He loved the idea, but remained somewhat skeptical of the murky plan.

After Josh left, Smith became withdrawn. Even Azure noticed his odd behavior.

"Look, I need to make this happen. That spy ship is there to monitor the deployment. We can't tip them off. My hope is that they won't notice our real operation. Then the destruction comes as a real surprise and it will be on them to come to terms with the how!" Smith explained.

"Won't they figure out from the decay that we used nukes and explosives on them?"

"The planet's surface is heavily contaminated. It also houses a couple of ammunition dumps from the war. It will be a perfect disguise. The only problem is whether we have the time to successfully mount the bombs . . ."

"So, they aren't missiles?"

"Not exactly. The essence of the missiles, the bombs themselves, are on their way to the Trixec." he checked his device for updates and continued: "So as the modified delivery and mechanism. Thirty megaton each." Smith frowned, reading it off the tiny holoscreen.

"Why the frown?" Asked Azure.

"There was no other option, as there was nothing low yield around. We can get our hands on such a short notice . . ."

"So, the devices will cause a larger detonation?"

"Perhaps too big. The bitch of it is this: If we go too low, the destruction will be minimal and they figure it out who did it. If the destruction is too big, it could have catastrophic consequences for the region . . ."

"Like all five outposts be destroyed?"

"No, not just them. It could break the planet apart . . ." Smith's frown deepened.

"Shit!"

“Yeah, not to mention the fact that we have to mount those things on the AOCP machine. Thirty-second is way short time. It basically ensures nobody has a chance to do a damn thing with it. On the other hand, if I get involved, will that influence their future plans, who knows . . .”

Azure frowned. “Oh, you mean retaliation?”

“Exactly. If we prolong our answer, they could adapt this exotic weapon to other scenarios. I wouldn’t want them to have that impression. That’s why I have to deal with this right now. I need to think . . .” Smith left her on the bridge.

He withdrew to the DSR’s mast to think about it all.

*

“All I can tell you that they formulating a plan . . .” Commander Danek replied to Amerlee’s repeated questions. They were standing in the corridor, just outside of her temporary cabin. Soldiers strolled by, robots on wheels rolled across the pristine floor that was cleaned by nano robots, overseen by Victor. Izim quietly stood by the cabin’s door, partially watching them, partially the traffic. While the possibility of something would happen to Amerlee was pretty low, one would never know, she thought of. It was obvious to her Amerlee was worried about Evan Smith. She was constantly pushing the Commander to reveal more of his cryptic answer, but he was standing his ground, and eventually she gave up for a moment to probe him from a different angle.

“So, before he became the Emperor, what was his hobby? What did he like to do?”

“Um, dunno.” Danek frowned. “It was a long time ago . . .” he finished the sentence, but that did not satisfy her. He saw that. He did not want her to ask mission related questions, so he actually forced his brain to remember. Way back . . . They were fighting. Round after rounds, battles after battles. The grinder . . . Smith got into fixing airplanes after one of the mechanics screwed his engines up. It almost cost his life. Smith only eased up after he found the Albino, but that was much later. They hang out in the bars sometimes. Smith used the holo fighter sim to train himself, he used to call out for opponents, and sometimes Danek wagered on him to make an extra buck or so. Soon nobody wanted to fight against Smith. He had to frown. There was not much besides sleep, sorties and shorties. Smith flirted with the radar operator girl a lot. That was, of course, before he got his own Trimaran. *Think Danek, think*! He forced himself to dig deeper.

Amerlee's question shook him back to the present.

"Say what?" Danek forced himself to look into her face.

"Did he play any games? Baseball or Soccer?"

"Nah, I never seen him doing that." Danek thought he would remember to such an oddity.

"Maybe he was into bikes?"

"Bicycles, perhaps. He did not like motorcycles." Danek frowned.

"Why?"

"He thought them as being dangerous . . ."

"As opposed to be a teenager pilot out in space, facing an alien race who wants to destroy humanity?" Amerlee had difficulty to digest it.

"Huh, that's an interesting view. I don't think we looked at it that way." Danek replied.

"So, bicycles?" Amerlee flinched. "How about card games?"

"Some he played . . . Listen, lady, we were busy most of the time!"

"With what?"

"The war . . ." he gloated at her.

"Yeah . . . I got it." Amerlee thought of him having an empty childhood. She remembered of the warm nights she spent as a kid with her parents. She used to play with her daddy, while mom ordered the servant droids around. She wanted to learn of his childhood to connect better, but it seemed he had none.

"After the Klon ship ran havoc in the Capitol City, he stayed there for couple weeks. He got a homework of sorts, to be a cop."

"Excuse me?"

"Yeah, it was after Kabnul. He told me he was a cop, chasing this thug a lot and discovering hidden parts of the city. This guy, he was a thief named Monk who was in love with Iman Telis, the singing star we used to adore . . ." Danek began to perspire. He used to dream about her so many times. Imagine her body, him being very close by . . .

"Did not she die or something?"

"She perished sometimes after Super City was being constructed. I think there were too many things going on with the city and Smith decided to demolish the entire thing. He hoped to have a genesis event, forget the old shit, the bad stuff with the Capitol City and have it re-morphed into Super City that could fight better against a future Klon invasion."

"Which it did!" Amerlee remembered.

"Yeah, twice, if I remember correctly. Smith had a secret file on his laptop he carried everywhere. He used to show me how some buildings would transform into battery stations in case of an emergency. He was fixated on that . . ."

"So, what happened to this thug, did he ever catch him?"

"Monk? Yeah, sure. Soon after a big concert of Iman's he arrested him and offered choices."

"What choices?"

"Smith like choices, like rot in a prison cell or go with him and be a trained fighter . . ." Danek shrugged.

"I see. There is a recurrent theme emerging there, right?"

"Yeah, I think so . . ." Danek realized he himself is a good example of that policy.

"So, what happened after?" Amerlee tried to get him back on to the right track.

"Smith got back to space, onboard the Trimaran to fight. We got separated as I remained on the Cloud Cruiser until it was blown apart. Then I was rescued by intersecting a route with his escort ships. They were trying to find him as he became erratic and went out of route. Then Te'lek happened. I was not there, but heard of the heroic battle. I think once he lost his Trimaran, and by that time he was an Emperor, not an elect, he went back to Down Earth to grab the Prince Force. If my memory serves right, he took off with the entire armada, all the ships of the Prince Force fleet while they were still being assembled, and that's when he got acquainted with Baby Haas as well!"

"The Honor Guard leader?"

"Yes. Smith told me once that the original Honor Guards that supposed to protect him consisted of thirty-two genetically engineered girls, developed by an off world, owned by the Ancient Man. I guess at that time they had a good relationship . . ." he wondered.

"That's good. I never heard of that story!" Amerlee pressed her lips.

"What story?" Captain Aa got within an earshot.

"Ma'am!" Commander Danek snapped into saluting position.

"Oh, come on!" she called out at his XO's behavior, but she returned the salute.

"We were discussing Evan Smith and how he became the Emperor!" Amerlee chatted happily. She was unaware of these things and they were very interesting indeed!

"There was only one more thing I wanted to mention,

miss . . ."

"What is it?"

"That as the young Emperor took off with the fleet, he knew the location of a new, regional Klon command post. It was in today's AOCP territory, near a planetary system that was back then not part of the Empire."

"What do you mean, not part of . . . ?" Captain Aa became curious.

"I mean the Magistrate or Ministry . . . Oh, I don't know how they were called. They were the ones whom sent agents into humanoid culture to assess their development before they were being contacted . . ."

"Yes, I know what you are talking about, Commander. Their building now located on SWEi Prime!" Captain Aa remembered the water fiasco and what eventually led her to Agross V. undercover . . .

"That's the one. So, Smith err, the young Emperor needed skilled soldiers, and he had the list of these embedded agents. He thought of them as pretty good ones. He knew of this humanoid system and sent out a call to the sleeper cells. At nightfall he made the landing and picked them up."

"Amazing, what happened to the humanoid culture?" Aa was interested.

"I don't know, but I think the Klon's were mounting a devastating attack while the um, the Emperor, made the order to retrieve the agents. You know, now Captain Josh Kulighan was one of those agents."

"What?" Aa shouted, bypassing Amerlee's own exclamation.

"Yes, and if what Smith told me is correct, Mr. Kulighan was in deep dodo at the time, because he had fallen in love with a local and their relationship produced a child!"

"Oh, no!" Aa covered her mouth.

"Yes. And allegedly Josh Kulighan knew Smith from before somehow. So, he asked Smith to save his then girlfriend and child, but Smith had other grand plans and he did not want to be bothered with the entire stuff so he told him he would save one only, not both of them. I don't know how it ended, but I know Josh was a respected governmental agent; he was on his next to the last mission before retiring and was upset Smith and the Klons were messed it up."

"I bet!" Aa nodded feverishly. "Continue, please!"

"Not much to add. Smith promised Josh a superb career and after that battle he set him free with a rank of something like a field command Rear Admiral to chase the Klons out of the Milky Way. Which he did . . ."

"Indeed, he did!" Aa nodded, realizing this was just another piece of the puzzle. A very important puzzle!

"Amazing!" Amerlee shook his head.

"Yeah, your boyfriend had a tumultuous life!" Danek nodded.

"This whole thing! Simply breathtaking!" Amerlee added, then turned to the Captain, "Did you want to see me?"

"Yes, for two things. One, I suppose, I can reveal that your boyfriend is busy fixing the mess at the Green Void. Apparently, like everything, this seems to be more convoluted than we originally envisioned. I suppose he missing Commander Tri'ng's close proximity as she and her powers would come really handy . . . Who knows, she might be summoned to here. The other thing was that I freed up couple hours for us to continue practice at the gun range. Commander Danek, care to join us?"

"Naturally!" The Commander began to follow them and the single but extremely capable Death Squad member who trailed the pair of women.

Chapter Twenty Three

The Stakes Just Got Higher

By the time Smith emerged from his location, it was evening. Jena and Baby prepared a report to him from Captain Mya, who forged digital keys to access the UNHL Accelerating Ring 534's secure transmissions. They found plenty of compromises, all in the root level that pinpointed to some serious players involved. The problem was the sheer number of possible players indicated the system was more compromised they previously believed it.

"Man, I wish Tri'ng would've been here . . ." Smith repeatedly shook his head, pointing to another part of the report: "Look, this is pure X-Force coding. And it's fairly new. What the hell the Krea'tor's people need this for? Then I see some stuff here that looks like our own clandestine services have a Trojan, a piece of shit coding here that I think is just some local crime syndicate and these," he pointed to the next pages; "These are again deep shit stuff, most likely AOCP . . . Its best to keep this report to ourselves!" he concluded.

"So, we won't alert the locals?" Baby scrutinized his face.

"We won't alert anyone! Advise Captain Mya to drop some new loggers and set up fake accounts for that." he scratched his chin. "I'll talk to Admiral Qaw myself. I'm sure he is in it too . . ." he added as an afterthought.

"Man, I feel like I'm in the whorehouse . . ." he glanced at his fingers, before addressing Toxic: "I'll have to get involved as the Emperor in this, so we need to appoint Baby Haas as the team leader!"

"What about me?" Azure pointed to her blossoming chest.

"You'll be her second!"

"That's better!" she sounded a tad relieved.

"What are you planning to do?" Toxic inquired, feeling anxious.

"Teleport us back to where Tarbuk is, then dock inside his Starboard POD!" Smith addressed her awful formal.

"What's in your mind?" Toxic felt a trap being sprung around her. Smith was planning something shady; she was sure of it.

"Our biggest problem is time, right?"

"You mean, while the device is exposed?" Azure asked.

"Yes." Smith nodded.

"Indeed, it is. I wonder what kind of delivery mechanism these casings of yours will have?"

"Nice, but that isn't the answer. I'll make time. I'll slow it down!" Smith flexed his hands in anticipation.

"I so hate that idea!" Toxic whined from the background.

"I know!" Smith nodded again.

"Do you think it's wise, boss?" Baby was not sure it was a great idea either.

"Meaning?"

"To use your special powers. Could this be a trap?"

"Trap for me?" Smith pointed at his own chest. It never occurred to him. He had to calculate that into the response as well. He weighed it for a moment then shook his head: "This is a truly exotic weapon. Might have come from the Klon Wars. I can't really see them spending so much money on a lone project like this. I mean, this is tailored to this particular scenario. It wouldn't work at any other place. Maybe they could evolve it to have a super-fast needle that would shoot across shipyards to create mass effect or a terrorism related endeavor pumping a planet with things like that, but this operation had to cost a fortune." Smith shook his head.

"And it would remain highly successful where we not realize what was going on . . ." Baby responded. "But again, are you sure this isn't a trap?"

"No, I can't be fully certain." he shook his head all of a sudden, uncertain of his plan. "How long do we have?" he asked from Toxic.

"About two days."

"Baby, I want you to go ahead with the plan. Have Jena supervise the reprograming of the Songolar 7B tactical killer missiles. We can't use remote detonation; it has to be pre-programmed. Figure out a timeframe!"

"Lots of variables." Baby frowned.

"Can't we start the countdown from the moment the tractor beam activated?" Azure asked.

"Good call!" Smith liked her idea, pointing in her direction.

Azure felt immensely proud. She contributed to the plan in a meaningful way.

"Do some work on it! Azure, you are with me!" Smith left the bridge, with Azure tickling him as soon as the door closed behind them.

"Hey!" Smith shrieked.

"Where are we going?"

"To our room!"

"I love it!" Azure began to grin.

"We're going to join . . ." Smith did not even hear her exclamation. He was thinking along the line to mentally scan for AOCP agents, but as soon as he turned around and she jumped into his arms, he realized their interests differed at the moment.

"No love, eh?" Azure noted his mood and jumped out of his arms.

"Focus, girl, focus!"

"I was focusing!" she sounded upset, but she obeyed his request and soon they were laying on their beds, mind joined into a tight grip, scanning hundreds of light years across for any trap the AOCP might have them in store.

They found agents onboard the AOCP spy ship and felt a brief communication between them and the AOCP rouge planet, but nothing beyond. They scanned thirty light years into AOCP space, but a dark shroud stopped them from looking further. No matter how hard did they tried to penetrate, it did not work. They tried to peek behind it, and they realized it was a perfect sphere. They quietly withdrew afterward.

"What the hell was that?" Azure sat up on her bed.

"Beats me . . ." Smith had a bad feeling about it, then called Toxic and asked her to project the star charts onto the side wall.

"I don't see any planets there." Azure said after going back and forth of the selected area.

Smith bit his lips. "Toxic, were there ever a space station there, perhaps?"

"Maybe. I have to look . . ." she trailed off.

"In the meantime, expand your ability and see if you notice the same sphere we felt, would you?" Smith asked her, and she complied.

Minutes later, the hologram formed before their eyes. Toxic gesticulated thru the hologram: "The dark sphere is there, but it isn't entirely uniform. I did as you instructed and I did not look into further, but in essence yes, there used to be a huge space station there once upon a time. It was the home of an elite force that helped you win at Te'lek back in the war. Records indicate that after the war it was mothballed for about twenty-two years, when unexpectedly it was taken out of the registry. I obtained a copy from Admiral Qaw regarding to the history of the Albert'fa-Coop station and it clearly states that it was still in the registry about six and a half years ago."

"So, it just disappears from the registry, no mentioning of being decommissioned, huh?"

"No . . ."

Smith winced. "I don't think we supposed to find this installation."

"What's your hypothesis?"

"It's a black site for some sort of cagey AOCP Section work. But it has to be something truly big or truly frightening. If it's a black hole, it is being guarded with impressively strong telepaths . . ." Smith licked his lips.

"What?" Azure noticed him.

"Something is going on there. For sure . . . We might have approached this from the wrong direction."

"Meaning?" Azure did not get it. One good look at the holographic projection and she was sure Toxic was clueless too.

"The planet from where the AOCP shoots the projectile at us could be a smokescreen, to blind us from the real issue."

"So, the black hole now an issue?" Azure was not sure she got it.

"Definitely an issue . . . Okay, so they use telepaths, and I will use my power to stop the projectile."

"About that projectile . . ." Toxic spoke up.

"Yeah?"

"Despite our best efforts, I was not able to break in."

"We went over this before." Smith turned to the projection, scoffing in the meantime. "Baby said the report she got went along the line that there were no ports to listen to. There was nothing that was broadcasted."

"Well, I found a short-range bidirectional port, sort of like a wi-fi station. I tried to communicate, but all I got back was garbled mess. So, I concluded it was pointless to deal with."

"Nicely left it out of your report, eh?" Smith was not sure where she was getting at.

"I recently finished analyzing Captain Mya's report. She notes different keyloggers and subroutines embedded in the root level of her interest, but I also found things that by coding technique seemingly matched the garbled mess I dismissed earlier."

"So, what are you trying to tell me?" Smith was losing his coolness.

"That what I thought was a garbled mess might not. That it is a new kind of protocol that we just don't understand. Akin to a never heard of language . . ."

"I don't like it at all!" Smith shook his head.

"It would mean the AOCP is using an entirely different protocol for communication!" Toxic finished.

"Fuck!" Smith jumped from the bed and ran out of the cabin.

“I think we should follow him.” Azure said after recovering.

“God idea.” Toxic was not sure what got into Smith all of a sudden. Sometimes humans were so cryptic to her.

“Smith?” Azure found her partner in the conning tower. He was sitting in front of numerous holo screens, watching different reports.

“This could be it . . .” he mumbled, eyes large as a watermelon and then turned to Azure: “The stakes just got much higher!”

“What do you mean?” she asked him, but instead of an answer all he did was contacting the Admiral and asked him to slowly remove excess assets from the area.

“You never mentioned him the garbled transmissions.” she noted.

“No, I did not!” Smith left at it, then asked her to follow him back to the primary bridge where Baby showed some preliminary calculations. Smith scrolled over the screens. It preoccupied his mind, Baby could tell. She would ask him what it was about, but he would never respond. Eventually he began to nod: “Toxic, please contact our spy assets and re task them.”

“To do what?”

“Have one of them spy on the AOCP spy vessel. Passive only, the other one should aim its listening arrays toward the Albert’fa-Coop station. Capture everything!”

“May I ask what for?”

“The enemy is adapting, that’s why . . .” Smith remained cryptic.

Toxic glanced at Azure, but she was clueless.

“Would somebody call Captain Mya and ask her to start watching those illegal Trojans with undecipherable coding?”

“So, we no longer concentrating on the Green Void?” Toxic asked. She felt confused at the moment.

“Oh, we are, but so as they and it’s prime time to observe them thinking we aren’t onto them!”

“Are you okay?” Azure touched Smith’s forehead. Its temperature felt normal, drawing additional frowns into her otherwise smooth face.

“So, the plan is going ahead?” Asked Toxic.

“Full power!” Smith was busy nodding.

*

“I think you’re steadily improving!” Captain Aa watched Amerlee emerging from the cubicle. It was a sim room, this time simulating a war zone. The trodes were hooked to Amerlee’s forehead. Their red imprint lingered as she disconnected them so quickly. She hated an apocalyptic city scape, hated even more that it was the Capitol City. She recognized some storefronts and corners from her own memory. All in all, she fared relatively well, only being killed by thirteen times in the past four hours. Time flew quick in the simulation chamber. This was of course after two hours in the gun range. Time flew quickly there as well. Captain Aa went out of her way to teach her, and that piqued her interest. As far as Amerlee saw, Aa was also interested in her boyfriend, yet her approach seemed genuine. She decided to get to the bottom of this, so she said to her, “I think I’m going to have my hair cut short!”

“Why?” Aa looked at her from top to bottom like a disaster.

Amerlee shrugged. “Azure has some long hair. Longer than mine, so maybe it would interest Smith if I would appear different.”

“I don’t think so . . .” Captain Aa shook her head.

“Do you ever thought of having an orgy?” It slipped out of her mouth so quick, it petrified her.

“Excuse me?!” Aa seemed highly upset for a moment.

“It’s obvious you harboring feelings for him.” Amerlee responded quietly.

Aa shot back an ultra-quick: “No!”

Amerlee squinted. “Yeah, right . . .”

"Okay, so I might have feelings for him, but he knew of it a long time ago. He never moved forward." Aa shot back angrily.

"Have you been persistent?"

"Oh, yeah, I have been! He plays a pussy in those scenarios!" Aa frowned.

"It's obvious you have been with girls, so why the utter decline for a groupie?" Amerlee asked her candidly.

"I would like him for myself. Why would I want to share that?" Aa asked her matter-of-factly.

Amerlee thought she had a point there: "Perhaps you like a setup with him . . ."

"I won't entertain myself with that anymore!" Aa shook her head again. It felt disturbing; like a force that awakened in herself, to try something utterly sinful. Something that would empower her as well. She glanced at Amerlee, who giggled to mask this utterly disturbing conversation. "I was just joking!"

"No, you did not!" Aa scoffed.

"Okay, so let's shelve the thought, eh?" Amerlee thought it would be best to withdraw.

"Deep!"

"Agreed!" They nodded in unison.

"So . . ." Aa forgot what they would do next.

"So?" Amerlee was eager to learn more.

"Commander Danek pushed a message to me while you were inside the chamber. Smith is doing fine. There seems to be an AOCP connection to the blowing up spaceships just as I thought so!" she lifted her chin. It did not go unnoticed either.

"He is going to put an end to it, right?"

"Yes, he is. There are certain things in motion already. All we have to do is to wait for the big bammm and then you would end up in his arms again." Aa tried to smile.

"And you?"

"Me? I would be on my way to somewhere." Captain Aa misunderstood her entirely while continuing: "Perhaps under the wings of the Admiral or perhaps a Monarch mandate propels me in a different direction, why?"

"Nothing."

"Don't worry, I am a good girl!" Aa thought she understood her earlier question.

"I don't think that goodness suits you!" Amerlee looked at her.

"Meaning?"

"Meaning, that I would expect some devious way for you to stay at arm's length for my Smith!"

"Nonsense! I have a military carrier to live for. I want to make the Emperor proud!" Captain Aa had to remind herself to say that.

"That's not just it!" Amerlee walked around her, looking for a twitch in her face that would explain the Captain's true motives.

"No. I want to make my father proud as well!" Aa admitted.

"Father? Oh, that's nice! Well, for now all I have to say that whatever happens in the bed I'm gonna steal his love!" Amerlee bobbed her head.

Aa tilted hers, trying to see something. It was obvious Amerlee had some sleazy dreams about Smith, but how one would go to steal someone's love in the middle of the act was beyond her. "Go home, Amerlee!" Aa shook her head and walked away. It baffled her. What if anything Smith saw in Amerlee? She was not in the military, yet she tried. She was not aggressive, yet she tried.

She was not vicious, yet she tried.

Then again, she was persistent.

More than herself.

She looked back, seeing Amerlee deep in her thoughts, flexing her left arm, imaging aiming a gun in it.

Chapter Twenty Four

Execution with complication

"Battle stations!" Smith was overly excited as he allowed Toxic's nanites to strap him into the bed. He lulled himself to a deep state, where he was hyperaware of his surroundings; even outside of the Toxic herself!

The daunting task of supervising the entire maneuver fell onto Baby, who had done important missions like this before. Three huge silver bullets hung from a rail like device beneath the DSR. Azure and two Honor Guards spent half a day in zero G to affix the deadly devices. As Toxic said, if any one of them goes off, they would be instantly vaporized. She tried to pay no mind of her back then and now, as she, Izim and Jena were tasked with the important task of manually navigate each individual missile into a designated spot in space. The idea was that the missiles would lock onto the AOCP asset on three different sides. Soon it was T minus one minute and tensions rose exponentially. Nobody knew for sure whether it would work, nobody knew whether AOCP would target the designated uranium ore vessel at all. But as the claxons went off on board the Toxic Smith focused, and soon time took up an entirely different meaning.

For human senses, space was always at a standstill. A manmade object occasionally would hurl across the field of vision or field of observation, and then humans would realize time was moving. This time it was eerie different. As soon as the AOCP object dropped out of hyperspace, time slowed considerably. They were able to see as the uranium ore hauler buckled under the enormous pressure, how it instantaneously ripped apart by the strange object and how seconds later the object made contact with the Green Void, then began to bounce off of it. As soon as the object began to turn to expose the protected positional thrusters, Smith slowed time to a screeching halt. Soon it was Azure and her partner's time to spring into action. The girls used a strap on holster to propel the missiles to their approximate position. Once in place, they de-mated the Songolar 7B from the strap on and used their only option to activate the missiles. By that time the AOCP object repositioned itself and began to hurl toward its home base. In the meantime, Toxic began to move away from the scene.

The now active missiles mated onto the extremely heavy object, and moments later they made a positive magnetic lock.

Smith battled with time to maintain focus. It was difficult for him to maintain it, as so many things were dependent on this being successful. After Azure mentally sent him the all-is-good signal, the relived Smith lost his focus and time returned to normal flow.

He was exhausted, and the nanites worked hard to relieve him of his accumulated sweat. A holographic screen appeared out of thin air, showing the grainy, distant feed, relayed to them by the Eclipse. The AOCP vessel arrived at its destination, and it slowly began to descend. It was just about to disappear under the moon's surface when everything lit up. It seemed two detonations hit simultaneously after the first one.

Smith was sipping from the water bottle as he watched the telemetry with great joy. The truly great news was, the planetary object was not blown apart. The bad news was that the entire region was literally up in smokes!

"The locals will learn of this unusual occurrence in less than an hour!" Toxic warned him.

"Good. Keep the mine laying operations alive, like nothing happened. Have Captain Mya continue her operation and have the Colonel aid her! Send the Avroras back to Captain Aa. Say if the AOCP spy . . ."

"Smith!" Toxic's voice changed. It suddenly became urgent as she cut him off in mid-sentence.

"What?"

"The targeted spy vessel just sent a burst of transmissions toward the AR-534!"

"I'm coming to the bridge!" Smith pulled up his pants. By the time he arrived, Azure and her companions were there as well.

"What's the situation?" Smith asked repeatedly.

"AR-534 is still okay . . ." Apparently Toxic was worried for the same thing as Smith was. Namely, if some hidden charges might blow it to shreds.

"Where is the spy vessel?" Smith demanded to know.

"Well, it turned around and headed straight toward our black hole in AOCP space!" Toxic admitted.

"And the AR-534 is still operational?" Smith did not get it. He was fearful the dormant AOCP trojans would unleash their true payload, whatever they were.

"Captain Mya reports in!" Toxic did not wait for approval; she brought the feed to the main screen.

"Captain!" Smith acknowledged the woman.

"My Lord! We've intercepted several garbled transmissions from the AOCP spy vessel. It activated two of the dormant Trojans we've been observing. They sent their payload to other AR's in the region, but after transmitting they erased themselves. We recorded the entire operation and we will simulate and reverse engineer it soon. As far as we could tell, the payload the Trojans released was a similar garbage style, sent out to four ARs: One by Danal IV, another one at Tetran7, and another one somewhere into the Hudris triangle, deep in AOCP space. The last one was destined to one of the many GalSat nodes operating at the CTP!"

"Very interesting, Captain! Monitor for twenty-four hours, then withdraw to the Trixec's staging area to meet up with us and bring the Colonel too!"

"Yes, My Lord!" she bowed respectfully.

Smith felt trapped for a moment. He was about to have a panic attack. Perhaps he missed something and just getting caught up with it now, as he saw this garbled transmission that nobody saw before. To calm himself, he automatically expanded his mental aura, then contracted it, but not before briefly contacting with Toxic and Azure as well. At the moment as their aura met, a message filtered thru deep space. It was just a single word, almost cut off; a mental outcry before the captors realized what just happened: 'Hilderin'.

Smith spun around, toward the general direction of AOCP space, and frowned.

Azure observed him visually and mentally. She saw it piqued his interest; she felt his mental turmoil he was quick to contain. What she did not see or felt was how the hair felt to be standing up on his back.

Smith slowly licked his lips, then turned back to the hologram: "You felt it too?"

"What?" Baby became alarmed.

"I felt it!" Azure chimed in.

Smith blinked, looked confused at her direction, then back at the main viewscreen that dimmed as Toxic displayed the solar system called Hilderin.

"What's that?"

"Hilderin . . ." Toxic announced, then added more relevant information.

"What?" Jena was looking for clarification around the bridge.

"So close to the AOCP border." Smith walked closer, still shivering.

"During the recent occupation they set up bases there." Toxic activated another holo screen beside the main one to show them the files.

"And they're evolved how?" Smith was lost trying to find a relevant sentence.

"They were just admitted to the UNHL two years prior the AOCP attack, expansion or occupation, whatever you want to call it." Toxic responded.

"So, they aren't sophisticated?"

"No. Their first fusion reactor went online five years prior. That's when the Ministry of Extraterrestrial Culture Integrations, you know, before the split of AOCP-UNHL, decided to send agents to the planet. They're humanoid. They had a permanent space station that had dual use."

"Dual use?" Azure was unfamiliar with the term.

"Yes. They had a civilian and a military section. They were more than certain they weren't alone. The military extension gathered radio communication from the nearby trade route. The Ministry of Extraterrestrial Culture Integrations concluded that because of that and their first fusion reactor, they pose little risk to the neighboring planets, but lots of internal risk as a society, so they made their move and sent agents to the planet. After successful exploration, they issued the order to make an announcement. While it was immature, they believed they were able to contain the shock wave rippling across the planet. The inhabitants on four continents, about three billion total humans, were angry and scared at first, but the Ministry of Extraterrestrial Culture Integrations worked out a decent plan, due to the planet's potential."

"What potential would that be?"

"Very pure water! The deal with the four continent's leaders were made to export decent sums of water in exchange of low-level technology that could push them forward in evolution."

Smith made a face. "What the fuck?! How is this connected to our mental outcry?"

Toxic continued with a kind voice: "Even you, or rather the companies you own transport water, about fifty thousand gallons a year to Gnem . . ."

Upon hearing one of his worlds connected to the newfound trouble, Smith took a second to think of it: "So how far is this?"

"Four thousand light years from here. Due to the borders and angry planetary systems, the ride would take couple days as there are too many break points between our current position and . . ."

"So . . ." Smith dismissed her concern with a hand move. He remembered to the recent past: "So, a couple years ago once we stuck at Tical, and the AOCP took over the old GalNet and stranded everybody apart in the Milky Way without communications, I assume they expanded to Hilderin as well?"

"Correct. They blew up the planet's extensive space station, killing thirteen astronauts in the process. Then they landed. We don't know too much about the occupation, but what we do know might be interesting in light of what we witnessed in here."

"Let's hear it then!" Smith became impatient.

"As you all know, after what went down in the history books as the 'Battle at the TCP' the UNHL gave one week or a hundred and sixty-eight hours for the AOCP to withdraw from the occupied territories. Well, there were couple cases when the deadline was not met. The analytics shows that the average withdraw concluded under five days, but in the case of the Hilderin it stretched out to almost two full weeks!"

"They had something there . . ." Smith leaned forward in his chair.

"Possibly. UNHL representatives visited the planet about a month after the deadline. Robotic response was of course within the withdrawal period. The locals were unhappy and between denouncing their alliance and threatening shooting representatives onsite, they asked for reparations for their demised space station and the loss of life. As far as I know, the representatives left, but we had not come up with formal reparations."

"Why?"

"The Ministry of Extraterrestrial Culture Integrations believes they will come to their senses if the AOCP wonders to their space again . . ."

"Great policy, huh?" Azure crossed her arms over her chest.

"Seventy-five thousand miles from the planet. The Armistice line is way too close on that one."

Smith flinched. *And the UNHL had other things to do besides honor low level agreements*. "We have to keep a low profile there." he realized.

Chapter Twenty Five

Preparations

"So, what do you make out of this?" Toxic asked him later, playfully bumping into him onboard the Trixec. They were taking their seats in the conference room. He did not reply and did not acknowledge her physical closeness either. That bothered Toxic. Smith's mind was obviously preoccupied. All she could do was wait for his impending speech.

Smith waited until everybody arrived, including the Admiral, then he slowly rose from his post. "I want to congratulate to everybody involved in this convoluted operation. I will meet with Captain Aa to congratulate her sideline involvement soon after this meeting adjourned. As you all know the Toxic made a slight detour so I could have a meeting with Admiral Qaw. I asked him to extend our borrowing of the Mya and the Eclipse. This mission turned out to be very different from what I envisioned. First of all, I would like to announce that we accomplished our primary object. We destroyed the exotic AOCP weapon along with the five interconnected bases on the AOCP moon! We do know that several rescue ships converged above the moon and they're running many scans. The mine laying SCC, completed her work, near the border and offered our help to AOCP, but of course they declined. Upon reviewing all information, I asked the Admiral to fold this position as our job seemingly concluded. He agreed to stay in position for couple more days to simulate further expectation of mysterious civilian cargo disappearances. Now for our second goal. I would ask anyone who don't have top secret clearance to leave the room now!" Smith glanced around.

The Admiral's XO, Captain Ke'hn left along with Jena and the Death Squad members as well. Smith glanced around again, then he stopped at Captain Mya. The Zenin woman was seemingly uncomfortable in her chair.

"Captain Mya. I need you to take off and head to one of the two UNHL based Accelerator Rings of the Green Void and covertly search its databanks for clues. Perhaps we need to discretely infect it for later use. It's best done locally. Colonel Re'kl you will do the same thing with the other AR then meet with your Captain. Temporary you two are under the 26th UNHL Fleet, working as advisors. Your home port will be the Destination Unknown, trailed by Captain Josh Kulighan and his expeditionary forces. We need to get to the bottom of the transmissions we observed upon the exotic AOCP weapon's destruction. I believe the stakes are really high. I'm certain that what we've seen were part of their newest Sygma Operating System and if that's true we need to decipher it or at least penetrate it because it is entirely different platform than a

Sygma 9 . . ."

Azure made a face at Toxic, who responded in a similar fashion. Spy work . . . Back to square one!

"So, what now?" Azure asked from Smith once they left the conference room.

"We're going to meet with the DU. I need to pick Amerlee up, calm her, and then we'll play it by ear . . ."

"What do you think those transmissions were about?"

"Remember the past? How we learned AOCP dual utilization of the military Sygma Operation System for their own, nefarious reasons?" he turned to her warningly.

Azure nodded silently.

"How we learned by very unfortunate means of their embedded backdoors that led to a very cold state between us? How we spent enormous money designing a new system for the UNHL so we could not be double crossed again?

"I do remember." Azure nodded once, yet again. Keeping her baby face serious.

"And how we learned, basically me and my closest comrades, that these operating systems being developed by extremely talented AOCP Section Agents, whom they meet telepathically to design it, work on it remotely? Minimizing chances of discovery? Huh? Remember the crazy space stations with all those hallucinations?" he lifted an eyebrow for emphasis.

Azure covered her mouth with a silent scream as realization hit her.

"Even if Sygma 10 isn't operational, we've seen nodes being contacted, and that's important for us to weed out local spying rings. If it's operational than we've just witnessed that it moved with virtual impunity and we need to stop that being happening! Then again, with Hilderin in the picture, we must go there. Perhaps it's already late, who knows? In either way, we have work to do!" he folded his hand behind his back. It was the serious sign Azure was waiting for. Now she knew he was not joking! She folded her hands behind her back as well and ran after him.

Amerlee could barely contain her enthusiasm once she spotted Evan Smith approaching her. Captain Aa, in the background, felt to be like a mother who made sure her child was ready for the world.

Commander Danek watched them all. He knew time was too short of getting Amerlee ready, but believed the woman was on the right track.

As Amerlee's lips parted from Smith, she felt his tensions emerging.

"What's wrong?"

"An Emperor's job is never finished!" he responded wearily.

Amerlee tried to read his face, but could not. She turned to the uncomfortable-looking Azure, who shrugged. "Welcome to the black ops world . . ." That's, of course, not what she wanted to say, but it was best to leave it at that. Azure secretly hoped she would be back at the Villa-Castle with Smith, but now it seemed that won't be the case anymore. She, however, wondered how will Amerlee receive the news. Just as she thought, Amerlee seemed confused. Apparently, she was under the same assumption that they would head home.

"Let me talk to the Captain for a minute." Smith excused himself, leaving Amerlee with Azure.

"So, what's this sad look on both of your faces?" Amerlee asked her, gloating toward Smith and Captain Aa, thinking about what she told her about Smith over the past couple of days.

Azure rolled her eyes. "Well, now of course it seems we won't be getting home anytime soon."

"Complications?" Amerlee tried to learn more.

"We can say that . . ." Azure sighed heavily.

*

Captain Yoyo on board the UNHL Planet Destroyer Trinity was not expecting a late-night visit from the Admiral's official couriers. It surprised her, to say the least. The last thing she heard was the successful conclusion of the Emperor led mission. She was under the assumption she would trail either Admiral Tarbuk or Captain Aa, but to receive a military grade data crystal with undoubtedly secretive stuff on it heightened her insecurity. The Emperor was correct; by working for the 26th UNHL Fleet, she would barely have time to visit her family . . . That conversation happened years ago.

She called the bridge for a confirmation; the courier ship had indeed returned to the Trixec. Its sole mission was to hand deliver the encrypted information, something that could not be trusted even to a sight-to-sight communication! After digesting the news, she sat down in her chair, placed the data crystal into the socket and laid back to receive the new orders. The Admiral's gloomy posture on the holographic projection did not elude her attention: “Captain Yoyo, you are now on a black ops mission!”

Upon hearing, she almost fell out of her chair. She was beyond excited. The moment she was waiting for! She had to pause the recordings to concentrate on the voice again. “It is disguised as a part goodwill, part checkup mission to a pre designated route. At o’ eight hundred two of Captain Josh’s SCCs will join you. One of them is a multipurpose, the other is a training ship. At first the three of you will head to Galler, a world not far from the Zenin-Kron Empire where an ammunition ship will replenish your needs. Standard ops, but like any ammunition transfer, it’s not without its own risks. Once all of your ships received ammunition and spare parts, you are to head to the armistice line along the following coordinates . . .” The recording paused to give space to a crude map where a dotted line represented her proposed route. It touched upon five planetary systems. Then the recording continued: “These systems are within earshot of Hilderin, a planet where the Emperor is staging an operation. Your job is to listen in, to see if he needs your help. Hilderin falls within the armistice line, so I don’t need to explain the sensitive nature of the situation. Be the souls of the Emperors guide you on your journey!” The Admiral was seen saluting on the screen at the end of the recording.

*

“Anything to enlighten poor me?” Amerlee massaged Smith’s stiff shoulder in the Toxic’s cabin.

“What do you want to know?” Smith raised an eyebrow.

“Yeah!” Azure drooled from the other side, earning a deep frown from Smith.

“I saw those soldiers with the Trixec’s logo on their shoulders, so I know we are going somewhere!” Amerlee protested.

“Fascinating!” Smith rewarded her with an approving nod. Such a miniscule detail caught her attention.

Amerlee delightfully grinned. “So?” she poked his side.

"We are following up on something that might be nothing. How 'bout you? Do you want to join us or shall we drop you off

at . . ." Smith stopped as Amerlee's expressions changed, for the worst.

"If I may intrude!" They all heard Toxic's voice reverberating in the room.

"Don't let me stop you!" Smith laid back on his bed, waiting for Toxic to produce a holographic screen where statistics began to roll down.

"What's that?" Amerlee leaned forward.

"That's stuff we gathered about Hilderin, our destination!" Toxic responded.

"They use an extensive network of roads?" Amerlee read it.

"Apparently. And they not too fond of us."

"Are we going in disguise?" Toxic formed a hologram, and that holographic presentation turned to Smith.

"Yes. Prepare to change the ID and the looks of the DSR!" Smith regained his leadership role.

"To?"

"We're going to borrow another DSR design."

"Is Admiral Qaw onboard?" The hologram frowned.

"With my plan?" Smith asked, then nodded, "You'll take the 776-Vidra call sign and

looks."

"She is blue!" Toxic sounded a tad sad, referring to that DSR series exterior paint.

"Yeah. Is that going to be a problem?"

"No. I can make it happen!"

"Good. Jena and Baby with the Honor Guards and the Death Squad members are just part of the deal, as you noted, my love!" he fiddled with Amerlee's finger to Azure's not so covered anger.

"So, they're elite guards?" Amerlee was not sure.

"Yes. Originally thirty-six of them." he gave her a quick history lesson. "Then we have two Dream Fighters affixed to the half pods as a good measure, but we will do this on a quiet mode. First, we'll extend the boom and make accurate readings of the planet. Then we will do seismic readings and so on. We need to read the situation and I won't be there as the Emperor for sure.

"A corporal, maybe?" Toxic made an offer.

"Maybe. I don't know yet. It depends on how fast Captain Mya can rejoin us. We need her ship's expertise, so we will not land on the planet before." Smith replied confidently.

He was less confident a week later as the Toxic, under the disguise of the Vidra, made her endless flips around the planet near the AOCP border. While Baby and Jena with the Honor Guards made themselves extremely useful in the ongoing mapping situation, Smith had another potential nightmare to face with; namely that one of the continents just invaded the other!

Chapter Twenty Six

Hilderin

Captain Aa quietly sat in her chair on board the Destination Unknown's bridge. The space ship encircled Danal IV. Josh Kulighan, and his numerous SCCs were running various exercises in the neighboring planetary systems. Colonel Re'kl returned from his dubious mission just last night. He asked for fuel transfer and the replenishment was underway. She tasked an Avrora8 spy plane to run by Agross V, and she anticipated its return any time now. She gave Commander Danek wide berth to conduct various flying exercises. Some were quite elaborate, she observed. She got the hint from the locals calling her ship periodically that their continued presence now is less than welcoming for them. Just the other day, Danek was contacted by Danal IV Space Navy to ask for clarifications of their continued presence.

Her hands were itching for fight, but knew the crew needed exercises. She was pleasantly surprised when Captain Murdoch showed up with his pristine looking Victory IV.2D Planet Destroyer. He invited Captain Aa for a tour, and she gladly accepted it. Commander Danek could surely hold the 'fort' for couple hours while she would be away. She barely heard the first call of her rank; she was so into her thoughts. Then her attention snapped back to reality.

"Communications Officer, is there anything to report?" she asked.

"Captain Mya of the 0999-Mya arrived. She is reporting in!"

“Send me the feed!” She straightened her back as the small holo screen appeared front of her face.

“Captain Mya reporting in Ma’am!” The short blonde saluted with her bridge visible in the background.

“Was your deployment successful?”

“It was. My officer is prepared to send our reports to you!”

“Have it delivered it by person. Does your ship need any replenishment like Colonel Re’kl’s?” She inquired, out of character of a ship captain, but in line with Smith’s handling of friendly forces.

“My crew could use a short R n R and our telecommunications tower needs some repairs as well.” she replied with minimal hesitation.

“Have your ship land in the Port Side POD as the Starboard is currently reserved!” Captain Aa responded.

It was unusual for her to play the host and was not familiar with all the nuances of it yet. She was somewhat saddened that Smith took her out of the equation. She would much rather to be with him running the show than be sidelined like this, *but I suppose it has its merits as well,* she wondered. Not to mention it was beneficial for her carrier.

She withdrew to the Ready Room to meet Captain Mya while candidly Victor showed a quick holographic model of the DSR. Indeed, the green, needle like military space ship was damaged. It seemed their main communications array suffered something like an impact!

A bit later she learned it was space debris, as the DSR had to escape Tetran 7’s snooping security forces. Captain Mya called her assignment a success and did a quick demonstration of it by pulling data from the now live feed her ship possessed. It visibly impressed captain Aa. The malware dropped within the computer network of the Tetran 7’s Accelerating Ring filtered presumed Sygma 10 protocol perfectly. They found the supposed AOCP dormant malware and extracted a copy of it to try to reverse engineer, but according to Captain Mya it may take a considerable amount of time. Meanwhile, the DU's workers already began repair work on the 0999-Mya . . .

It was way before Smith would call it the early morning. Azure, of course, could not sleep, was up since four AM local time onboard the Toxic. She quietly slipped out of the upper bed and dressed up, then sat down by the holo display and began to browse thru the scanned information from last night. She knew well that the ship was more than capable to identify anything she might come across as interesting, but she was curious herself. The operation was well advanced; over a week and a half passed since the beginning of it. At first, things weren't going so smoothly. Evan made mistakes on his own, but of course he wouldn't say it out loud. The crew remained extremely obedient to his wishes, but she could feel the tensions rising. Everybody wanted to find the missing piece, as Smith called it. Nobody did. Smith to speed up operation spent about an hour every afternoon with the rest of the crew in the crowded galley where Toxic displayed past information about the planet. Smith called these the seminars, Baby joked about the daily 'reeducation camps', but even Azure could not deny that they were useful. For example, she herself did not know the full term of the AOCP withdrawals or that after the initial UNHL contact with the planet they worked out a trade agreement. Apparently, the fact that the Ministry of Extraterrestrial Culture Integrations set up the contact so hastily pissed Smith off, but eventually he calmed down, nodding that he understood the fast-tracked operation was due to the changing galactic climate. Back then, due to UNHL push, the Ministry of Extraterrestrial Culture Integrations was forced to reexamine every potential first contact situation along the AOCP border. SWEi Prime reasoned the potential planets would just fall under AOCP territory shall they decide to expand. It was a strategic move, one that Azure herself understood quite well. Unfortunately, and predictably, it caused a cultural shock to the planet's inhabitants. The Ministry of Extraterrestrial Culture Integrations worked out a deal with them to exchange the abundantly available and pure local water for standard energy cells and their power generating equipment all the while they pushed for planet wide ban on nuclear equipment. The Ministry of Extraterrestrial Culture Integrations also sent technicians to the planet to understand and study the planetary effort to finish their first fusion plant with the hidden motive to accelerate the local's effort. Of course, things did not go so smoothly as the population leaders demanded more answers. All the negotiations broke down as AOCP occupation began. Hilderin was abandoned by the numerous delegations sent by the Ministry of Extraterrestrial Culture Integrations, evacuated by the only UNHL frigate in the planet's vicinity. Then the AOCP occupation began and nobody had a way to find out about Hilderin's evolving internal politics under AOCP 'supervision'. Nor was it important. After the occupation, the Ministry of Extraterrestrial Culture Integrations sent a survey team to make contact. The planet's leaders behaved colder than the last time, understandably, since AOCP built a listening post on their land without permission from the locals. While AOCP military choose not to exterminate the living creatures on the planet, they did annex sizeable swaths and enforced a no entry to those lands. While Hilderin's people protested and occasionally attacked the annexed lands, every attempt by them was a failure. They never got past the perimeters and after an above planet bombing raid that decimated two of their major cities on the main land a form of truce was formed that both sides accepted. During the AOCP withdrawal that fell outside of the 168 hours mandated by the Emperors, they removed every equipment they could, blew up everything else. They knew well the planet's inhabitants would devote their entire population to dissect and understood the technology that killed many of them. They would not allow, and so it was one of the few planets where the withdrawal was lengthier than was allowed. The UNHL never pursued this failure and after a UNHL destroyer passed by, the UNHL abandoned it as a possible military beach head. Politicians on both sides demanded a DMZ, and Hilderin fell into that. Eventually the Ministry of Extraterrestrial Culture Integrations reopened their embassy, albeit very limited in nature. They helped to rebuild a destroyed space station for the planet and even fixed the space elevator. It was the way the preoccupation exchanges took place. When the Emperor demanded to know how if AOCP agents are still on the planet—that was his suspicion—could receive messages sent from the Green Void, the simple answer was that the space elevator also acted as powerful transmission tower. Apparently, the Ministry of Extraterrestrial Culture Integrations was thinking big when they built it!

Azure made a gesture, and the screen switched mode. She studied the people below them and their four continents. The so-called Main Land was huge; coastal cities everywhere, busy shipping lanes in every direction, while the internal land laid somewhat unused. They spotted couple of industrial hubs, remnants of a melted nuclear power plant, but since Smith believed the AOCP if they remained would keep agents away from populated areas, they were tirelessly scanning the Million Island chains. He was fixated on the almost continuous archipelago of close by islands. The locals spread out on it, devoid of major cities, and used fishing and tourism as a main source of income. Not far from the Main Land, another landmass stood less than six hundred miles away. Seemingly, they were the military powerhouse. Their military sea fleet was impressive, so as the arsenal of other weaponry they spotted on their preliminary over flights. Smith was certain AOCP wouldn't hang there . . . Then there was a lone land mass, seemingly far from everything else, sitting on the other side of the planet. Rich agricultural farmlands covered almost three quarters of it. Azure shook her head. It was suspicious for her that AOCP ran out of their allotted time to leave the planet. It would point to a huge operation on the planet below. But Smith did not want to use his powers to scan the planet, and conventional methods were time-consuming. She brought it up just yesterday and got a lecture in front of everybody from Smith on the bridge. He reasoned that the scanning operation is just the question of resources. He wanted to keep a low profile; hence, they were alone.

Jena's job was to fly one of the Dream Fighters closer to the AOCP border. She dropped buoys to act as a perimeter fence.

As far as Azure considered it, they were stuck at Hilderin for good or worse. She glanced at the sleeping couple: Smith and Amerlee, then back at the screen, thinking about how to help the spaceship in its mapping operation, when suddenly the claxons went off without any warning. Green light pulsed from the corners and Smith banged his head good into the bunk as the noise woke him abruptly.

"What, what's happening?" he held his head, blinking hard.

A lone drop of tear from the pain ran down of the corner of his left eye.

Azure jumped to him and quickly examined his head, knowing well it was nothing serious.

Amerlee was yawning beside him. Apparently, she was sleeping too.

"Are we under attack?" Smith yelled toward the middle of the room.

Soon light particles began to form and Toxic appeared out of thin air: "We are fine. However, my long-range sensors detected a nuclear detonation on the planet's surface!"

"Maybe some sort of test . . ." Smith held the bunk's side as he stood up, feeling slightly disoriented.

"I do not think so." The hologram swayed her head than a holo display appeared in midair, depicting a nighttime inferno over one of the Main Land's coastal city.

"It's a shame we matched our working cycle with the island chain's day time operation." Toxic added.

Smith made a nasty look toward the hologram, then grabbed his pants.

"So continent number three just invaded number one, is that it?" Smith hovered over the bridge's main holo display. He was more than dismayed. He hoped to snoop around undetected, but seemingly that was out the window, so to speak. He also hoped to convey the UNHL's continued vested interest in the planet. That seemed to be up in smoke as well.

By then, two more nuclear detonations killed well over two hundred thousand innocent people as the military nationals attacked the Main Land. Toxic offered high resolution scans, re-tasking her surveillance equipment to begin scan of the presumed military endeavor.

"Seems they hell bent on taking over!" Baby frowned.

"Casualties must be near half a million by now . . ." Azure flinched.

"What a massacre!" Smith held his head.

"Maybe we could've avoided it, huh?" Azure wondered aloud.

"How, exactly?" Smith growled at her all of a sudden.

"Um. Maybe if you would've contacted them as soon as we got here . . ." Azure became hesitant upon seeing Evan's anger focusing on herself.

"Why would've I have done that? Oh right, to ask them if they saw any occupiers renting a flat, yeah?" Smith was openly sarcastic. His anger stemmed from the trigger-happy locals fighting each other, and his inability to find a solid clue to his suspicion.

Toxic so humanly attempted to clear her throat to raise attention.

"Guy, guys!" she activated a new layer of holo screens and began to point to the left corner.

"What is it?" Smith took his eyes off Azure, who was about to repel the verbal attack.

"Look!" she repeatedly pointed at the screen.

"What should I look at?" Smith lost steam, then his mouth began to hang. When he regained his senses, he pointed at the screen: "Is that a Wongel class AOCP heavy frigate? In the sand. . . ?" he tilted his head.

"Eight of them." Baby added as Toxic zoomed out.

"Is that a coincidence?" Azure asked from them.

"This is not a coincidence!" Smith stepped closer and examined the screen. "How did they crash land so perfectly lining up?"

"Their main body aims toward the ocean." Toxic said.

"Are their engines working?" Smith began to think.

"I can't determine that from this angle."

"Force fields?"

"Multiple! Some might mess with your perception to believe nothing is there . . . While it seems they are abandoned, the body mass indicates they aren't just an empty shell!" Toxic added.

"Life forms nearby?" Smith snapped.

"As I said, seems abandoned. My equipment can't detect anything from this distance."

"Can you send a drone or something?" Smith wanted to know every bit of information.

"Something . . . We are too far and we can't abandon our equipment just like that, but perhaps with the help of a Dream Fighter?"

"Jena Suit up!" Smith snapped, his hands itching.

"Yes, boss!" Chirped the slender woman, and the next moment she was thru the bridge's blast doors.

"I need more options!" Smith slammed on the armrest.

"Like what, honey?" Amerlee asked for the first time.

"Where Is Josh Kulighan?"

"Captain Yoyo is somewhere nearby." Amerlee reminded him.

"I need a tactician!" Smith almost panicked. "I want Josh!" he added.

"He is cruising with Captain Aa . . ." Baby reminded him.

"Would someone call him and tell him to turn his SCC around!" Smith barked.

"It will be at least two days before . . ." Toxic could not continue as Smith lifted his index finger. Toxic abandoned the protest. "I call him right away!"

"Tell him to bring company. At least three more SCCs!" Smith's attention snapped back to the holo screen. This was what he suspected, but hoped he wouldn't find. Still . . . Eight Wongel class heavy frigates? They were at least forty years old. What good use the AOCP had for them to keep it around? Perhaps they modified them to keep working from inside. It did not make sense at all. But it piqued his curiosity. Amerlee gently touched his arm, and he found a rare moment to reassure her with a smile: "We're in business!"

"Not the one you hoped . . ." she responded, understanding the situation.

"Not . . ."

Suddenly another set of warning light were activated.

"What now?" Smith stared across the bridge. He still had not had his breakfast, and it made him jumpy.

"A Flying Wing type of super freighter just entered to the solar system at high speed." Toxic calmly informed them.

"Commercial?" Smith was not sure anymore.

"Yes. It doesn't broadcast anything; but I can ping it when they get closer. Um . . ."

"Um what?"

"It launched two smaller space vessels."

"Are they armed?"

"Doesn't seem to be the case . . ."

Smith bit his lips. "No way to determine what they are from this position, huh?"

"Sorry."

"Baby, take the other Dream Fighter. Snoop around them. See if they commercial or what exactly their intent is!"

"Maybe they here for the water?" Amerlee suggested.

"Could be . . ." Smith slowed down, then turned to the hologram; "Do we know if the UNHL reestablished the exchange program?"

"The time frame does allow it, but I don't have the means to confirm it at the moment." Toxic replied.

"Fuck!" Smith felt to be in the binder here, then suddenly a thought emerged from within: "Can you check whether the escalator is moving?"

"The what?" Azure thought she lost out a couple of sentences.

"To explain it crudely," Smith turned to the girls, "It's like an endless rope with multiple buckets on it. So, since its couple hundred kilometers tall, it's a complex system and to speed the rope up from zero to the desired speed might take a week as the strain on the machinery is pretty enormous. So, if it is moving, it would indicate they are expecting a load to arrive soon." Smith explained.

Amerlee nodded and spoke before Azure could: ". . . and if it's not moving, it would indicate something else entirely!"

"Good girl!" Smith kissed her, alienating Azure in the process, who uttered angrily, "I thought the same too!"

"Let me see . . ." Toxic began to profile the station as it just appeared on their horizon.

Smith cursed himself for how low profile he chose for this mission. They can't abandon their position now, and he only had two fighters to begin with! Toxic noted that Jena's fighter just entered into the high atmosphere, so she was out of communication right now.

"Send an update to her about the company we're about to receive."

"We got some time, about a full day before the Flying Wing gets here." Toxic added, then as Smith was about to ask as of why, she explained: "Depending their gross weight they going to use a slingshot type of deceleration. Frankly, I'm just as dismayed as you are."

"Why?" Azure asked both of them before Amerlee could get in the middle of this conversation.

"Because they aren't meant to navigate within the solar system." Toxic replied.

Smith scratched his head. "First of all, they aren't meant to dock with space stations at all. They're heavy haulers with several million of metric tons of cargo. It's simply wasteful to operate them in this manner. They would just use smaller freighters whom it would operate from the planet's surface. The small freighter would catch up with the Flying Wing, unload the cargo and move on. This type of maneuvering is highly suspicious!" he scratched his face, reminding him of the fact he skipped shaving this morning.

"Baby launched!" Toxic reported. "You, Smith may have to contact Captain Yoyo."

"I want to avoid commotion! It could raise attention from the AOCP side!" Smith cried out loud.

Toxic's hologram shrugged. She knew they could not just retract the surveillance equipment on a whim.

"Okay!" Smith sighed, giving in. "Contact Captain Yoyo and ask her to send reinforcement to us, now!"

"So not her ship or big SCCs, but maybe some landing ships?" Toxic was not sure anymore.

"Heavy bombers and a Spec Ops freighter will do!" Smith agreed. "I'm hungry!" he exclaimed.

"Here is a biscuit!" Amerlee offered helpfully from a small tray she smuggled onto the bridge.

"Azure, don't you have that ugly look!" Smith had to laugh. He kissed Amerlee's forehead that just further infuriated Azure, who believed there was some kind of an unspoken battle between her and Amerlee to win his arms.

"What do you think about the Flying Wing?" Toxic asked Smith as he was eating the biscuit.

"Suspicious . . . I really need some answers." The still warm food delighted Smith, not to mention of causing happy feelings emanating from his greedy stomach.

"Baby will be in range within two hours. Jena should be back by then. The drone is a high endurance one with very sophisticated detection equipment. Will get answers, don't worry!" Toxic explained.

“I worry when people say don’t worry!” Smith snapped.

“I’m not exactly a human, so that should count!” The hologram winked.

“Are you two bonding again?” Azure crossed her arms in defiance.

“Uh oh . . .” Toxic changed the holo feed showing the seemingly abandoned space elevator.

“Not moving . . .” Smith’s frown deepened.

“Trouble, I presume?” The always polite Amerlee tried to read between the lines.

*

Meher grabbed his binocular and began to scan the perimeter. He took a deep breath of the dry air. It was just past dawn, and he wanted to check on the semiautomatic equipment. The gigantic trawlers moved slowly across the deserted land. He had to laugh every time he saw the gigantic heavy equipment in his land. People said he was crazy. Why buy practically abandoned land right next door to the aliens who occupied their planet? Because it was cheap, he replied all the time. He made sure the poles were all active to tell the land movers to begin their turn so the AOCP force field wouldn’t disable them. He saw the pictures from the TV couple years ago, during the last attack on the installation. It was pathetic. Whatever they threw at it just blew up harmlessly. Of course, the so-called occupation was the past now. The Main Land government decided not to poke into the annexed land despite the military junta’s objections. They tried to buy him out several times, but so far, he refused. The land was not the best location or composition, but pristine, untamed by the radioactive midland that was abandoned twenty years ago. People moved into big cities. Urbanization was the slogan. Meher refused to move. He used his house as a bargaining chip to buy another swath of land. After the second season, he reinvested all his profits to the lands again. His wife was not happy, but she saw he was right. Meher believed his location was the correct one. If one day the so called UNHL aliens would buy his grain, he only has to get a trucking business going to a distance less than six hundred miles and he would be at the space elevator. He was already thinking big!

"Dad, I'm hungry!" his daughter chirped beside him on the open jeep. Meher stopped daydreaming and patted his daughter's shoulder. He opened the food basket and began to fiddle between the sandwiches when his daughter pointed at the light blue sky across the deserted land, "Look, a white line!"

Meher tossed the sandwich at her lap and grabbed the binocular again. He pulled to his eyes.

She was correct. There was a white line, high across the land, but it drew not one but two white lines! It was immensely high and shrinking by the seconds. Suddenly the lines stopped growing and the tiny dot before them disappeared.

Meher, who was always curious and served in the military, knew this was something really high tech.

"Turn on the radio, honey!" he flinched. No airplane can disappear without a trace. It had to be there. He repeatedly searched for any sign of it, but then he spotted or he thought he spotted it way higher! A half minute later it was gone forever. He glanced at the ground, thinking hard. It perhaps meant that the plane was not a plane; maybe it was a spaceship. As far as he knew, the Main Land has not restarted their manned space program yet. "Maybe we were dreaming . . ." he glanced at his daughter, who listened intently to the noisy radio.

"What is it, Mysha?"

"Dad, the radio said that the military junta attacked us overnight!" she was breathing shallow.

Meher had to sit down in the driver's seat. He turned on the radio to listen to the frail voice of a reporter talking about mass casualties at the expensive City Line, the Belhar-Mentol axis of cities that grew into each together in the past fifty years. He fearfully glanced at the blue sky. Perhaps it was the junta's stratospheric plane they saw, cruising high above the continent. He had to report it. He remembered to the airport, a military outpost less than twenty miles away. He turned the key in the ignition and the jeep fired up its internal combustion engine. He was about to steer the jeep when the unexpected earthquake hit.

The ground shook, loosen soil like waves of an ocean rose from the ground and covered them the next second. Meher stopped the jeep and after making sure his daughter was okay, he turned around. There was a crater below them with something smoldering in the middle of it. He grabbed his shotgun and slowly approached it while sternly deterring his daughter to follow him. The object was oval, about a meter and a half long. Almost like a torpedo, except it was not. It was dull brown, a bit red perhaps, and it was smooth at every angle he could look at. He could not see any opening on it. He fearfully touched the surface, and it was hot. He glanced at the edge of the crater where his daughter stood; folding her own hands, apparently worried for her father.

"Mysha!" he yelled to unleash his anger at her, but she pointed beside him: "Watch out, Dad!"

Meher turned around and now the torpedo like device levitated! It emitted a strange noise while slowly repositioned itself to face Meher, who turned pale. He lifted his arms, but nothing happened.

"Don't kill me, please!" he uttered and shut up as he heard a loud clack from the levitating thing. Two small holes appeared on its side, then a blade like device extended on both sides, unpacking itself into wings. The device slowly moved away and out of the crater.

Meher climbed out of it and watched as the levitating device moved closer to the barbed wire fence. He huddled his daughter and pushed her into the jeep while still watching the alien device. He was sure of that now.

The brown levitating thing reached the fence, began to cruise alongside of it until it reached an old gate. There, it faced with it and soon the smell of a stench hit Meher's nose. He was trying to restart the jeep frantically.

"Dad?" Mysha grabbed his arm. Meher turned toward the object that bore across the fence than sped up, while moving close to the ground.

“We would be dead if we try that!” Mysha shook her head in disbelief.

“No doubt!” his father mumbled it, put the transmission into gear and floored the pedal.

*

“Jena is back!” Toxic announced on the bridge.

“What did you find?” Smith asked her while she replaced a burned-out energy cell on the fighter. She was pretty good moving in zero-g.

“I dropped the surveillance unit and left the atmosphere. I saw a small airstrip where I can land and pick it up six hours from now. The last message I got from it was that the entire area is under a force field erection, but it has spotty base, so I believe it chose to bore across the outer protecting fence.”

“The force field is active?” It surprised Smith.

“Yes. It’s a military camo style.”

“Hold on!” Smith turned to the hologram.

“The images we saw about the AOCP space ships . . .”

“Yes?”

“Have you used any kind of filtering or that is a natural camera feed?”

“Come on Smith, you know that it isn’t!”

“So, what do the locals see?” Smith defensively crossed his arms.

“Oh! I haven’t thought of that . . .” The hologram scratched her head, imitating slight confusion. She re ran the feed and showed it to them.

“Nothing!” Azure summarized it in one word.

“So, they think it’s abandoned, huh? Is that a low powered energy field?”

“Yes, it is. So low in fact that without specialized equipment it is undetected!” Toxic added.

Azure frowned, “Why leave it on if it’s abandoned?”

“Is it?” Smith poked into Azure’s eye.

"But once the occupation was over, AOCP would have to know we are coming back, that we are going to snoop around . . ." Azure remained skeptical.

"Maybe they rode the shotgun." Amerlee tried to be helpful.

"A what?" Smith turned to her.

"Gamble that we aren't. After all, it is in the border region. The withdrawal prohibits military installations this close to the border. So, if UNHL isn't allowed to set up permanent installation, this backward planet will remain under the guidance of its own people. The UNHL has no reason to establish presence. Not a military one, and it's just plain easier to send them energy cells in return of water from space than to remain in their business." Amerlee explained.

"That girl . . ." Smith pointed his finger at Amerlee. "She is a businesswoman at heart!"

"However, that Flying Wing is, I think will be trouble." Amerlee added.

"I don't like it either." Smith returned to the barrage of holo screens.

"Captain Yoyo is sending us a military package! They are going to be here within three hours!" Toxic reported.

"Good!" Smith bobbed his head.

Within the hour, they got Baby Haas's report.

With the tail number of the Flying Wing, they were able to identify the bird, presumed to be lost two-and-a-half years ago at the end of the AOCP occupation at the Marazza Triangle. With that news in hand, Smith ordered Toxic to reel back the equipment they were constantly towing. He reasoned that they found the base. For the Toxic's question of there could be another base Smith just responded mean.

"It will take a day to dismantle the equipment." Toxic responded.

"Never less we are on the right path."

"Are we?" Toxic asked.

"Why are you saying that?" Smith asked back.

"Baby Haas's second part of the report!" she pointed at the holo screen.

"Not a good sign!" Azure's right hand naturally reached her gun holster.

Smith flinched, seeing the two small, but armed space planes flying along the huge Flying Wing. Only one of its perimeter lights was working, and the right-side wing pod seemed to be greatly damaged.

"Did you say that the two smaller space planes weren't armed?" Smith probed Toxic's hologram.

The hologram chuckled: "Oops . . ."

"Pirates perhaps?" Azure offered a clue.

"Contact Baby and tell her to drop a small relay buoy before she returns. Let's compose a warning message, shall we?" Smith sat down in the captain's chair.

Thirty minutes later they knew the Flying Wing's operators weren't legit. As soon as they forward deployed a relay and sent a message thru in the name of the 'local' UNHL outpost, the Flying Wing blasted it out of existence.

"Fairly decent firing capability to find and hit the relay from a great distance, don't you think?" Toxic gauged Smith's response. Seemingly he got very concerned: "Would somebody hail the real UNHL outpost on the tip of the space elevator and ask if they are expecting a load? Say that we're a passing UNHL frigate or something!" Smith became impatient.

"I'm on it!" The Honor Guard named Nyikha hopped down to a corner station, to Azure's delight.

A minute later, while still in her chair, Nyikha turned around: "My Lord, they say they scheduled nothing!"

"Blast it!" Smith slammed his fist at the console pad. He had to think and think fast. "Man, where is Josh Kulighan when I need him!" he cried out loud, then shrugged and with a resigned voice he barked into the air: "Tell Baby to drop the other buoy so we can send another message and send a long-range message to the DU.

Ask Captain Aa to send Qaw's two DSRs if they are done with their mission!"

"This message to the Flying Wing, is it in the name of DSR Vidra?" Toxic inquired.

"Yeah. Mask my image with its current captain."

"You would wonder why blast the relay buoy out of existence instead of just leaving it." Amerlee finally said what bothered her.

"Perhaps they were angry?" Smith shrugged.

"I mean, it's a waste of energy unless they would think the local military would use that to ask for help." Amerlee added.

"Why would the UNHL military need help? It's a commercial cargo ship with two interceptors. We can take care of that!"

"Could the commercial pods be repurposed?" she asked.

"I guess . . ." Smith began to have a bad feeling in his stomach.

Few minutes later he faced with a towering man named Zaluk. Apparently, he owned the Flying Wing and warned the crew of the 'Vidra' to leave while they can. Zaluk promised destruction and broadcasted some internal feeds from one of his Wing pods that showed landing ships and a ragtag bunch of soldiers checking their equipment. Eventually Smith disconnected the feed and the Flying Wing destroyed the communication buoy as a response.

"Annoying as hell!" Smith announced, then typed something in his holo pad.

"Contacting Captain Yoyo?"

"It's obvious Mr. Zaluk could not pull this off without helpers on the ground. By the sound of his grandiose plans and already submitting a claim for the planet on SWEi Prime, we can conclude he is committed. No, it's best to get him stopped as soon as possible! Not to mention of his wing pod full of landing ships. I mean, it's obvious he will siege the planet and take over . . . Ah, Captain Yoyo!" he glanced at the holo screen facing with the young woman.

"My Lord!" she saluted hard. "My package is under way!"

"We need you, Captain Yoyo. Apparently, we are having an intrusion and the captain is hell bent to carry out his plans. We are transmitting what we learned. Please help us out and deal with it! I need you to be the cop and learn everything you can while remove the remnants of his ship from this solar system as soon as possible!"

"We are on our way!" she saluted again.

"I have to go . . ." Jena stopped by the bridge to inquire about how things were going.

"How do you expect to recover the surveillance unit?" Smith asked her.

"I have a perfect way to do it without the local's interference!" she grinned and left.

"Is Baby still nearby of them?"

"She is on her way to us!" Toxic responded. "Why?"

"I was thinking she could engage them, but perhaps we should wait . . ."

"Waiting is the best course of action!" Toxic responded seriously.

*

Mysha was playing with the radio buttons. Occasionally she glanced up to survey the deserted land. Not too many trees littered the landscape. The jeep was standing between the airstrip and the main building. His father went inside to tell them what they saw, but was skeptical upon seeing the decay around the base. Once upon a time it was fenced up and housed thousands of soldiers. As the occupation ended, the government defunded the base, moved the solders and the airplanes away. Now, two transport planes with badly needed paint jobs just took off with ammunition toward the faraway coast line that was attacked overnight. She was just past fifteen and some loitering soldiers looked at her funny. There was a handgun under the seat and she hoped she wouldn't have to defend herself. She repeatedly and wearingly glanced to her right, up to the tower where her father should be.

"Listen Mr. Meher, I understand your concern, but it's highly unlikely the Junta would conduct over flight operation this far from the front lines!"

"I told you before that I think its alien in origin. I think the stratospheric plane dropped this object I saw and left, but it has to come back to pick it up!"

The Commander tried to cover his laugh. "The Junta gains nothing by this. Go home Mr. Meher and prepare for a fight! As a past soldier, your knowledge may come handy again . . ."

"What's that mean?" Meher took a step back, frightened by the prospects.

"We need skilled workforce like you!" The Commander replied. No more amusement on his face.

"No. No, I'm out of the military! I'm a civilian now!" he vehemently shook his head.

"At the moment! But the junta nuked some of our cities with the clear intent to bog us down while they move inland. Our preliminary assessment is that their intent to take over the space elevator, our means to contact and conduct business with the UNHL. We can't allow that to happen, so we are mounting an offensive to stop them. It's a mayhem out there. Why would they try to retake the annexed land? It isn't making any sense, sir!"

"That's why this was an alien ship!" Meher stood by his beliefs.

"The UNHL clearly stated they don't want to step on this planet for a long time." The Commander worked hard to discredit him, but Meher was sure he was right: "Maybe it's AOCP. Is it possible they have returned?"

"Then everything is pointless!" The Commander shook his head than offered his hand: "Don't worry about it, Mr. Meher. My soldiers are airlifted out of the base as we speak. By now there is just a skeleton staff remains to oversee the nearby ammunition factory."

The response dismayed Meher. They escorted him out of the building. The two soldiers left after saluting.

"Dad?" Mysha watched him walking around the jeep. He seemed to be disappointed.

"Let's go home, darling!" he seemed sad as he sat in the car's driver seat and started it.

"They did not buy it?"

"Of course not, but they are the smart men and our country is under attack. They have an important task to perform." he drove along the service road beside the landing strip. Mysha looked behind and the control tower was just a box in the desert. Suddenly their engine cut off.

"Piece of sh . . ." Meher pounded on the steering wheel.

"I wonder what else could go wrong today?" Mysha helped his father open the hood.

While his father checked things, she glanced around. Suddenly she grabbed his father's arm. "Dad!" she said alarmingly.

"What? I can't see anything wrong with . . ." Meher protectively stepped front of his daughter as she was steering at the alien object hovering nearby. It emitted almost no sound.

"Where the hell is this coming from?" Meher uttered.

"Look, Daddy, another plane!" Mysha pointed straight at the other end of the tarmac. A rapidly growing dot just landed. The airplane was big and wide. Much wider than anything Meher ever saw, even in the military. Its meticulously clean, white body was occasionally covered with deep blue and black areas. Two huge nacelles extended out of its main frame.

"Is it ours?" Mysha stared at the aerodynamically sleek war bird.

"I have never seen anything like it!" Meher shook his head, wondering where the soldiers were as the airplane taxied beside them. The turbines winded down and the mirror like cabin cover retracted, revealing a slender woman in a jumpsuit with a helmet on. She hopped out of the plane and took off the helmet. She had a short black hair and brown eyes; totally mesmerized Meher and his daughter.

The pilot showed the sign of 'V' and talked in an alien language. She turned toward the hovering unit, spoke to it, and as a response the unit responded with a series of high-pitched noises. The woman listened intently, then pointed at her fighter plane and the object slowly began to move toward it while folding up its wings.

The pilot turned toward the locals and produced a stick from under her gear. She touched its top, then patted her throat twice and when she spoke, they could understand her. "My name is Jena, sorry for the intrusion, I and the surveillance unit mean no harm!"

Meher stepped closer, while hiding his daughter. "We mean no harm either!"

"Good. I've only got couple minutes to affix him, would you help me?" she bent forward and disappeared under the fighter plane's belly. Meher followed her suspiciously.

"Just hold it, like that!" she moved swiftly, and they were done in a minute. She escorted him back to the jeep and pointed at the four-wheeled vehicle: "Don't worry, it will start once I'm gone! I had to erect a dampening field so I can land here and pick him up." she pointed behind her.

Meher half measured her and the airplane; "Are you AOCP?"

The slender woman frowned and pointed at the patch on her shoulder: "UNHL forever! You guys don't recognize the emblem?" she pointed at the vertical tail of her fighter next.

"No . . ."

"I belong to the Honor Guards." she said, but upon seeing their reaction she explained: "UNHL Honor Guards. We are the elite soldiers of the Human Emperor. We represent the will of him wherever we travel! As a matter of fact, my employer isn't too

far . . ." she smiled pleasantly, then turned serious: "Do you aware the fact that the other continent invaded yours?"

Meher nodded silently.

"Stay here, it's a good place to be. I think the military continent wants the bread and butter for themselves."

"What?"

“The space elevator . . .” she added. “Do you guys live nearby?” she was in a pleasant, almost chatty mood.

“We live on a farm, that way!” Meher pointed in the direction they headed.

“I think I saw that before I dropped the unit,” she nodded. We might come by to visit again . . . Don’t get enlisted in the military. I also have a haunch it will end rather badly for the Junta.” she hopped to the wing of her fighter with such an ease it shocked them both. As the canopy extended again, the turbines spun up and soon the airplane was moving again. After a short time on the runway, it lifted its nose straight to the sky and soon it was just a tiny dot.

Meher turned the ignition, and just as the alien pilot would say, the engine started.

“Let’s get out of here!” he turned to his daughter, who agreed: “Who would’ve thought that we would meet an alien today?”

“Certainly not me!” Meher shook his head while driving away.

*

Captain Yoyo’s hand was itching for action. Despite the Emperor’s initial request to only send a small contingent she was here, in person with her majestic PD, the Trinity. As her XO counted back from thirty, she called the alert fighters for takeoff. As the Trinity, her huge UNHL warship dropped out of hyperspace, the six fighters took off like bullets. The enormous Flying Wing could be seen thru the blast windows.

“Man, it’s big!” Somebody close to her uttered.

“Have two squads with incendiaries ready for takeoff!” she decided to be on the cautious side. “Put me up!” she stood behind the Communication’s Officer’s seat.

“This is Captain Yoyo from the UNHL Planet Destroyer Trinity! You are entering into an operational zone! State your business!” she waited for a minute, then gently patted the officer’s back.

“They got the message, Ma’am, but chosen not to reply!”

"Okay, put me up one more time!" Yoyo took up a defensive posture and with a serious face she spoke. "Power down your main engines and prepare to be boarded! This is your only warning!" she stepped away for a second. She needed some information about the Flying Wing's presumed weapons. She authorized a scan that determined the sure existence of multiple laser cannons on the wings and some kind of torpedo tubes along the main body.

"Order the alert fighters to fire across the bow for added emphasis and launch the two squadrons along with another squadron of protective fighters!"

"Yes, Ma'am!" Her XO began to relay the commands. Captain Yoyo half measured the approaching commercial vessel. "They have to know they can't win. . ." she was about to order the activation of the shields when suddenly the Planet Destroyer shook. The sound that reverberated thru the frame was almost like a metallic battle cry. Claxons went off, and the bridge came to life. Orders flew across the stations; her XO reported that they received some kind of kinetic weapon charge that not just tore some hardened plates off the ship but blasted a hole thru the port side wing's tip!

It took another second for her to realize it was a rail gun projectile. "Shields up!" she yelled then asked the Weapon's Chief to have salvo fire to be loaded into the main gun.

"I really don't want to do this . . ." she uttered thinking what the salvo fire might do to the commercial grade composite materials. Probably bore right thru of it, incinerating the cargo ship. If the Emperor needs answers, she can't do that.

"XO, have our boarding parties trail us, engines all ahead full!" While she thought how the moment of opportunity slowly but surely was slipping away.

"Engines ahead full!" The XO reported firmly.

"Yaw negative thirty degrees!" she ordered for corrections after observing the 3D holo screen.

"Enemy is launching fighters . . ." The XO reported, nervousness in his voice.

Captain Yoyo spun around. One look at the screens and she realized the XO was right. Only the Emperors would know what those enemy scrap fighters have. "Establish defensive posture half a click from them!" she folded her arms in defiance as the top side cannons began pounding the incoming fighters.

It was bold and also unusual from a commercial freighter to launch an attack. They can't turn around; they have to know that . . . She frowned. "Launch defensive fighters and order them to engage all incoming objects!"

"Ma'am, something is happening!" The XO pointed at the screen where the Flying Wing was extending its size. A quick look and the Captain realized it was shedding its wings! Whatever the reason, it could not be good, so she was a tad relieved when Captain Mya and Colonel Re'kl announced their arrival. She sent them in on a different approach vector to fly by the wing pods for observation and attack the freighter from the rear. Her fighter squads did a great job taking out the scrap fighters, but their sheer number was a true concern of her.

Then the dreaded words came again: they fired the rail gun again from the belly of the freighter. Their shields kept most of the damage occurring, but the projectile did cause additional damage to the bow of her ship.

She took one split look at the screens before ordering the salvo guns to be fired. She modified the trajectory to be a near miss, but just not. They were really close, the freighter never changing trajectory; less than half a kilometer away. When the belly of the freighter caught fire, she knew she was on the right track. She turned to the Weapons Chief: "Port side cannons one thru eighty-six, fire when possible!"

"Yes Ma'am!"

They were just beginning to pound the freighter's exposed side when its rear engines blew apart in trillions of small pieces, thanks to the two DSR's orchestrated attack on it.

"Enemy ship is drifting!" she heard the joyful words.

"Maximum turn, do not expose our engines to them!" she warned her crew. This will be an expensive repair she knew . . .

About an hour later it was over. She had a tremendously huge task to do; to oversee the Flying Wing's scrap fighters being dragged into her PD, the arrival of the multipurpose SCC that helped to secure the drifting wing pods. Keeping in her mind that the Emperor wanted the debris out of the solar system as soon as it was possible, she had to coordinate that as well. Then there was the question of interrogating the Flying Wing's commanding staff, including the Captain who resembled to a drunk sailor from a high sea more than a respectable freighter captain. After running fingerprints, she came to the conclusion that Mr. Zaluk was a gun for hire, although being associated with questionable entrepreneurs that would be little more than thugs with money. She contacted the ICID, the UNHL federal police to make her formal logging of the events and to stop the criminal gang to make further advance on other worlds, because as it turned out they had 'big' plans in that regard. Luckily, the two DSRs helped her scarce forces to effectively clean up. Once she did that, she contacted the Emperor and used a transport ship to send her official report to SCC 26-54 that arrived along with three other SCCs.

"Rail gun?" The Emperor seemed quite puzzled upon hearing the news.

"Yes, My Lord!" she responded. "Cheap, but effective if you have plenty of power. And they had all the power from the main fusion reactor. It is still pretty destructive, as you can see!" she explained the damage done by the two projectiles.

"I concur. It is interesting to see some exotic weapon making a dent, although I would be happier if we would've done that to others." The Emperor mulled over, then glanced at the screen: "You've done well Captain . . ."

"Most of the high praise goes to my crew, My Lord!"

"Yes, of course, every man and women and the droids as well!" The Emperor seemed to be hasty about it. He just stared at the screen quietly and when Captain Yoyo was about to break the silence, he spoke again: “Take care your ship, but I need you to remain here. Can that be realized?”

“My Lord, I need emergency repairs done on the hull. The Trinity is exposed at the moment, a situation any competent captain would highly dislike!”

“I see . . .” The Emperor frowned, then after pausing he said, “Seek repairs at Danal IV, the DU should have competent crew and plenty of resources to manufacture emergency plates, but I need you back here in three days, is that understood?”

“Yes, My Lord!” she bowed deep.

*

“This fine vessel and now we’re just a repair ship?” Captain Aa fumed behind closed doors.

“Well, we could certainly learn new traits with this event . . .” Commander Danek tried to downplay the issue, but instead received glaring looks from his Captain.

“We have to please the Emperor at any rate.” Victor decided to enter into the mix.

“I give him a please!” Aa’s fist was about to blast the light practices apart by punching the hologram.

“We have the technology, but to actually do anything under the extremely tight deadlines, even we have to prioritize.”

“How much ore do we have onboard anyhow?” Captain Aa disliked her situation. She wanted to be where the Emperor was. Fight and learn, not playing rear end to his operations.

Before the Commander could answer, the hologram replied: “Minimum amount. We should seek help from the planet below to replenish our metal pellet storages and skip the ore processing all together for this job.”

“Can we make acquisitions?”

“I better get going and coordinate that.” Commander Danek was about to leave.

“Victor, please contact Captain Yoyo and ask her to send a list of additional replenishment she might need . . .”

"Even emergency force fields?"

"Whatever required for her to be in acceptable shape when she leaves in seventy-two hours!" Captain Aa turned away from the door. As the light beams scattered and she made sure she was alone, she slammed her palm at the desk: "Damn you, Empy!" While fully understanding his needs to remain hidden and keeping a low profile, she missed him and his guidance terribly.

Chapter Twenty Seven

A Tactician's Mind

"So, what do you think?" Smith asked him about the third time now. Josh Kulighan did not exactly expect a situation like this. Limited resources and towering demands . . . He glanced over the holographic screens, trying to see something.

"So?" Smith's voice became erratic.

"Hm . . ." he glanced up from the holo screen.

"Say something!"

Josh rolled his eyes. "Damn inconvenient that you can't use your powers." he elaborated.

"Tell me something I don't know!" Smith glared at the tactician.

After some hesitation Josh closed his eyes, trying to imagine the scenario. "In either way we will have to introduce ourselves to the locals and undoubtedly to the AOCP spy contingent as well. What do you think about how many of them are down below? A hundred or perhaps two?"

"Three hundred tops. Those old AOCP ships can't sustain more in the long run."

"Maybe they go fishing on the weekends . . ." Josh zoomed in on the coastline, while trying to be light on the jokes.

"So, what do you think?" Smith stepped closer. "I need options and I need them as soon as possible!"

Josh glanced around on the Toxic's bridge, noting the quietly rocking Azure in the Captain's chair, the equally quiet Amerlee on the Navigation Specialist's chair. His gaze returned to Smith; "You will have to contact the leader of the Junta and offer him something to stop this war!"

"I don't want to do that! I don't reward stupidity!"

"Look, they are rapidly moving inland. The Main Land military unequipped and untrained to stop them. In about a day, they will threaten the space elevator and they could blow it up devastating the planet if we aren't careful!"

"They should be careful then!" Smith shot back.

"If you are so interested what's behind the annexed land, why don't you just go there and snoop around?"

"I want to slow down the Junta so I can have the time to do that."

"I can achieve that from here!" Josh snapped.

"How?"

"They use a form of global positioning system." Josh brought up another chart to illustrate it. "So, we could just take them out entirely. Shouldn't take long with all the resources we have. While at it with the use of the DSR's we have an excellent opportunity to map their assets as they undoubtedly try to activate those."

"Can't we just disable them?"

"Takes forever to do it quietly."

"Blow it up then!" Smith quickly changed his mind.

*

Mysha heard the knock. She was closer to the door. "I'll get it, daddy!" she ran toward it, hoping it wouldn't be the postman bringing a drafting letter to her father. She opened the door wide and upon recognizing the tall and slender woman, she froze.

"Who is it?" His father asked from the kitchen where he was helping his wife.

"Daddy . . ." she mumbled, still holding the door.

"So, who is. . . ?" His father dropped the cloth he was cleaning his hands with and swallowed hard upon seeing the fighter pilot. She wore a slightly different dress, or body armor, he was not sure.

The woman tapped her neck twice than said, “Greetings Mr. Meher!” she spoke with an alien accent.

“What can I help you with?” Meher stepped front of his daughter, shielding her upon seeing the thick holster on the alien woman’s belt.

“We would like to have a couple of words with you, if you would follow me, please!” she stepped backwards, in hopes to convey her less than intimidating nature. The man of the house popped out his head, looked around, but saw nothing behind the young woman. “Where is your fighter plane?” he asked.

The tall, slim woman smiled. “Silly man, I’ve got it strapped to the DSR . . . Come on, follow me!”

“What is a DSR?” Meher followed her down the steps and on the path toward the main highway about a hundred foot from the house and the couple trees around it on the otherwise barren land.

“You’ll see it, soon!” she walked over the asphalt and into the whitish-beige soil, occasionally stepping on a patch of grass.

“All right, a hint, Toxic?” she hollered in the direction she believed the cloaked DSR was, then turned around. “Don’t be afraid!”

“From wha . . .” Meher’s mouth hung as the scenery began to change; the air rippled and for a half a second, he could make out a towering green-blue shape before it disappeared again. By that time, they were walking up on a green ramp.

Meher’s eyes were rapidly moving around. It was all alien to him; the green indented walls, the funny-looking ceiling. Then he spotted a couple of awful young women standing at the opening. “There are no men onboard?” he inquired, his eyes moving in between the two young women.

“Here I am!” A tall, slim man in his late twenties or early thirties offered his right hand to him. He accepted the ritual and shook on his strong hand.

“I am Meher, I own the land and had an encounter with the tall fighter pilot beside me.” he was uncertain why did he meet these people, these aliens.

"Yes, Mr. Meher. I'm here because I need a favor from you!" The tall man invited him in deeper. They led him to a room with a bunch of chairs and more women.

"Are you owning these, sir?" Meher heard of owning people was customary in space, a highly disgusting thing as far as he was concerned.

"No. Not at all. They are all Honor Guards . . ."

"Not me!" Another brunette appeared in the door, folding her arms on her chest.

"Ah, her name is Amerlee, my girlfriend!" he led Meher into the room.

"Why am I here?" Meher felt to be in a surreal dream. Certainly, he heard of stealth technology, allegedly possessed by the alien humans, but never believed it for a second. Now he was in real doubts.

"You are here, sir, because I need to keep this spaceship around and I want your permission to that." The man replied, "by the way, my name is Evan Smith!"

"Are you a civilian?" Meher measured him from top to toe.

"No. I'm a military contractor with certain special skill sets that's in high demand in the UNHL . . ." The man shook his head.

"Why bother asking me? If it's invisible, then nobody can see it!"

"But you can bump into it and so we will make her into a huge barn."

"Why?"

"A barn has doors. We can keep things in the barn if we need to."

"It doesn't make any sense. How do you going to build a barn this big in only a couple of days?"

"Two hours . . ." Meher heard a sensual female voice from nowhere in particular. He spun around on the chair looking for the source of the voice, but to her biggest amazement a bunch of light beams formed front of his chair, depicting yet another slender woman in deep green military dress.

"Who are you?" he leaned backward, standing front of a chair.

"My name is Toxic. I am the ship! In disguise running under the call sign Vidra . . ."

"Are you an AI?" Meher slowly touched the light particles, swaying his fingers and causing a ripple effect in the image that nodded. "A leap of faith, huh?"

"A what?"

"Thinking that I'm an AI. From a primitive human race like yours it's practically a leap of faith thinking of that!"

"So, you aren't?" Meher seemed surprised.

"No, I am something entirely different!" The hologram imitated blowing a kiss at him, then stepped backwards, allowing Smith to reenter into the picture.

"So, as you know, we are interested in this annexed land of yours. I am intending to snoop around, but it's really annoying that the military Junta invaded this continent."

"I can use other words too . . ." Meher turned angry upon being reminded of that. "But . . ."

"But what?" Smith asked.

"The Junta already established headquarters on the continent, and my government entered into continuity mode early this morning. Disappointedly, the way things are going, this will be over in a week." His head slouched, feeling sad.

"Well, hopefully not. First of all, the Junta will have to learn to use maps again pretty soon." Smith frowned.

"They have GPRS receivers. And of course, we bought into their system, so since they jamming us, we have nothing now!"

"As I said, they will have to use maps soon!" Smith dismissed his concern. "See, my problem is this!" he pointed to a 3D holo map above the table, showing his land, the road and as they zoomed out of it, the red circle, the forbidden land came into view.

"It's annexed . . ." Meher nodded once.

"The Junta might want it now that they think it's abandoned."

"It's not?" Meher glanced around with fear in his eyes.

"What do you see when you look beyond the fence?"

"Empty land."

"Look what I see!" Smith nodded and the red circle disappeared, revealing the eight AOCP heavy cruisers pointed toward the sky.

"Those are real?" he fearfully pointed at the rusting, alien spaceships aiming toward the sky.

"That's why I'm here, to find that out. Here is the thing sir," Smith looked into the farmer's eyes: "If they're abandoned than we just land and stop the Junta. We have the resources and frankly the automated, mechanized robotic force is pretty advanced. We can stop this mess in two days. However, if the AOCP violated the treaty and they are still here, they will do everything in their power to stop it and they don't care who remains alive from the locals. Do you understand what I'm trying to accomplish here?" Smith looked into Meher's glassy eyes.

"I think so . . ." Meher shifted his weight from left to right.

"So. I would like to keep my space ship here while me and my entourage snoop around. Once it's over, you will be greatly compensated for your trouble, I promise. Now," he warned him, "do not enter the barn; just claim it as your own if anyone asks. And here is a little delicacy from one of my worlds. Hopefully, you will like it!" he gave him a white bag with seven round disks.

"Canned food?" Meher skeptically took a peek into it.

"Yes, but eat it with bread or something alike. It's expensive, made from fish eggs . . ." Amerlee warmly reminded him from the side.

Meher walked back to the house where his daughter first hugged him then asked what was in the bag: "Some sort of food, I think. Where is your mother?"

"Here I am!" she appeared from upstairs.

"I have an interesting story to tell!"

"Daddy, since when do we have a mound with a barn door?" Mysha ran back from outside, looking excited.

"That's another thing I have to tell you . . ." Meher scratched his head, thinking how to begin.

Chapter Twenty Eight

The Deepest Secrets of All

A bizarre entourage on an antigravity sled approached the Annexed Land from Meher's farmland. The occupants of the vehicle left from the overnight erected barn and Smith hoped dearly nobody would see them or the alien vehicle zipping about three feet above the asphalt road without wheels. They slowed down front of the gates Jena's drone found the other day.

"Very sparse meeting with the locals . . ." Baby Haas joked while she fiddled with the gate's lock. She just affixed the AOCP code breaker.

"Yeah, nothing fancy, right?" Smith glanced around. Jena's device did not detect any nanites, sensor net or old-fashioned cameras either.

"Creepy!" Amerlee glanced around, holding Smith's hand.

"I still think you should've been stayed behind!" Smith, feeling distracted, played with her hair.

"But I wanted to be with you." she smiled at him with love and his anger dissipated.

"I am also here, you know!" Azure mentioned it to them, sounding somewhat angrily.

"I know . . ."

"Let's go!" Baby pocketed the small but handy device as the thick blast doors were receding.

They all hopped back onto the antigravity sled and zipped across the gate.

“Anything?” Smith repeatedly tried to get a better view at Jena’s equipment screens.

“Deserted. Even at long range.” she implied at the eight AOCP Wongel heavy frigates.

“I don’t like it!” Smith had a bad feeling.

“Why can’t you just accept that the AOCP withdrawn and left these here?” Amerlee was interested.

“Not like them. Especially knowing that our standoff wouldn’t resolve quickly and we would analyze everything they’ve left behind. It’s a tactical error. No. They have to be here!”

“Did not Captain Mya’s report say that the space elevator’s software repository seems intact?” Baby turned her head for a second.

“Yes, more suspicious that way . . .” Smith hollered back, shouting above the winds.

“To whom?”

“To me, of course!” Smith eyed Jena’s device again.

“Nothing, boss!” she shook her head.

They pulled up to one of the frigates and realized instantly that none of them were flying ever as their engines were ruptured. With Baby’s lead, they entered into the closest one. Smith protectively tucked Amerlee behind him as they made their way in the dark.

“Interesting . . .” Suddenly they heard Jena’s concerned voice.

“What is?” Smith snapped.

“There is a low-level power source still running!”

“Coming from where?” Smith grabbed his gun, feeling jumpy.

“Deep below. I think the reactor is still alive, but it’s in sleep mode.” Jena corrected herself.

“Let’s find a station, this way!” Smith turned left at the next corridor. “Try not to leave a digital footprint, okay?” Smith reminded Jena, who nodded: “Of course. Here we go!” she brought the screen alive.

Smith watched as the girl dug deep into the OS, then she glanced up and the question mark in her eye was all Smith needed to know, to feel creepy again.

“All eight frigates are connected. All their power sources are in sleep mode, but the passive radar is on. All this is, one giant defense battery, aimed at the sea and the sky!”

“So, if an airplane say would fly toward it . . .” Amerlee made a hypothesis.

“Bumm!” Jena shook her head in disbelief.

“Strange . . .” Baby rummaged around.

“What now?” Azure asked impatiently.

“Jena, check if any escape hatch was used recently.”

“For?”

“Do it!” Smith was really concerned now.

“What is it?” Amerlee tried to read his love’s face.

Smith shook his head. “The perimeter fence would discourage anyone to enter. If they do, I’m sure robots or ground forces could repel the intruders. The batteries aimed at the sky and sea, to thwart off intruders, and we know there is nothing above,

so . . .”

“So?”

“So, it has to be underground!” Smith shook upon realizing it.

“Beneath the soil?” Baby felt it was a bad joke.

“Jena?” Smith urged her again.

“I’ve got an activated entry to the frigate’s inner core about six months ago.”

“Take us there!” Smith double checked his gun, before grabbing Amerlee’s arm so hard the girl told him to be gentler on her.

A good thirty minutes later, they stared at a dark pit as Baby overrode the security to the hatch. Baby and Jena argued about how to proceed when Smith used a flashlight, then grabbed the rail and disappeared below.

“Shit!” The girls looked at each other, but it was late.

When they caught up with him, he was staring at a paper map hanging from the wall. Apparently, they were standing on a platform. There were rail tracks coming from somewhere, heading away in the opposite direction.

"This points to a massive operation!" Smith pointed at the map.

"So, we're the red dotted line?" Amerlee glanced around, not seeing very well at all in the almost darkness, unlike Azure, whose enhanced eyes picked out the smallest details in the tunnel and its creepy white ceramic tiles.

"Yeah. Seven more, and what is this brown going in a circle? We need to . . ." Smith stopped, then suspiciously turned left.

"What is it?" Azure turned left as well. "I hear it. What is that?"

"Hide behind the columns and lights off!" Smith demanded with great urgency in his voice.

The next moment they felt the wind, and then the noise turned metallic in nature. With a great whoosh, three lit metro cars flew by.

"I spotted about thirty soldiers on it . . ." Azure frowned.

"You still think this is abandoned?" Smith glared at Baby Haas, who uttered 'shit!'

"Smith, why the soldiers had full gear on?" Azure tried to use her special glasses to hook to any wireless signal, but the tunnel was devoid of them.

"We need to get to the brown line!" Smith used the flashlight to look below the platform. There was a skinny, narrow walkway leading into the darkness. "Jena, you first!"

"Me, second!" Baby pointed to herself.

"Let's go, princess!" Smith grabbed Amerlee while Azure closed ranks.

After a good ten minutes of almost running, they reached another deserted platform. Above their head, thru the cracks of a steel lining, they spotted another set of tracks. Azure found a freight elevator in the darkness and, as she pointed out, they were on the red level. "Look how many other levels!"

Smith frowned. "They really dug into the rocks here. I wonder why . . . Let's go to the brown line. Is there anything less claustrophobic than an AOCP freight elevator to the unknown?"

he looked around and soon discovered concrete steps leading upstairs. They all went up on them. The brown line was sparsely lit and soon they spotted two separate metro cars whooshing by.

“Big operation, wouldn’t you say?” Smith tried to joke.

“I guess they did not get the memo for evacuation two years ago!” Azure added.

“I don’t think that was the intention at all! What is this thing?” Smith looked around and soon he found another map. He tried to decipher it, then with an a-ha, he left toward the darkness. Soon he whistled at them. “Come on, I found a maintenance shaft!”

Behind three doors, they entered into a meeting point of some sort with a window. Upon getting closer to it, Smith almost fainted.

“What the heck?!” he stared out the thick window at the strange object. It was like an inverted raindrop, about forty stories tall, three to five hundred feet of a diameter, brightly lit, a bit of purple and very bright.

“It says A-12 . . .” Azure pointed below them at the real walkway where a bunch of soldiers marched away.

“Many walkways I see . . .” Smith observed the horrifying sight.

“What is this place?” Amerlee cuddled up to Smith, feeling the other’s nervousness.

“Some sort of intelligence operation, I think . . . But it doesn’t make too much sense, because they are all underground and they don’t communicate with above ground.”

“Obviously they spent tons of money to create it, so It has to have a meaning!” Azure shook her head, then added, “My glass tells me that there is a general warning went out seconds ago, but nothing to do with us!”

“Then with what?” Smith was afraid somebody discovered their entrance into this object and now the hunt was on.

“It says something to stay away from the walkways and wait for package reload . . . Smith, what’s that mean?” Azure turned to him.

"Dunno . . ." Smith had hard time understanding the nature of the operation. It made no sense at all! "Fuck, fuck, fuck and fuck!" Smith got angrier and angrier.

"Baby?" Amerlee tried to calm him down.

"I thought it would be over in an afternoon, or two. But this?" he cried out loud. "This is a massive problem!"

Then all of a sudden as Smith was just about to remind them about the Junta's invasion, a bright white light blinded them all and when it died off and their eyes got used to it, they saw plain clothes of people along with soldiers walking away from the object.

"What the heck was that?" Smith massaged his eyes.

"Different name . . ." Azure tried to comprehend what she saw.

"What?" Smith did not understand her until she pointed the sign above the walkway on the object. It said G-7.

"How many letters in the alphabet?" Baby stared at Smith, who mumbled amid shaking; "Teleportation! Of course. The pit and the extra space . . . Man, this is some deep shit!

Has to be some spy ops. We're so fucked!"

"Where are these men go?" Amerlee asked, pointed to another group of people leaving the object.

"They have to disembark the planet. I guess from underwater. We can check this out. Azure, please record everything you found here!" Smith began to shiver. This was anything but what he imagined it would be!

"Jena, give me your recording package!" Smith opened his hand toward the girl.

She obeyed to his request and gave him a thick black necklace of a sort when Baby asked, "What are you going to do?"

"I'm going in!" Smith frowned, constantly shivering beneath the clothes. A moment later he realized he was scared!

"But. . . ?" Amerlee looked at him with her big brown eyes, worried and all.

*

Meher just made sure Mysha was in her bed. He quietly walked down to the living room, where his wife watched the war news.

"Honey, they say that we hit one of their supply lines and that the Junta seemed disoriented. Good news, right?"

"Maybe?" he kissed her hand as he sat down beside her. Frankly, he was skeptical about it all. He remembered when he was in the military. Disinformation and propaganda were the tools not just the oppressing enemy, but a desperate home government as well.

"But look at the blurry footage!" she pointed at the screen where friendlies pounded enemy barracks.

Meher inspected the footage and thought it could be authentic, but a sinister voice in the background of his mind told him that it could be blurry because they rendered it on a computer farm and it wouldn't stand up to close scrutiny. He flinched. "Our visitors said that the enemy would have to learn to use maps . . ."

"You think they would destroy satellites to do that?" his wife turned at him.

Meher shrugged. "They could destroy an entire planet if they wished to. But whether they would go to the trouble, that I don't know. I am sure it cost lots of money."

"They have the money . . ." she said it to herself, occasionally nodding.

"Don't be too hopeful about the Junta, my love!" he brought her back to reality.

"But look at that!" she pointed at the TV screen showing an entire industrial plant being missed by the Junta's smart munitions.

It brought hope to Meher as well, seeing the plant virtually unharmed, and the ground bombed to hell beside it.

"Let's go to sleep!" he wanted to have hope, so he turned off the device before it would bring more bad news again.

"Okay . . ." she smiled at him obediently and escorted her husband upstairs.

Meher woke up in the middle of the night. He dreamed something really stupid about his parent's old farm in the Midwest. He looked to his right where his wife slept quietly. He slowly turned, not to disturb her, and tried to go back to sleep but could not. He slipped into his shoes and walked to the window. The land was dark, scarce light at the nearby town and the military base at the other direction, but nothing else. Then the strange object caught his eyes. He was so busy calming his family he forgot to check on the 'barn' that just appeared out of nowhere along with the mound. It was bigger and way longer than he thought it would be. It was at least six hundred feet long, with the big doors at the front. It was almost dark down there. He glanced up to the sky, to see the stars, to wonder why his planet was chosen to be visited by humanoid aliens in the first place. The only male in the spaceship told him not to venture inside the barn, but occasionally he thought he saw light flickering thru the doors. Maybe it was a fire? Now he got scared. He ran downstairs, out to the cold night, but stopped front of the doors. He smelled into the air, but sensed no burn smell. He cracked the door just a hair and what he saw was just amazing! There was a bunch of haystacks inside and the earlier met alleged captain with a different outfit tried to talk to a four-legged animal.

"What the . . . ?" he stared at them, utterly surprised.

The four-legged animal turned around, emitted a snorting noise, then smelled into the woman. It was so surreal to see a green disc hovering above both of them that Meher just stood there, appearing speechless.

"Did not my master say something that you not supposed to be coming here?" The girl beneath the green disc tilted her head, then took off the weird, oversized hat.

"What is that?" Meher pointed at the animal.

"It's a horse, and I supposed to be a cowboy, can't you tell?" she pointed at her hat and the jeans she wore.

"Cowboy? What are those green objects above your heads?"

"Oh." The girl, the hologram, seemed relieved for some reason. "Those are our emitters. We can't exist outside of the ship without them!"

"Um, the horse is just a light thingy too?" Meher seemed dumbfounded.

"Yes, it is. I am running a simulation on how to feel to be a cowboy in the West. There is no better way than to relive it, yeah?"

"I would not know . . ." Meher suddenly thought he got more what he bargained for.

"It's just a horsie . . ." The hologram patted the equally hologram horse's back for added emphasis.

"Is it common from where you from?"

"What is?" The girl, the hologram, walked closer and with it the green disc also moved.

"The four-legged animal, the horsie as you called it . . ." Meher asked shyly.

"Now that's a trickier question than you might would think so, sir!" she winked at him with a sexy smile.

"Why. . . ?"

" 'Cause horses were common at one point on Earth. Do you know what that is?"

"A planet, maybe?"

"Yes. It's where humans originated from. Long, long time ago . . ." she added.

"How long?"

"That's another tricky question, Mr. Meher, as it's not only happened in the distant past but also in a distant parallel universe!"

"A what?" Meher thought she lost it.

"Um. Let's see . . ." she imitated, thinking hard. "So, imagine that your planet and the sun and the solar system of yours and the galaxy end everything else you see at night is in an incredibly big box and that normally you can't go outside of that box, so you would not know, that you are inside of a box. Now if you would go outside of the box, you would learn that there is infinite minus one boxes out there."

"Why minus one?"

"It's a super box, one nobody was ever able to see in, even if you travel between boxes. Knowledge holds that this super box was the original universe, from where all other universes transcended." Toxic watched Meher's transformation and there were multiple. She saw he got lost in the realization. She needed to get back to the original path, and she took a step closer, held his face in her holographic arms. "So, to get back to your question, while you are inside your box, humans originally lived a different box. But they were a greedy bunch of fuckers and got what they deserved; almost total extinction! To escape from annihilation, they teleported their planet from that box to another, but made a mistake and ended up in a totally empty box. From there they discovered a pathway into the box where you live in and began to seed humanity into multiple worlds. That is how you came into existence!"

"What?!"

"Yes, Mr. Meher, the irony of the keen resemblance to the aliens you see is because your race and humans are distant

relatives . . ." The hologram chuckled.

Meher had trouble of comprehending it all. "No, we, my race, originated from monkeys in the northern hemisphere of . . ."

"Save the talk, honey!" The hologram shook her head. "I can tell that you are pretty much an earlier version of them. Don't worry, there are thousands of worlds just like yours out there in the Milky Way. Full of humans. At least you are the majority in the galaxy. How that feels?" she inquired by walking around him, intimidating Meher to his core. "Of course, it happened about twenty thousand years ago, a long time at any rate, so this information isn't even widely distributed among humans. Actually, only a select few know of this."

"Your Emperors, huh?"

"For example!" The hologram acknowledged his lucky guess with another hot smile.

Meher stood there for a moment, thinking about it all, then asked: "So the Emperor is running the UNLH?"

"UNHL, United Nations of Humanlike Life-forms, and yes the Emperor runs it, but they are from this planet that came from the other box so to speak, called Down Earth. It's a broken paradise. where horses once were used to move people around. Help them fight their pity battles and move heavy objects. Now it's mainly a recreation item, but they use them for racing as

well . . ." The hologram frowned.

"You aren't from that planet?"

"No . . ." The hologram shook her head, looking sad.

"I can see the sadness in your face if I can say that!" Her presence truly intrigued Meher.

"Thank you, my creators worked hard for that . . ."

"Creators?"

"Yes, you see, I am a very special thing, if I may say that!"

"But somebody had to build you, not? How other way can you be?" Meher could not even find the correct words.

The hologram touched Meher's face; the light particles caressed his cheeks before turning around. "They did not build me in the exact meaning of the word. It's true that there were others before me, but see I was born, because I am alive! This hologram is just an avatar to allow you to communicate with me."

Meher stared at the hologram and the horse, shook his head and then said, "It's a big secret, right?"

"Bigger than you think. You see me now I am not an Artificial Intelligence, I am beyond that. I am a conscious being here to serve my master while observe the surrounding universe!"

When Meher opened his eyes, it was past eight o'clock in the morning. His Daughter already served breakfast. He held his head in his arms, thinking of this weird dream of talking in the barn, and infinitely big different boxes that the universes are inside. "Nonsense . . ." he washed down and headed downstairs.

*

Amerlee just stood there, in the empty, damp and alien room, staring at Smith, who was busy with Azure. She felt lonely, suddenly disconnected from the people she used to know, from the surroundings she came to know. Smith instructed Azure to zoom on the soldiers leaving the object so he could learn the uniform's style. For minutes nothing happened, then she slowly began to notice the transformation. Evan Smith no longer looked like a renegade leader, but more like a soldier. His uniform changed; became an exact replica of what Azure saw down below.

"What, why . . . Why do you look so different?" she glanced up and down at him.

Smith turned back to her, quickly smiled, and grabbed her by the shoulders. "Good, it's mean it is working!"

"While I don't feel the presence of any particularly strong telepath," Azure spoke, "you should watch yourself!" her voice was full of worry.

"I will . . ." Smith replied darkly.

Azure sighed, feeling vulnerable for the moment, and cried out loud; "Why do I feel like when I lost you for years? When telepaths suppressed your memory on that prison ship?"

"It won't be that way now. I'm a different man!" Smith tried to reassure her.

"I strongly dislike your decision!" Baby Haas voiced her opinion. Jena nodded in the background.

"Don't go!" Amerlee pleaded.

Smith smiled sadly; "It's my duty, my life as the Emperor, to seek redemption and safe harbor for my people. It is my job to learn more about this threat to all of us and neutralize it. Clearly, we stumbled upon something we not supposed to know. I have some ideas about how big the operation is, but I need to be inside that thing." he pointed thru the smeared windows. "Don't worry, I'll find my way back to Toxic if I have to, just make sure she doesn't leave! Keep her beside Meher's house. If I wouldn't return in forty-eight hours, send a continuity message to Captain Aa to contact my master!" Smith told Azure, whose eyes grew bigger and bigger as the severity of the situation sank in.

"I love you . . ." Amerlee uttered at first, then said it louder and more firmly.

"I love you too!" Smith kissed her in front of everyone.

"My heart is in pain thinking of you leaving!" she admitted amid crying.

"It's my life . . ." Smith shrugged it off, looking sad. "Can't do anything else about it now. For a long time now . . ." he added with a heavy tone. I love this planet somehow. I love the cold wind, the blue sky and the clay ground. I wish I could spend more time here!" Somehow, he felt the need to tell them, then turned back to the window and watched the object in question. He watched for minutes, while he compartmentalized his personality, built the hardened mental walls, then focused and became the soldier who was born for the job. When he walked out, he did not even say goodbye.

Amerlee stared after him, uttering a *sweet goodbye* before turning back at the window to take a peek at him, walking alone at the walkway toward the purple object. Others walked by, but they did not notice anything.

"How come . . .?" Amerlee uttered in confusion.

"As his transformation complete, he became someone else." Azure explained. "I saw this trick before, but never this precise. I guess he perfected it over the years." she wept quietly. Smith was in grave danger!

"Let's go!" Baby patted Amerlee's shoulder. "We have to get back to the Vidra undetected, and then we have to deal with Toxic. She will not like that we returned without him!"

"Yeah!" Azure's arched lips turned downward. She was there once before, knew the DSR could be extremely stubborn.

"Baby . . ." Amerlee pushed her head against the dirty window, feeling lost.

"Come on!" Azure gently hugged her, then offered her hand and pulled her away from the window.

*

Smith or Ormon, the soldier's base profile he greatly enhanced over time, was moving quietly and swiftly thru the gate. Once inside the gigantic inverted raindrop like monstrosity, he stepped to the nearest terminal and brought it to life. Seemed to be for him that the general assumption was that whoever was inside the object had clearance to a wide range of data. He quickly learned that the next teleportation event will occur in sixteen hours. He obtained a data card thru the lost and found service and with it he had a place to stay as well; a small, one-man compartment. Once inside, he used the place's terminal to read up on the program. It was apparently a long running operation, but to get the history of each mission, he had to interface with the so-called Nexus. He hoped to find it after the next jump as he curled up on a cot, half asleep, half resting.

*

Toxic sensed their return, but something was amiss. Azure broadcasted sadness, but calmness as well. Upon the antigravity sled's arrival at the barn, she 'noticed' Smith's absence. She got angry and worried at the same time, and before her particles would form the hologram itself, she was already grilling them. "Where is Smith, My Master?"

"He had to stay behind . . ." Amerlee still held Azure's small and warm hand.

"What?! This was not the plan!" The hologram yelled angrily.

"He changed it!" Baby walked by the hologram toward the bridge.

"Wait a minute now!" Toxic shouted after her, but Baby kept on going.

"It all blew up in our face!" Azure seemed sad. "You know him. He wants to have all the facts before moving on, and it seems Guvojan practically violated every law there is!"

"War again?" Toxic could not comprehend what could've been inside those eight frigates to vindicate this type of response.

"Could be . . ." Jena seemed to be concerned as well.

"What is it?" Azure noticed her.

"I better tell the bad news to the farmer!"

"Do that, then come back. I need to compose this message to Captain Aa!" Azure did not sound happy at all, noticed Toxic, who also noticed the two women holding each other's hand like they grew together.

"Don't worry, it has been worse before . . ." Azure tried to reassure Amerlee as they walked toward the bridge.

It did not surprise Meher at all to see the tall and slender woman at his doorstep again.

"Would you want to step in?" he asked her, trying to be polite.

"Rather not." Jena shook her sad face.

There was something dark, a bit sad in her voice, so Meher decided to listen to her at the door.

"A slight complication arose, and my employer had to remain behind for a while. That means we are staying too." she flinched.

"For how long?"

"About two days for sure, but could be longer."

Meher flinched, too. "You know, you just missed my buddy from the nearby military base. He stopped by to ask me how long did I had this big barn here. I told him it was here for ages, but if they turn suspicious, there will be a standoff and I have a family to protect!"

"We understand. My employer likes this land, appreciate your gratitude and will repay it once it's over."

Meher made a face. Somehow it did not look like it will be over anytime soon. The morning news talked about mass casualties rising at the City Line. The Junta moved a quarter million soldiers to the beachheads, and their intention seemed to shift from the coastline to the inner land; toward the Space Elevator . . . Upon voicing that, the tall brunette nodded. "We will have to get involved deeper to stop this!" And with that, she left.

Meher got a taste later on that day what that deeper involvement meant when the digitally broadcasted TV stopped and after fiddling with the old analog antenna on the attic, he got the main TV channel reporting that all the satellites they used for communications over the planet went dark.

Chapter Twenty Nine

Asymmetrical Warfare

Josh Kulighan was hard at work. He set up his war room just below the SCC's bridge, from where he oversaw the cyber-attack; Captain Mya and Colonel Re'kl ran against the Junta. Earlier in the day, they disabled almost all satellites around the planet. He learned of some sort of complications from below, albeit Azure remained extremely cryptic about it all. He understood one thing; whatever Smith found warranted him to be extremely negative about not just Hilderin's future but about the entire galaxy's. What that was he was not sure, but got a bigger picture in the evening when a spy space plane from Captain Yoyo's Trinity made a transmission to his location, bringing light to some AOCP secrets; namely spies on a cloaked vessel were leaving the planet where no AOCP military should have remained in the first place! He glanced back at the holo map where he was running simulations against the Junta. The first such attack involving seventy-seven fighter planes was being conceived.

*

"Major Haj!" Master Sergeant Meij saluted hard as he entered into the hardened command vehicle.

"What is it?" Major Haj was overseeing the aptly named Defense Line 2 as the Junta broke across the first one some eight hours ago with such ease it told no great tale about their fates . . . He had two squadrons of helicopters ready for takeoff, about two hundred battle tanks, another hundred light tanks and over six hundred anti-aircraft batteries to hold the line, overseeing the valley. They already lost the cities some hundred miles below them and it horrified him thinking of the millions of casualties he could not do anything to prevent.

Master Sergeant Meij stepped from his left leg to his right, holding his dirty hat in his hands; keep trying to tie a knot on it.

Major Haj noted his subordinate's impatience, but he had other things to worry about. They lost all networked communications during the day, and the IT guy's assessment was that it was lost forever. It did not sound reassuring at all during their disastrous retreat after retreat style of fighting. The only good news he got out of it that it was not just them, but the enemy lost all connections as well!

"So? What is it you could not wait with? Have our engineers reestablished limited connection to Major General Andor's think tank?" The Major was hoping to get good news.

"No sir! Um, yes sir. We do have a landline connection now, but that was not the reason I came so urgently!"

"So then?" Major Haj pointed at the maps and monitors around him. "I'm busy trying to stop the enemy!"

"Well, it from battery station Alpha . . ."

"Forward base, so?"

"They are being jammed!" Master Sergeant Meij was seemingly about to eat his hat.

"So, it began!" Major Haj's gloomy mood returned.

"Well, yes, and no . . ." he stepped from one leg to another.

"What? Speak clearly!"

"Um, sir, it's not just us, but the Junta is being jammed as well. The only radar station that has something is rear radar station Gamma and um, sir, you should see it!"

"What? Why? That old system is till good for something? I thought we phased that junk out a decade ago!"

"We can't understand what we see, sir . . ."

"Are they Jenk-22s? Or Talon7s? What other advanced planes the Junta have?"

"No sir, so it's multiple fast-moving objects heading this way. They first appeared about

fifty-two thousand feet and rapidly descending!"

"That's obviously a mistake. We don't have anything like that in our arsenal. Not even drones or missiles!" Major Haj shook his head.

Suddenly his aide stopped his conversation with the Master Sergeant: "Sir, if I might grab your attention, we have a message sent on the clear."

"On the clear?" Major Haj straightened out upon hearing it.

"Yes, sir. It's one sentence; 'stay out of it'. It's been appearing on our screens as well!"

"Can I see what Gamma sees from here?" Major Haj thought the enemy sure picked an interesting disinformation campaign.

"No, sir. We have radio communications only as we no longer have uplink to the sat . . ."

Major Haj almost slapped his aid as he ran out of the communications container, then abruptly stopped. He glanced up at the night sky and looked around. He heard a faint noise; some sort of unmanned planes flew over their positions. Soon, he saw a bright blue eruption over enemy positions. Then another and another happened. He grabbed his night vision set and looked into it. Seemingly, some enemy advancement broke down. Some moved on. He was thinking about what just happened when his aide ran after him. "Sir, we have sporadic power outages. Our forward stations report malfunctioning electronic equipment. The more advanced the electronics are, the bigger the problem is!"

"Somehow I don't think our people cooked this up . . ." Major Haj scratched his head. He heard of EMP as a byproduct of the nuclear weapons, but far as he knew it was in development stage only . . . Soon, multiple, low-flying cruise missiles advanced on their positions from behind. The sleek weapons flew toward the darkness, hiding the enemy, bypassing their own automatic batteries, flying overhead and hitting enemy targets one by one beyond the valley.

“Who authorized this?” Major Haj barked at his aide, who shook, “it’s not us, sir! It can’t be! We don’t have this kind of technology!”

“We have cruise missiles!” Major Haj shook his head.

“Not like those!” the aide pointed at the carnage below.

“Why not?”

“What I’m saying, sir . . .” The Major Sergeant appeared beside him. “They not on the regular radars. Only these old ones see it. That’s why our batteries did not shoot at them. They simply can’t see it!”

“Damn it!” Major Haj ran back to the C&C module but saw nothing but total chaos inside. He stared at the operators, saw the loss of order, and wanted to run away. And what was the worst part of the situation; they did not have the chance to get involved yet! The Master Sergeant closed the door. His face was one big confusion.

“What’s now?” Major Haj turned to him.

“I thought we were told of clear, starry skies . . .” he wondered as he stepped inside and sat down to the first seat he saw.

“Major Haj, we’ve got video feed from radar operator Gamma! You should see it!” his aide grabbed his arms and began to pull him away.

“Hey!” he brushed him off and with big steps he hopped behind the monochrome display showing a non-descriptive cloud swiftly approaching.

“What is that?”

“A cloud, sir . . .”

“We can see clouds?”

“We can see this . . .” the operator was just as confused.

“This is the last time I’m going out! This is a useless tin can!” Major Haj barked angrily and unbolted the deadlock, holding the thick armored door securely.

He saw as the stars began to twinkle in the sky and soon, they totally disappeared. Somehow, he calmed, but he shivered at the same time. Thick, low-flying clouds ran over their station and it moved forward into the valley. As the edge of it reached the enemy positions, it began to fire! From somewhere deep within missiles and lighting shots appeared, hitting an enemy target each time. The Junta began to fire everything they've got against the superior attacker, but nothing ever happened. The cloud slowed down, began to hover while the rockets and smart bombs volley after volleys hit their intended targets. It was over in less than an hour. The cloud dissipated from the radars and from the sky as well. As the stars returned, they looked down to the ground and saw chaos and carnage. If they could see inside Major Haj's C&C module, they would've surprised to see the screens showing just two words: 'get'em now!'

*

"A word, Ma'am!" Victor appeared out of the blue in the back of the bridge.

"What is it?" Captain Aa mulled over Commander Danek's report. Sixteen hours after the UNHL PD's arrival, the outer armored plates finally began to ship to the Trinity so her crew could begin to swap out the bad ones. It was obvious they wouldn't have the time to finish the job, but Aa still thought they might be able to fix fifty percent of the damage. That was considered a very good result, given the initial hurdles they faced acquiring refined ore and ready-to-use pellets from the locals. She glanced up from the screen and, with dreamy eyes, she asked again. "What is it, Victor?"

"If I may . . ." the hologram pointed behind the bridge, toward the Ready Room.

Captain Aa frowned.

"I can explain it there!" the hologram added.

"Okay." Captain Aa left her chair, watched the hologram walking front of her. "Accurate, hmmm . . ." she watched the light particles forming his rear.

"Excuse me?" the hologram turned around, but she played in her earlier daydreaming mood and dismissed his inquiry with a single head shake.

"So, what's this about?" she crossed her arms on her chest as the sound dampening field kicked in for privacy.

"Well . . ." Victor imitated scratching his head. "If I were to be a human, I believe I would characterize our situation as suspicious!"

"What way?" Captain Aa frowned. She saw the visual incompetency of the hologram to explain the situation and wondered whether something was threatening her ship or perhaps the threat was more distant. To give the required nudge, she asked: "Is the situation on my ship?"

"Well . . ." the hologram tilted his head, appeared to be thinking hard.

In the meantime, the Captain was losing the little patience she had left. "Is this regarding to the aid they required us to give to the Trinity?"

"No!" the hologram shook his head adamantly.

"A—ha!" Aa was lost. "So, what's the hesitation to my question before the last one?" she was well aware that the AI was a young one, not really mature, and therefore he often got lost to explain things when sentient life forms were involved in a situation.

"Because in a vague sense it is on the ship now, but was not before . . ."

Aa's eyebrows almost kissed each other. It was akin to an interrogation, only worse. She had to know the right words, except she obviously did not. "Let's start at the beginning, Victor. What happened?" she exhaled deeply, signaling the AI her willingness to listen. It seemingly worked because about twelve holo displays appeared out of nowhere, showing various screens. In the meantime, the hologram began to talk unusually swiftly; "So this morning we've received long overdue mail from home port."

"Oh, you mean Down Earth?" Aa's eyebrows slightly parted from each other.

"Yes. It's purely electronic and among other things, it contained navigation updates along with material requisition replies. Then another part of the compressed transmissions were crew letters from their families. I promptly disseminated the stream and forwarded to the crew's mailboxes. Upon verification, however, I noticed garbage in the stream. I caulked up to CRC errors, but there were too many of them for that. So, I began to analyze the garbage and I no longer think it's only that . . ."

"If it's not an error or a partial message, then what's that?" The Captain still did not understand, or rather she believed the story did not end there. She was correct. The hologram nodded. "Yes. I realized that there was other garbage in the full stream and molded it together. I am certain it is a message, but . . ."

"Let's hear it then!" Captain Aa began to itch for action. Perhaps a secret message from the Emperor? Maybe from her father?

"Well, see Captain, they compressed the message in a rather peculiar way!" the hologram trailed off.

"Meaning?"

"I am still analyzing the encryption method, but it doesn't conform to any known cryptography key. Not any that's used by UNHL today. However, there are certain markers in it that I can already see and the way are being left would only raise suspicion with an AI, not even remotely with a human. So, what I am trying to communicate that there is a message, and it was being assembled in a way only I would notice it. It's not made by human logic and neither by a common computer language so the sender is either an alien or another AI and that is a worrisome revelation!"

Captain Aa tilted her head. "Indeed, it is . . . Do you know what the message is about?"

"No idea, Ma'am!"

"Is it possible to decipher it?"

"Yes."

"Get working on it!"

"It might take some time, as this exercise is clearly meant for me!" the holo Victor scratched his head.

"Call up your dormant nodes to speed up operation! I want to be presented with an answer as soon as possible!"

"Ay—ay!" the hologram disseminated in the air, leaving Captain Aa in her thoughts. Perhaps something bad has happened, but what that can be? Now, it was possible that the message sender was Diana from the Sky Riders, or perhaps Gabriel from the Starship Azure. It could have come from the AI of Down Earth's Supercomputer or even from the Toxic, but why any one of them would select such a cryptic method was beyond her.

Azure let herself into the green room onboard the Toxic. She found Amerlee curled up on the lower bunk, hugging her knees, rocking herself back and forth amid crying and weeping.

"Hey, hey!" Azure ran to her, then began to pat her shoulder and hand as she realized she was not hurt, at least not physically.

"I have this big twisted knife in my heart!" she brought her big brown eyes to Azure, who emphatically nodded: "I know, I felt that way the first time too!" she remembered.

"And . . . and that just something twisted in him and did not even say his goodbyes, just left!" she whaled.

"He did, indeed he did!" Azure tried to caress her, and she was good at it, so she had to be careful there . . .

"He did not sit down with us . . ."

"No, because we all understood him. All, except you, honey!" Azure added emphatically.

Amerlee stopped rocking and watched Azure. "What do you mean?"

"He is a patriot. The Ancient Man must've seen this in him all those years ago to choose him to lead us. He understood the implications of the AOCP having such a thing and went to investigate. His task is a difficult one, and he knows it. He did that just before he went to prison with the Ancient Man and he walked, willingly. We must respect his decision and abide by his wishes. In his absence we work, fight and advance! I know it's hard because it was hard for me, but with time I understood. It was difficult, but eventually I reasoned and I gathered allies to rescue him. In this case we don't know whether he was captured or not . . . We hope for the best but prepare for the worst!" she hugged her again.

*

"So, there is no new news?" Josh Kulighan stared into the camera.

"None what so ever!" Azure shook her head before adding: "You'll be the first one we contact! Azure out!"

Josh stared at the blank screen for a good minute, then at his wife, Telis, who stepped out of the shadows and said, "you just going to have to play couple more rounds with the Junta!"

"I was seriously hoping Smith would call their leader and talk some sense into him, but now with the disappearance of the Emperor this task befallen me." he snorted. He was truly annoyed.

"All you have to do is work them more!" she was confident her husband can do the work.

Josh fumed in the background. "Of course, the only reason I'm still in charge, if we can say that, is because I was already called in. He supposed to do all the talks and I, well I supposed to stay around to show some power if needed . . . And instead of this, the last word I heard from him; Josh, take care of it! And he off to something more important. Not even Toxic would tell me what it is. His directive stands of not tipping off the presumed AOCP spy guys on the ground, but where he went, we not supposed to know or care. Thank you, but where can I opt out of this?!" he glared at her after adding, "I'm really getting annoyed by this!"

"I think you have to take this as an opportunity and stop whining. He needs you, and here you are. Now if you think, just ask for reinforcement, repeat last night's pitch perfect attack on the Junta's forces by SCC-26-48 and hold them off indefinitely!"

"Yeah, but what you don't get is I'm in a deep pickle here! How do I supposed to go ahead? Threaten the guy myself? Reveal that he has no choice or keep nitpicking with his forces?"

“Did not the Emperor allow Captain Aa thirty-six hours to work on the Trinity? She’ll be back soon, and if I’m not mistaken, she has ground forces on board. Not to mention some planetary bombardment package . . . You are a tactician; use your head, honey!” she stomped the ground.

Josh nodded at her: “You know, you might know something there!” he sniffed into the air then stepped to the con: “Commander Rick, get Captain Mya on the horn!”

“Yes, Captain!” he heard it in return. He began to grin. “Mya better know how to break into their network so I can make my phone call!”

Two hours later, he wished he would’ve not had to be in the shoe he was. Captain Mya just assured him he was on standby, waiting for the final go to talk to the Junta’s head. General Maximoso, Supreme Leader of the Junta. Kulighan gave the go, and he watched the grainy picture provided by a drone high in the atmosphere, aiming its cameras at the ground. The middle-aged man was doing his morning walk in the walled garden. He was talking to someone. Josh did not know, nor did he care, who was on the other end of the line . . .

“Sweetheart, I assured you last week that once we take control of the Space Elevator, we will amass so much wealth we never have to think again!” Maximoso assured his daughter. Suddenly the line on his private, secured, and encrypted cell phone became static.

“Hallo? Hallo!” he yelled into the slim device.

“Listen carefully, General Maximoso!” the male voice sounded calm and cold.

“Who is this? Do you know who you messing with?” the Supreme Leader yelled into the phone, but the calm, accented voice continued, “We’ve already stopped one of your advanced battalion last night. We will do so again. You must cease your war against the Main Land immediately!”

"You piece of shit, this isn't your ordinary phone prank! My men will get you and kill you along with everyone who ever known and cared for, do you understand?" General Maximoso was not kidding, but turned around because he was afraid a sharpshooter might have breached his estate's perimeters.

"Stop looking around, General, you're looking in the wrong direction!"

"You can see me?" the man pointed at his wide chest.

"I can see that you pointed at your chest, sir! Now give the general order to withdraw and you won't have to meet my forces. If you don't, the Teccena Research facility of yours won't blow up eight hours from now!"

"You fool!" the General hung up and began to yell at his ever present and nervously lingering aides.

Josh watched the feed in his room. "This went as well as I expected." he winced, then called up the DSR Eclipse to devise a run at the earlier mentioned facility where the Junta was hard at work to devise a bio weapon. He knew the General wouldn't believe him, but he had to know about his destroyed battalion. *That should cause some doubts in his head and if not enough, oh well, eight hours from now* . . . He snickered, his hands itching already.

Chapter Thirty

Revelations

General Maximoso was beyond mad, he was raging! "How could you not stop the attack? I told you when will it happen! Now all I can see is the ruins and the public relations nightmare that would soon to follow!"

He was yelling at two generals whom were in the unfortunate situation to face him. Although both of them had ample warning regarding to the Teccena Research facility, they choose to ignore the rumor about the impeding attack. They reasoned; nobody would be fool enough to actually carry out a large-scale attack against a well-defended land-based object. Now both hoped they could roll back time, and actually do something different about it. That seemed to be a nonexistent option.

"Sir, the facility was well defended!" General Bartak calmly defended his position.

"Well, it's in ruins!" General Maximoso barked at him angrily.

"Which means we should open up negotiations with however done this!" the second general, General Bolak, spoke.

"With some rebels? Are you insane?" the Supreme Leader yelled at him with full force.

"I don't think they were the rebels, sir!" the first one spoke. "We had active defense over it, like an impenetrable tomb!"

"Impenetrable?!" What do you take me for???"

"Sir, my dear leader," the General softened his tone "We tried to shoot at the attackers, but could not achieve a lock on the target.

It is clear to us it was not any special ops unit from the Main Land. All reports indicate something more robust and serious happened earlier. We believe it is the work of the UNHL. Last night attack on our forward battalion at the . . ." he could not finish as the second Admiral was cut down by the Supreme Leader's harsh words; "I won't stand down for anyone! Not for you, not for some imaginary enemy! I want my space elevator and I will have it! While we're at it, I also want the annexed land as well! The AOCP left a long time ago! We shall use what they have left behind, even if my men have to go thru the field with a fine brush and sweep up everything!"

"Yes, sir!" General Bartak saluted. Upon seeing this, his partner done the same.

"Now, go and make my dream happen!" the Supreme Leader pointed at the door.

Once outside the younger man, General Bolak glanced at his mentor; "Why stop protesting if you disagree with him?"

"Because I value my life very much so. But . . . But I believe there are forces who don't want us to succeed." General Bartak mulled over. "If that's the case we need to learn what they want so as we may satisfy them and save our asses in the mean time!"

*

"I have a worrisome revelation!" Victor formed a hologram around midday to let his Captain know of his advances.

"Go for the revelation!" Captain Aa was at the end of her shift, wondering whether her presence was required at all during repair works. She was slightly tired and mildly annoyed Victor was yet to be able to translate the message. She was sure he ran into other difficulties.

"I am almost one hundred percent sure that the message was composed by Toxic and that the sender is Azure. The message is for you. What the message is, I am yet to decipher it."

Aa wanted to contact the Toxic right away. Then, as she calmed down, she decided to contact Kulighan instead, against Victor's advice.

The legendary tactician seemed tired. He glanced at the monitor and camera. "Captain Aa, what can I do for you?"

"Is . . . Um . . . Smith around?" Aa asked shyly.

"I was left in charge of the operation . . ." Kulighan frowned, thinking the Captain might not aware of the situation. Although he himself was not aware of the entire situation. *Whatever*! He gave up thinking about it.

"What operation?" Aa frowned.

"Stopping the Junta and have his position fold on the Main Land.

"Okay . . ." Captain Aa backed down. It was obvious to her, whatever the situation was, required no mentioning of the Emperor. "If you need help from me, just ask!"

"We'll do, Captain!" Josh said his byes.

"So, we know anything more?" Victor asked her.

"We know that the Emperor isn't around and that he is either unwilling to explain or he can't. Work on that damned message and wake me if you have to when you got it! Let Commander Danek know also!"

"Right, got it!" Victor dissipated instantly. He felt her annoyance radiating from her words.

Aa was about to retire for the night when her comm went off. She made an ugly face, then hopped to the device. "Who is it?"

"It's Victor, Ma'am!" the voice said.

"Materialize then!" the Captain frowned. She turned around upon hearing the sizzling noise. The light beams focused and soon the tall man in bronze suit formed. He saluted and spoke from all the microphones of the room: "I finished translating the message!"

"So where is it?"

"I just sent it to your workstation. You may want to sit down for this!" Victor said as the hologram fell apart, leaving the Captain alone in her room. With slightly trembling hands, she gestured at the holo TV and activated the newly arrived message.

Even before she began to play back the message, she identified the background as the Toxic's deserted bridge. Azure was standing in the middle, looking strong, chin high up and saluting hard. Captain Aa swallowed big. That was a bad sign. She saw her as another soldier and not the Emperor's girlfriend or bodyguard. She flinched and sat down on the big sofa; her shoulders slouched forward. As she un-paused the recording, Azure finished her salute and began talking: "Captain Aa, this is a continuity message! In the absence of the Emperor, I was chosen to forward it to you. Our present location is well known to you. We are staying and waiting for his return. The time stamp clearly dates this message. You have forty-eight hours from that moment on to prepare for your task, shall the circumstances require it. We've come upon a discovery on the planet that threatens the peace of the entire Milky Way. We embedded some of our discoveries in this stream. Upon the expiration of the forty-eight hours and the non-reappearance of our Emperor, you, as the Apprentice of him, are required to hand deliver the discoveries to the Ancient Man himself! Be the blessing of the Emperors follow your path!" Azure saluted again and the recording abruptly ended.

*

Ormon/Smith felt the abrupt shake and woke immediately. The teleportation was underway. Once it ended, he checked his terminal, made sure the so-called Drop arrived at the Nexus, then left. Along the way he stopped at one of the galleys where his card allowed him to choose from a wide variety of menus. Naturally, he chose something from his home world; Tattun, an agricultural planet where he spent his childhood. On his way out of the facility, he ran into an unexpected line of fellow soldiers. Without hesitation, he stepped in, obeying the signs. The man in front of him in the line turned around. "I so hate the waits! I mean, teleporting home should be like a reward. We worked hard! Open all the gates, let the agents disembark or transfer to other Drops! How hard is it? We do all the background works for the various missions, planting evidence and assassinating UNHL citizens, they should not test our loyalty this way!"

"For the Love of Guvojan, I totally agree!" Ormon/Smith nodded, approving his rant.

The guy grinned. "That's right!" and as the line began to move, he pointed to the bright lights beyond the gate, "Nexus, home sweet home!"

Ormon/Smith had to compose himself as he realized what the guy implied of. Their Drop was just one of the many, arranged in a circular pattern around an immensely tall cylinder. They were still underground, somewhere else, obviously. Luckily, admission into the Nexus was a breeze. His Drop issued card was a welcome token of all the system needed. Not even fingerprinting was required! One that Ormon/Smith was sure to pass as his skin long changed to better represent the soldier profile Smith painstakingly forged over the years.

Chapter Thirty One

Desires

"I so hate waiting!" Azure just finished her short breakfast. Amerlee popped her head in, just to ask the obvious. Azure was sure by now; Toxic would tell any new information to the poor girl if she comes it across. "Hop down by me!" Azure pointed at the seat. Four Honor Guards were also sitting, talking quietly about some stuff around them.

"It's been more than two days now!" Amerlee sobbed, nursing a bio drink, looking sad.

Azure flinched, Smith would've too. It drew a smile on her face, remembering his face.

"What's the laugh about?" Amerlee was shocked to see the smile on Azure's face under the circumstances.

Pointing at Amerlee's drink, she responded, "He hated that. I think by nature . . ."

"What do you mean?"

Azure swayed her head. "I don't know. He never elaborated, but I think they have sent him on long duration missions thru space where no other protein was available."

"It's good. It gives me the precisely required number of calories . . ." she defended herself.

"Perhaps there is some Tri'ng in your blood as well!" Azure laughed while drinking her raspberry fruit smoothie. She placed the plexiglass on the table, licked her lips and said, "Smith will be away long, I presume. Hm. Presume or not, his words, not mine . . ." she reminiscent of his way of talking. Suddenly, she slammed on the table and said, "The AOCP device's teleportation just occurred while we were there. Knowing the immense power it requires, I don't think they do that every hour, heck might not every day either." she shrugged. "Then again, he wowed to find out as much as he can about it. We're lucky if he is in AOCP territory by now!"

Amerlee found herself in a peculiar state. All of a sudden, she felt claustrophobic. She wanted to leave the spaceship, and both Toxic and Azure disagreed with her about that. She was not about to give it up so easy; climbed the DSR's tower and watched the view thru a camera system. Something about the blue sky caught her mind. Perhaps it was the clay ground and the blue sky all together. She wanted to feel the sand beneath her bare legs, feel the wind against her skin, the sound of crying birds, and listen to the whoosh of the wind. She was hard at explaining these at the airlock a while later as Toxic naturally caught her.

"What's the obsession about it?" Azure did not have such yearning, and therefore she did not understand the need. Now running, she wanted, but could not at the moment.

"I want to, need to!" she replied passionately.

Azure contemplated the pros and cons, then nodded, "Toxic, call Jena and two of the Death Squad members here!"

"Done!" the voice instantly replied, then asked with a curious voice, "What's your plan?"

Meher and Mysha were just about to leave the house when the tall, slender brunette came out of the 'barn'. He decided to wait for her as she most likely wanted to talk to him, plus there was still ample suspicion left in him about their true intention.

"Good morning, mister!" the brunette greeted them with a warm smile.

"Likewise," Meher measured the woman who pressed her lips.

"I . . . we were wondering how safe is this land around here?" she looked around.

"What do you mean?" Meher expected lots of weird questions, but not like this one.

"Well, surveillance and such. Tell you what. We have a civilian onboard who wants to be outside for an hour or so. What do you think?"

"Of?"

"How safe it is? Does the men from the nearby military base snoop around a lot? You know, we don't want to be cornered." Azure tried to explain herself.

"Well, this is the main road to the highway, but I don't think that supposed to be a big problem. They're on a lockdown," he added, holding onto his daughter's hand firmly.

"Would you mind if we joined you along the way a bit? Wherever you are going?" Jena waved toward the barn. Its door opened and an interesting group of people left it.

Meher naturally frowned upon seeing the young women, especially the all black two in the rear. He waited until they got closer and passed by him.

His daughter wanted to say something, but his fingers, like a grip of the vice, grabbed her arms. She disliked and voiced her opinion, but he silenced her with a single look.

One of the fully robed girls stopped and turned to him, looked deep into his eyes. He stared back at the green eyes, mesmerized, then uttered, "You must be gorgeous . . ." then he spotted the sword on her back and frowned.

Jena watched him, then snored as she picked up the pace, "You're lucky . . . Immensely!"

"Why is that?"

"Standing so close to them as an outsider, looking into their eyes to see their unconditional loyalty to the One and live to talk about it!"

"Who are the robed girls? They look so young!" Meher bobbed his head. They did not look too dangerous to him, but rather extremely creepy!

"Death Squad members . . ." Jena left the sentence hang in the air.

Mysha moved closer to her father. The words rang like a cold dead fish in her ears.

"Who are those?"

"You don't understand our culture? I would've thought these frightening tidbits freely circulated on your planet by now!"

"Frightening?"

"Most frightening indeed. If you thought we're badass, they're absolutely maniacs!" she lifted her chin.

"So, all of you girls are just taking a day off here, on our planet?" Meher tried to change story line.

"We are waiting for his return. Our boss, our employer, I mean. He might not even come back to here, but never less until we hear from him, we are staying . . ." she replied, then asked, "Where are we heading?"

"I was going to inspect my automated fleet of agricultural tractors with my daughter here. We are going to climb on those shallow dunes." he pointed to a group of a rising mound of sands with their gentle, grassed hills.

"How is the war going, mister?" Azure asked from three rows ahead.

"Good, I would say, or bad from the enemy's
standpoint . . ." he mulled over his answer.

"Great news for my people!" Azure bobbed her head.

"Did you girls have something to do with the fact that for now all satellite communication is down?"

"Almost certain that it's a permanent thing!" Azure slowed down to walk beside him.

"I had to adjust my antenna to get analog feed now." Meher snorted, revealing his personal displeasure regarding to the subject.

"Yeah, see, the Junta was about to use them for troop communications. They could be pretty resourceful when they want to be . . ." Azure's good mood evaporated.

"But you must've done other things because they supposed to wage battle for the Space Elevator and they're nowhere near it! Heck, they could not even climb the hills much beyond the City Line. A cousin of mine tells me that there was a night battle of some sort and their systems were taken over. A single line of 'don't-get-involved' appeared on the computer stations while a mysterious cloud massacred the enemy . . . Well unofficially, because our government made a great spin off about it."

"Oh, I love it in here!" Amerlee turned toward the sun, opening her arms and feeling the breeze.

Meher stopped dead in his tracks and watched the woman enjoying the sun and the wind. She even threw her sandals away.

"Is she all right?" he mustered her.

"Civilians, you know how undisciplined are they!" Azure shrugged, then realizing she was bashing her master's girlfriend, she was looking a way out of that. "But hey, she is the one who had those canned food thingies for you, so like her!"

"Yeah, that was good. We only ate one can so far. You were right; it tastes so much better with bread!" Meher added.

"Glad you like it!" Azure bobbed her head.

"Well, we better get going . . ." Meher retrieved a thick tablet like device while pointing at the distance, where big, slow-moving vehicles pulled long objects behind them.

"Good. Thanks for the chat and be careful!" Azure said her byes, but the man's daughter stepped out of his shadow and asked, "Why can't you stop the Junta? They're killing so many of our people!"

"We are doing everything we can under the circumstances, young lady!" Azure bobbed her head toward her as an acknowledgement.

"Can't you do more?" Mysha persisted.

"Not under the special circumstances you guys are in. But don't worry, we will deter them, just that the Junta's leader pretty convinced he can have what he wants. We don't want to resort to assassination as it would lead to a civil war here. But we will do what we must, except it might won't matter . . ." Azure flinched. Her bad mood returned, despite the wonderful landscape.

"Why?" Mysa and her father asked the same.

"Because if galaxy wide civil war does break out, this planet will perish like countless others will . . ."

*

"I don't want to bombard them!" Captain Josh Kulighan explained his position to Captain Yoyo face to face. The UNHL PD, Trinity, just returned several hours ago from her emergency repair near Danal IV.

"The Emperor was clear on that. No compromise can be made or the AOCP will find out about us and all hell breaks loose!"

"We do have infiltration units onboard . . ." The Captain tried to offer help. Her Planet Destroyer, the Trinity, parked outside of the solar system just as she was told to do.

"Meaning?"

"If you can't deter the Junta's leader, we can send our units to the ground to cause dissent or assassinate him. We have the drones on board. They won't even know what hit them!"

Josh frowned, imagined as the tiny drones infiltrate enemy systems, paving the way to the assassin drone to deliver its micro explosive device, inject it to the bloodstream and baaam!

"We have to calculate the feasibility and the outcome of such a scenario . . ." he seemed withdrawn as he was thinking of the likelihood of it.

"We can get the package ready!" Captain Yoyo offered help again.

"Get it ready!" Josh nodded darkly, then as the meeting concluded, he and his advisors left.

Once back on his Space Craft Carrier, he called Commander Rick and by the time he walked into the crowded C&C room; they made the connections to the others required by the mission.

"Is Captain Mya in range?" he asked and soon an affirmative yes came back as an answer.

"Make the call!" Josh mentally prepared himself for the conversation. To be mean and dark, yet firm, took him a second to be. By the time Captain Mya facilitated the call, Colonel Re'kl's DSR, the 0709-Eclipse, was descending into the planet's atmosphere to execute the threat he will deliver momentarily.

General Maximoso was inside his palace, where he felt safe. Lately, ever since the threatening calls, he was getting paranoid about things. He even had his generals with him. When his cell phone went off with the numbers of multiple zeros, he barked at General Bartak, his trusted friend, and he yelled for security while they set up the trace.

"This is General Maximoso, supreme leader of the J . . ."

"We know exactly who you are, sir!" The cold, calm voice on the other end reverberated.

"Then you know I will not back down!"

"We hoped to deter you from that path! Our actions regarding to your chemical warfare facility and the continued setbacks at the Main Land's City Line should've signaled our intentions quite clearly. Why have you not backed down from your foolish quest?"

"I will win!" he promised in a strong voice.

"That's not a nice way to treat me or the call. I know you are tracing this, but it won't do no good!"

General Maximoso turned pale.

"Tell you what. I'll give you a nice round eight hours to change your mind about ending the war. After that, there will be no more phone calls to you. To emphasize my request, I have to set free your underground facility at the Malop mountains!"

Maximoso stared at the phone, unable to comprehend how someone could enter into the heavily guarded mountain range undetected. "Contact the Malop Mountains ballistic missile reserve!"

"General?" Bartak turned at the Dear Leader.

"Do it, now!" he yelled impatiently.

Bartak himself made the call and returned to the room minutes later. His pale face said all Maximoso wanted to know.

"How could the rebels do that?" he tried to recover from his shock. Around the room, the military personnel tried to look away, give wide berth to the raging leader.

"Sir, we have to take the possibility seriously that our enemy might be the UNHL or the AOCP!" Bartak remained realistic.

"No! AOCP left for good and the stupid UNHL wouldn't dare! Oh, so politically correct ones no! It has to be the rebels! Search suspected rebel strongholds and execute everyone found there! That will send them a message!"

"Mapping is complete!" Commander Rick reported to Captain Josh Kulighan three hours later.

"So, who is the best candidate to approach?" he asked.

"A man named Bartak, a general, longtime friend of the Supreme Leader. He partially devised the invasion, according to our sources."

"Will he take it kindly?" Captain Josh mulled over the options. He hated to send good men to a risky operation.

"No way to know, but the package of drones that infiltrated General Maximoso's compound for intelligence purposes were really thorough. Captain Yoyo's infiltration package is exceptional!"

"Don't forget, my son, it's only exceptional because the technological level of the planet below has not matched us. Our built-in dampening fields on every UNHL warship makes this kind of warfare kind of mute, don't you think so?"

"Yes sir, I mean Captain!" Commander Rick composed himself. The Captain was correct, of course.

"So, our general . . ." Josh trailed off. He forgot his name already.

"General Bartak, sir!" Rick helped him out.

"Him! Where does he live? Does he go home?"

"Yes. His family lives on a ranch just outside of the capitol. Pretty big, Colonel Re'kl won't have a problem landing there cloaked!"

Josh Kulighan nodded. “See, our Emperor would’ve solved this by now with one meeting. We, on the other hand, have to do everything mechanically. Can’t fight the Emperors or his will, but today Mr. Bartak can’t fight us!” He shook his head and walked back to his post.

Chapter Thirty Two

The Offer

The aides helped General Bartak out of his military limousine. Earlier he observed the two heavy tanks posted on both sides of the road as the limousine turned off from the main road. He was always happy and relieved seeing the big family house; his father's family. The soldiers at the entrance saluted at him and all he did in return was a single nod. That was enough.

His wife and five children greeted him happily. He hugged them all, then asked for a drink and headed outside to the back of the building, where a garden of retreat was neatly maintained. He wanted to have a quiet hour or two, to think about his future, about the Junta's future. He asked not to be disturbed. As he walked thru the maze of flower gardens, he looked to the left. The three-football field wide green grass looked awful quiet this afternoon. Not even the wind would bend the tall grass . . . He frowned and made the last turn into the small plaza guarded by tall, deep green, neatly trimmed bushes. At first, he did not notice the military man holding a cigarette in his hand. When he did, he froze up.

"Who are you?!" he tried to back out greatly alarmed, but seemingly out of nowhere, two black-robed people jumped out like cats. Quiet and swift, the hallmark of assassins, he had no doubt.

The military man patted his throat two times, then spoke with a deep accent, "Time to talk, General Bartak! Heave a seat, please!"

The General was about to scream for help.

"No need for that, sir!" he pointed at the two girls blocking his exit. They revealed their shiny swords, and it cooled the Admiral instantly.

"What is this about?"

"It is about your loyalty to General Maximoso, of course!" the military man smiled.

"Who are you again?" Bartak glanced around swiftly, looking for out of this unfortunate situation.

"I would prefer if you wouldn't try to leave. Those warriors would have to cut you to pieces, and your family, of course . . ." he added, chuckled, then tossed a thin tablet on the table.

"What's this?" Bartak carefully turned the device around.

"Feeds from your estate. See, we are following your family for some time now!" he snickered, puffing his cigar, then tapped the top of the glass tablet, switching between thermal and real time feeds.

Tarbak spun around, glancing at the sky, looking for something.

"There is nobody around, sir . . ." the military man shook his head.

"Where are the helicopters? Bartak stared at him.

His conversation partner frowned, then realized what Bartak had meant. "Such a crude instrument . . ." Laughed. "No, we have other means to infiltrate. See, your estate was not the only one!" he switched apps, showing General Maximoso's estate. His loyal soldiers, the inside of the intricate layout, the Dear Leader himself in real time! There were hidden cameras in his personal office too! Bartak was gasping for air.

"Who are you and what do you want?" With a pale face, Bartak had to sit down. His conversation partner chosen again to avoid explaining the first part.

"See, we made a phone call to General Maximoso some time ago, asking him kindly to stop this nonsense of invasion. He rejected our call. We will have our way, sir!" the man looked into his eyes. "My name is Colonel Re'kl from the Thirty-Second UNHL Fleet, but I fail to see how that helps you to get out of the hot seat!" he puffed from the cigar again. He was waiting for so long to smoke again; it was bigger relief than to negotiate the message to the right person.

Bartak blinked at him with empty eyes. Suddenly he was open to suggestions. "What can I do?"

"We are prepared to make some kind of leadership change in your country's structure to deter the Junta from occupying the Main Land. Don't look at me so surprised General; I'm sure your history is riddled with similar takeovers! Normally UNHL doesn't get involved this way, but we're in a binder here. Simply put, we can't have anyone get near the Annexed Land."

"This isn't about the Space Elevator?" Bartak totally misjudged the enemy's intentions.

Re'kl nodded. "Can't say we weren't getting uncomfortable with the object falling into the Junta's hand, but hey if you guys decide that you don't want to hear from us again, we were prepared to make that happen. Sure, we don't have an insidious interest in this planet or mostly any other planet either, but as it turned out that Annexed Land isn't quite deserted, so . . ."

"But, but it is! The AOCP left! We observed the evacuation. They took everything and said that we are not allowed to enter to the annexed lands. We believe it is a deterrence tactic, and nothing more!" Bartak shook his head.

"Well, you are wrong there!"

"We conducted stratospheric flights, and we took pictures. There is nothing there!" Bartak disagreed.

"You fool! We have all this technology to observe without you knowing. You don't think we did not use it on that site fist?"

Bartak wanted to object, then shut his mouth and watched the feed on the tablet. "Remarkable!" he observed enthusiastically. "Is it some kind of cloaked helicopter?"

Re'kl had to laugh. "Think beyond such crude devices, sir! Well, to not to deviate from my objective here, my mission involves getting you on our side!"

"What do you mean?"

"We have the mean to kill General Maximoso, but we need an insider guy, one who takes over. Hopefully, you would declare open elections too, we sincerely hope . . ." he added with emphasis on the hope part.

Bartak frowned. "I, I can't be part of this!"

"You already are! We told your leader he won't get more calls, but we never promised others won't. If not you, then somebody else." he shrugged as casually as he coud. "I would think it's better you then . . . somebody else . . ." Re'kl added, emphasizing their wide options.

"How and when would this unfold?" Bartak massaged his forehead. He developed a sudden headache.

"The sooner the better. We have everything in place. It would be best if you would gather your most trusted men for this, set up somebody with a plausible intention and have him framed for the act, but it's up to you how exactly do you want to do it."

"Why to go to all the trouble with this? If you guys are so powerful, I'm sure you could bombard our planet from space . . ."

"We can and we would. We have the power to do so, but it would unleash a galaxy wide civil war that would simply consume your planet as it was here where we discovered a breach to the Treaty. See, it wouldn't matter where you are on this planet!" Re'kl saw the transformation in Bartak's eyes. He could always frighten the man more and he decided to do so, to give him the necessary nudge in the right direction. "Our now dormant Solar System Destroyer would annihilate all you call home and then some!"

Chapter Thirty Three

The Report

Captain Aa patiently waited as the door opened and she walked across the thick entrance. Commander Danek jumped from the seat and saluted hard. “All sentries recalled, support ships in formation, Ma’am!”

“Have the nav computer calculated the route?”

“Yes Ma’am!” The Commander glanced up and down at the woman. She wore her sparklingly clean dress with her military ribbons all affixed on her chest. He chuckled as she took his place.

“Prepare for a jump!” she seemed to be content as the stars began to turn into streaks and the UNHL warship; the majestic SPD Destination Unknown jumped to light speed.

Diesel walked through the Final Victory’s quiet and deserted halls. He slowly made his way around the cordoned off area, where the largest Planet Destroyer ever built sustained devastating damage from the II. Klon Wars some thirty years ago. His master decided never to repair beyond restoring strength to the SPD itself. He wisely said, “let that be a reminder to all . . .”

The gunslinger, personal bodyguard of the Ancient Man, had a strange but most likely vitally important information he needed to share with his master. His hands were itching as he entered into the huge room full of computers and screens. His master laid in a recliner type of floating device, jacked directly in to the data stream to better comprehend the data feeds.

“My Lord!” he exhaled to project calmness.

For a minute or so, nothing happened. Then the holo screens, one by one, folded and the tall man opened his eyes. “Why is the abruption into my search?” he slid off the elevated recliner and stood firmly, front of his bodyguard.

“My Lord! There were inquiries made about your location some time ago . . .”

“AOCP spies?” the Ancient Man frowned.

“No. It was UNHL. Presumably. A contact of mine reached me first about a day or so ago. He is a trusted one. He told me that a UNHL Captain made discrete inquiries of our location. He said he did not know the name or ID of the person. They did it thru encrypted electronic mail.”

“Did you reveal our location?” the Ancient Man frowned. This did not happen too often.

“I changed the exact coordinates. It’s a bit off from our present location.”

“I hope it’s not beyond the event horizon?” he chuckled.

“No, My Lord! Safe distance from us and from the black hole!” Diesel referred to the gigantic black hole, a gaping well in the fabric of space and time; the center of the Milky Way, eating stars and chewing space dust forever now.

“What is your guess, who will be our visitor?” the Ancient Man ratcheted up his normally distant human emotions.

“I believe it will be a very special event . . .” Diesel trailed off.

“Indeed. Tell the Captain to prepare for possible hostiles . . .” the Ancient Man replied coldly.

“. . . Still, an educated guess could be derived from all available data!” Diesel felt the need to share his own hypothesis.

His mentor tilted his head. A wry smile accompanied his tilted head. “Meaning?”

“I had the Final Victory monitoring UNHL troop movements since the first contact. Moments ago, part of the 26th UNHL fleet jumped to hyperspace from near Danal IV. As far as I can tell, it was an unscheduled, unannounced jump. Not even a single message could be found on the military networks. In your discretion, I contacted Admiral Tarbuk moments ago and made an official inquiry. He had no idea that one of his ships and its supports left prearranged position, though he did note that the particular space ship and troops were under the direct supervision of the younger Emperor . . . Designated as a back end of an urgent operation he is involved in."

"What ship?" the Ancient Man's eyes twitched.

Diesel moistened his lips, "SPD Destination Unknown . . ." he watched as his mentor shook. It did not get lost on him how great of a turmoil his mentor went thru upon mentioning of the SPD's name.

The Ancient Man sniffed into the cold air, signaling he understood. "The Apprentice of the younger Emperor coming to see me . . . I can almost spell the word doom! She would not come unless . . ." he swiftly turned around, his hands behind his back. He glanced upward and spoke: "Prepare for her arrival. I better change!" And with that, he disappeared in a white fireball.

*

Ormon/Smith had no trouble walking thru security. Once inside the Nexus, he got separated from the previous group and wondered around until he got to one of the terminals. He utilized it and browsed thru the public content. Only dates and operation names were public. Those numbered in the hundreds . . . With a delighted face that he was part of such an important task force walked away, got into several turbo lifts and about ten minutes later he walked outside of a plaza. He was in an inner court of an all-glass building; a mega complex, spanning half a city. He looked up to the hazy yellow sky, then he glanced at the city below him. He had to find out where he was. The nagging question somehow ruffled his feathers, as the planet was not the CTP . . .

*

Captain Aa stepped off from her shuttle. It was one of the newest one, came off the assembly plant less than six months ago, a kind thought from the younger Emperor. Now it was not the time to think of that, she reminded herself. She cleared her head, knowing the Ancient Man was an intrusive telepath. Troops from her SPD lined up as she proudly walked away in the wide and seemingly abandoned hangar. The shiny, black floors made her wonder. It was old; she has not seen that since the floor tiles were light gray blue nowadays. It was almost like a bad omen. Some fifty meters away, another line of troops greeted her. These were more abundant and very professional. Two men stood at the end of the line. One he recognized instantly; Diesel, bodyguard of the Ancient Man. Although the bodyguard was tall, the man beside him was at least a half head taller. He was skinny, mean looking. Sparse gray hair covered his otherwise naked head. Not much to look at, but she guessed she wouldn't look much better closing on her eight hundred birthday either.

She stopped, first bowed, then dropped to half knee in front of him. "My Lord! I have a message from the younger Emperor!"

"Stand up, my child!" The Ancient Man glanced at the young woman. Her special traits glowed like an invisible force field around her; worthy of only other specials! No wonder, he thought, Smith began to shape her long time ago.

The young Captain of the UNHL navy's proudest SPD stood up, glanced at the Ancient Man, then her eyes slipped at the bodyguard standing beside him.

It irked the Ancient Man. He was curious of the younger Emperor's message, but at the same time he recognized the need to break the so-called ice. He remembered centuries ago, when he was being trained, he probably had the same reservations as she had about him now . . . A touch of softness he recognized and upon realizing he scoffed; such a human emotion and he promptly discarded the weakness.

Captain Aa noted the presumed irk toward her presence and definitely turned away from the immortal, while worried for her life.

"Apprentice of the younger Emperor!" The words came clear, cold and harsh. She shook upon hearing it.

"You would have not come unless your master wanted it such way therefore you presumed to be ready to walk with the immortals, so LOOK at me when you about to talk to me!"

"Yes, My Lord!" she forced herself to look at him.

"Better!" he acknowledged her. "Now walk with me and tell me why have you traveled to the center of the Milky Way!" he turned around, hand behind his back, face strong and began to walk toward the exit with Diesel on his left side, Captain Aa on the other.

Servants offered complimentary food and a drink of Deghna to her as she explained the settings of Hilderin, how the younger Emperor was led there by presumed AOCP telepaths or UNHL prisoner with telepathic ability. She saw his mood transforming upon hearing her story, the implications of his disappearance underground, and what his team discovered so far.

He quietly nodded at the conclusion of her report. "Who is running operation in his absence at Hilderin?"

"Captain Josh Kulighan." she replied.

"Good. The fate of the planet and the younger Emperor's orders are in safe hands!" he nodded again. "We will make our next move together." he then turned to Diesel. "Order general mobilization from the far end of the galaxy! Don't let AOCP take notice! Then come back and we will send a message worthy of Guvojan's attention!"

"Sir. Um, My Lord, you believe he was aware of this?" Aa was shocked hearing it. It mounted to akin to preparing for war . . .

"He had to be. If he did not than he is incompetent and he is not!" The Ancient Man closed the argument.

Aa admired the immortal to make such life-altering decisions on a whim. She would mull over things like this for months! Even Smith would. Perhaps . . . She did not notice, as the Ancient Man had her full attention. Upon noticing it, she shook.

"To answer for your question, it is yes. As you grow older, you will begin to see certain patterns. As you know, I'm much older than the younger Emperor. I know President Guvojan for many years now. That system you have described to me is something that was authorized for entirely different reasons during the last phase of the war against the Klons. It was a way to mobilize a vast amount of ground forces; drop them to important planets to fight the enemy. It used to be a robust plan. I never knew they developed it until now." The Ancient Man explained, not looking at her, not seeing her mental questions erupting.

"My Lord, if I may . . . I never knew you would explain this to me!"

"You are special, that is for certain . . ." The Ancient Man turned at her. "Your fate is undecided. I see as you will rise to be in the position the younger Emperor envisioned you would be. But then . . . Like great things that will end too. Why, I can't see clearly, but by now he must know it too. You will, however, survive as an independent woman that is written all over you. You are stronger than you believe you are. Perhaps time does it . . ." he brooded over his half empty glass. He slightly nodded and started a different thread: "I see you capable to heal others . . . I am surprised you never tried your gift on yourself!" he smiled lightly.

"Excuse me? My Lord?"

"Yes. See, you can heal yourself, not just others. And that's makes you almost immortal. Which means you will live exactly as long as you wish to!" He lifted another glass of Deghna toward her. She mirrored his presumed well wishes, lifting another glass toward him. Then they both drank it all.

*

Azure found Amerlee in her bed. She wanted to see her as the crucial time had passed; it was past forty-eight hours since Smith left. Past the deadline she had to convey certain facts to Captain Aa, who had to be on her way to the Ancient Man by now. . . Surely Amerlee realized this, too. That and the worry toward her emotional state made her look after her. Amerlee could be strong, but could be unstable once things began to revolve around Smith. It meant she was extremely caring toward him. Perhaps more than she herself was. She wanted to know, to understand this. To understand why she was more worried for him than she herself was? Was it because she was a fellow soldier and Amerlee was just a civilian, or she really loved him more than she did? That whole thing bothered her, but at the same time annoyed her as well.

"I'm so sacred!" she was wiping her endless tears.

"Listen . . ." Azure hopped down beside her. Actually, she was tired of keep convincing her, then as the day progressed, they were back to where she began . . . Upon seeing this was the case again, she cried out loud revealing her annoyance: "Jesus Christ!"

Amerlee stared at her with big eyes. She even forgot to cry. "Who?"

"Johnny used to say that . . ." Azure frowned, thinking about her previous life. "Nothing

really . . ." she made the thought disappear. "Stop crying!" she patted her hand.

"You don't understand! I'm so scared!" she shook her head.

Azure wanted to reassure her, but instead the defiance of a soldier and patronizing the one she cared for the most came abruptly to life. "That's a problem then, because this is almost normal for him. It's his job, it's his life! He won't change. If you can't take it, you better stay home and just wait for him!" she shook her head, looking frustrated.

Chapter Thirty Four

Supreme Leader, Bartak

General Bartak massaged his right hand. That was all the nervousness he was willing to display as his limousine entered into the Supreme Leader's estate. He was thinking all yesterday afternoon about how to proceed, but could not come up with anything. He had nobody to set up, nobody to frame for . . . He was not sure the UNHL stopped watching him or his family or whether they were behind every lamppost on the planet. It drove him crazy. He thought about yesterday's visit from that military guy and the two assassins. Perhaps they were loyalty testers from the Supreme Leader himself! It was good he did not commit verbally to them! He was in mental chaos as he walked thru the metal detectors. The estate's lavish interior completely eluded him as he walked thru the maze-like building; took the elevator to the underground levels to meet General Maximoso. All of a sudden, the Supreme Leader wanted his presence on a Saturday . . . Today! He had no idea why, but hoped to live long beyond this day. He exited the elevator, nodded at the two military security officers as he walked past them. He shook, half expecting ringing shots as the last thing he would hear before being killed, but that did not happen either. He made the turn at the corridor, walked on the elegant carpet and opened the big, heavy doors to the meeting room. The carpet changed to deep blue, the walls ruby red with occasional white lines for decoration along the multiple paintings hung from the walls. Inside the huge room, about fifty staffers talked in small groups. His former apprentice, General Bolak noticed him, and with a big smile on his face he approached him: "General Bartak, so good to see you! Our Supreme Leader has a big surprise for us!" Bratak was not sure whether he was the surprise himself or there was something else, but with weak legs he walked into the middle of the room. He saluted hard at the wide shouldered man, who grinned like it was prom night.

"Welcome, my dear friend, tonight we'll teach those weak Main Landers to a new lesson! Come," he invited him to the middle of the room where a hastily set up screen showed them the Main Land and the coast lines around it.

"What is this about?" General Bartak remained suspicious.

"Since the land units have such a hard time advancing, I asked my navy to annihilate the Main Land's major military bases and remaining strongholds. They needed couple days to realign our strategic nuclear missile submarines but finally we will send a decisive blow at them!"

Bartak's eyes grew wide . . . It was not about his loyalty, but then this just became a nightmare, just the same! The world will engulf in flames and he and his family will perish like they were never alive! He glanced at his former apprentice, General Bolak, who nodded happily.

"My friend," The Supreme Leader offered a drink from a gliding server's plate, "Tonight we will rewrite history!"

Minutes later, he pulled Bolak to the side. "How did this materialize?"

"I believe the Supreme Leader grew tired of us not delivering and tasked the lean navy to do something about it. We should consider our asses lucky that we still alive!" his former apprentice replied.

"What about the Malop Mountain's ballistic missile reserve?"

"Oh, all reports indicated massive detonations at all entrances. Our people stuck inside. They have water and air reserve, but we not even sure they're alive, so we lost our land capacity to restock our forward based silos for some time, hence the brilliant move from our Supreme Leader!" General Bolak was happy to inform him. Bartak, however, remained very nervous. If the UNHL did not know about it, could be a big trouble, but they did not exactly leave a way to be contacted either. “When is this show supposed to begin?”

“About an hour from now. All twelve of our strategic submarines are in their zones, preparing to launch all sixteen tubes. And as they informed me, two of them equipped with our advanced MIRV warheads, quadrupling the possible targets!”

*

“Commence targeting and start the clock!” Captain Josh Kulighan announced in the CIC (Combat Information Center). The room around him came to life. Officers began making calls, relaying information, and the screens above their heads began showing multiple locations and data. He was informed about the Junta’s next strike about four hours ago as the military arsenal mapping concluded. At first, he was skeptical about knowing how the Junta disliked navy operations, but upon learning the existence of their strategic nuclear submarine fleet, he immediately went on devising a tactic to disable them.

It was relatively easy to track the surface battle ships and luckily, they all converged on locations where the submarines were presumed to be. He discovered no less than twelve huge submarines running high speed toward the coast lines. Of course, then they were still couple hundred nautical miles away, but by now he expected them to be in their designated region. The question of how to deal with them became mute with Captain Yoyo’s infiltration package being present at his will. Two SCCs from his fleet were on a slow and surprising descent into the planet’s atmosphere, assuming they knew all the passive Junta radar locations. Fighter planes on his SCCs were just given a go ahead with special pods beneath their main bodies. Some of those pods were delivered from the UNHL PD, the Trinity, as his forces lacked atmospheric infiltration to the scale it was required. Soon

Commander Rick reported that the cavity torpedoes from the pods were dropped into the ocean.

Another phase began after the launching of the deterrence fighter planes and the unguided, so called smart loitering munitions that would take eighteen minutes to reach their intended striking area. If they sense the launching of anything dangerous from the Junta's warships, they would counteract that with high precision. And if a missile or rocket launch would be successful from them, the deterrence fighters would deal with it while the loitering munitions would blow them to pieces.

The minutes seemed to be hours as he waited in the room. People around him were busy coordinating the attack, and he was proud of them. This was an unusual war theater, asymmetric in some form, and so far, they were executing his orders to his liking!

Somebody updated the maps, showing most of the cavity torpedoes reaching the submarines. They offloaded the nanites, and the torpedoes themselves stuck each submarine's propulsion systems. The now active nanites had two reasons to be there. For one, they submitted telemetry and information about the damage, and if it was needed, they themselves could be detonated or activated for structure dissemination. That was the case of target No.7 that somehow survived the cavity torpedo's premature detonation. His officers sprang into action and a minute later the now hull bound nanites began to bore thru the layered structure while some of them attacked the propeller base . . .

General Bartak began to sense General Maximoso staff's impatience. As he calculated by now, the nuclear-tipped missiles should've been launched from almost all locations. That has not happened. Then a flash from one of the screens showed two missiles being launched, but as they eclipsed over enemy territory one went dark, the other separated to four separate warheads. One by one, missiles that seemingly came out of nowhere took the warheads out.

Bartak frowned. He was searching for General Bolak's presence. Seemingly he was confused, like everybody else in the room.

Bartak licked his dry lips. Something had to go wrong . . . Very wrong . . .

"Supreme Leader!" Personal aide Ender cut thru the personnel and reported to the Supreme Leader.

"What is happening? Power outage that I can't see my warheads?"

"My Dear Leader, we've got S.O.S from one of our subs. They reporting system-wide malfunctions!"

"What? How could that be? They're isolated from the surface by the water! They were all thoroughly tested at the port!" General Maximoso was unable to comprehend the failure. "Contact the support ships!"

"They seem to be busy repelling attacks from all directions!"

"They're under attack?" General Maximoso could not believe. "The Main Land had puny sailors on old rusty buckets! Check your sources!"

"The S.O.S. from the sub reported sudden hull compromises, but before it all began; they had a close-range detonation underwater as they were ascending from a general depth of two hundred eighty meters and twenty-seven knots!" the aide responded amid shivering and not from the cold.

"Nobody has weapons like that!" Somebody replied as skepticism spread thru the room.

General Bartak watched as the Supreme Leader turned away from him. And then he spotted the anomaly: A bubbling dot beneath his skin on his neck! He took a step closer to look. Then, as the bubble grew in size and General Maximoso began to complain of a sharp pain in his neck, he began to trail away. The next moment the Supreme Leader yelled in pain and agony as the soft detonation ruptured his spine and he fell toward the floor.

Bartak reached for his service weapon and aimed at one of the service employees who happened to freeze up and stare at the Supreme Leader lying on the floor.

“You! Stop moving!” General Bartak aimed his gun at the man, who dropped his tray and began to turn and run.

Bartak thought of setting up someone and yelled: “He had a puncture device!” And pulled the trigger repeatedly, hitting the innocent man three times on his back. He fell and within seconds, dark blood spewed thru the garments and spread across his immaculate white suit.

Somebody yelled for a doctor, but all they could do is to announce the sudden death of the Supreme Leader. Bartak dropped to the floor beside General Maximoso and checked his neck. The lumpiness quickly faded, and he became desperate for an alternative to how he could’ve been killed. He quickly altered the storyline and secured the notion of someone was an assassin with multiple means for delivery and execution. As he still huddled the late Supreme Leader, he turned him around and used a moisten napkin from his jacket to quickly wipe the fallen man’s lips then moved to the dead waiter and placed the napkin into the guy’s jacket.

“General Bartak!” General Bolak practically screamed from across the room, looking helplessly.

Bartak glanced up while pretending to search the guy’s pockets. As he found the napkin, he carefully pulled it out from the pocket.

Ender, the now fallen leader’s aide, yelled: “Guards! General, be careful! It could have poison on it!”

“You’re right!” Bartak stopped fiddling and held his trembling hands open.

Security locked the room while guards whisked away the presumed attacker’s body.

Bartak seemed to be shaken by the events, like others, but General Bolak glanced around: “Who is the second in command? Who takes over our great nation?”

Nobody stood out from the crowd, but Ender, late Supreme Leader’s personal aide, gave a wet towel to General Bartak: “I believe it should be you as the one who took out the assassin!

Nobody had an understanding of the situation, but you! I believe you're a worthy successor of the late General!"

"Supreme Leader Bartak, what is your first order?" General Bolak saluted at his former mentor, who almost fainted . . .

Chapter Thirty Five

Almost Twenty Thousand Years Ago

Ormon/Smith sipped from his hot tea. He was sitting on the balcony of a protruding café shop and glanced below. People, mostly agents and men in suits, walked around on the concrete tiled park. He felt to be the slightly curious type. As always. He counted over thirty agents in ten minutes. That told him the operation was pretty big, with wide-reaching implications. With a sudden move he jumped up from his seat and walked back to the building he came from. He utilized one of the terminals to visually see all the possible Drop locations. There were one hundred and thirty-two locations across the UNHL territory. Others resided in AOCP territory, about a third more. He glanced back at the previous screens. Out of the one hundred thirty-two, two were in the Kingdom of Sahsalos, seven in the Zenin-Kron Empire, and the rest, seemingly, were thrown across all UNHL territories. He found it curious to have so many locations in UNHL space, but noted that there was none on SWEi Prime. "Funny . . ." he mumbled. He was so into reading the screen, he did not notice three guards approaching his location. Suddenly he heard a loud 'hands up!' notice. He glanced from the screen and noted two of the guards. "Shit!" He moved away from the screen, looking for a way out of this. He was certain someone flagged his activity somewhere. All he knew, he could not be caught. For why? That eluded him. He waited until the guards got within his reach, then he used a quick move to knock the closest guard's face, then jumped behind him and used the other guard for a shield to jump behind a corridor as they fired shots at him. He was looking for doors. Those would give him a second of relief. Why? Again, he had no idea. The corridor he found himself in was littered with offices. He stormed into one of them, across the lobby, never acknowledging the secretary's 'hey!' and he disappeared into the men's room. He jumped into one of the rooms with a toilet sign and noted he was breathing heavy. He heard yells from the outside, looked down at his evaporating hands, and he was about to scream in panic as he disappeared in a great, white fireball . . .

That moment Smith regained full operation over his consciousness. He was between states; no longer on Belmar, known from its huge concentration of diplomats and the AOCP State Department's secondary location, but not quite yet at his destination either. He wanted to be on a safe place, inside his house or onboard the Sky Riders and for a split second he panicked, not sensing either of them, then realized that those were in another Parallel Universe, so he looked for the next best option: Toxic. But that split of a second already ruled out millions of destinations. He sensed Toxic's presence on the planet he left behind in the beginning of his journey, but could not quite pinpoint it, so he just made a haphazard decision and materialized . . .

*

Both girls woke up instantly. It was really early morning, before dawn.

"He is here!" Azure exhaled with a sense of calmness.

"I felt him too . . . Strange!" Amerlee grabbed her pants.

"Smith is back!" They heard Toxic reporting what they already knew. "Why isn't my master onboard me?" Toxic wondered aloud.

"Maybe he is in trouble?" Amerlee placed her hands on her chest.

"He isn't too far." Azure frowned at first, then pulled up her pants too. It was time to find him. She also began to worry. He did not make a mental connection, but she could feel his presence. It was obvious to her; he did not want to advertise his location on the planet; no sane person would under the watchful eyes of AOCP Spy ops.

"Call Baby Haas and Jena to the bridge now!" Azure jelled into the room, addressing Toxic of course, while grabbed her tank top.

"My Smith!" Amerlee exhaled deeply. "Strange that I felt his arrival! I am not telepathic at all." she wondered.

"You two have a special connection now!" Azure replied, rather annoyed that they really do have it!

*

Somebody was knocking on the front door really hard. Mysha grabbed her robes and ran up to her parents' bedroom scared: "Dad, somebody is outside . . ."

"All right, all right!" she heard the familiar baritone that belonged to his father. Soon he opened the door and with big steps he walked beside his daughter.

"Who is it?" he yelled outside, not opening the door. He glanced behind, looking for his rifle. His daughter helpfully held it in her hands.

"It's Jena. We need your help! It's urgent," she added.

"Damn neighbors!" Mr. Meher cracked the door open first. He saw the tall woman alone at his doorstep with the dark blue night and the sea of stars as a background. It was an interesting contrast, one that he was not interested at the moment as he was irked when somebody woke him. "What now? The barn isn't enough?"

"That's not it! We need your help and a car, preferably!"

"What for?" he snored. He was still half asleep.

"We need to find our guy! He isn't too far, but we are unfamiliar of the land, plus we don't want to cause unnecessary surprises.

"I betcha!" he slammed the door shut. All he could think of that if this is the reason they stayed, his pesky and decidedly strange neighbors would be gone soon. His life would return to normal! “Give me a couple of minutes!” he ran upstairs, past his daughter who wanted to come as well. He was too confused to shut her up, and instead he vaguely nodded toward her. Mysha took that as a yes, grinned, dropped the rifle, and ran back to her room to get dressed.

“So, your very important guy suddenly appeared, huh?” Meher tried to get an understanding out of his star-visitors. They took the open top jeep as his annoying neighbors pointed in the direction of the flat-top mountains toward the desert. Unfortunately, their general direction pointed across the military zone as well. When he expressed his concern, they all replied that it was okay as long as they can go around it.

“I think so!” Amerlee wailed.

“What’s wrong with her?” Meher glanced back. His daughter was sitting beside him, the two girls in the back seat.

“Love sick . . .” Azure shrugged, but inside she was longing for him, too.

“And you think he is in that direction?” Meher turned off from the main road. Upon instructions, he lowered the headlight’s intensity, but it also slowed him down.

“Is this road safe?” Azure glanced around. Her enhanced eyes picked out four-legged animals in the distance.

“Yeah. It’s a country side road. It leads to the mountains, but it evades the military zone by wide.” Meher frowned and switched to a lower gear.

“It’s okay.” Azure nodded with Amerlee, who added, “I know he is just descending.”

Azure frowned in her direction. Their bond must be strong. Stronger than she initially thought.

Mr. Meher saw the expression. He just had to ask: “So your girlfriend here is his lover?”

“We both love him!” Azure responded before she realized what it means.

"Two girlfriends? Does he know that?" Mysha turned toward his father. This was new.

"Well, he can have any combination of four . . ." Amerlee clenched her fingers together, looking nervously into the darkness. She did not see anything, unfamiliar scenery and all. She needed Azure's help to stay alive, so she gently leaned toward her. Azure noticed and patted her shoulder. "It's okay, you know. We are getting closer!"

"I know!" she uttered, looking very concerned.

"Weird people!" Mysha glanced at his father, who responded: "Maybe they're rich and goofy . . ." he offered an explanation that used to just work.

"Goofy perhaps . . ." Azure responded, shocking them at the front.

"You can hear us?" Mysha turned around to face her. Azure nodded. "I'm an enhanced human, if you can call me as such. I was engineered and as such my maker dialed up certain selectors in my nature!"

"Is the guy we are looking for created you?" Meher made the wrong deduction.

"Nah, not even close!" Azure had to laugh.

"So, what does, um, your friend means any combination of four?" Mysha was interested in the mating rituals of off world people.

Amid Mr. Meher's high scoffs, Amerlee explained about four wives or girlfriends or the combination of them. At the end she rushed to add in her defense of UNHL way of living. "But it only pertains to him."

"So, he is special?" Mysha grinned, barely hiding her smile.

"Yeah, he is!" The girls replied in unison.

"It seemed to me that Miss Jena was also nervous for him. Is she another . . . ?" Meher left the sentence hang in the air.

"Oh, no. She is a bodyguard. I am too, in a sense." Azure frowned, realizing that.

"What's the difference between the two of you, then?"

"Um. I'm poor and in the military, but Amerlee was never in the military and perhaps can be called as wealthy." Azure replied, thinking about anything else that might be considered as a big difference and can be explained rather quickly.

"You certainly have more memories than I would ever collect, so in a sense you are rich too!" Amerlee grabbed the side rail as the jeep made a sharp turn on the rugged road.

"Yeah, I do."

"Why?" Mysha was interested.

"Because, my darling, this is my seventh life!" Azure forced a smile. She could tell it rattled the cage in both of at front.

"Seventh?" Mysha echoed the words like they were forbidden.

"In essence, my consciousness is saved and overwritten periodically. If and when I die, they just remake a new body around the last saved consciousness. Well, if Evan wants it to." Azure stopped.

"Evan?"

"The guy we're after." Amerlee explained.

"So, you fought in the war with the Klons?" Meher tried to gauge the girl's expertise.

"Yes, but only in the first one . . . With Johnny, I mean." Azure added.

"Johnny?" Amerlee echoed her, trying to put a finger on the guy, but it came back empty.

"I was born in a sense in Mars, property of KHI, Karalan Heavy Industries as a pleasure model, but by the time my line was perfected the civil war on Earth ended and the enforced rules prohibited the sale of pleasure models so my line was converted to soldiers." she shrugged like it was nothing.

"So that was before the Fall!" Amerlee realized, eyes big.

"Yeah, so Johnny was the public name of the almost mythical person otherwise known as the Doctor."

"The man who saved humanity!" Amerlee nodded as an expression of respect. "I have not realized that. Then you saw all that was before the Fall. It had to be disheartening to see all human advances go up in flames!"

“Yes . . .” Azure turned her face away, memories flooding her brain. “My parents and the workers; the Martian Humans sacrificed themselves to give time for Earth to escape.”

Amerlee patted the girl’s shoulder as she expressed her caring and understanding.

“How long ago that was?” Meher was unfamiliar with all what just they explained.

“Almost twenty thousand years ago . . .” Azure sounded remorseful as she looked into the darkness, trying to spot Evan.

“Um, what?” Meher became alarmed, and his suspicion did not cease to exist, even after Azure repeated herself.

“I met Evan Smith back in my time as he and my Johnny became trusted and good friends.” Added Azure.

“How could he meet you that far in the past?”

“He traveled back in time to restore a distorted timeline.” Azure said like it was an everyday thing, then asked him to stop the car. She stood and probed the horizon.

“Miss Jena said that we are the seeds of past humans from around that time, is that true?” Meher watched his steering wheel intently.

“Possibly . . .” Azure was not paying too much attention to him anymore. “If it is, it had to happen after the Fall. After 9752. I was not around by then. Evan would know all the answers you looking for . . .” she gauged the land before her, then pointed her fingers like a dart: “There!”

*

Smith had a mental conversation with himself. He was pissed he could not just teleport to the Toxic, but then he would reveal his location to the AOCP telepaths, possibly spying on the local citizens. Based on what he learned just recently, it was a very real possibility. No, he concluded, the best thing was to just keep on walking. Sometimes when his anger boiled, he blew off the steam by allowing his mental waves to create real swirls in the air; miniature sand storms by his legs and behind him. He was thinking of Amerlee and Azure. Somehow, he missed them both. Possibly because he tried to hide from the looming and rather uncertain future by way of being with them. He half way expected active military shelling or bombardment by now. The Junta's advances were impressive. Since the land was quiet, the nearby military airbase was not in total darkness, he had to believe they slowed the Junta down. "Perhaps Josh did something to them . . ." he mumbled under his breath. His old pal would do something like that. Perhaps carry out a half order to slow them down so he would have to deal with it later. He would scare the shit out of the Junta. That made him laugh so badly he stopped and wiped off his happy tears. Then he heard something in the distance and froze up. He had nothing to defend himself with; no guns or weapons, but he had multiple options. He cleared his mind and began to walk to confront the noise.

"Smith!" Azure repeatedly yelled in the dark.

"Evan . . . ?" Amerlee sounded utterly hopeful.

Meher and Mysha stood by their jeep, glancing into the pitch-black desert. They saw nothing, but just for caution, the rifle was nearby.

"Girls?" They heard a faint but familiar noise.

"Smith!!!" Amerlee took off into the night.

"Damn it!" Azure ran after her.

Five minutes later, a trio emerged from the darkness. Amerlee was practically hanging from the guy, kissing him all over while Azure walked beside them, holding Smith's hand. As they approached the jeep, Smith appreciatingly nodded toward the father and daughter. "Thank you for coming and get me!"

Smith sat between the caressing girls, looking exhausted. Mysha helped them into the car and pointed at Amerlee. "She seems to be madly in love!"

"Youth . . ." Azure shrugged. "You know, love knows no boundary. And she is very devoted . . ." she made an ugly face and hopped beside them.

Half way back to the 'barn' Smith patted Mr. Meher's back and leaned forward. "I heard you were really nice to my crew in my absence!"

"We tried to be neighborly . . ." Meher was not sure what to answer.

"I heard you have questions." Smith pressed on.

"They can wait if you have to go."

"A matter of fact, we have to go. Urgently, but I'll be back. I have unfinished business here and I haven't properly thanked your help either."

"I understand . . ." Meher nodded while thinking that this guy had to be some kind of top spy.

Smith had to laugh. The girls looked startled at each other.

"What is so funny?" Mysha looked at the guy in his early thirties. He was tall and a bit cute, but not really her type.

"I'll live . . ." Smith smiled at her.

"Excuse me?"

"About me not being your type, and my smile was directed at your father, thinking me being a top spy!"

Mysha and her father glanced at each other, horrified.

Once the jeep pulled front of the barn, they heard all kinds of noises.

"Toxic, contain yourself!" Smith hollered toward the doors.

The noise died down instantly.

"Thank you!" Smith offered his hand to Mr. Meher, who took it.

Others watched with enormously big eyes.

"Why is everybody looking at me like that?" Meher uttered toward Smith.

"Touching me is a big thing, even if for a single handshake where I'm from. Stupid ritual, if you ask me!" he patted the farmer's back for even more awe from his people.

"But why . . . ?" Meher asked from no one in particular.

"You are blessed to be touched!" Baby Haas turned toward him.

"A handshake?"

"Touched by an immortal . . ." she added for clarification.

"A what?!"

"We are leaving, sir!" Smith waved and disappeared inside the barn. His people followed him, too.

"Immortal? Dad, who was that guy?"

"I don't know . . ." Meher held his daughter ever so tight as the barn dissipated, revealing a bluish body of a spaceship called the 776-Vidra. It lifted its bow toward the morning sky and as it made a run for it, also disappeared; teleported away.

Mysha and her dad felt the wind and looked into the rising sun, utterly confused.

Chapter Thirty Six

A Hesitant Decision

Toxic appeared directly front of Space Craft Carrier 26-54; floating in space. Captain Josh Kulighan's assigned space ship and he ran past and current operations from there. After clearing the initial confusion, Toxic made the call and soon Smith was staring down at Josh's face. "Hello my friend!" Smith was wary, but in a good mood.

Captain Josh Kulighan saluted, then replied, half joking. "With friends like you, who need enemies! By the way, I made a regime change in the Junta's ranks and they stopped advancing. Far as I know, they are opening negotiations and withdrawing from the Main Land!"

"What happened to that Maximoso guy?" Smith was shocked to hear a radical end to the war.

"Um, well, he was not obeying me, so I had him killed. We framed a waiter who was also killed so he wouldn't be able to tell his side of the story. The guy who is in charge was the late leader's right hand, but not a bad one. I had Colonel Re'kl pay a visit to him so he is frightened and plays along!"

"Nicely done! I expected chaos and carnage!"

"Well, the situation was very fluid at the time, so I had to make some decisions without consulting you first!" Josh replied varyingly.

"I knew I left the situation in capable hands!" Smith added and hinted to remain around for the time being. Once the transmission was over, he turned toward the holographic representation of Toxic. “Take me to my former mentor!”

“Ay-ay!”

Captain Aa was told of Smith’s arrival. Victor made sure of it. The DU and its support ships were sailing alongside the Final Victory. Victor told her before Commander Danek could tell her the news. She was much relieved, but the lingering nervousness did not cease. She realized that because the picture of galaxy wide war still hung around them like an ever-present bad omen.

“It is nice to see you again!” The Ancient Man greeted the younger Emperor, who was unhappy to set foot on the Final Victory. It reminded him of stark times and horrifying decisions . . .

“Likewise!” he responded. He was the only one who came from the Toxic. The small DSR, like a kneeling cat, waited for him in the deserted main hangar.

“How do you want us to proceed?” His former mentor wanted answers.

“It has to be a clear message to Guvojan!” Evan Smith pressed his lips.

“I agree. I quietly began mobilizations from the far end of our territories!”

The younger Emperor stared at his former mentor. He half thought the same, but was horrified hearing the words, actually. The Ancient Man saw it in his eyes and responded, “it’s a clear violation of the Treaty!”

“Yes!” the younger Emperor admitted. “I have all the recordings, and with that we know exactly where the so-called Drops are. By the way, was this a contingency plan during the Klon wars, perhaps?”

“Yes. It’s a big operation. Guvojan has to know about it. Matter of fact, he does. He okayed the go ahead too, not just me!”

"So, we can preposition our forces to all one hundred and thirty-two locations before we send a message to him."

"That is how we going to play it, huh?" his ex-mentor glanced at him.

"There will be a blowback from them for sure." the younger Emperor nodded, the decisions weighing heavily on him.

The Ancient Man tilted his head instead of asking the question.

Evan Smith saw the confusion and opened his mouth: "The deadline we must set will be too short for the AOCP to remove all its agents, so the question remains, what will be their fates?"

"Kill them all . . ." his former mentor responded without any emotion in his voice.

"If they go down quiet. Somehow, I don't think so." The younger Emperor shook his head. "They might resort to terrorism; they might just blow themselves up to cause panic among the unsuspecting civilians. After all, part of that was their original roles."

"Should we contain them?"

"We can leave it up to the governments of those worlds or we can lock them down, a form of barricade and cleanse the planes ourselves. In either way, I expect casualties from the local population." he mulled over.

"So . . . We just have to see it, right?"

"Right. And so, to get back to the present and how to deal with it, we need a messenger who takes our demand to President Guvojan and I can't be that . . ." the younger Emperor realized.

"I can facilitate that. Diesel will happily play his role aboard the SPD Unforgivable."

"Are you prepared to send Admiral Jandailh into such dangerous location?"

"She is an adept person."

"Your Jandailh?" Smith clarified himself.

"Yes. After all, you sent Captain Aa to me. The Unforgivable and its support ships won't have a problem penetrating CTP

(Central Trade Planet) defenses to reach their destination, I can promise!"

"So, we not going to warn them?"

"No!"

Chapter Thirty Seven

The Message

Macell clearly remembered the last time he had to bother the President with horrifying news. It was years ago when UNHL made a bravely heroic run against the Orion-7 Star Yard. Of course, it has been rebuilt since, but the devastation in both manpower and ego left such a bruise in President Guvojan he punished Macell for years to come. Now, while he was not sure what exactly was going on, he knew one thing: he wanted to live! For his luck, President Guvojan was already on the regular Sunday morning Intelligence Committee meeting, deep inside his Presidential Palace, towering above the CTP. The AOCP killing droids moved aside upon recognizing him and his implants. He hurriedly moved across the chairs, the virtual reality devices, and sat down beside the President, who seemed annoyed. "What is it Macell? Don't you see I'm buried in paperwork regarding to finance this ballooning mess?" he referred to the ever-growing black budget.

"Um, perhaps in a way they're completely related!" he paused for a second.

"And the reason you bothering, is . . . ?" The President grew angry.

"Moments ago, we had a perimeter breach at our territory! UNHL forces are on their way. Their presumed destination is us, the CTP!" he exhaled rapidly.

Guvojan stopped for a second, weighted his aide's sanity, then laughed at his face. "Clever way to spice up my Sunday!" But as

Macell's expression did not change, he had to consider the rational here. "How bad is it?"

"We don't know for sure. Their emission signatures are highly masked, unusual for them, especially knowing that at least one of their spaceships is a Super Planet Destroyer. Which one, we can't know for sure until they get closer . . ."

"What is their ETA?"

"Less than two hours."

"Alert the Presidential Guard and Admiral Motf of the military forces!"

"They were notified as I came!" he nodded, looking serious.

President Guvojan had to think. "They wouldn't dare to break the Treaty so bluntly. Do we have an estimate on their numbers?"

"About seven to ten capitol warships and their accompanying forces." Macell replied, sounding strong.

"It has to be a message . . ." he began to nod, as he believed he was right. He cleared his throat: "Except the Section Chiefs, all must leave!"

People stopped debating and looked at each other.

"Do I have to repeat myself?" Guvojan was short on patience.

People grabbed their pads and other projection devices and left in a hurry.

Once the room lost over two quarters of its occupants, President Guvojan looked at them: "We have an intentional border breach, so I want answers. What kind of high-profile operation do we run against the UNHL? Now!" he pressed on.

"Over a hundred, I'm sure!" Admiral Melnor responded. He ran most of the Top Security operations.

"I need prompt answers!" Guvojan warned them again.

"We are preparing for the next mission, but it's in preliminary stages." Section-6 Chief rose, rather nervously.

"Could they get wind of it already?"

"The Time Dilation nature of the mission forecasted more than forty percent chance that in case the UNHL has a chance, they will return in time to prevent it . . ."

Guvojan disregarded with one dismissive hand move. “Not good enough. What else?”

“We have ongoing destabilization operations in the upper two hundred with mostly help from NGO’s.” Admiral Melnor added. The probability was high the UNHL would find a link and tie it back to them, although the very nature of the soft penetration would not result in a hard response. he frowned. It had to be something else.

“How is our Sygma 10 implementation working?” Guvojan himself was thinking.

“Good. We are in the midst of flushing our older cells operating in hostile environments.” Another Section Chief responded.

“Could they be responding to whatever debacle happened in the Green Void?” Guvojan remembered the fresh incident about a month ago. Although reports remained inconclusive whether UNHL had any involvement in the loss of the exotic weapons lab just across the border, near that damned planet he could not remember, he could always miss another report.

“No, Mr. President!” Admiral Melnor shook his head. “That was a weapons error. Its exotic nature required a toxic engine, and the planet had four labs with connecting railways beneath the surface. Once the leaked fuel was ignited upon the weapon’s impact, it was only a matter of minutes before we declared the whole thing a total loss. Naturally, the UNHL snooped around. Reports indicated part of the 26th Fleet being involved, but not their capitol ships. That told us all we needed to know of their interest. We can thank to all the Gods that they did not discover the transport facility. The last telepath was just evacuated to Nomm before we lost the planet!”

“And you sure the UNHL never discovered the way station or the obfuscating nature of the operation?” Guvojan leaned forward.

“We can never be one hundred percent sure, but I believe if they would’ve discovered the true nature of our operation, we would be facing war by now. As they would run out of any other options.” Admiral Melnor reacted.

They all watched the main screen where a bunch of blue hue dots jumped around, indicating the masking of emission signatures.

"Are they cloaked?" Guvojan frowned.

"No, Mr. President." Section-11 Chief responded. "They're running in stealth mode, at or near exact light speed. Slower than they should, but the added resonance is distorting their already obfuscated emission signature. It's very clever, and it tells me that there are serious about their intentions. They also want us to know this; therefore, they will want to speak with either somebody high up in the armed forces or with you, Mr. President!" After pausing, he added: "If they want to speak to anyone at all . . ."

"It's also possible," Admiral Melnor cut in, "that the Super Planet Destroyer is an older model. One that we have on file, but due to the masking and other methods, they keep us in doubt."

"It's working . . ." Guvojan slammed on the table, then stopped. "Admiral, since we running so many concurrent operations in destabilizing nature, how are we transporting our agents around undetected?"

Admiral Melnor stopped chewing on his nail. "We built an extensive fleet of cloaked warships."

"Stealth? Is that what's eating up my budget?" Guvojan rolled back the virtual pages of a report the intelligence community prepared for him. He glanced into a couple of pages, then shook his head. "No. Stealth is increasing, but the budgetary deficit comes from support related issues. What are those? Anyone knows that?" he looked around in the room.

Section-10 Chief glanced at the Admiral, who pretended not to see his increased insecurity, but it was late. Guvojan picked up on the mental disturbance. "Would somebody tell me what I don't know?"

"Mr. President, for deniability's sake, it would be best if you don't know!" Admiral Melnor responded calmly.

President Guvojan's shuttle just left the landing pad. He had couple minutes to compose his thoughts. His head was in disarray. He just learned of the Nexus and its expanded operation. He knew there were more than a hundred locations within the UNHL they regularly transported agents to. The ballooning Stealth program itself was a black box, hiding behind the Nexus program's trails. There was no magic stealth component his Section Chiefs discovered five years ago. There was no magic bullet his advisors came up with destabilizing the UNHL. Those whom told him to agree to the Treaty were all neglected to tell him what they worked on his behind. But at the end, could he blame them? Sure, he could, but it would be unwise. The Nexus program was a big-ticket item. It held great promise. And it still does. After all, if that's what the UNHL found, they could still utilize the portion within the

AOCP . . . He glanced at the fake windows. They were monitors. Super high resolution 3D monitors. The Central Trade Planet shrunk to nothing more than just a little ball as the personal shuttle ascended into low orbit to step onboard the Unforgivable. He remembered to the war battered warship. It was old. His advisors were correct. The near light speed operation of it was a novel way to mask the emission exhausts.

The shuttle shook as it landed in the SPD's main dock. His Honor Guard lined up upon his exit and were met by twelve elite soldiers from the UNHL side. His advisors disagreed, rather vehemently, against UNHL Admiral Jandailh's repeated insistence to come aboard. He shook them off. He knew he won't be harmed and upon seeing the tall, broad-shouldered man standing beside the slender Admiral, he knew he was right.

"Mr. President, welcome onboard the Unforgivable, my SPD!" Admiral Jandailh's frosty tone did not go unnoticed.

"I am pleased to establish dialogue!" he responded dryly.

"It won't be a long one, I promise!" The tall man beside her said, then added, "we're here to deliver the Emperor's message. They stand firm behind their case!"

"Mr. Diesel, right?" Guvojan was sure.

"Indeed! Please follow us into the Executive conference room! We have an issue to discuss!" The Ancient Man's bodyguard was mean and to the point. Professional. He could not blame him, either. They led him thru a maze of corridors, presumably into the near top section of the SPD. It wouldn't be too difficult for him to learn the exact location later, but it was all history. It was not important, so he shelved the idea and watched the assigned soldier's face and mental aura. They were either told nothing or they were unaware of who he was. That was unlikely. He fought hard not to show any sign of surprise as they led him into the conference room. There, he saw multiple holo-monitors displaying multiple items. Some were visuals of planets, empty fields, abandoned factory buildings, while another holo monitor tied them together into one screen. He glanced back and forth at the monitors. Beside the main monitor, the information presented was useless to him.

"Do you need a history lesson in regard to the Nexus—Drop symbiosis?" Diesel asked once the doors closed.

President Guvojan blinked at the monitors. So, they did find out about it . . . A pity!

"No. No, I don't think I need. I know the story myself. It was a secret project for troop movements across the galaxy, beneath the soil during the II. Klon Wars. Its origins fall before my rein, but upon ascending to my position they briefed me about it." he turned to Mr. Diesel. The man nodded; his hands folded hard behind his back. Guvojan always admired the augmented human. He represented what a real soldier should've been all along! If he would have an army of cloned version of him, he could achieve his goals without any opposition. Not to say AOCP did not try, but genetics were an expensive experiment, one that was riddled with setbacks. He flipped an eyebrow and returned his sight to the main holo screen. "I presume you view this as a breach of the Treaty, yes?"

"We have detailed information about all the one hundred and thirty-two locations in UNHL space. The Emperors, as always, will give you multiple directions to go from here!" Diesel watched the president intentionally. He was not surprised; therefore, he had to know in advance there will be choices offered to him. He continued, "you must recall all your Drops from UNHL territory by midnight CTP time. We will destroy all locations!" He could see the transformation on the president. He obviously expected something like that, but with a greater deadline as he shook his head. "We need more time to withdraw orderly!"

"Denied!" Admiral Jandailh shouted with anger.

"That's correct, Mr. President. I am sorry to tell you that your actions angered the Emperors to great heights." Diesel added calmly. "They gave me options to convey to you, but the deadline will remain! Also, by midnight the main Nexus terminal on planet Belmar has to be shut down!"

"Why?"

"I think you know the answer . . ." Diesel replied darkly.

"We will meet any breach of the territory border with deadly force!" President Guvojan fought back the urge to kill them both on the spot.

"No, Mr. President!" Diesel dismissed his threat. "The deadline is midnight, and the evacuation is also midnight or . . . we will curve back to the original idea of war. But this time there will be no mercy. The Emperors will publicly and galaxy wide disseminate the info you see here. They will explain in great detail how they got their hands on this and the public will rally behind them as one. They won't find peace until someone publicly hung you. I would presume your hands would be tied hard as you would have a hard time to explain publicly what moral reasoning you invented to justify this!" he pointed at the screens.

Guvojan knew the deadline was way too short. Assets, agents would be in danger. He also realized somebody got information directly from the program; therefore, UNHL spies were present on Belmar . . . A weak trail to go by.

"What about AOCP assets on UNHL territory?"

"You should've thought of it before authorizing this. The door is this way!" Admiral Jandailh stepped to it.

Less than half an hour later, as the Admiral and Diesel watched telemetry on the Ready Room behind the Unforgivable's bridge, she turned at the Ancient Man's emissary. "This is very risky! If they would find out about our less than clean slate of nature being here, we would face their best troops!"

". . . Surely you wanted to add that by now . . ." Diesel reminded her.

She quietly watched the President shuttle's telemetry approaching the first defense bastion around the CTP. Just before the gate, they saw a tiny flash on the screen. It was a visual sign of another silent operation that just began.

"I still don't understand how a less than two meters long cloaked missile can travel as far as to Belmar!"

"It is cutting-edge stealth technology. Guaranteed to work and throw of the President's spy chief." Diesel watched telemetry as additional tiny flashes represented additional spy work in motion.

"I think it's not honorable to fight this way!" she shook her head, disgusted, and left the Ready Room to give orders to her crew, leaving Diesel alone, who watched information fade on the screens. He watched her from behind the thick composite glass to give orders, then shut down the screens and erased the saved feeds. No, she, just like the younger Emperor, was naïve in that regard. War was coming one way or the other. It was better to be ready when the fireworks began . . .

President Guvojan returned to the Intelligence Committee's underground bunker as the midnight drew closer. He just could not sleep. The hint of personal neglect and guilt lingered around. A shred of humanity, his psychologist would characterize it . . . Admiral Melnor greeted him with mostly good news. As the clock turned midnight, almost all the one hundred and thirty-two Drops were teleported to safe underground chambers within the AOCP territory. The Admiral did not think the Primary Nexus facility in Belmar was in danger, but at the personal order of the President they evacuated all essential persons while the perimeter was strengthened and the best droids swept the facility for hidden bombs and or foreign assets. They found so far nothing, and that pleased the Admiral.

As the huge digital clock turned to two minutes past midnight and the facility remained standing, the tightening feeling in Guvojan's stomach eased. A high smile appeared on his face. "They bluffed!"

"We need to run calculations whether this threat on their part was a way to flush out our assets!"

"Did not we leave behind some?"

"A lot. Indeed, we had to. Last information packets from UNHL territory indicated increased UNHL military presence. I don't think they bluffed when they threatened us. We will see casualties and political fallout from this debacle!" the Admiral reminded him.

"Can you forecast the possibilities?" the President asked.

"That report alone could be dangerous! It would be best to wait and see. It will take months to learn the full extent. Not to mention that our cloaked ships will have to withdraw orderly or some of our agents will turn sides. We don't want to anger our own."

"Can't we kill them remotely?" The President remembered some sort of secretive program to that regard.

"Some . . . We have the capability. It will fall onto the Section Chiefs to execute that as they see fit."

"Send a memo to them!" Guvojan pressed. Suddenly one of the screens went blank, then another three joined it.

"What's happening?" Guvojan felt the earlier stomach churn returning.

"Something . . ." Admiral Melnor stepped to his holo keyboard and tapped it. Deep clouds appeared on his forehead and amid apologizing, he pointed at the main screen. "The Belmar facility is completely destroyed! Preliminary reports indicate four separate detonations occurred!"

“Shut down operational space around the planet and have them scour and scrub every cubic meter around the planet with robots!” Guvojan was battling with his stomach muscles not to throw up. He felt disgraced!

“Mr. President, our defense was not breached! We littered space with objects around the planet months ago. Without the correct guiding, no mother ship could approach it undetected!”

“I want answers!” President Guvojan slammed his fist on the desk. “Somehow, they managed to bypass your measurements, and it was not the Emperors personally or our indicators would’ve lit up like an armed bomb, right?”

“Right . . .” The Admiral was not sure. In the past two decades they spent tremendous effort building and managing systems and projects, monitoring the Emperor’s mental auras. He was sure they would’ve caught them if they enter into AOCP territory. But if it was not them, nor was it a vessel, it had to be something tiny but at extremely high speed. Perhaps a rocket of some kind . . . That would take some time to learn, and even then, they might not find out for sure.

Chapter Thirty Eight

Prologue

Toxic changed call sign back to 776-Vidra as she landed on planet Hilderin. This time there was a ceremony held at the fast-withdrawing Junta's main military airport, near the Presidential Palace. The Honor Guards and Azure accompanied the Emperor, while Amerlee watched it from within. Smith deemed the situation too dangerous for her to follow them. She was angry, but at the same time she understood that this was a well-founded precaution.

After a rushed reception, the younger Emperor had a short but private talk with the interim Supreme Leader, a man named General Bartak. They talked outside in a garden, accompanied by Honor Guards whom stood in a distance.

"I was told to walk with you here, outside, as the Presidential Palace was still bugged . . ." the Human Emperor turned to the big man. He had to weight over three hundred pounds. Never less he walked rather evenly and swiftly on his curved legs.

"Yes. Um, My Lord. I was told that you are the leader of the UNHL."

"I am an Emperor, true, but I am not the sole leader of the UNHL. There are others, not to mention the true leaders of the UNHL are the souls, the people and other life forms. And to emphasize this point, I was told that you will step down from your Supreme Leader position in less than ninety days as general elections will take place. Is that still the plan?"

"Yes, um, My Lord. Unless of course they elect me." he began to grin.

The Emperor stopped and turned to the wide-shouldered man. “See that the elections will be impartial and free! It would be best if you would ask the UNHL’s help to monitor the elections! I would really hate to return to this planet!” The Human Emperor probed the man. He was full of confusion, but saw the flicker of worry on his face.

General Bartak nodded: “I will do so!”

“Good!” The younger Emperor nodded and began to walk. “The park is nice. The previous leader had a good taste. And I do know how did you manage to grab the position, so it would be truly unwise to deviate from the free election path!” he reminded him again, then after a pause he added. “We noticed that a battalion still on the Main Land. Care to elaborate as of why?”

“They are helping to withdraw our wounded and the military equipment.”

“Stop lying to me!” the Emperor raised his voice. “We noticed movements toward the Space Elevator.”

“We aren’t going near to it!” General Bartak replied honestly.

The Emperor probed the man’s brain, then nodded. “No. I see that you’re telling the truth, but still, the presence of those men is . . .” he pressed his lips as he spun at him again. “The Annexed Land. No. General, you must withdraw. That land is neither for you nor for anyone else!”

“But we just like to . . .” Bartak inched forward.

“Forget it! Anyhow, the UNHL already contacted the Main Land’s leadership and re-annexed it. It belongs to us now! Military operations already commenced. Of course, it won’t be ours forever. Months and years and it will return to its rightful owners, to the people of Hilderin.”

Smith and his entourage just returned to the space ship when Amerlee indicated that he had a call.

“Who was it?” Smith was annoyed.

“It’s from the Ancient Man. He needs to see you!” she replied nervously.

"You talked to him directly?" Smith frowned deeply.

"Yeah, my love!"

"Huh . . ." Smith did not expect that answer from her and was thrown off by Amerlee's accompanying sweet smile.

"Focus, Smith, I'm here, too!" Azure grabbed his hand.

"Yeah, I know!" Smith became confused for a moment. "Damn that old bugger! I used to have couple weeks down time between missions. Now it's not even that. I used to like old times better!" he imitated being angry and hurt, then ordered Toxic to fly to Mr. Meher's house. "I guess I just have to cut it short with my neighbors again." he shook his head.

Baby quietly turned around upon hearing that. Something in the back of her mind, something of a task she forgot to do . . . Something she used to do . . . She swiftly walked to the Toxic's bridge, opened the unused hatch behind the Captain's seat, and disappeared into the dark tunnel. She skipped the last six steps and hopped to the ground. Sparsely lit corridor welcomed her, and she moved quick. Soon she made a left turn and found herself in the Space-Time Continuum Observation Room. She sat behind the curved monitor and brought it alive. Perhaps Smith's old mentor spotted something? She wondered. She enlarged the time frame they were in, but saw nothing unusual. She took a deep breath and exhaled slowly. The weight was suddenly off of her chest. They were still in the realm they supposed to be . . . Then, as she zoomed out ahead in the near future, a blip occurred. She stopped using the console and watched the region, but nothing happened. She frowned. "Maybe I just imagined it . . ." she said to herself, for calming purposes. She was not sure she supposed to scan ahead. Smith often told her confusing stuff about the unwritten future and the predetermined destination, so she was not sure if a blip in the near future meant anything. She shut down the machine and left. But all along the way back to the Toxic she thought she might have to say something to her boss.

Two hours later Smith was sitting around a hastily set up garden furniture. Mr. Meher and his wife sat across from him, while Azure and Amerlee sat on his sides. They were eating dinner and Smith liked the food so much he even commented on it.

"It is just so strange that your Vidra is a space faring ship, sitting on its legs beside my house." Mr. Meher pointed at the towering ship behind them.

Smith had to smile. "It supposed to be this easy. So, I was told you have questions. Name them!"

Mr. Meher put down the fork and wet his lips: "Are you living on a planet called Down Earth?"

"Yes." Smith nodded.

"Ah!" he nodded. "Is it really very different from this place?" he made a sweeping gesture with his hand.

"Not exactly. There are cities with older technology than in a major metropolitan city in your country. If you look at our cities first, the difference might not be evident, but some of our cities are highly advanced. As humans evolved on the planet, some branched off to an entirely different route than others."

Mr. Meher frowned. He did not understand.

Azure glanced at Smith, frowning too. Did he imply the ancient city, Bristol?

Amerlee leaned forward, likewise thinking of things similar in nature.

Smith clutched his hands, resting on his full belly as he lounged backward on his chair. "Deep underground we have self-sustaining nations living in total seclusion. Long, long time ago their brain pattern was digitized as they wanted to part from materials and their bodies. They understood technology well, so they built a digital city. They live there. Jacking into this city is possible, but not recommended. I did it once or twice. It is alien. They branched off as I said . . ." Smith leaned forward.

Azure's jaw hung as she stared at him. "You never told me this!"

"I never heard of it either!" Amerlee responded with awe.

"No. It's one of the many secrets of the Central Supercomputer . . ." Smith began to chew on a salted cookie.

"I, I was told that my people are a branch off, if you would like to call it that way." Meher lifted his index finger.

Smith turned at the man, scrutinized for a bit, then nodded. "Yes. Ninety-eight percent similar."

"I was also told that other humans in the galaxy are the same way. Why?"

"The Ancestors seeded humanity to a thousand planets." Smith frowned. "That happened long time ago."

"Why?" Meher asked again.

"They were beaten and humiliated . . ." Smith shrugged, making a face.

"A beaten nation wouldn't have the resources to travel to a great distance!" Meher's wife disagreed.

An evil smile appeared on Smith's face as he grabbed his paper napkin and marked two points on it with a piece of ketchup. Once he did, he showed to them: "Tell me what is the shortest distance between the two points?"

Mysha grinned. "Easy," she said before her parents. "A straight line connecting them!"

Smith's smile softened, then with a superior face he folded the napkin. "I asked this from others and like you, they all answered wrong. The shortest route between the two endpoints is exactly

zero . . . Thinking differently is a key to understand our Ancestors and a long extinct nation; the ZONs who built great Starships with teleportation engine that allows to fold the fabric of space, to do just like this!" he held up the smeared napkin. Its wet edge blinked by the setting sunrays. Smith squinted. "Want to know more?" he asked, but already knew the answer.

Contents

Books By This Author

Hope

As a far away human civilization in the other side of the galaxy slowly rise from its own ashes - a nuclear war-, a venerable police chief with a dark past hunts for strange clues in a mass murder case and falls in love with a beautiful blonde woman who befriends his teenage daughter, Zoe. Nothing as it seems, the blonde wasn't even born on that planet and there are more agents from other humanoid civilizations converging on the planet called Agross V, all looking for the same thing; however some to save it, some to destroy it while holding entire populations of other planets in hostage.

Agent Sasha

The Monarch in the Milky Way series Book 1

Taking many of the fantastic traits and much-loved tropes of classic galaxy-spanning science fiction, Agent Sasha takes us out of our world and into Down Earth, a realm where humans run the Milky Way. We meet war heroes and beautiful femmes fatales, all of whose lives revolve around the Emperor, who is only recognizably human in some of his manners and ways. As we meet new alien races and travel to exotic new places, so unfolds an intriguing plot of a battle for survival in this truly unique world.

www.ingramcontent.com/pod-product-compliance
Lightning Source LLC
LaVergne TN
LVHW020519100826
845148LV00010B/1278

* 9 7 8 1 7 3 4 3 8 8 7 3 2 *